She watched the subtle rippling of muscles beneath his bronzed skin.

Although she knew she was playing with fire, she reached out, needing somehow to reassure herself one more time that this was not a dream. When she placed her hand against the warm skin of Alessandro's back, she felt him stiffen, but he did not move away.

"Sandro?"

"No one calls me that."

Adrienne smiled. "Good. Then I will." Her fingers spread in a reflexive caress. "Good night."

He turned his head a little so that she could see his straight profile. "Don't touch me again, Isabella, unless you're issuing an invitation."

She tucked her hand under her cheek. "Another threat?"

He heard the smile in her voice. Admiration and amusement warred with his ill temper and won. When he spoke, there was an answering smile in his voice. "No, Isabella. Just another friendly warning...."

Dear Reader,

This month brings another exciting first from Harlequin Historicals. A time-travel story. But *Across Time,* by author Nina Beaumont, is not an ordinary time-travel. It is the story of a young woman catapulted through time into the body of her ancestor, the evil Isabella di Montefiore. Don't miss this passionate tale of treachery and desire.

And just in time for the new year comes another daring love story from DeLoras Scott, *Spitfire.* When the headstrong daughter of a wealthy rancher runs away to find her *bandido* lover, gunslinger Lang Cooper is sent out to bring her back.

For those of you who enjoyed *Beloved Deceiver,* we have a new book from Laurie Grant, *The Raven and the Swan.* Awarded a former abbey for his loyalty to the Tudor crown, Miles Raven is shocked to find himself the protector of an innocent young orphan who seems determined to wreak havoc on his well-ordered life.

Readers of contemporary romance will surely recognize the name Muriel Jensen. In *Trust,* the author's first historical romance, the sparks fly between a woman with a notorious past and an ambitious businessman in turn-of-the-century Oregon.

Keep a lookout for next month's titles wherever Harlequin Historicals are sold.

Sincerely,

Tracy Farrell
Senior Editor

Please address questions and book requests to:
Reader Service
U.S.: P.O. Box 1325, Buffalo, NY 14269
Canadian: P.O. Box 1050, Niagara Falls, Ont. L2E 7G7

NINA BEAUMONT

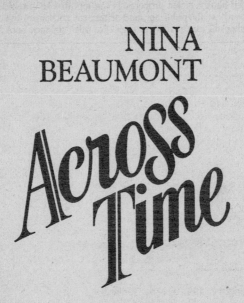

Across Time

Harlequin Books

TORONTO • NEW YORK • LONDON
AMSTERDAM • PARIS • SYDNEY • HAMBURG
STOCKHOLM • ATHENS • TOKYO • MILAN
MADRID • WARSAW • BUDAPEST • AUCKLAND

ISBN 0-373-28803-4

ACROSS TIME

Books by Nina Beaumont

Harlequin Historicals

Sapphire Magic #101
Promises to Keep #153
Across Time #203

NINA BEAUMONT

is of Russian parentage and has a family tree that includes the Counts Stroganoff and a Mongolian Khan. Born in Salzburg, she grew up in Massachusetts. In 1970 she moved to Austria, where she lives in the country with her husband and an overly friendly schnauzer.

An avid history buff, she enjoys traveling, which gives her the opportunity to use the five languages she speaks. She also loves music, books and the French Impressionists.

Her writing keeps her more than busy, but she also finds time to work as a translator and teach adult English classes.

To Tracy Farrell, friend and editor par excellence. Thank you for letting me do something really different.

Chapter One

Normandy, France
March 1794

Although the March sun that was beginning to burn through the morning mist was warm on the back of her neck, Adrienne could not shake the chill a long, sleepless night seemed to have settled in her very bones. Her hands deep in the pockets of the ragged breeches one of the stable boys had left behind, she lingered along the path, loath to return to the château, where the walls seemed to echo and close in on her now that the last servants had departed.

Her mission had gone well, but despite the relief, her nerves were still jangling. Every time she stood on the beach with the cold surf swirling around her feet and watched old Père Duroc's fishing boat push out into the Channel with its human cargo, she waited for the fear that curled in the pit of her stomach to disappear, but it never did. She'd tried to ignore it. After all, she'd become very good at ignoring things she could not change. But she could never quite manage. Instead, she'd become accustomed to it.

Rolling her shoulders against the tension, she haphazardly kicked at the gravel gathered in clumps from the rainstorm two days ago. Her generous mouth curved in a small, sad smile as she suddenly remembered how the path had looked when it had been tidily raked with that slightly wavy pattern her mother had insisted upon. She allowed herself a small sigh at the memory but blinked her eyes furiously against the threatening tears.

A faint sound had her head snapping up. Her dark eyes narrowed, she turned around slowly. But all she saw were the still-bare bushes and trees in the overgrown, neglected park.

Then she heard the sound again. Even before her tired brain had consciously identified it as the whimper of a child, she began to run. Skidding to a stop near the jungle the rose garden had become, she called out softly, but there was no answer. Ignoring the thorny branches that caught at her shirt, she ducked under the broken trellis, moving quickly—so quickly that had the child not cried out again, she would have walked right past.

Pivoting, Adrienne pushed aside the thick, almost waist-high weeds that had withstood the winter. A young woman, her thin face streaked with dirt, crouched in the shelter of the high grass. With both arms she pressed a small child to her breast.

"Please, don't hurt my child." The woman's voice was pleading, but her eyes were fierce and determined. "You can do whatever you want with me, but don't hurt my child."

Adrienne dropped down to her knees so that she was eye to eye with the woman. "It's all right," she said softly. "No one will hurt you here."

The woman's eyes filled with tears. She'd been expecting violence. Instead, the soft, gentle voice seemed to sap the remainder of her strength. "Aren't you one of them?" she whispered, her eyes darting back and forth. "They saw me on the road. I'm sure they saw me."

"Who saw you?"

"The men." She swallowed convulsively. "The men who followed me from Paris." The woman's eyes blurred and she stared past Adrienne's shoulder. "The men who killed my husband." She focused her gaze again and her shoulders seemed to straighten a bit with some remainder of pride. "I am Charlotte de Lambert. Jean de Lambert was my husband."

Adrienne recognized the name of the nobleman who had tried to steal the little dauphin away from his jailers and paid for his courage with his life. "I will help you."

"Who are you?" she managed.

"I am Adrienne de Beaufort."

Realizing herself at the goal she had almost lost hope of reaching, the woman slumped and lowered her face to her child's hair.

Adrienne reached out to touch her shoulder. "Did someone send you to me?"

The woman raised her head and nodded, unable to speak through the tears that ran down her face.

The ache between her shoulders forgotten, Adrienne slid her arm around the woman and helped her rise. "Come on, let's get the two of you to the château."

They were almost there when Adrienne heard the baying of the dogs.

Her stomach knotted, but her hands were steady as she guided the woman toward the château, pulling her along to speed their steps. Once inside, she took the time to lock the heavy oaken door behind her.

Her ears trained on the sound of the dogs, she tried to gauge how far away they were. She would manage, she told herself. It would be close, but she would manage.

Quickly, softly, although there was no one to hear her, she spoke to the woman. "I shall hide you in a secret chamber. You will be safe there until I can come for you."

The woman stopped. "Oh God, please, no. Don't make me go into some dark, closed place." Her fingers bit into Adrienne's arm. "I couldn't stand that."

But Adrienne pulled her on. "There are candles," she soothed. "You will be all right." She tried to smile, although the baying of the dogs was closer. "There is food, too, and water. You can rest, and I will come for you as soon as I can."

The woman began to cry softly and the child, too, began to whimper. Adrienne would have liked to stop and comfort them, but she knew she could not spare even a moment.

Pulling them through the library, she slipped inside the small study. Letting the woman go, she rushed forward. Adrienne heard her slip to the floor, but she could not afford to stop, even when the child let out a wail.

Her breathing was uneven, but she forced her hands to be steady as she reached the painting that guarded the entry to the chamber. As always, she looked into the eyes of her ancestress, Isabella di Montefiore. They looked back at her, cool, distant and imperious, but Adrienne felt the habitual jolt of intimacy. The cool eyes had never fooled her. Not even before she'd read Isabella's diaries and become privy to the woman's passions and secrets.

Placing both hands against the inside edges of the ornate gilt frame, Adrienne carefully slid her hands toward the center of the portrait. When she felt first one barely detectable bump beneath the canvas and then the other, she pressed down and stood back to let the painting spring away from the wall on its well-concealed hinges to reveal a small door.

She swiveled and gestured to the woman. "Come quickly. There is no time to lose."

The woman shook her head wildly, her eyes huge and frightened.

Adrienne ran back to her and pulled her toward the chamber. Once inside, she took time she could ill afford to light a candle. Gripping the woman by the shoulders, she shook her gently. "You will be all right here. Do you understand?"

The woman's crying had subsided a little and she managed a shaky nod.

Adrienne smiled and laid her hand against the woman's cheek. Her heart heavy, she slipped out of the chamber, closing the door behind her.

She ran back through the rooms. As she took the stairs two at a time, she was already pulling her shirt over her head.

Tossing shirt, breeches and boots into an armoire, she slipped into a simple gown with more speed than elegance. She was still barefoot when she heard the pounding at the front door.

Adrienne opened her window and leaned outside. "Who's there?" she called loudly, although she knew full well that her uninvited, unwelcome visitor could only be Marcel Fabien. Her lips curled with contempt. Fabien. She hadn't forgotten that he had worn Beaufort livery. Just as she hadn't forgotten that her father had threatened to take a whip to him before he'd thrown him out of the château for abusing one of the maids.

Now Fabien preached the revolution, but he wore lace at his cuffs and had appropriated the Count de Louvelle's carriage and hunting dogs when he had intrigued his way to becoming chairman of the Committee of Public Safety in Calais.

A large, thickset man appeared around the corner of the château. "Citizen Fabien has come to speak with you, Citizeness Beaufort," he barked up at her, obviously dissatisfied that he had to crane his neck upward.

"I will be down in a moment." Adrienne shut the window loudly.

Picking up a shawl, she went down the stairs as slowly as she dared. Perhaps it was petty, she thought, but that small gesture of defiance sweetened a little the bitterness of being at Fabien's mercy.

As she opened the door, Fabien greeted her with a charming smile that did not quite reach his eyes and a bow casual enough to be an insult. Even as his gaze took a leisurely trip over her body, he continued to tap his silver-topped cane against the brick step.

Adrienne's mouth thinned as she fought the impulse to step back and shut the door in his face. "Is there a particular reason you have come to call on me this early in the morning, Monsieur Fabien?"

The man's bright blue eyes narrowed. "I could have you arrested for that alone." He leaned closer. "Or perhaps since you refuse so steadfastly to address me as Citizen Fabien—'' he drew a finger down her cheek ''—you would prefer to call me Marcel?''

Adrienne felt an icy shiver travel down the length of her spine. It wasn't the first time Fabien had come to harass her with his suggestive remarks, but he had never dared to touch her before. Her nerves were jumping and when she spoke, her tone was cooler than was wise. ''It is not my habit to address strangers by their first name.''

Fabien placed a slender, well-cared-for hand against his chest and shook his head. ''I am hurt that you think of me as a stranger. I had hoped that you would come to think of me as a friend.''

''Indeed?'' With a toss of her head, she flicked her thick black braid over her shoulder.

Fabien's hands tightened on his cane at the disdain that was so vividly audible in that one word. Smiling to disguise the rage that had begun to smolder within him, he asked, ''May I come in?'' His tone was deceptively light. ''I would speak with you.''

Reluctantly Adrienne stepped back from the door to let him pass. She pushed the door closed and preceded Fabien into the salon, where cold, stale air greeted her.

Wrapping her shawl more closely around her shoulders, she strode to the window. Her hands stilled on the window latch when she saw Fabien's henchman on the path she had taken with Jean de Lambert's widow and child just minutes ago. The hounds were whining and barking, pulling wildly against their leashes.

''They seem to have picked up an interesting scent.''

Caught off balance, Adrienne whirled around at the sound of Fabien's voice close to her ear and found herself flush against him.

"Is something wrong, Citizeness Beaufort?"

Adrienne fought down both the fear and the angry, direct retort that rose to her lips. "Yes." She moved to step past him, but he reached out to grip her shoulder.

Forcing herself to stand still, she met his eyes. "Yes, something is very wrong, Monsieur Fabien."

He heard the slight emphasis on the last two words and understood well the insult that lay behind it. His hand on her shoulder tightened.

"I am not accustomed to being accosted and manhandled in my own home."

Fabien heard the centuries of breeding in her icy tone. For a moment, he needed all of his control not to throw her down onto the floor and take her on the spot. But there would be time enough to show her who the master was these days. His handsome mouth curved in a smug smile and he released her. "My apologies." He stepped back. "But perhaps you should accustom yourself to the manners of the day."

Scathing words on her tongue, Adrienne opened her mouth to speak but closed it quickly as she remembered the distraught woman in the secret chamber.

Although she would have liked to put more distance between herself and Fabien, she remained where she was and met his eyes squarely. "Just what is it that you want from me?"

"You don't know?"

The softly posed question sent a shiver down her back, but she managed a cool smile. "No."

Fabien felt the fury close his throat. "I want you, Adrienne," he rasped, all the subtlety, all the carefully rehearsed words forgotten. "I have always wanted you. And I am going to have you."

He reached for her again, but this time she avoided his hand. "Don't I have any say in the matter? Or are those rights so touted by your revolution only for the male of the species?"

"Do not bring the revolution into this, Adrienne." He lunged for her again. "This is between you and me."

"No!" Adrienne felt the panic rise and lodge in her throat. She remembered the knife that was strapped to her calf and felt a flash of relief. But that was gone as soon as it had come. If she used the knife, she realized, Fabien's pet butcher out in the garden would be upon her in a minute. Then both she and the fugitives in the chamber would be lost.

Fabien gripped her shoulder and dragged her back to the window. The hounds, whining with excitement, were retracing the path back to the château. "Where are they?" She could feel his hot breath against the side of her face. "I know you've been harboring fugitives. I have known it for months."

"There is nothing to know." Adrienne fought to keep her voice even. "Besides, if you did know anything, you would have arrested me before this."

"Ah, but, Adrienne, what good would you do me in prison?" His hold on her gentled and became a caress as he turned her to face him. "Do you think that I wish to see that pretty head separated from that lovely body." His hand slid down, molding the curve of her breast.

Nausea rose in her throat at his touch and Adrienne instinctively struck his hand away. "I don't know what you're talking about!" she cried. "Where is your proof?"

"Proof?" Fabien rubbed his wrist where Adrienne had struck him. She would pay for that, too, he thought almost gleefully. And he would enjoy extracting payment. "I do not need proof, my dear. Whose word do you think the revolutionary tribunal would believe? Yours or mine?"

Adrienne felt her throat closing. Desperate, she played her last trump card, although she was more than a little unsure of the truth of her words. "My brother, Charles, might have something to say about that."

Fabien laughed softly. "Your brother has other worries now."

"What do you mean?"

"It seems that Charles has fallen out of favor with Citizen Robespierre." He toyed with a ring that had once graced the hand of an aristocrat, but his eyes remained on hers. "A small matter of misappropriated funds. The incorruptible Robespierre was very grateful for the information."

"You!" Her hands fisted, she moved forward. "How dare you?" She despised Charles for selling himself to the revolution in exchange for the safety of his aristocratic neck, but he was still her brother.

"Do not do something you may have cause to regret later on, *chérie.*" He smiled, but his eyes remained cold. "If you behave yourself, I may even be moved to help that hypocrite brother of yours."

As the implications of his words sank into her brain, Adrienne stopped so suddenly that she almost overbalanced herself. Not only her own safety depended on her submission to Fabien's desires, she realized, but Charles's safety and the safety of the woman and child in the chamber behind Isabella's portrait.

"So you are going to be sensible. Good." Fabien rubbed his palms together slowly. "On the other hand, I would not have minded a little rough and tumble."

He moved past her and unlatched the window. "Jacquot!"

Adrienne watched him beckon to the stocky man who had summoned her earlier.

"Leave me one of the horses and go back to town. And take the hounds with you."

The other man's broad face seemed to split in half as he grinned, showing more gaps than teeth. "Go to it, my friend." With a wave he moved around the corner of the château.

Still staring out the window, Adrienne did not even notice when Fabien turned toward her. She was still seeing Jacquot's face breaking into that lewd grin. No, she screamed silently, she wouldn't do it. Not for herself. Not for others. She still had the knife, after all. After she used it, she'd think of something.

"Come along, Adrienne." Fabien stepped closer so that they were separated by no more than the breadth of a hand. "I have wondered for years what it would be like to lie with you in that virginal white bed of yours." He slid a finger down her neck. "And now I am going to find out."

She needed time, Adrienne thought desperately. Just a few minutes until Jacquot was gone. She raised her eyes to Fabien's face. "I need a little time. Please." She let her eyes flutter closed and swayed.

"You disappoint me, my dear. I would not have thought you the type to simper and faint." Gripping her arm, he pushed her down into a chair and paced across the room.

Adrienne leaned back, her eyes closed, concentrating on the sounds outside. When she heard the crunch of the gravel beneath the wheels of the carriage, all her muscles tightened in anticipation. She let a minute go by and then another. Then she opened her eyes a crack and carefully, surreptitiously, reached under her skirt for the knife. When it was hidden in the folds of her gown, she rose, telling herself that she would have the courage to use it.

Fabien stopped his pacing the moment Adrienne stood.

She was very still as she watched him walk toward her, his slow steps a menacing promise. The knife's carved handle bit into her palm, which was slick with sweat.

He was close now—less than an arm's length away. And still she did not move. Even when he raised his hands and reached out, she remained motionless. Then he smiled and Adrienne struck out at him with the hand that was empty.

"No!" She fell back a step. "Do not touch me!"

"Do not make me come after you, Adrienne."

He spoke so softly that she could barely hear him above the hammering of her heart and her ragged breathing.

"Come here." Fabien stretched out his hand, palm upward, toward her.

Adrienne shook her head.

He took a half step forward. Then his hand moved as quickly as a cobra striking and he hooked his fingers into the neck of her gown and pulled.

The sound of the material tearing was like an explosion in Adrienne's ears. Instinctively she brought the knife up, aimed squarely at Fabien's belly. But instead of finishing the movement, her hand veered aside, sending the blade through the flesh at his waist.

Barely registering his cry, Adrienne ran. The study! she thought. She had to reach the study! She didn't hear the vase tumble to the floor and shatter as she jostled a table. She didn't feel her shoulder collide with a doorjamb as she skidded into the library.

When she slammed the study door behind her, her breath was burning in her throat, and for a fraction of a moment she leaned back against the door, a crazy pattern of red and black swirling in front of her eyes. Then she was moving again.

She twisted the key in the lock and dashed toward the portrait. Almost as an afterthought, she detoured toward the French doors. Perhaps he would be fooled if she opened them. Clumsy with panic, her fingers fumbled with the stubborn, rusted latch. In a burst of frustration she struck the door with her fists and her hand went through the glass. She saw the blood but felt no pain. She struck the door again. This time it sprang open and she turned and ran toward the portrait.

Her fingers were sliding over the canvas when she heard Fabien's fist ram the door. She jerked and her hands slid upward. Beginning again, she placed them on the edges of the painting. There was a shout and a crash behind her. She twisted her head back and saw that the center panel of the door was beginning to splinter.

For a moment Adrienne froze, then her hands began to move again—feverishly, frantically. She knew she had to slow her hands to find the right place at the edge of the painting and move inward, but she could not make her hands obey. Her fingers raced over the canvas again and again.

There was another deafening crash behind her. Adrienne looked into Isabella's eyes. "Help me." Her lips formed the words, but no sound emerged. "Help me."

Suddenly Adrienne felt a jolt. Then she was being drawn into a void—completely black, completely silent. She wanted to struggle against it, but she could not move. She wanted to cry out, but her voice was paralyzed. Panic rose within her until she thought she would suffocate.

Then, as suddenly as it had sucked her in, the void seemed to spew her out and she found herself staring at a painting she had never seen before. A painting depicting a plump, alluring Venus cavorting with a handsome, virile Mars.

Afraid to move, Adrienne shifted her gaze and saw elaborately carved posts and aquamarine velvet curtains gathered by tasseled golden ropes. She was lying on a bed, she realized, and the voluptuous painting lined its canopy. How had she come to be here? Had she fainted before she had reached the secret chamber?

Sitting bolt upright, she saw that she no longer wore the blue gown that Fabien had torn at the bodice, but a nightgown of the finest white linen, covered by a wide-sleeved robe of a richly patterned brocade in scarlet and purple. Unbelieving, she drew her hands down her body.

She looked around the room, disoriented. More than once she closed her eyes and shook her head, wanting to clear it. Surely she was in the midst of some mad, opulent dream. But every time she opened her eyes, she saw the same lavish bedchamber. The furniture was dark and richly carved. The walls were covered by tapestries and hangings of brocade and velvet.

Adrienne slid off the purple coverlet and stood. Carefully, unsure that her legs would carry her, she began to wander around the room. A table loaded with decanters of ruby red wine, platters of sweetmeats and bowls of fruit caught her attention. How strange, she thought. It was as if preparations had been made for guests.

She wandered further. On a low oblong table a large casket made of finely inlaid mother-of-pearl spilled its precious contents onto the polished wood as casually as if they were children's toys. With hesitant fingers she reached out to touch, barely believing that what she saw was real. Golden chains, strings of sapphires and emeralds, a ruby as large as a pigeon's egg, ropes of pearls—white, pink, gray, black—shone up at her. She dipped her hands into the jewels for a moment.

Then she looked up and found herself staring at a clever painting made to resemble a beveled mirror. Lifting her hands to touch it, she saw the movement reflected in the glass. She shook her head, certain that it was some kind of a trick. The movement of her head was reflected back at her. Her disbelief gave way to panic.

Adrienne moved closer and ran her fingers over the features she saw reflected in front of her. Instead of the pert, heart-shaped face with its upturned nose that she was accustomed to seeing, she saw elegant cheekbones and classic features. Instead of black curly hair, she saw hair the color of spun gold, which curled gently over her shoulders and fell to her hips. She stared into the mirror, shock turning into recognition.

She met the golden brown eyes that looked back at her. Eyes she knew well. A minute passed. And then another. Finally the moment came when she could no longer deny that through some quirk of destiny, she, Adrienne de Beaufort, had slipped into the body of Isabella di Montefiore.

Chapter Two

Covering her face with her hands, Adrienne spun away from the mirror. How could this be? she asked herself frantically. Was this a dream? A nightmare? Was she hallucinating? Had she gone mad? Opening her eyes again, she turned around in a circle, hoping against hope that she would see something familiar. That by some miracle she would find herself in the surroundings she had known since childhood. That the next time she looked into the mirror, she would see her own features.

But as her gaze skimmed over the beveled glass, she saw the fall of golden hair over her shoulders, glimpsed features of an imperious beauty. The room remained a luxurious bedchamber of a bygone era. But then her eyes settled on the far wall and she saw something she had missed when she had first examined the room. There, almost within touching distance, hung the portrait she had grown up with. The portrait of Isabella di Montefiore that guarded the entry to the secret chamber in the Château de Beaufort.

She approached it slowly, step by step. Just as she was raising her hand to touch it, the door burst open.

Adrienne whirled around and watched as a crowd of revelers led by a dwarf in the multicolored clothes of a jester filled the room.

"There she is!" he cried, and danced up to her. "Our blushing bride." He cackled and brandished a puppet on a stick, making its bells jingle.

Her heart in her throat, Adrienne retreated a step. Beneath the long wide sleeves of her robe, she clenched and unclenched her hands. Her gaze skimmed over the crowd attired in rich, festive clothes. But it was not clothing she was familiar with. Although her mind was spinning with confusion, she recognized the ornate dress of the Renaissance.

Her eyes came to rest on the dwarf. Gianni. The realization that she knew his name struck her like a lightning bolt.

I had the dwarf, Gianni, whipped today, but only with silken cords. Perhaps that will fire his imagination a little so that he can better amuse me.

Adrienne felt a strange lurch in her stomach as she remembered Isabella's offhand comment. She had always wondered what the poor fellow looked like. She shook her head. No, she thought, this could not possibly be happening. This had to be a bizarre dream. Surely she would wake up any moment and find herself in her own bed.

The dwarf pursued her, his oversize head bobbing as if his thin neck were too weak to support it properly. He jumped up on a tasseled hassock and leaned closer to her, so close that she could smell the spiced wine on his breath. When she retreated a step, he turned to his laughing audience with a grimace.

"Isabella *la bella*." Gianni looked up at her again and something—surprise or perplexity—flickered in his sad clown's eyes. "Why do you stand there like a cornered doe when you have a night of sport with our new master to look forward to?" He vaulted down from the hassock, hunching his shoulders and pulling in his head as if he were trying to avoid having his ears boxed.

When the blow did not seem to be forthcoming, he straightened. "What's this?" he demanded, capering out of reach of his mistress's hands just in case. "Is this the Isabella we know?" Sending his audience an oblique look, he slowly moved his head from side to side. "The Isabella who can slay a man at twenty paces by merely raising an eyebrow?" He pressed his hands, which seemed overlarge for his size against his chest and again shook his head.

The crowd laughed uproariously and proceeded to make their own ribald jests.

Adrienne watched the scene with disbelief, her mind insisting that it had to be some kind of illusion. And yet a mounting feeling of horror told her that some supernatural power was at work. She understood what these people were saying, she realized. It was the same melodious cadence of the archaic Italian she had painstakingly learned so that she could read Isabella's diaries. It could not be, she thought desperately. It was impossible. Surely if she repeated that often enough, it would be so.

But no matter how her mind, schooled in the logic of the Enlightenment, fought against the realization, it seeped into her until slowly she knew that it was undeniably true. Somehow—by some sorcery or grotesque quirk of fate—she had traveled back through time almost three centuries.

She shook her head as a hysterical giggle rose in her throat. It could not be true, her mind insisted, and yet in some strange, mystical way she knew that what had happened to her was as real as anything in her life had ever been. The mind and soul of Adrienne de Beaufort had traveled back through time to enter the body of Isabella di Montefiore on her wedding night.

"She is shaking her head," the dwarf shrieked, hopping from one foot to the other. "Does that mean, Madonna Isabella, that you do not want a night of sport with our new master?" He rattled his puppet again.

A young woman in a dark blue gown rich with precious stones pushed through the crowd. "How could she not want it, my friends?" Her voice was as high and melodious as the notes a musician coaxes from a flute, yet Adrienne shivered at the sound. "A night with Alessandro, the most beautiful man in Siena." She raised a goblet of the finest Venetian glass and drank deeply of the ruby-colored wine within. "The first of many nights," she added, her mouth curved in a knowing smile.

With a practiced toss of her head, the woman sent a wealth of reddish gold hair over her shoulder. Putting her goblet into another's hand, she fixed her gaze upon the man who stood in the doorway, arms crossed in front of him, his expression as dark as his coloring. "Come forward, Alessandro, and claim your bride." She laughed. "We cannot wait to see if your prowess and stamina is as great as those who extol your strengths would have us believe." Hooking one arm around Adrienne's shoulders, she beckoned to Alessandro with the other.

Again Adrienne felt the lightning bolt of recognition. Luisa. This was Luisa Barbiano, Isabella's bosom friend, with whom she had shared so many secrets. Why then did she feel an icy shiver snake along her spine? Why did she feel an aura of malevolence that seemed to surround the beautiful young woman like a noxious cloud? She jerked away so that Luisa's arm dropped from her shoulders.

Adrienne saw Luisa's sky blue eyes narrow and she met the suddenly appraising gaze as resolutely as the terrible feeling in the pit of her stomach would allow. The smile on Luisa's lips did not waver, but she did not try to touch Adrienne again.

As she glanced at the colorful crowd and beyond, Adrienne met the jet black eyes of the man who stood in the doorway, his brows drawn together in a frown. His hair, the blue black of a raven's wing, just brushed his shoulders, framing a face of such perfection that it might have been chiseled of Carrara marble by a master's hand. Her eyes skimmed over him and she could not help noticing how his doublet and breeches of white velvet slashed with gold and scarlet were a perfect foil for his dark beauty.

I saw Alessandro di Montefiore face-to-face for the first time yesterday when we signed the marriage contract in the great hall of the Palazzo Montefiore. I burned with hatred for him as I had been taught all my life. I burned with hatred, but from the moment I looked into his black eyes, I burned for the night to fall. Burned for him to share my bed.

Adrienne's eyes widened as she stared at him, and her hand fluttered up to lie between her breasts as if it could still her heart, which had begun to pound like a dozen horses galloping in a dead heat. So this was

Alessandro di Montefiore, she thought as Isabella's words spun around in her head. Alessandro, whom Isabella had hated, loved and betrayed. Alessandro, whose death Isabella had atoned for with her own.

As her heart drummed against her hand, Adrienne looked into Alessandro's beautiful face. No matter what she had been taught, how could Isabella have felt hatred? Adrienne asked herself. No, she thought, in her heart there was no hatred for this man.

Looking beyond the frown, beyond the arrogant challenge in the jet black eyes, Adrienne saw something she could not quite define. What was it? Intensity? Power? Passion? Violence? Yes, she thought. All of them. This was not a restful man. And yet there was something more, Something softer. Something that made her want to reach out...

Before she could think further, the women in the crowd surged forward to pull her toward the bed. Giggling and tossing about bawdy remarks speculating about the night to come, they had tugged off Adrienne's robe before she realized what was happening. When hands reached for the laces of her nightdress, she pushed at them and tried to turn away. But there were more hands than she could fight off and the laughter around her rose to a still higher pitch as the laces began to give.

Desperation lending her strength, she swung her arms upward, striking the grasping hands away from her body. Wheeling away, she managed to twist herself out of the circle of women surrounding her. Her breath hitching, she fell against the carved bedpost. Realizing suddenly what a picture of disarray she presented, she snatched up the bed curtain and with the aquamarine velvet covered herself where her night-dress gaped over her lush breasts.

"No!" she cried. "*Lasciatemi!* Leave me be!" The words echoed in her ears and her insides constricted as she heard a voice that was not her own speak in a language she had never spoken out loud.

There was a moment of utter silence before the babel rose again, even louder than before. The women surged toward her like a wave, gowns billowing, hands outstretched.

"Stop it!" The voice was mellow, but the unmistakable tone of command cut through the noise like a hot knife through butter. All sound, all movement ceased. "Leave her alone."

As Alessandro moved forward, the crowd parted to let him pass. He strode toward his bride, stopping an arm's length from her when he saw her dark golden eyes widen still further. What kind of game was this? he asked himself testily, a good portion of his irritation directed at himself for allowing her performance to touch him. Why was she playing the role of modest, shy virgin when rumor had it that she was not a virgin at all? He had seen her hand flutter helplessly to her heart when their eyes had met across the crowd, seen the gamut of emotions on her face—shock, distress, bewilderment, fear, wariness. If she was really this good an actress, he cursed silently, she would lead him a merry chase.

His gaze swept over Isabella again, taking in her expression, her stance. He saw the knuckles of her hands, which clutched the velvet curtain, whiten still further and his eyes narrowed. This could not possibly be the woman who ordered her servants to be dealt twenty lashes as casually as she commanded a jester to divert her. The woman who whipped her horse until the beast bled. The woman who, it was whispered, had lain with more than one man—perhaps even with her own brothers.

The din behind him began again and he made to turn around. As he saw Isabella's hand reach out to him, tremble and return to clutch the velvet curtain, he stilled.

"Please." Her whisper was barely audible. "Make them all go away."

His dark eyebrows curved upward for a moment. Surely she was aware of the customs. Surely she knew that a marriage like theirs was consummated before witnesses to make certain there would be no grounds for annulment later on. His gaze flicked over to the long table filled with refreshments for those who would spend the night here, making coarse jests and keeping a record of how many times he broke the lance. Despite himself, Alessandro felt his blood begin to heat at the thought of taking this woman.

"Please."

He might have resisted the urgent whisper if he hadn't looked into her eyes. Although he saw fear there and confusion, it was tempered by a resolute spirit that glowed in their depths. He had seen less courage in eyes he had faced over the length of a rapier.

Even as he cursed himself for a fool, he turned around to face the crowd. "Leave us." Silence fell, but only for a moment. Ignoring the agitated murmurs, Alessandro continued. "This marriage will be consummated in private."

Two young men pushed through the crowd. "If you think that we are going to let you get away with this, you are wrong." The shorter of the two men spat the words at Alessandro. "You will have no reason, damn it, to repudiate our sister and ask the pope for an annulment."

Adrienne took half a step back as she recognized the same golden brown eyes, the same golden hair she had seen in the mirror. Piero and Alfonso Gennaro, Isabella's brothers.

"I would think you would be pleased." Alessandro's voice was dangerously soft. "Think of the rich dowry that would return to your hands." His mouth curved in a chill smile. "To say nothing of the beautiful sister to be sold again to the highest bidder."

The shorter man started forward, but a narrowing of Alessandro's eyes stopped him in his tracks.

"What's the matter?" the taller man taunted. "Afraid that your performance will fall short of your reputation?" His soft mouth curved in a derisive smile, but he did not move forward.

Alessandro let his eyes travel down Alfonso Gennaro's body and then up again to his face, as much to give himself time to control his temper as to show his contempt. He placed his hand lightly on the jeweled hilt of the dagger at his waist. "Be grateful," he said, keeping his voice low and light, "that you are guests of our house." His anger eased a little as he saw Alfonso swallow and take a step backward.

An older man strode forward, brushing the Gennaros aside easily with a muscular arm. He planted himself in front of Alessandro and glared past him at Adrienne. "Enough of this foolishness," he growled. "Stop your whimpering, girl, and come forward."

As the man with the grizzled beard reached for her, Alessandro shifted to block his way.

The man's eyes moved to Alessandro's face, but the steely look in them did not soften. "Think well, my son, before you make this decision."

Alessandro curbed the desire to look back over his shoulder at his bride. "It will be as I have said, Father."

Francesco di Montefiore shrugged and shot another surly look at his daughter-in-law. If she brought peace to his troubled state, it would be worth it. And if she caused any trouble, there were ways of taking care of that, and her. He turned around and swept the crowd with his gaze. "Out."

One of the Gennaros began to protest again, but Francesco quelled his words with a single look. He remained motionless until the chamber had emptied. Then he turned to face his son again. "The witnesses will examine your sheets in the morning." His voice was crisp and matter-of-fact. "I would mislike it if you made a laughingstock of yourself—for whatever reason."

Alessandro looked into his father's face, so devoid of any deeper emotions. When he had been a small boy, he would have done anything to please his father. Anything to see his father's eyes light up for him as they did when he looked upon the woman who was his wife. Now Alessandro did what he had to and for the rest pleased himself. "Have I ever done less than my duty?"

"No, my son, and I have always been proud of you." Francesco di Montefiore sighed, feeling older than his fifty years. "If your mother had been my wife and not my mistress, perhaps I could have given you more." He clapped his son's shoulder and turned away.

Adrienne watched the two men, but the words they exchanged were too softly spoken for her to understand them. When the door closed behind Francesco di Montefiore, she felt her stomach knot at the thought of what would come. She had gotten what she wanted, she thought. The people who had crowded the chamber were gone. But now she was alone with this beautiful stranger. The stranger who would in a few minutes take her as his wife.

She opened her mouth to speak but closed it just as quickly. What could she say to him? How could she make him understand that she was Isabella in body only? That she—the woman inside the body that was not her own—came from another time, another place? What words could she use to make him believe her? She could feel the fear pumping through her bloodstream, and yet... and yet an odd certainty wove through the fear like a fine gold thread weaves through dark cloth. A certainty that it was here that she belonged. That in this time, this place, she had things to do. Vital, important things.

Alessandro looked at his bride. He could have sworn that when they had stood face-to-face in the great hall to sign their marriage contract, her eyes had rested upon him with as much cool calculation as a slave trader's. Now she looked so guileless, her eyes wide and full of questions. Had she always looked so? Had he simply refused to see it because he had grown to adulthood despising everyone who carried the Gennaro name?

Slowly he reached toward her and, his eyes on hers, began to loosen the fingers that still clutched the bed curtain so tightly. One by one he pried her fingers from the velvet until it fell away. Only then did he allow his gaze to slide downward.

The laces hung undone, her linen shift falling open just far enough to hint at the curves of her lush breasts. As he stared at her, he saw the soft, firm flesh quiver from her accelerated breathing and he felt his own body tighten in answer. He reached out again and, taking a lace into each hand, began to twine them around his fingers, pulling her toward him.

She did not resist, but he saw her flesh begin to flutter still more strongly as her heartbeat started to race. He brought her closer and closer yet until they were separated by mere inches.

When she felt Alessandro's hands begin to work her fingers away from the curtain that shielded her, Adrienne felt a quick flash of panic. No! she screamed silently. She could not allow this! She could not! But as the protest rose to her lips she met his eyes.

They were as black as his hair, without a trace of any other color, yet they were filled with light. It was that light that beckoned to her and made her fingers pliant, allowing him to ease them from the cloth until it fell away from her with a soft rustle.

Her eyes still fastened on his, she felt the first tug as he pulled her toward him by the laces of her shift. Her heart began to hammer, propelled by the fear that rose within her. But it was not fear alone that had her heart beating like the wings of a songbird caught in a cage. No. A strange sensation she had never felt before reshaped the fear, both blunting and sharpening it in the oddest way. A sensation that had her body tingling in answer.

She had to pull back, she told herself. She had to strike away those slender, dark hands drawing her ever closer. She had to find words to explain that she was not Isabella. But she could do none of these things, caught as she was in the changeable light of his eyes. She saw and acknowledged the flicker of challenge and the flare that she recognized as desire. But it was the glow of something more gentle that held her prisoner.

Lifting her hands, she laid them against his chest. "Alessandro, *ti prego...*"

"What?" he asked softly. "What do you beg me?"

But whatever words she had wanted to speak left her and she could only shake her head helplessly.

Suddenly he jerked the laces he still held toward him, bringing her flush against his body, imprisoning her hands between them. "What kind of game are you playing?" he demanded. "Who are you?"

Adrienne opened her mouth to tell him the truth, but the words died in her throat before they could reach her lips. If destiny or magic or God had sent her here, to this man, to this moment, was it not her fate to play out the role assigned her? Even before her mind answered her question, she had tilted her chin up at the man who was scowling down at her.

"I am Isabella di Montefiore." Her voice was firm. "Your wife."

Chapter Three

"**Y**es. My wife." Alessandro felt his body spring to life at the thought that this woman belonged to him. He would guard his mind and heart and guard them well, he vowed, for no child of the Gennaros could be trusted. But he would take her body and bring himself pleasure. Bring them both pleasure. He released the laces and slid his hands onto her shoulders.

Even before Adrienne realized that he was no longer restraining her, his hands were on her shoulders, sliding over the thin linen of her nightgown, upward over the sensitive skin of her neck until he cupped her head. As his face came closer she felt that quick jolt of fear she was already so familiar with, followed by that sharp-sweet sensation that made her body throb in the oddest places.

As Alessandro lowered his head toward Isabella, his last rational thought was that this must be what selling one's soul to the devil was like. Then he was lost in the honeyed taste of her mouth.

The taste of wine and candied almonds was on his tongue as he filled her mouth. But there was another taste that Adrienne recognized with some instinct she had not known she possessed. The taste of passion lay on his tongue. Passion just a step away from violence. She made a small sound of protest and pushed against him, although her hands were still trapped between them and gave her no leverage.

Alessandro felt rather than heard her soft sound of protest. Reacting automatically, he gentled his mouth and sipped where he had drunk greedily, soothed where he had unsettled. Where he had taken before, he began to give.

He traced the curve of her cheek with his lips, then retraced it with his tongue. The softness, the fragrance of her skin reminded him of the roses in his mother's garden. His mouth found a pulse that beat frantically below her ear. He teased the pulse with his tongue, the scent of roses rising to intoxicate him as surely as a strong, sweet wine.

She was pliant against him, her lush curves molded against his aroused body, her hands resting lightly on his hips. As Alessandro raised his head to look at her, she opened her eyes, and they were glazed with incipient passion. He smiled. This he could be sure of, he thought. He had seen enough women in all stages of passion to be a competent judge.

Sliding his hands down until they lay between the curve of her breasts and her collarbone, he began to push her shift aside. All the laces hung open and the soft linen slipped off her shoulders without impediment.

The cool air on her breasts barely penetrated the sensual haze that surrounded Adrienne. Before she realized what he was doing, Alessandro had shifted her hands away from his hips to allow the nightgown to fall to the floor. Her eyes flew open as she felt the material slither down her body, but before she could even begin to tense, he had lifted her in his arms and laid her in the center of the bed.

For long moments she lay there unmoving, her mind hazy, her body still languid with the passion Alessandro had aroused. She watched him move around the chamber with the careless grace of a large cat. He tossed the heavy gold medallion and chain he wore onto the table to lie next to the jewelry that spilled out of the inlaid box. Undoing the ruby buttons of his doublet with one hand, he walked to the table. He filled a goblet with wine, then left it untouched.

Without so much as a glance in her direction, he dispatched his clothing quickly. Perhaps it was that casual neglect more than his lack of modesty that made Adrienne suddenly aware that she was lying naked on a bed and that within minutes a stranger would invade her body. Desperate, a flush heating her skin, she sat bolt upright and snatched the coverlet of purple silk to shield her nakedness.

When Alessandro turned to face her, her breath caught in her throat at the sheer physical beauty of his partially aroused body. Although the impulse to hide herself was strong, Adrienne met his eyes. She watched him pick up an apple in one hand and his jeweled dagger in the other and move toward the bed.

As he approached, her heart pumped beneath the coverlet she clutched over her breasts. A few feet away from the bed he stopped. Taking a leisurely bite from the apple, he ran his gaze over her with a cool insolence that had anger pushing aside all the other confusing emotions within Adrienne.

Then, without warning, he tossed the apple toward her. Automatically she held out her hands to catch it, realizing too late what his intention had been when the coverlet slid down into her lap. Again anger surged within her at his trick, and without thinking, she hurled the fruit back at him, barely missing his shoulder.

He threw back his head and laughed, the warm, rich sound filling the chamber. "Thank God. I was beginning to think I had married a mouse." Still smiling, he came forward and sat down on the bed.

"How dare you..." Adrienne began, the words dying away when she felt the cold tip of the dagger sheath press lightly against her left breast.

"I dare anything I please." He smiled again, but this time the smile did not reach his eyes. "It would behoove you to remember that, *mia cara*. Your duty is to warm my bed and bear my children." Pulling the dagger back, he flipped it once, then caught it easily and bent forward to slide it under the pillow.

"Are you threatening me?" she demanded.

"Threaten?" His black brows curved upward like the wings of a bird of prey. "Do you take me for a barbarian?" He reached out and cupped her chin in his left hand. "No, *madonna*. Not a threat. Just a friendly warning."

Forgetting that she was not Isabella, forgetting that she had been set down in the midst of someone else's life, Adrienne again felt anger slice through her. Operating purely on instinct, she brought her arm up and slapped his hand away from her face. Before she could draw a breath, his fingers had encircled her wrist and were imprisoning it as securely as an iron manacle.

Alessandro stared at her, fury and admiration balancing each other out. What a mass of contradictions this woman was. She apparently possessed more courage than wisdom. Even now, as he held her wrist hard enough to leave marks on her skin, the anger was winning the battle against the fear in her eyes. Why then did she act the immature girl, afraid of the rituals of the marriage bed?

Even though he did not release her hand, his fingers gentled and his thumb began to rub the soft inner skin of her wrist. "Easy," he whispered, much as he would to a skittish mare about to be mated. Leaning forward, he brought her hand to his mouth and, keeping his eyes on hers, replaced his thumb with his lips.

As his lips and tongue and teeth traced circles on her wrist, he hooked his other arm around her waist and pulled her closer until her breasts brushed his chest. Even as he felt the tremor that went through her at the contact, he lowered his face into the curve of her neck, fragrant with the scent of roses.

He leaned forward, nudging her back down to the soft mattress with his body. When she lay on her back, his hands, his mouth began to drift over her, discovering the lush curves, the rose-petal skin. His blood began to swim with desire and quickly, more quickly than he would have wanted, the demands of his young body grew insistent.

Pulling back, he propped himself on an elbow, thinking to cool the heat driving through him. But as his gaze traveled over Isabella—over her thighs, which hid the solace he craved so badly, her breasts, which quivered with her quick breathing, her lips, which were slightly parted and seemed to invite his kiss—he knew that his patience was stretched as tightly as his body.

His mouth had worked magic on her skin, tracing circles that seemed to reverberate through her whole body. As her senses began to whirl, Adrienne found herself forgetting the arrogant words he had spoken. Forgetting the casual assessment that had been in his eyes. Forgetting even the cold tip of the dagger's sheath he had held at her breast.

When she felt a chill, she opened her eyes to find Alessandro looking down at her. His eyes glowed like live coals with the reflection of his desire. The nostrils of his straight nose quivered slightly with passion. His bronzed skin, sheened with moisture, rippled over his tightly stretched muscles. Despite her innocence, she understood just how badly this man wanted her. Understood that he was a breath away from taking her.

Suddenly the panic speared through her again. Even if this body was not hers, how could she allow it to be invaded by a stranger? And although he had kissed her, touched her, made her tremble with pleasure, this man was still a stranger.

Not knowing where she got the courage to do so, she lifted her hand and placed it against his chest.

"Alessandro?"

He curved his fingers around her hand and lowered his head to brush her fingertips with his mouth. "What is it?"

"Please, will you wait?"

He frowned. "Wait? Wait for what?"

Adrienne took a deep breath and spoke the words quickly, before she lost the courage to say them at all. "Wait to make love to me until we are no longer strangers."

Unmoving, he gazed at her for a long time before he spoke again. "You mean it," he said slowly. "You are actually serious."

She said nothing, but her gaze did not waver from his.

Alessandro felt a surge of anger, fueled by his arousal, fueled by the impossibility of her request, fueled by his absurd impulse to yield to the plea in her eyes.

"Do you not understand?" he burst out. "Our marriage should have been consummated before witnesses."

Adrienne stared at him as she remembered Isabella's words.

Alessandro came to me five times in the night and I cared not that prurient, envious eyes watched us. I saw the desire in his eyes again and again and I will know to make him a willing slave of my body.

Her lips parted in a mute gasp as the realization hit her. If this was not an insane dream, if she was truly here, now, then she, Adrienne de Beaufort, had already in one small way changed the history that Isabella di Montefiore had lived.

"And this? What of this?"

Jolted back by the hiss of Alessandro's voice, she watched him jerk her hand downward and press it against his aroused flesh. Felt him surge against her palm. Although she did not recognize it, her body throbbed with an answering heat. She tried to wrest her hand away from him, but he held it fast.

"And what of the witnesses who will examine our sheets in the morning?" He flung her hand away. "Their eyes will be especially sharp after that little performance you put on." His hands flexed as he fought for control. "Do you think that I will allow myself to be made a fool of by you when they find neither a trace of your blood nor my seed?"

His eyes narrowed to obsidian slits. "Or are you just trying to find a way to disguise the fact that your vir-

ginal blood was spilled long ago?'' Wrapping his hand
in her hair, he pulled her closer. ''Are you?''

*There was suspicion in his eyes when he plunged his
body into mine the first time. Suspicion that did not
fade until he saw my blood running red on his own
flesh. Then I knew just how clever I had been to guard
my maidenhead during all those pleasurable love
games that Piero and Alfonso taught me.*

''You are hurting me.''

Instead of releasing her, he tightened his grip on her
hair. ''Answer me.''

''Will you believe me if I tell you that I have lain
with no man?'' Her heart gave a jolt as she spoke the
words that were both the truth and a lie.

''Do you swear it?''

''Yes.'' Her gaze did not waver from his eyes.
''Upon the head of my firstborn son.'' She tilted her
chin up. ''Of our firstborn son.''

He released her then and, bending his leg, crossed
his arms on his knee. Propping his chin on his arms,
he studied the woman who was his wife. He must be
mad, he cursed himself. He should have bade her to
hold her tongue and taken her quickly, before she had
had the chance to worm her way into his soul with her
soft eyes the color of wine from Jerez. If he gave in,
he would be opening himself to mockery, to shame, to
blackmail. Even as he told himself all this, he knew
that she had won.

Adrienne watched him as he wordlessly reached for
the dagger he had put under the pillow. Even though
fear lanced through her as he slipped the finely honed
steel from its jeweled sheath, she did not move, some
sixth sense assuring her that he would do her no harm.

His hand steady, he flicked the tip of the blade across his wrist and calmly watched his scarlet blood trickle onto the white sheet and spread into a bright stain.

Her stomach knotting with agitation and gratitude and guilt, Adrienne raised herself onto her knees. Snatching up her nightgown from the floor with hands that were as tremulous as Alessandro's had been steady, she quickly ripped a strip of material from the garment and wrapped it around his wrist. There was blood on her hands when she finished—his blood. She stared down at them. It was as if he had given her part of himself, and she felt inexplicably, irrevocably bound to him. Picking up the ruined gown, she slowly wiped the blood from his hands and hers.

Sitting back on her haunches, she looked at Alessandro for a long, silent moment. "Thank you," she said softly, lifting her hand to touch his cheek. "You will not regret it."

Even as the words left her mouth, an ominous foreboding began to gather in the pit of her stomach. How could she make such a rash promise? This night had to be a trick played by a spirit, and it would be over as quickly, as suddenly as it had begun. How could she make promises she would not be here to keep?

Alessandro saw the doubts and anxiety flicker through her eyes, but he was too weary, his nerves and his body stretched too tightly, to categorize them. "For your sake, I hope so." He kept his eyes on her face. "Now cover yourself before I change my mind." His voice was brusque.

Adrienne lay down, pulling the coverlet up to her chin. Turning his back to her, Alessandro slid down onto the soft mattress. She watched the subtle rippling of muscles beneath his bronzed skin. Although she knew she was playing with fire, she reached out, needing somehow to reassure herself one more time that this was not a dream. When she placed her hand against the warm skin of his back, she felt him stiffen, but he did not move away.

"Sandro?"

"No one calls me that."

Adrienne smiled. "Good. Then I will." Her fingers spread in a reflexive little caress. "Good night."

He turned his head a little so that she could see his straight profile. "Do not touch me again, Isabella, unless you are issuing an invitation."

She tucked her hand under her cheek. "Another threat?"

He heard the smile in her voice. Admiration and amusement warred with his ill temper and won. When he spoke, there was an answering smile in his voice. "No, Isabella. Just another friendly warning."

As he lay there, eyes open, body tense, Alessandro heard Isabella's soft breathing even out in sleep. He turned over and looked at her. She lay there like a child, her cheek pillowed on her hand. Against the rich purple silk of the coverlet, her skin gleamed like alabaster.

The needs were still driving through him and the temptation to forget the unspoken promise he had made and reach for her was so keen that his body leapt at the thought of sinking into her. Again, he cursed himself for a fool. But he had made a promise, sealed with his own blood, and—although it was not something he would have cared to admit in public—for his

personal sense of honor, a promise made to a woman
was no different than allegiance pledged to a warlord.

His gaze resting on Isabella, he touched himself to
complete the fraud of a marriage consummated.

Adrienne emerged from sleep, her heart pumping
from the onslaught of unfamiliar sensations. She lay
half-pinned under a man's body. A possessive hand
was splayed on her midriff, the fingertips grazing the
undercurve of her breast. His leg had been slung over
hers, bringing his body into intimate contact with her
thigh. Dazed but ready to fight, she tensed and half
raised herself.

The man's head lay on her pillow, his long black
hair partly concealing his face. But the chiseled profile left no doubt in her mind as to the identity of the
man who lay with her so intimately. Relief coursed
through her, even though her heart continued to race.
She fell back onto the pillow and closed her eyes. So
it had not been a dream after all. The past night came
to life behind her eyelids—vivid, with all its tastes and
scents and textures intact. She had lived it. She had
truly lived it.

But what was she going to do? The question
thrummed through her head like an insistent drumbeat. She did not know by what power she had come
here, but she could not stay, she thought desperately.
She had to find a way back to her own life. In the thin,
early light that filtered through the windowpanes, she
remembered all the things that had drained out of her
mind in the heated, atmosphere of the bedchamber
last night.

There were people depending on her. Jean de Lambert's widow and child were in the secret chamber,

where they would die of hunger and thirst if she did not go back to free them. And more people would come after them. People who would fall into the hands of Fabien and his ilk unless she was there to help them.

She began to struggle, trying to twist herself out from under the man's limbs, but he murmured something and his hand moved upward to mold her breast. Twin streaks of heat and weakness shot through her and she lay still, her head turned to face him.

Sandro. She tasted the name on her tongue. This was not some nameless man that a fluke of fate had thrown her together with. This was a man she knew. From the time she had spent at his side last night. From the pages of Isabella's diaries.

His face was relaxed in sleep now, with none of the tension that had been there earlier. She lifted her hand to touch him, his beauty tempting her as strongly as the serpent's apple had tempted Eve. Then she remembered what he had said about touching him and issuing invitations and her hand fell away.

Still she continued to watch him. Did he know? she asked herself sadly. Did he know in some secret part of his being that he would never see children born of his loins? That none of the plans, the dreams that he cherished within him would ever be fulfilled? That he would go to a terrible death, betrayed by his wife?

Forcing herself to look away from him, Adrienne scanned the room. If only she could find some clue to how she had come to be here, perhaps that would help her find her way home. Her eyes passed over the portrait of Isabella that she knew so well, then returned to it. The longer she stared at it, the more a strange, agitated restlessness built within her until her body seemed to hum with it. As the restlessness grew, so did the assurance.

This was a visible connection between her life and Isabella's. Perhaps it was a clue, a sign. If the portrait existed in both lives, perhaps, by some secret means, it had been her vehicle to this room. If that was so, it could be the vehicle back to her own life.

Moving more urgently than before, she managed to disentangle herself from Sandro's limbs. He murmured something again but did not wake. Sliding from the bed, she tugged the curtain closed. She started walking toward the portrait, then stopped. It was insane, but she needed to look at him again.

Retracing her steps, she supported herself against the bedpost and gazed down at him—young and beautiful and doomed. Her heart was heavy, as if she were already grieving for him.

"Isabella."

Horrified, Adrienne heard his sleep-blurred voice. She wanted so badly to stay. To stay while he woke. To stay and be the wife he deserved. But she knew she could not. Begging him silently for his forgiveness, she dropped the curtain and ran toward the portrait.

She began to move her hands over the canvas, registering vaguely that the texture was smooth, without the cracks in the paint that three centuries had wrought. Nothing. Her hands moved ever faster, as the panic within her rose.

"Isabella? Where are you?"

His voice was husky and it beckoned to her. Beckoned so strongly that she almost pushed away from the painting and returned to the bed.

"Please," she whispered to whatever power had brought her here. "Please take me back home." Her palms slid over the canvas.

"Isabella?" The voice was stronger now and held a note of irritation.

Adrienne heard movement behind the curtain and another jolt of panic flashed through her. She had already started to turn around when she was catapulted back into the blackness.

Chapter Four

It was dark when Adrienne opened her eyes. She lay still for a moment, strangely drained of all energy. Winded, as if she had run for miles, she inhaled a lungful of air in an attempt to even her breathing. The scent that filled her nostrils was not the heated air of the opulent Renaissance bedchamber, saturated with the perfume of Turkish rose oil, ripe fruit and arousal. Instead she could smell the mildew that had seemed to settle everywhere once she had stopped heating the château, overlaid by the faint tang of the sea. She had succeeded, she thought bleakly. She had returned to the Château de Beaufort.

Forcing herself to sit up, she looked down at her body. She was once again wearing the familiar non-descript gown, the bodice torn, the skirt pushed up to her knees. Had it been a dream after all? Perhaps a fantasy to escape the reality of being raped by Fabien? No, she thought as the memory washed over her like a scented summer breeze. She remembered that heated night too vividly—its colors, its scents, its textures—for it not to have been real.

She shifted and a ray of thin moonlight fell across her, highlighting a dark smear across the knuckles of one hand. Adrienne touched it lightly with her finger. She knew—her brain knew—that it could be anything. But her heart knew with an absolute certainty that this rusty brown smudge was the blood Sandro had shed for her. Somehow she had taken the reminder of his sacrifice with her across the centuries. Adrienne lowered her forehead to the back of her hand. As the terrible choice she had made filled her awareness, tears welled and overflowed.

Oh, she understood well enough that she could not have lived with herself had she not returned to bring Charlotte de Lambert and her child to safety. But as the tears ran down her cheeks, she wondered how she would be able to live with herself knowing that, had she let her spirit stay in Isabella's body, she might have had a chance to save Sandro from betrayal and death.

She had made the decision—one life for two. One life that was none of her concern for the two lives entrusted to her now, and for all the other lives the future would confide to her. Roughly she wiped away her tears and stood up. She had work to do, she reminded herself. And although her life stretched out before her like a desolate wasteland, she knew that she would do what she must.

Suddenly her head snapped to the side as an impression of some vague inconsistency crystallized. Stumbling to the French doors, she looked up at the sky, where an almost full moon hung like a lopsided lantern. Her fingers tightened on the wood that years of salty air had roughened. How could there be a full moon tonight, she asked herself, when two nights ago she had stood on a beach lighted by a misty sickle and watched Père Duroc's boat with its human cargo sail for the English coast? And she had been away but a night. Or had she? Her mind spun as she tried to sort out the possibilities.

Pushing away from the doors, she turned back into the room. When her gaze fell on the portrait, she fell back a step with a gasp. The painting looked as if it had been attacked by a madman. So many cruel slashes and gouges covered it that it was barely recognizable. And the knife she had used on Fabien was now embedded at the base of Isabella's long slender neck. Adrienne felt an icy sheen of sweat cover her skin. This was what he might have done to her, had she not been carried away across the centuries. This was what he might do to her still if he ever got his hands on her again.

Even though the mutilated portrait made her skin crawl, even though she wanted to run from it, she knew what she had to do. She stepped closer. By some miracle the portion of the canvas that hid the mechanism had remained intact, and carefully Adrienne manipulated it, while sweat began to trickle down between her shoulder blades. When the hidden door sprang open, she sagged a little with relief.

She had barely stepped inside the secret chamber when she was almost knocked off her feet by the impact of Charlotte de Lambert's body.

"*Dieu merci,* I had given up hope that you would come." She gripped Adrienne's arm so tightly that Adrienne's nails cut into her flesh. "I have lost track of the time, but we have been here for days." Her voice rose in near hysteria. "Days!"

"Days?" Adrienne repeated, bewildered. "But I was there for but one night."

"Where? Where were you?" Charlotte shook her arm. "How could you go away and leave us?"

Adrienne shook her head, remembering the change in the moon that had perplexed her earlier. Staring into Charlotte de Lambert's wide, frightened eyes, she began to understand that while she had traveled across the centuries, time had somehow shifted. It had gone off balance, stretching or contracting in some bizarre way, making a few hours the equal of a day.

She freed her arm from Charlotte's grasp and began to pace. She had to do something. Make plans, arrangements. But even as she told herself that, she knew that she could not risk staying at the château another hour. They had to leave now, this minute, while it was still dark, before Fabien returned to finish on her what he had started on the painting. If she could only manage to get them to the village, Père Duroc would hide them until he could ferry them across the Channel.

Half-dazed still, her mind confused with a jumble of memories and feelings she was at best half-aware of, Adrienne turned to Charlotte.

"We have to leave here. Quickly." Her hand curved over the smaller woman's shoulder in an automatic gesture of comfort. "Will you be able to walk a ways?"

Silently Charlotte nodded and Adrienne hurried the woman and her child out of the chamber.

The light of the moon made the descent to the seaside village both easier and more difficult. On the one hand, they could negotiate the slippery, rocky path with its treacherous drop-offs more safely. On the other, they had to edge along the shadowed side of the rocks, not knowing who might be watching them.

When they came in sight of the cluster of humble fishermen's huts, Charlotte shrank back.

"No! Do not make me go down there!" Her high voice was made higher still by the wind that swept in from the sea, carrying a taste of rain.

"You will be all right," Adrienne soothed. "There is no one there who will hurt you."

"You do not know that," the woman cried, her eyes turning wild. "I cannot risk something happening to my baby." She hitched the child higher. "Not when I have come this far."

"You will be safe." She ran her hand lightly up and down Charlotte's back.

"No!" Charlotte's voice rose in a wail and the child began to whimper. "No!"

Adrienne tensed. She would trust these fishermen with her life, but there were so many others about these days who were more than ready to report a suspicious word. Turning Charlotte to face her, she gripped her shoulders.

"Not another word. You will come with me." Her voice was firm but not unkind, and carried the innate authority of someone accustomed to giving orders and having them obeyed without question.

The resistance went out of Charlotte as suddenly as it had come and she swayed. Adrienne ignored the stab of guilt and cupped the woman's cheek for a moment. "Good girl. You have been so brave to come this far. It would be a shame to risk it all now. *Pas vrai?*"

Slipping from shadow to shadow, they reached the Duroc hut. It lay in darkness, as did the rest of the village. Adrienne crept forward and scratched on the window once and then again. She heard a murmur, the shuffle of feet and then the creak of the door as it was cracked open.

"It is me, Adrienne de Beaufort," she whispered urgently.

"C'est la petite comtesse." Even as he whispered the words over his shoulder, Duroc threw open the door and began pulling Adrienne inside.

Adrienne gestured to Charlotte, who had wedged herself into the shadow of the thatched roof, and, taking her by the hand, slipped inside the hut.

A light flared and the smell of the lard-dipped rag that served instead of a candle joined the odor of fish that pervaded both the dwelling and its inhabitants.

"Comtesse Adrienne!" His natural reserve and all rules of proper behavior forgotten, old Duroc gripped Adrienne's hands. "Fabien, the filthy swine, has been turning the countryside upside down looking for you. Where have you been?"

Adrienne shook her head. "It is not important. Listen, Père Duroc. This woman needs to be taken away and quickly. Men from Paris are looking for her. Can you help her?"

Moving his massive shoulders in an eloquent shrug, the old man rubbed the back of his hand against his stubbled jaw. "Not until the moon wanes. Now, with Fabien's informers digging around everywhere like pigs rooting for truffles and the moon lighting up even the most secluded cove..." He shook his head.

"It is too dangerous for her to stay here for more than a day, two at the most." Adrienne put her hand on Père Duroc's arm. "If they come to search the village, they will recognize her."

Père Duroc drew his bushy eyebrows together and looked toward the young woman. Then he nodded. *"Bon."*

That one taciturn word told Adrienne all she needed to know. With a soft sigh of relief she gave the old man's hand a quick squeeze, knowing that more would only embarrass him.

"And you, Comtesse Adrienne? What of you?"

Adrienne shook her head. "What of me?"

"You cannot stay here, either. If Fabien gets his hands on you, he will use you like the cheapest whore and then send you to the guillotine." Duroc touched her shoulder. "Go to England with them. You will be safe there."

Adrienne looked up at the old man. "But I have to be here for the others who come needing help."

"If you stay, you will be able to help no one," Duroc said roughly. "Not even yourself." He gripped her arm. "He will kill you, I tell you, or worse."

Adrienne stared at Duroc, the first tremulous beginnings of an idea germinating within her.

"The first time I ever saw you, Comtesse Adrienne, you were three years old." The old man's voice softened. "You had run away from the château to gather shells on the beach. I would rather lose you to the English than to Fabien."

Her eyes glazed, Adrienne stared unseeingly at Duroc. She heard the sound of his voice, but the words did not register. The idea burgeoned within her, expanding, intensifying, until it became a vision. There was a place she could go, she thought. A place where she belonged. A place where she was needed.

"Comtesse Adrienne?"

She gave no answer, the questions and doubts beginning to push at her. If she had truly been in that bedchamber, how could she be sure that she would be able to return? Would Isabella's portrait take her back in time again? Would her mind and soul again slip into Isabella's body, supplant her mind and soul? And could she live with the beautiful stranger with whom she had spent that strange night—so wanton, so chaste?

But he was not a stranger, she reminded herself. He was the man who had treated her kindly when it would have been his right to use her as roughly as he pleased. He was the man whose beauty and grace made her heart beat faster. He was the man whose future she knew in all its bloody detail. It took no longer than a heartbeat to make the final decision.

Suddenly she felt Duroc shaking her shoulders.

"Comtesse Adrienne, have you heard a word that I have said?"

She shook her head as if to clear it. "I am sorry, Père Duroc."

Outside, the sky was lightening with the first signs of dawn and Adrienne felt an urgency driving her. With some sense she had not known she possessed, she knew that she had no time to spare—in this world or in the other.

"Listen to me, Père Duroc. I have a place to go. A place that is far away." The old man started to speak, but Adrienne shook her head and the words kept tumbling out. "Take care of them for me. Them and the others who will come." She curled her fingers around his rough hand. "Will you do that for me?"

"Yes, but where..."

"I do not know if I can get there." She gave his hand one more squeeze. "Pray for me."

The urgency was there, pressing against the back of her neck, and she whirled away toward the door. She heard voices calling her, but she ignored them and began to run.

Within minutes she was back on the path above the village. She slipped on the slick rocks again and again, but she did not feel the cuts and scrapes. Every breath burned in her throat like fire, but she did not stop. Her legs felt like wax that had been left out in the sun, yet somehow she kept on moving.

The château was within reach, wrapped in the mist and the thin gray light of dawn, when Adrienne tripped over a fallen branch and fell facedown on the gravel. She lay there unable to stir. The impact seemed to have jarred the last of her energy from her. It was then that she heard the dogs.

Run, Adrienne, run, she exhorted herself. Yet she lay there, motionless, eyes closed, as if she had already capitulated to her fate. Then the image of Sandro's face appeared behind her eyelids and she felt a surge of energy. Still it took long, precious moments before she managed to scramble back up on her feet. Drawing on a hidden wellspring of strength, she raced toward the château in one last mad dash.

As she reached the French doors, she was pulled to a halt. At the thought that Fabien had captured her after all, a scream rose in her throat. Twisting around, she saw that it was only her sleeve, which had caught on the jagged glass. Barely noticing when the glass sliced into her thumb, she freed herself and tumbled into the study.

Her legs beginning to falter again, she lurched toward the ruined portrait and ran her hands over it. The sound of the dogs was closer now, their baying high-pitched and excited, and Adrienne knew that they had picked up her scent. Where had she touched the portrait before? Where?

The dogs were close enough now that she could hear the sound of their claws digging into the gravel as they strained against their leashes. Then their barking changed. As she glanced over her shoulder she saw the lead dog of the pack framed in the open doors, his eyes savage and red-rimmed, his tongue lolling between vicious fangs. Within seconds they would be upon her.

Adrienne screamed, her hands still pressed against the painting. As the sound filled the small room, she felt a jolt and then she was hurtling through the silent black void, the echoes of her own scream still ringing in her ears.

Even before she opened her eyes, Adrienne knew that fate had taken pity on her. She inhaled deeply and all the lush scents she remembered filled her nostrils. Opening her eyes, she saw that she was sprawled on the floor, as naked as she had been when she had journeyed from this room just a few hours ago.

She pushed herself up against the wall, the top of her head touching the frame of Isabella's portrait. The room was silent, the aquamarine bed curtains still drawn as she had left them. Had she been away at all? The sudden flash of doubt had tension gathering at the back of her neck. Had it been a dream, a nightmare, an illusion? Did she still have the journey to release Charlotte de Lambert and her child before her? She

balled her hands into fists. A throbbing in her left
hand nudged her out of her inertia and she looked
down and saw the jagged cut on the pad of her thumb.

As she ran a finger over the cut, from which blood
still seeped, an image rose before her, so real she
thought she could smell the tang of the sea. She saw
herself frantically working to disentangle her sleeve
from the broken glass that had caught it. She saw the
glass slice into her finger. She saw herself stumble toward the mutilated portrait.

Looking down at her body, Adrienne searched for
the other cuts and scrapes she knew she had sus-
tained, but her golden skin was smooth and unblem-
ished. She closed her eyes. It was as if she had been
given that one wound to take with her across time as
a sign. A sign so that she would know for certain that
she had truly fulfilled her duty.

Rising, she walked toward the bed. Her stomach
muscles knotting, she held the aquamarine velvet
aside. Sandro. He slept as she had left him, his chiseled face half-buried, childlike, in the pillow. A maze
of emotions rose within her. Adrienne recognized the
tenderness, the need to keep this man from harm, to
cherish him always. But she could not have put a name
to the strange, boundless feeling that sprang to life
within her heart and quickened her pulse.

She drew the curtain aside and lowered herself onto
the bed. As she pulled the coverlet of purple silk
around her to shield her nakedness, she glanced toward the window and saw the light of early morning.
She sighed with relief, deciding that she had been fortunate. This journey had been accomplished without
the wrinkle, the shift in time that had almost caused

her to be too late to save Charlotte de Lambert. Smiling, she settled down to wait for Sandro to awaken.

The minutes trickled by gently like sand in an hourglass as she watched Sandro sleep. She wanted so much to touch him, but she waited. The air was warm and scented. The silk that covered her was sleek against her skin. Her eyelids began to drift closed.

The next thing she knew, she was being roughly lifted up from the soft mattress.

"Where were you, damn you?"

Jolted from half sleep to full wakefulness, Adrienne found her heart beating in her throat, blocking her vocal chords.

"Answer me!" Sandro flung her back down on the mattress, only to pick her up again, his fingers biting ruthlessly into her arms.

Adrienne shook her head helplessly. Even if she had been able to speak, what could she tell him?

Sandro lifted her so that she knelt on the mattress facing him. "When I woke up yesterday, you were gone." He shook her. "If my father were not ruler of Siena, your brothers would have killed me." His beautiful mouth curled with contempt. "Or tried to."

He looked at her for a long, silent moment, eyes narrowed to obsidian slits. "I do not know what kind of game you are playing, Isabella, but I do know one thing—" his hands slid upward, over her shoulders, until they curved around her neck "—you are not going to play it with me. Do you understand me?" The overt anger was gone from his voice, but the low, velvet tone held even more menace.

"Your brothers accused me yesterday of having done violence to you." His fingers tightened around her neck—just a little. "I would greatly dislike it for them to be right." His thumbs pressed lightly against her windpipe. "Do you understand me?"

Adrienne managed to nod jerkily.

"Good."

Sandro released her and it was by pure willpower that Adrienne kept herself from collapsing on the bed.

"I will have an explanation now, *madonna.*"

Adrienne picked up the fallen coverlet to shield herself and felt the mad drumbeat of her heart against her hands. What could she tell him? she thought desperately. He would never believe the truth. How could he, when she barely believed it herself?

"I did nothing dishonorable." She felt the brush of panic as she again heard a voice speak that was not her own, but she ignored it. "I needed time alone."

"You needed time alone," Sandro mimicked her words, his voice heavy with sarcasm. "And left me to be a laughingstock of the whole court. To face your brothers who were frothing at the mouth like mad dogs." He gave a disgusted snort. "Left me to hear my own father decree that I would be kept prisoner in my apartments until Madonna Isabella returned, well and unharmed."

Battling back her own panic, Adrienne studied him. He was not simply angry, she realized. His pride had been injured, his honor insulted. And although she did not how she knew it or why, she suddenly understood very clearly what that meant to a man like him.

"I am sorry," she said softly, aware of the inadequacy of her words. "If I could, I would undo it, but I cannot." A smile trembled on her lips. "Will you forgive me, Sandro?"

"I told you that no one calls me that," he snapped.

Her smile grew stronger. "And I told you that I would."

He stared at her. "I should thrash you for your insolence." His voice was rough, but when he had spoken, he laughed.

His laughter emboldened her and her smile bloomed fully. "But you will not."

He reached out and ran a slender finger over her shoulder and down her arm. "It would be a shame to mark skin like this." He felt a sharp flash of desire. This time, he thought, this time he would take her and none of her pretty pleading would stop him.

Moving back, he slid off the bed and stood. "Come. You will show yourself now."

Still clutching the coverlet to her breasts, Adrienne stood. As Sandro moved toward the door, she held back. Surely he did not mean that she should show herself like this? But he did, she realized, remembering what she knew about the mores of the time that was now her own.

He was almost at the door when Sandro looked over his shoulder to see Isabella standing next to the bed as he had left her.

"May I please dress first?"

She was playing her game again, he told himself, and she was doing it flawlessly, right down to the fear in her eyes, which she seemed to be fighting so courageously. Why then did he feel the urge to believe her, to grant her every wish?

He returned to stand before her. "No, you may not."

Adrienne opened her mouth to protest, but he silenced her, placing his fingers lightly against her lips.

His eyes met hers and held them. Comfortable as he was with the unapologetic immodesty of the age, he found her behavior odd—and, just as odd, his strangely unquestioning acceptance of it. Taking the coverlet from her, he wound it around her in the manner of a Roman toga, leaving one shoulder bare. When he was done, he tipped his chin toward the door in silent command.

Side by side, they moved forward.

Striking the door twice with his fist, Sandro stood back. When the door swung open, he saw his brothers-in-law with their blond hair and their weak chins.

"Isabella, *carissima.*" Both young men spoke in unison and started forward, but an imperious gesture from Sandro had them skidding to a stop. "Are you all right? Where were you? Has he hurt you in any way?"

Although she was covered at least as modestly as a gown would have covered her, Adrienne could feel her skin heating with a flush. "I am perfectly all right."

"But where were you, *piccolina?*" The shorter of the two brothers reached out to her. "And how did you leave your chamber without anyone seeing you?"

It was Piero who had spoken, Adrienne realized, recognizing him by the thin white scar along his jaw. She met his eyes, recoiling from the coldness she saw there. "This is not the only door."

"But where were you?" Piero insisted.

"I have told my husband where I was," she said clearly, ignoring Piero's hand. "He is the only one who needs to know this."

Quickly controlling the small start of surprise at her words, Sandro held out his hand, palm upward. "The key."

"But..."

"I dislike repeating myself, *messere.*"

His eyes blazing, Piero Gennaro slapped the key into Sandro's hand.

"*Grazie tante.*" Sandro's voice was softly mocking. He stepped forward and tapped the bit of the key against Piero's shoulder. "Tell my lord father that Madonna Isabella has returned and is safe from harm."

With a casually elegant movement, he swung the door closed and turned the key.

When he faced her again, Adrienne understood that the time she had asked him for had run out. But she felt no fear as she had just a few hours ago. Instead, tension and excitement mingled within her, making her pulse scurry.

"Now, *madonna,* we will see if the blood I shed was a poor joke or not." He took a step toward her and then another until merely a handbreadth separated them. "Do not insult either of us by begging."

Adrienne understood that he was going to take her. Somehow, through some secret instinct, she understood, too, that if they were to have a true chance together she had to give before he could take. Suddenly it seemed so simple. He was no longer the stranger of a few hours ago. He was, after all, the destiny she had consciously, deliberately, chosen for herself.

"Sandro." Adrienne placed her palm on his chest.

"Do you remember what I told you, Isabella?"

She nodded, feeling the strong beat of his heart accelerate against her palm.

"Are you issuing an invitation?"

Her fingers spread in an unconscious caress and she smiled. "Yes."

Chapter Five

Adrienne's heart almost stopped beating when she saw the heat shoot into Sandro's eyes. Alarm snaked up her spine, and she could not prevent the light shiver that shook her. She started to lift her hand away from his chest, but he covered it with his, effectively pinning it down.

"Were you planning to take the invitation back, Isabella?"

"No." Her whisper was barely audible.

"What, then? Second thoughts?"

She wanted to squirm under the black gaze that seemed to probe into the deepest recesses of her mind and heart, but pride stiffened her spine instead. "Yes," she admitted.

Sandro felt the hand beneath his tremble. "Afraid, *madonna?*" Although his voice was soft, his eyebrows lifted in a mocking curve.

"There is no shame in fear." She tilted her chin up defiantly. "Only in fleeing from what you fear." Pausing, she deliberately met his eyes and held them. "And I do not intend to flee from you, *messere.*"

His hand slid down to close around her wrist. "But you fled before."

"Not from you."

Sandro looked down at her, amazed, distressed at the violence and venom of the jealousy that bored into him like the point of a rapier. Jealousy that went far beyond the socially acceptable refusal to share his wife with any man. Jealousy that was intensely, fiercely personal. "Where did you go, Isabella?" His hand tightened. "Tell me."

"I cannot tell you more than I already have." She took a deep breath. "There is no more to tell."

"You do know what happens to unfaithful wives, do you not, *madonna?*"

Adrienne bit back a cry of pain as his fingers tightened still further. Suddenly the fury in his eyes lost its heat and turned to ice.

"The executioner's sword is always well honed," he murmured. "You would do well not to forget that."

Forcing herself to remain still when she would have retreated before this cold rage, Adrienne let her gaze drop to where his fingers were still curved viselike around her wrist. "You are hurting me."

Immediately his hold loosened, but he did not release her.

"There is no need to threaten me. I did not lie when I promised to be your faithful wife."

He laughed gruffly. "It would be the first time that a spawn of the Gennaros did not lie or cheat."

The trace of a smile curved Adrienne's lips. "Someday you will beg my forgiveness for your words."

"Are you so courageous, *madonna—*" Sandro's eyes narrowed as he gauged her "—or merely so insolent?"

"I wish you many healthy years to find an answer to your question." Adrienne lowered her gaze again, afraid that he would be able to read all the emotions she was sure were reflected in her eyes. If he only knew just how much she wished him many years, just how much she wanted to give him those years.

Sandro frowned. There was an inflection in her words, an undertone, as if they somehow held a second meaning. An odd feeling moved through him, but it was gone before he could define it. He hooked a finger under her chin and tilted it upward, needing to look into her eyes again. But the golden brown depths seemed to hold no secrets, no deception—only a smile that he absurdly wanted to believe in. "I cannot make rhyme or reason of you, Isabella." He shook his head, unused to puzzling over women.

"You have a lifetime for it."

His hand drifted down her arm and back as her soft voice flowed over him, as seductive as a breeze in a summer garden. His anger of a moment ago already half-forgotten, he took her hand and raised it to press a kiss into her palm. It was then that he saw the blotches on her wrist, which were already beginning to darken.

He felt his stomach knot. He had never before bruised a woman's skin except in the turbulence of passion. How was it that he, who had always not only taken pleasure from women but given it as well, had marked his wife's skin before their marriage had even begun? He felt a surge of anger. At himself for not controlling the violence he knew lived within him. At her for pushing him over the edge.

Adrienne watched the gamut of emotions mirrored in his eyes and the fear that was still flickering within her sputtered and died. Instead, the boundless feeling she had felt earlier as she had watched him sleep swept through her again, giving her the courage to lift her other hand and touch her fingertips to his face.

Her gesture seemed so artless, so genuine. Even though all logic told him that it was practiced seduction, Sandro felt his anger fade. Keeping his eyes on hers, he set out to entice, to seduce in his turn. Capturing her fingers, he drew them toward his mouth. He slid her fingertips, which smelled faintly of roses, over his lips, once, twice, and watched her eyes widen.

Her reflexive response and the soft skin of her fingers on his mouth made his body spring to life so swiftly, so powerfully, that the wish to take her here, now, quickly and without preliminaries, was almost irresistible.

He released her hands and with the flick of a finger loosened the purple coverlet that was still tucked around her. The silk glided to the floor with a whisper. For a moment he allowed his gaze to travel over her body with its golden skin, its gentle curves with their promise of lushness. His hands slid around her ribs and lifted her toward him.

Tantalized by the caress of his lips across her fingertips, Adrienne did not protest when he carelessly swept the silk that covered her aside. She felt her skin heat beneath the fire of his gaze, and before she knew what was happening, his hands were sliding around her, lifting her toward him. When his aroused flesh slid between her thighs, she cried out softly as surprise and a touch of fear mingled with the sensations of her own body.

He was so filled with desire that all he heard was the rushing of his own blood. But he heard her low cry.

His hands were already sliding down her back to fit her to him when the realization struck him that it was not solitary satisfaction that he craved. For some reason he could not understand, he wanted more from this woman than to be the receptacle for his seed.

"Put your legs around my waist." His voice was hoarse.

"What are you doing?" she whispered, even as she obeyed him.

Sandro's hands slid down to cup her bottom. "I am taking you to bed," he said as he moved across the room.

As he lowered himself onto the soft mattress, Adrienne felt his aroused body flex under her and she felt an answering tingle in her core. Wanting to capture the sensation again, she instinctively shifted over him and was rewarded.

"I want you." He drew his hands upward until his fingertips touched the soft curve of her breast. It was more than mere wanting, he realized. He had wanted women before, but it had never felt like this. This was need. As clear, as pure a need as the need for air, for water. How had he lived to this day without her? Even as the words formed within his brain, he rejected them. He could not allow himself to need her like this, for that would mean surrendering himself into her power. And that would be the same as turning his back to an enemy in a dark alleyway.

He fought to distance himself from her, but she drew him toward her although she remained perfectly still. When his mouth brushed hers, her lips parted, inviting him in. His tongue dipped inside and he was lost. She tasted like some luscious, forbidden fruit and his mouth grew greedy.

Adrienne struggled not to fall under the spell being wrought by the light touch of his fingers on her skin. Some still-rational part of her bade her to remember that she was not Isabella di Montefiore. It bade her to remember that she was Adrienne de Beaufort, who had a life of her own in another time, another place. An eddy of panic swirled through her as she asked herself what she was doing in this web of supernatural deception.

But then Sandro's tongue plunged into her mouth, possessing her as if their bodies were already joined. As he filled her with his taste, Adrienne reminded herself that she had chosen this man to be her destiny. As she had chosen to be his.

With a sigh she yielded to his kiss, offering herself as a wave offers itself to the sea. She felt his hands slide up her back to bring her closer. As their bodies met, she moaned softly, sure that there could be no greater pleasure. But then he drew her tongue into his mouth, provoking her until her tongue began to move against his. As the heat raced through her, her hands tightened on his narrow hips.

With a single fluid movement, he rolled over onto the bed so that they lay face-to-face. Even as his body clamored to be joined to hers, he untangled himself from her. Leaning on one elbow, he looked down at her as she lay there, her eyes closed, her skin lightly flushed with arousal.

"Look at me, Isabella."

Adrienne opened her eyes. He was watching her, his black eyebrows drawn together, the nostrils of his straight nose fluttering lightly, his mouth gone thin. If she had understood more about male passion she might have been afraid. Since she did not, she reached up and touched his face again, wanting somehow to signal to him the emotions that were racing through her.

He captured her hand. "Do not touch me."

Her eyes clouded at his harsh tone. "Ever?"

"Are you so naive, Isabella?" he demanded. "Or are you such an accomplished actress?"

She shook her head, not understanding him.

"Do you not see that I am at the end of my tether?" He drew in a breath that was not quite steady. "If you touch me now, I will take you without regard for your pleasure."

Pleasure? Adrienne had a vague memory of her mother's words to Antoinette, her older sister, on the eve of her wedding. But that had been so long ago and she had been but a child. There had been much talk of duty and pain and none of pleasure. And yet she was sure that there could not be more pleasure than his kiss, his skin upon hers. She would have wanted to tell him that, but she kept silent. But when he began to touch her, she understood what he had meant. She understood that what she had felt before had been but a mere harbinger of pleasure.

He traced her lips with a lazy finger, and when they parted, he dipped the finger inside to touch her tongue. But he did not linger there. Instead, he drew the moistened finger downward. Down to the base of her throat, where a pulse had begun a mad drumbeat. Down to her left breast, where her heartbeat stirred the soft flesh. Then he lowered his mouth to taste.

When she arched up toward him, his control began to slip. While his mouth stayed at her breast, his hand drifted down, mapping her curves, finding still another spot to tease, to arouse. When his fingers slipped through the soft curls at the apex of her thighs, her legs opened as a besieged fortress opens its gates before the conqueror.

But instead of continuing his foray toward the tender flesh she offered him, he trailed his hand down the petal-soft skin of her thighs and then up again. Only when she arched against his hand did he allow his fingers to glide into the soft folds that shielded her ultimate secrets.

Raising his head, he watched his hand caress her and the desire in his loins burned hotter.

"Look at me, Isabella," he murmured, and waited until her lids lifted over eyes unfocused with arousal. "Tell me what you want."

"I do not know," she whispered, but her hips moved, bringing her still closer.

Sandro watched the sinuous movement of her hips and wondered if she was playing a game with him. Had she lain with a man like this before? Had she driven another man to a frenzy of desire with that seductive combination of shyness and abandonment? Just the thought that she had opened herself like this to another was enough to make the fury rise within him. But instead of quenching the flame of desire, his fury made it blaze even higher. His hand still cupping her, he rose to kneel beside her.

When he swung himself onto his knees, his lithe grace, the subtle movement of sinew and muscle under his bronzed skin distracted Adrienne for a moment from the heat within her. But then she felt it pour through her even more molten than before, like a stream of lava, until it pooled within her. There. Where his hand cupped her so possessively.

She saw the play of emotions on Sandro's face. She saw the anger, the suspicion, and she knew that he had every reason to feel them for Isabella. The other Isabella. But not for her. Never for her.

Unable to tell him the truth, she needed somehow to show it to him. Lifting her hand, she slid it along his muscled thigh. Her eyes flew up to his face when she heard his sharp intake of breath.

"I told you not to touch me."

"But I need to touch you, Sandro." Her hand moved again. "I need to show you—"

"What?" He covered her hand with his. "What do you need to show me?"

There were so many things she wanted to tell him. Things she had not yet even defined within herself. Things she would never be able to say aloud. She shook her head helplessly. "That I am yours."

Tightening the muscles in her belly, she pulled herself up to a sitting position and reached for him. The movement made her shift against him and she cried out softly as his fingers glided over her slickness.

Sandro felt the last sorry remains of his restraint give way like a frayed rope. He bore her back, invading her mouth as he would invade her body. Shifting, he moved over her and fitted his body to hers. The slick heat that awaited him goaded him to plunge into her. But even as the white-hot need pounded through him, he stilled.

"Look at me, Isabella." His whisper was hoarse. "I want to see your eyes when I take you for the first time."

As her eyelids lifted, he pressed forward until he felt the barrier of her virginity block his way. Twin surges of joy and pure male pride swept through him and he framed her face with his hands. "You are mine, Isabella. Mine."

Drawing back, he knelt between her legs and, sliding his hands under her, lifted her so that his thighs supported her. Again he fitted himself to her, and as his fingers caressed her, he pushed forward to join them together.

As he began to fill her, Adrienne tensed, but his fingers were working their magic on her, and even the quick, sharp pain as he pushed past the barrier was forgotten as heated pleasure coiled through her.

For a moment he rested inside her and then he began to move. Even though his needs drove him, he moved in slow, gentle strokes. He might not have admitted it, but he did not want to take this journey alone.

Adrienne felt the pleasure—exquisite and languorous—curl through her as he caressed her. Pleasure she had never dreamed of. Then suddenly something changed. What had been so light, so easy, became dark and fierce. Without warning, she found herself caught in a vortex that was spiraling out of control. Caught in a blaze that threatened to consume her.

"Sandro?" She whispered his name on a shudder. All of a sudden he was the only familiar entity in a new universe and desperately she reached for him and held on.

He felt her begin to flutter around him at the same moment she whispered his name. Wanting to give himself the gift of watching her crest, he tried to hold back his own completion, but as she arched and tightened around him, he could contain himself no longer. With a cry of triumph and surrender, he erupted into her.

Needing to feel her skin against his, Sandro bent forward and, sliding his arms under her, brought her toward him until she was cradled against his chest. Burying his face in her hair, which held the faint fragrance of jasmine and roses, he felt the aftershocks of climax pulse through them both.

Even as sated contentment filtered through him, he knew he wanted her again. Yes, the edge of that consuming hunger was gone, but now he wanted to make love to her for hour after leisurely hour until they were both drunk on pleasure and fulfillment.

But even as he acknowledged the desire, he put it aside. He would not make love to her now. Not now, when he still wanted her so badly. He needed to resist the temptation of her body, to prove that she had not—within the space of an hour—become vital to him. He needed to know that he could forgo the pleasures she offered. He would have denied that he would not make love to her now because he did not want to use her roughly. Just as he would have denied that he wanted to cradle her in his arms and watch her sleep in the aftermath of passion.

Her arms around him, Adrienne lay against his shoulder. Her body felt boneless and yet the energy that seemed to pulse through her blood and over the surface of her skin made her feel stronger than she had ever felt before. And all her senses were so acute that the impressions they brought deluged her. The scent of Sandro's skin and of passion spent was in her nostrils. Her hands against his back picked up the staccato beat of his heart. She ran her tongue over her lips and knew that it was his taste that lingered there. A lazy curl of desire drifted through her.

She drew back her head, needing to look at him. "Will it always be like this?"

The aloofness Alessandro had prescribed for himself dissipated like a puff of smoke as he met her dreamy gaze. Before he could stop himself, his hands trailed down her back to rest on her slender hips. "I do not know." His lips curved as he brushed them over her temple. "We will have to try it again and see." The mere thought of making love to her again brought his body to full readiness.

"Now?"

"Later."

Adrienne laughed softly. "Now." She felt wanton as the memory of the pleasure teased her. How was it that she, who had never even enjoyed a kiss, found herself wanting this beautiful, dangerous man to make love to her again? And again. She was no longer Adrienne, she reminded herself. She was Isabella. Or was she?

His body flexed within her and she found the questions draining out of her mind. She moved against him in instinctive invitation, but she found her tender body protesting the movement and she winced.

"Later." His control was fraying again and Sandro gripped her hips, stilling her.

Carefully he lifted her away from him and laid her back as one would a child. But the desire within him did not lessen, and fighting for control, he turned away. As he reached for a linen towel, he saw a pale crimson streak on his still-aroused body. For the others that would have been scant proof of Isabella's virginity, he thought. That was why men took their brides like barbarians—to make certain there was enough blood on the sheets. But he knew that she had come to his bed untouched.

Needing the distance, he stood and walked to the table, which was again crowded with refreshments. Leaning his hip against the rim, he chose a pear from one of the bowls and bit into the juicy fruit. He told himself that he would not look to where Isabella lay, but his gaze disobeyed him. She was curled on her side, her hip-length golden hair spread over her body like a thin, shimmering blanket.

She was perfectly still, but without knowing how or why he knew it, he was sure that she was crying. The tears that women seemed to cry so easily had never touched him, but Sandro found himself wanting to stanch Isabella's tears. Tossing the half-eaten pear down, he picked up a bowl of *confetti,* the candied almonds that were a staple at every wedding, and as an afterthought broke off the torso of a nymph that was part of the elaborate marzipan sculpture in the center of the table. His need for distance half-forgotten, he moved back toward the bed.

Adrienne felt Sandro brush her hair aside, but she resisted as he tried to turn her to face him. Burrowing her face still further into the soft pillow, she willed her tears to stop flowing. Would Isabella be crying? she asked herself as her eyes overflowed with a fresh surge of tears. When he had separated their bodies and left her alone in the bed that carried the scent of their passion, would Isabella have felt so bereft, so forsaken? Would she have been helpless against the tears that had come?

"Do not cry." He lifted her heavy hair and kissed her behind the ear. There, too, her skin held the faint fragrance of roses, and forgetting that he had wanted merely to comfort, he trailed his mouth down to her shoulder.

He was beginning to lose himself in the taste and texture of her skin, when a small sound from her reminded him that he had not wanted to touch her. And why. He sat up, irritated with himself and her that she could seduce him merely by being. "I would not have thought you a woman to cry easily."

Adrienne heard both the challenge and the irritation in Sandro's voice. Wiping away the traces of tears with her hands, she turned onto her back to face him. "You are right." Her voice was still a little blurred from the tears, but steady. "I do not cry easily." Suddenly it seemed terribly important that he understand that.

"Why did you cry?" He propped an elbow on his bent knee and waited for a shrug, a smile, an easy evasion. Instead, her eyes were serious as they deliberately met his.

How could she explain that she had needed a gentle embrace? "Because I wanted you to hold me—" her fingers gripped the linen sheet to prevent herself from reaching out to him now "—afterward."

"Why did you not ask?"

"Would you have done as I wished?"

Sandro paused. "No," he said truthfully, shaking his head. When she turned aside, he gripped her chin and brought her back to face him. "I could not have held you and not made love to you."

Adrienne smiled. "Is that true?"

"Why should I lie when I admit that I could not have resisted you?" Letting her go, he turned away, his beautiful mouth sulking.

Sitting up, Adrienne reached out, but as she remembered his warning not to touch him, she let her hand drop. "And that makes you angry?"

"Yes, damn you." He swiveled toward her, his eyes furious. He'd seen enough men so besotted that they forgot to watch their backs. "You are my enemy."

"I am your wife."

"And how long will my *wife*—" he accented the word contemptuously "—wait until she sells me to her brothers? Or to someone else, perhaps, who bids higher?"

The words flayed her like a whip. So he had recognized the danger, Adrienne thought, and still he had walked into the trap. Surely she, who wished him no harm, would be able to keep him safe.

"Can you not forget that I was born a Gennaro?" she asked softly. "Can you not take me as I am? As you find me?"

"As I find you?" He twisted a strand of hair around his hand. "You are the temptress. Delilah, biding her time to cut Samson's hair." Letting her hair go, he cupped her neck. "Judith, cutting off Holofernes's head after a night of love." Because he wanted to caress her, his hand tightened.

The heel of his hand was pressing against her windpipe, but Adrienne did not retreat. "Is that all you find, Sandro?" She reached out and placed her hands against his chest. "Truly all?"

He opened his mouth to tell her to take her hands away, but instead his own hand gentled.

"Take a chance and give me the benefit of the doubt. You are a courageous man, Sandro."

"Courageous but not foolhardy, *madonna*. My life is too rich a stake to wager on your loyalty."

She nodded, willing to accept his mistrust—for the moment. "I will prove that you can trust me. I can wait." She smiled. "For now, a truce?"

He looked at her for a long, silent moment. He was a fool, he told himself. Surely there was perfidy behind those soft, innocent eyes. But he found himself wanting to believe the innocence. Surely there was no danger in playing a game of pretend for an hour, a day.

Reaching over to where he had deposited the sweets, he held a piece of marzipan to her lips. "Truce. I have even brought you a peace offering."

Adrienne bit off a piece of the confection and then watched in fascination as he drew the end her mouth had touched along his own lips. The heat was already coiling through her when he slowly, provocatively, put the sweet into his mouth.

"Will you hold me now?" Her whisper was hoarse.

"You are playing with fire, Isabella."

"Yes," she said, and held her arms out to him.

Chapter Six

There was a murmur of voices as Adrienne began to stir. Still more than half-asleep, she stretched. She felt the tug of tired muscles she had not known she possessed and turned onto her side. Deciding to sleep a little longer, she burrowed her face into the pillow.

She had had such a bizarre dream, she remembered as she floated in that calm, delicious state between wakefulness and sleep. Bizarre but wonderful—as complicated, as erotic as an Oriental fairy tale. And so real that her body still throbbed and tingled.

"Tell Don Piero that we will be there."

She heard a voice, but it seemed too far away to understand the words. Was it part of her dream? she wondered. More of the dream began to come back to her—in images, in scents, in tastes. When she stretched again, her body protested the movement and she smiled into the pillow. She felt as if she had lived it instead of dreamt it.

"Wake up, Isabella. We will be late."

Her last thought and the voice, which she understood clearly this time, came simultaneously. Within the space of a heartbeat she came fully awake, remembering what had happened. No, not happened, but what she had done. Remembering that she had deliberately hurtled herself into a supernatural adventure that could cost her her life.

The wave of panic that flooded her was so powerful she found her breathing cut off. Where was she? *Who* was she? She felt disjointed, like a puppet made of two unmatched halves, its strings being jerked in different directions. But just as quickly as the panic had come, it receded, and in its stead, the hot, sweet memory of the past hours poured through her.

Sandro had made love to her again and again until all her senses were filled with him alone. Until her body was drugged with pleasure. He had told her that he wanted her, not only with his body but with words. He had fed her fruit and sweet almonds and cradled her against him with a gentleness that belied his dangerous eyes.

Although the panic was gone, her heart was still pounding, and she pressed her hand against her breastbone as if she could still it. Whose heart was it? Adrienne's? Isabella's? Whose mind was it that was racing now, full of unanswered questions? Did Isabella's terrible destiny lie before her? Or would she be able to make a new destiny of her own? She held on to the last thought and to the sense of freedom it gave her. She would be Isabella di Montefiore, she promised herself. She would be Isabella because she had chosen to be. But she would be her own woman.

"Wake up, *madonna.* I have sent for your women to help you ready yourself."

As her breathing became more even, she pushed herself up against the pillows and opened her eyes. Wearing a richly embroidered robe of wine red velvet that made his skin look like burnished gold, Sandro stood, hands at his hips, watching her. The memory of the past hours still warming her, Adrienne wanted to reach out to him, but there was a thin line of displeasure between his black eyebrows and his hooded eyes were distant and wary.

"Is something wrong?" she pulled the sheet more securely around her.

"We shall be late for the banquet. There have been two messengers already—from my father and your brothers—to make certain that we appear. Both of us." Sandro felt a surge of irritation at himself for his peevish tone. "We shall be late."

Relief bubbled up inside Adrienne. "You do not look like a man who would care about being late for a banquet." She smiled, taking the barb out of her provocative tone. "Why did you not wake me earlier?"

He shrugged. "You were tired."

"And you are still angry." Adrienne sighed. "Will you sit for a moment?" She spread her hand on the rumpled sheets beside her.

Sandro did not want to sit on the bed that carried her scent and his and the scent they had made together with their lovemaking. He did not want to sit within a distance of her that would make it much too easy to reach out to touch, to fondle. But, believing in his own discipline, he moved forward and lowered himself onto the bed.

"It will be difficult to make a success of our marriage if the only emotions that you allow yourself for me are anger and passion, Sandro." She laced her hands together to keep from touching him. "And I *want* to make a success of our marriage."

"I did not choose you, *madonna,* nor you me," he snapped. "And the success of our marriage will be judged by the number of sons you bear me."

His tone was so cold that Adrienne recoiled as if she had been struck. Could this be the same man who had made love to her so passionately, so tenderly? How could he look at her now with the chill, opaque eyes of a stranger after he had looked at her with such heat and desire? How could he doubt her when she asked for his trust? How could he doubt her when she had given up her own life because she wanted to save his? Heartsick, she lowered her eyes.

But he had his reasons for doubting her, Adrienne reminded herself. Better reasons than he even knew. And he could not know what she had given up for his sake. Perhaps because she knew there was no way to change that, a small fount of anger sprang up within her. She welcomed it, nurtured it, hoping that it would help her through the test that lay before her.

Alessandro hated the despondent look he had put into her eyes. Yes, he had wanted to provoke her, hurt her even, but he had wanted her to fight back with the same spirit she had faced him down with after her reappearance in the bedchamber. The same spirit with which she had met his passion. He was reaching for her when she tipped her face up to him, her eyes flashing with temper.

"How well do you know me, Sandro?"

"What a strange question." He frowned. "You know as well as I do that before our wedding day we saw each other only from a distance." His eyes narrowed. "If Pope Alexander had not decided to try his hand at matchmaking, the Gennaros would still be lurking in dark alleys trying to cut the throats of anyone even vaguely connected to the Montefiores." His tone was contemptuous.

He saw a brief flicker in his wife's eyes at his words. "I am not convinced that they are not still lurking." He saw the flicker again and this time his fingers gripped Isabella's wrist. "Or do they hire *bravi* these days to do their lurking for them?"

Adrienne tried to twist her hand out of his grasp but found it held still more tightly. "You will be a poor successor to your father," she bit out, "if you judge everything and everyone with bias and intolerance long before you go to the trouble of getting to know them."

"I suggest that you stop preaching at me, *madonna*."

"And I suggest that you stop marking my skin, *messere*." For a fraction of a moment Adrienne felt a flash of pure hatred. Oh God, she thought with horror, was this what Isabella had felt? Had this supernatural adventure gone yet another step further? Was she turning into that other Isabella with all her hatreds, all her cruelties, all her betrayals? Had she given up her own life only to become the same vindictive, perfidious woman Isabella had been?

The fireworks her eyes were throwing at him snapped Sandro out of his anger and he lowered his mouth to the wrist he still held, missing the look of horror that shot into her eyes. As he skimmed his lips over the soft skin on the inside of her wrist, he knew that even now, with his body sated, desire was not far from the surface.

Behind him, he heard the door open and he raised his head. "I have half a mind to dismiss your women and let the banquet, my father and your brothers be damned."

Adrienne would have liked nothing better than to stay here in this perfumed bedchamber and let the heat of passion purge the doubts from her mind. But there were too many things she needed to know.

She smiled at him and touched his cheek lightly with her fingers. "At the risk of hearing again that I am preaching at you, I would suggest that a little self-denial is good for your immortal soul, as I am sure your father confessor would agree." Her eyelids lowered a little, giving her eyes a slumberous, seductive appeal. "And you have not exactly been practicing a great deal of self-denial lately."

"Witch." Keeping his eyes on hers, he feathered his lips over her wrist one more time and rose. "There will be time to settle accounts later." He spun around before he could change his mind and brushed past the women who had come to help Isabella dress.

Adrienne's eyes followed Sandro until the door had closed behind him. Only then did she turn toward the women, who stood quietly, ready to do her bidding. Although their arms were burdened with linens and clothing, they curtsied gracefully and approached the bed.

As they came close enough for her to see their faces clearly, Adrienne let her eyes drop down to her hands to hide the horrified confusion she was sure was mirrored in them. She knew them! She, Adrienne, had never seen these women before, but she had a name to each face! Angela, Lucrezia and Renata.

The disjointed, fragmented feeling she had had when she had first woken was coming back. Who was she? When she had found herself in this chamber the first time, she had recognized people from descriptions she had read in Isabella's diary—Piero and Alfonso, Luisa, the dwarf Gianni. But these women she simply... knew. Something had drastically changed between then and now. But what?

She closed her eyes, needing a moment to calm herself, to accustom herself to yet another transformation. But her mind did not have a tranquil image to offer her. Instead, she saw Sandro as he had looked the first time he had taken her—triumphant, his eyes blazing with passion.

This was what had changed between then and now. Had theirs been a kind of mystical union? A metamorphosis from which she had emerged as the actual Isabella, leaving Adrienne behind like the shed chrysalis of a butterfly? The flash of hatred she had felt for Sandro moments ago returned to haunt her, but she fought it back, remembering the promise she had made to herself to be her own woman. Again she repeated it like a prayer, an incantation.

Opening her eyes, she saw a tall woman carrying a large basin of water and a basket full of small pots and bottles slip from behind the three women. She was dressed far more simply than the others in a plain dun-colored tunic with a corded belt, and her flaxen hair was braided and coiled tightly on top of her head with none of the ornaments or jewels that decorated the other women's coiffures. She knelt next to the bed, keeping her eyes lowered.

"May I wash *madonna* now?" Her words were fluent but carried a hard, foreign flavor.

Adrienne stared down at the pale blond head and knew that this woman had been given to Isabella by her father five years ago for her eleventh birthday—a slave, stolen from a riverbank deep in faraway Russia. Daria. Her name was Daria. She frowned. Where had that name come from? Isabella had always referred to her as Barbara. But somehow the name Daria wouldn't go away. That was another puzzle she would have to solve, she thought.

She slid her feet off the bed and stood, letting the sheet that covered her fall to the floor. "You must work quickly—" she hesitated for a second over the name and then went with her instincts "—Daria. Don Alessandro let me sleep far too long."

The woman's head snapped upward and Adrienne was stunned by the look in the incredible turquoise eyes. What was it? Hatred? Surprise? Fear? But the eyes lowered so quickly that she could not be sure of what she had really seen.

She turned to the other women, who still stood there with their colorful burdens. "Put everything down somewhere. I will call if I need you." She saw the women exchange quick, surreptitious glances before they curtsied again and left the room.

Quickly, skillfully, Daria washed her with the warm, rose-scented water. Adrienne found it odd to be washed like a babe and odder still that she felt no embarrassment. Had modesty been another thing she had left behind?

When Daria had finished rubbing sweet, aromatic oils into her skin, she sat back on her haunches. "Shall I call the others now, *madonna?*"

Adrienne looked at Daria, understanding from her question what Isabella's preference had been. Perhaps it was only a tiny thing, but the rush of relief that she had not taken on all of Isabella's traits after all was so strong that her head spun with it. The breath swept out of her lungs.

"No." She gave Daria a radiant smile. "Not unless there is something you cannot do by yourself." She felt a strange sense of kinship to this woman who was almost as far away from home as she was.

Daria bowed her head. "Yes, *madonna*."

With quick, efficient gestures, the young slave woman dressed her. The undergarments of linen were so finely woven they were almost transparent. The underskirt was of emerald green silk and the dress of heavy white brocade was covered with tiny flowers fashioned of gold thread, sapphires and rubies, circled by a belt made of intertwined ropes of white and gray pearls.

When Adrienne sat down on a stool in front of the mirror to watch Daria dress her hair, she saw that her hip-length tresses were hopelessly tangled from the hours of loving. Even though Daria drew the jeweled ivory comb slowly and carefully through the thick hair, it snagged. Drawing in a quick breath, Adrienne winced and lifted her hand to rub the spot. As she looked into the mirror, she saw Daria hunch her shoulders and pull in her head.

A wave of heat flowed into her cheeks as she realized that Daria had expected to be struck. Looking more closely at Daria's reflection, she saw a scar below one of the woman's high, wide cheekbones. Not knowing how she knew, she was suddenly sure that it had been Isabella who had caused it. How many cruelties had the other Isabella committed that she would be called to account for? And would she be able to atone for them all? Had she set herself a task she would never be able to fulfill?

Daria dressed her hair simply in a loose plait intertwined with strings of pearls. Around Adrienne's neck she placed a rope of pearls that carried a sapphire pendant in the shape of a teardrop. Then she offered a velvet-lined tray for Adrienne to choose her rings.

Adrienne had never seen such a profusion of gold and sparkling stones, but she hesitated only briefly and, following her own taste, chose two of the less ornate rings. Daria sent her a brief glance that was barely more than a lifting of her lashes, and Adrienne knew that she had again fallen out of her role.

She heard the door open and in the mirror she saw Sandro step into the room. Suddenly the temperature in the chamber seemed to rise. The blood seemed to pulse more freely through her veins. Her heart beat more joyously. For a fraction of a moment the impulse to open her arms and run to him was so strong that she almost gave in to it. Instead, she laced her hands and watched his progress toward her. A few steps away from her he stopped and looked around the chamber.

"Where are your ladies, *madonna?*" he demanded.

Adrienne turned on her stool to face him. "I sent them away."

"You prepare for the banquet with the help of one slave?"

For answer Adrienne lifted her right hand. "Your hand, Don Alessandro, to help me rise."

His eyebrows lifted at her imperious tone, but he obeyed and stepped closer. She placed her hand on his and stood. When he would have withdrawn, she curled her fingers to hold him fast.

"Is there anything in particular that you find fault with, my husband?" she asked softly.

Alessandro did not want to look at her too closely, for her fragrance was already making his blood run hot. Still, he took a step back and let his gaze roam over her.

"A man would be hard put to find fault with Isabella *la bella*." Sandro forced a mocking tone into his voice to mask just how much her beauty moved him. Again he began to withdraw his hand, but she held it tightly.

Adrienne stepped back and returned the favor. Today he was wearing gold brocade slashed with scarlet, the gold shades paler than his skin. Disdaining the velvet slippers of the courtier, he wore thigh-high boots of butter-soft kid leather. Her gaze flickered over the jeweled dagger fastened at his gold-studded belt, and she slid her fingers down to his still-bound wrist to tell him that she remembered. Releasing his hand, she reached up and pulled one side of his toque of white velvet down toward his temple, giving it a more rakish tilt. A small smile of approval curved her lips as she met his eyes.

"I believe that what Luisa said is true," she whispered.

Isabella's whisper seemed to skim over the surface of his skin, and Sandro's eyebrows drew closer as he fought its pull. "What?"

"You are the most beautiful man in Siena." She lowered her hands to his shoulders, but unable to resist touching him one more time, she twined a silky black curl around her finger and rubbed it with her thumb.

"How many women are you, Isabella?" he demanded in a rough whisper. "Seductress and innocent. Imperious lady and shy maiden." He clenched his hands into fists because he wanted to reach for her so badly.

She released his hair and brushed her fingertips along the angled line of his jaw. "At least one more than you think, Sandro."

There was something wistful and faraway about the smile that played around her lips, and despite himself, he would have wanted to insist on an explanation of her cryptic answer, but he could hear the insistent knocking behind him. He offered her his arm and together they moved toward the door.

The closer they came to the banquet hall, the louder Adrienne's heart pounded. As they approached the great doors, the raucous sound of voices, laughter and music swelled toward her like a threatening wave and her heart thundered louder still. Every muscle in her body seemed to contract until she was sure that she could not take another step.

Up to now she had coped with what demands her new life had placed on her. Now she would be facing people who knew Isabella and knew her well. She looked like Isabella. Apparently she sounded like Isabella. But what would happen when she did not act like her? How soon would people become suspicious—her brothers, Luisa? How soon would they realize that she was an impostor? What would they do to her once they did? Throw her in prison? Burn her at the stake for a witch? Would—could Sandro protect her? Would he want to? She masked the shiver that crept along her spine with a movement of her shoulders, but there was no way she could hide the trembling of the hand that lay on Sandro's arm.

Silent and deep in thought, Sandro walked at Isabella's side. Although he fought it still, he was honest enough to admit that he was falling under her spell—this woman of a thousand faces, each with its own special allure. But something did not fit, he brooded. She was like a mosaic that was missing some essential piece that would give the image a completely altered aspect.

Where did the key lie? he asked himself. With the woman who had awaited him in his wedding chamber? A woman of sweetness and passion and courage. Or with the woman who had stood beside him in the festively decorated hall as they had signed the marriage contract? A woman who had looked at him with both hatred and covetousness. With cold calculation and cunning. It was as if she were truly more than one woman.

He felt the hand that lay on his arm tremble and glanced at her. Her back was straight and her step sure, but he could see that her heart was beating against the bodice of her gown as urgently as a wild bird beats its wings against the bars of a cage. She was terrified, he realized, and fighting not to show it.

A burst of some new and strange emotion that he refused to examine more closely surged through him. This was the Isabella of the wedding chamber. And the only thing she had in common with the other Isabella was pride. It was that pride he would appeal to, he thought. And it would be that pride that would sustain her now. He willed her to look at him.

Adrienne wanted to turn and run, but then she felt Sandro's eyes upon her. She turned and met his gaze.

He was silent, but his eyebrows rose slightly and a provocative, challenging light came into his eyes.

Automatically her chin tilted up in answer and she felt her heart calm, her hands steady. Even though she answered the unspoken taunt with a flare of defiance, she was grateful. Had that been his way of giving her a little support at a moment of weakness, of need? she wondered briefly, but then rejected the thought. That would mean that he felt something for her beyond the desire he had expressed so freely during the past hours. That would mean that a little of the contempt he felt for her as a Gennaro had faded. No, she thought, unaware of the power that a single day had given her over this man. She would have to show him that she deserved more than the uneasy combination of desire for her body and contempt for her soul.

The great doors to the hall swung open in front of them and the two heralds in the blue-and-white Montefiore livery who stood at either side of the entrance announced them with a brief flourish of their horns. As they moved forward, the voices, the laughter, the music faded. In silence they crossed the wide expanse of black-and-white marble tile toward the dais, where Francesco di Montefiore, Duke of Siena, awaited them. .

Chapter Seven

Duke Francesco stood to greet his son and his bride. *"Evviva."* Although his greeting boomed through the hall, his sonorous voice seemed to lack warmth.

At his signal, the heralds who were positioned on the gallery raised their long brass trumpets, decorated with blue-and-white pennants carrying the Montefiore crest. An elaborate fanfare sounded, accompanying the cries of *evviva* that echoed from around the hall.

As Sandro bowed and Adrienne executed a deep curtsy, Francesco descended the steps from his dais. "Welcome, my son, Donna Isabella," he said, his voice ringing through the hall for all to hear. "I await an explanation—from both of you," he added in a murmur that was no less severe for its softness.

Sandro met his father's gaze and held it steadily. "There will be none—from either of us."

Francesco's pale blue eyes narrowed. "I will not argue with you here in public, my son, but we will speak in private."

"Indeed we will speak, my father." Sandro's chin rose by a notch. "But not of this." He could not have said why he was prepared to defy the father whose approval he had always sought. Nor could he have said why the urge to shield the woman at his side was so strong when doubt and suspicion were still keen within him.

Retreating for the moment, Francesco gave no answer but placed his hands on his son's shoulders and kissed him on both cheeks in the traditional greeting. Then he turned to Adrienne and repeated the gesture with her.

"Sowing discord can be an unhealthy pastime, *madonna*. Remember that."

The quick whisper was barely audible, but Adrienne understood both the words and the implication.

When they were seated on a dais at the other end of the damask-covered table that stretched the length of the hall, Duke Francesco rose again, this time with a jeweled goblet of hammered gold in his hands.

"Let's drink, my friends, to the marriage of our beloved son and heir, Alessandro, and the beautiful Isabella. May she bear him many sons."

As the cries and good wishes echoed through the hall, Sandro reached for his own goblet and offered it to his bride.

Adrienne did not take the wine cup from him. Instead, needing instinctively to make a public gesture, she covered Sandro's hands with hers and tipped the goblet to drink the ruby red wine that grew on the hills in the surrounding countryside.

Arousal flared in Sandro at the cool touch of her hands on his. Some softer, gentler emotion slipped through him, too, so surreptitiously—and for that all the more strongly—that he barely noticed it. He took the goblet from her and, keeping his eyes on hers, turned it so that his lips touched the rim where her mouth had been.

Through the voices that rose in shouts of approval and more or less ribald encouragement, Sandro heard the sound of a woman's mocking laughter. Setting the goblet down, he cupped Isabella's chin in his hand. Again he heard the laughter as he crushed her mouth against his.

The banquet began with a fanfare of trumpets that announced an interminable procession of domestics bearing huge platters of food, destined as much for the eye as the palate. There were roasted peacocks, which had been decorated again with all their brilliant plumage. Cooked venison and hare were ornamented with their heads and pelts. Spits the length of a rapier were full of tiny roasted songbirds. Large tubs of shrimp, cuttlefish, crabs and oysters rimmed with fried frog's legs were brought in. Dozens of jeweled dishes containing condiments and rich sauces, cooked vegetables and raw greens, cheeses and sausage all arranged in artful display filled the tables.

Everyone ate and drank with lusty abandon and, to her surprise, Adrienne discovered that the customary table manners held no secrets for her. Despite her apprehension, she found herself ravenously hungry and she ate with relish but drank little, well aware that she would need a clear head.

She speared a succulent piece of venison with her silver fork, and as she brought the morsel to her mouth, her eyes collided with Sandro's. They had spoken little here in the noise and turbulence of the banquet hall, but now their eyes spoke for them.

As she bit off and chewed a piece of the meat, spiced with wine vinegar and juniper berries, she felt a surge of heat that had nothing to do with the wine she had drunk.

Sandro reached out and covered her hand that held the fork with his. "Will you share with me, *madonna?*"

The torches that lighted the hall were reflected in golden points in his black eyes, emphasizing the heat she saw there. "Yes," Adrienne whispered, meaning far more than the morsel between them.

He drew her hand closer and bit off a piece of the venison. Then, plucking the remainder of the meat off the fork with his fingers, he held it to Adrienne's mouth.

More than half-seduced, Adrienne accepted his offering. She hadn't known that eating could be as sensuous an encounter as the boldest caress. As she resolved to repeat the experience in the privacy of their bedchamber, her lips curved in a secret little smile.

The slight movement of her lips against his fingers tested his control and Sandro drew back, knowing that it would be hours before they were alone again. "Temptress."

There was desire in his eyes, but again it was underlaid with the anger that seemed to leave him so rarely. She watched the man she had chosen turn away from her, and the pain in her heart was almost physical. For a moment, she gave in to resignation. But then her pride stirred, and with it her innate optimism, which would not allow her to lose faith for more than a moment.

For the rest of the seemingly interminable meal, Sandro lapsed into a moody silence. Awareness of the woman beside him, as sharp as the edge of his dagger, never left him. But that was something he could live with, he assured himself, even as he resolved to prove to himself before long that he would find other women as desirable. Less easy to curb and even harder to define was the soft feeling that would flow through him at odd moments, so unexpectedly that he had no defence against it. A feeling that made him want to reach out and lace his fingers with hers just for the pleasure of touching her, although he had never been a man to touch anyone without a reason.

Hours later, when the damask tablecloth was strewn with food scraps, its borders smeared from the guests wiping their mouths and hands on it, the desserts arrived. There were huge bowls of fragrant fruits and tray upon tray of tiny statues of mythological figures made of marzipan and sweet dough, decorated with colored sugar and gold dust.

As soon as the servants had offered the guests bowls of orange-scented water to wash their hands, the music changed from the lute-accompanied songs that had attended their meal to the stately strains of a pavane.

Francesco signaled to his son to open the dancing and Sandro offered his arm to his bride.

"Must we?" Adrienne whispered, horrified. Having lived in the country all her life, she could at best manage the round dances of the French countryside. She knew what to do when a mare was foaling, but, much to her mother's consternation, she had never mastered the intricacies of minuets and such.

Sandro frowned. "What ails you, Isabella?"

"I cannot."

"What do you mean, you cannot?" he said impatiently.

"I cannot dance."

"Do not be ridiculous." Sandro narrowed his eyes. "I have seen you dance myself."

She opened her mouth to make some excuse, but Sandro had already grasped her hand and taken the first step down from the dais. She would think of something, she told herself. At worst, she would fall down into a faint.

But when they began to move through the figures of the pavane, Adrienne found herself executing every step, every dip, every turn, every gesture with perfect grace. She still had not quite recovered from the surprise when the figure ended and both Sandro and she moved on to a new partner.

"Well, little sister, you look none the worse for wear."

Adrienne stared up into the laughing face of her brother. No! she corrected herself desperately. She must never think of him as her brother. Never. Only as Alfonso Gennaro, Sandro's enemy and therefore hers. But even as she repeated the words to herself, she recognized that she could not simply pick and choose what she wanted from Isabella's life and what she did not. If she were to be successful, there were forces in Isabella's life that she would have to accept. She would have to live with them and learn to turn them to her own advantage. And Sandro's.

As she examined Alfonso's flaccidly handsome features, an odd surge of emotion stole through her. Moving automatically through the stately steps of the pavane, she fought to define it, knowing that she needed to understand the nature of every emotion she felt. Needed to know whether it came from her— Adrienne's—heart, or in that mysterious, mystical way from Isabella's. But it remained nebulous, as if the time for it to be revealed to her had not yet come. Still, she could discern a trace of affection that made her want to return Alfonso's smile.

"Well, Bella, was it worth it? Was it worth saving your virginity for Montefiore, or would a little play-acting and a phial of chicken blood have done the trick?"

The smile that was beginning to curve her lips froze.

"What is the matter, Bella?" Alfonso's smile was suddenly replaced by a petulant frown. "Has a tumble with Montefiore addled your brain?" He sent his sister a baffled look, wondering why in the world she was staring at him with all the disapproval of a chaste nun instead of answering him in kind.

The affection Adrienne had felt only a few moments ago seemed to warp and spoil as it was colored by her revulsion at Alfonso's vulgar words and—even worse—at what they implied.

Suddenly she heard a peal of the same mocking laughter she had heard when Sandro had kissed her during the banquet and her spine straightened. Was the laughter aimed at her? She threw a glance over her shoulder and saw that the laughter had come from Luisa. But Luisa was not looking at her. Instead she was smiling into the eyes of her dancing partner. And her dancing partner was Sandro.

Adrienne turned away, stunned and confused by the flash of pure jealousy that rushed through her. The confusion was still in her eyes when she looked up at Alfonso.

"Why are you looking at me like that, Bella?" Alfonso's tone was that of a peevish child. "Have I suddenly sprouted horns in the middle of my forehead?"

Her eyes narrowed as she realized how much his offensive words of a moment ago still chafed. "Beware, brother, that you do not truly grow horns." She signaled over her shoulder with her eyes.

Starting at her own words, Adrienne had the strangest suspicion that they had somehow bypassed her mind before emerging from her mouth. But then, one by one, the pieces began to fall into place. She realized that she knew that Luisa Barbiano was Alfonso's mistress. She realized that she knew that nothing—not Alfonso and not she herself—would stand between Luisa and her ambition. And she knew that she had no intention of watching with equanimity as Luisa beguiled her husband.

Ignoring Alfonso's angry reply, she turned to look over her shoulder again, willing Luisa, who was still laughing at something Sandro had said, to glance her way. Their eyes met and in the space of seconds the silent warning was sent and received. As the warmth in Luisa's eyes cooled, Adrienne knew that she was no longer the friend and confidante of Isabella's diary. She knew that she had made an enemy.

But even though she was conscious of a light prickle of alarm at the back of her neck, her mouth curved in a smile. Again she had altered what the book of time had written.

As she took a long, gliding step toward her next partner, her stomach tightened. Although he had the same weak chin that Alfonso did, the lines around Piero's mouth implied both tenaciousness and cruelty, and Adrienne realized that he would not be as easy to fend off as his brother. But even as she examined his face, she could not deny the strange thread of affection that wound its way through her.

"Just what do you think you are doing?" His whisper was like the hiss of a snake. "What was the meaning of that little disappearance of yours? Where did you go?"

Adrienne met Piero's gaze evenly, although her throat began to constrict. Compared to his vicious tone, Alfonso's carelessly obscene greeting seemed almost benign in retrospect. Had she taken more upon herself than she could deal with? she asked herself as the enormity of her task stretched before her. If she could not handle her own brother, how would she handle the other danger that was to come—so much greater, so much more formidable?

"I have no intention of telling you anything, Piero." The dip and sway and glide of the dance seemed to quiet her raw nerves. "Especially if you do not moderate that tone of yours. I am not one of your slaves—" she paused "—or your mistresses."

A lascivious light came into Piero's brown eyes and his tongue passed over his lips. "Not yet." He bent and brushed his mouth over her wrist. "But someday soon. Remember your promises, Bella."

Adrienne stumbled as he touched his wet mouth to her wrist. She wanted to snatch her hand away and run. She wanted to call to Sandro for help. Instead she fixed him with a cold stare. "I forbid you to touch me like that, Piero." Her mind spun as the true nature of the symbiotic, depraved relationship between the Gennaro siblings dawned on her.

"You forbid me?" he sputtered. "How dare you?"

Even though she wanted to retch with the horror of her discovery, she forced herself to maintain her cool demeanor. Her only hope was that she could brazen this out.

"Do not forget that I am now Alessandro di Montefiore's wife."

"So?" His mouth turned down. "The thought never bothered you before."

"Exactly. Before."

"So what has changed? Besides the fact that in the meantime he has taken your virginity." The angry glimmer in his eyes supplied the words "which should have been mine."

Adrienne opened her mouth to speak. She wanted to say something that would end this revolting conversation. She needed to set herself apart from this man once and for all. But the figure was ending and she was already moving forward toward her next partner.

"Leave me alone," she whispered, half over her shoulder. "I warn you, Piero. Leave me alone."

He gave her no answer, only pulled back his lips in a cruel caricature of a smile and, slipping his hand under hers, slid a finger along the length of her palm.

Although she was trembling from that vile mockery of a caress, Adrienne moved forward with a graceful glide and smiled at her new partner.

It was late when they left the hall to retire to their chambers and Adrienne's head was spinning with exhaustion—both mental and physical. She could feel Alessandro watching her with his hooded black eyes as he walked beside her in silence along the torch-lit corridors. What would he say to her when they were alone? she wondered. Had he found her behavior strange? Her words unseemly? Would he look at her with desire? With that reluctant tenderness that gave her such hope?

When they arrived at the door of the bedchamber, he handed her through the doorway. Even as Adrienne turned to speak to him, he whirled around and strode away without a word or a glance, his step quick and angry.

When he was gone, Adrienne realized how badly she had wanted him to stay. How badly she had needed him after the long, enervating evening. The hours she had known him would barely make a full day, yet Sandro was the only stable point of her universe gone awry.

The three young women who had brought her clothes earlier that evening awaited her, but Adrienne, hurt by Sandro's wordless rejection, felt incapable of bearing the presence of these strangers, who would watch her and remember every word, every gesture, to repeat to the curious.

"Go away, all of you except for Daria." She waved a hand in their general direction.

Ignoring their curtsies, she moved toward the stool where she had sat earlier. She had barely reached it when her muscles gave way and she half sat, half fell down upon it. Staring into the mirror, she put both hands up to her face and traced her features as if to reassure herself that it was truly her own reflection that she was seeing.

The images of the past hours whirled in front of her eyes. She had passed the test, she realized. Whatever power had sent her here had apparently given her the visible, outward capabilities to assume Isabella's life. Needing something real, something logical to hold on to in a situation that was utterly bereft of any reality, any logic, she began to dissect the woman she had become.

She had Isabella's face and body. She spoke Italian with Isabella's voice. Without even realizing that she possessed it, she had apparently been given the knowledge Isabella had had—be it table manners, dance steps or faces to recognize and react to. Even a piece of Isabella's emotions were hers, she reflected, remembering the surge of affection she had felt for her brothers—despite everything.

What she had not been given were Isabella's memories. Or the ability to act as Isabella would have acted—not even if she had wanted to. Or needed to. It was still Adrienne's heart and Adrienne's soul that were caught here in Isabella's world. But how would she ever strike a balance between herself and the debauched, tainted woman Isabella had been? She could feel the courage seep out of her as if it were something physical.

Her eyes filled with tears and suddenly her reflection seemed to shift and waver. The room around her tilted. Oh God, she thought, was she going back to her own time, her own body? No! No! She wanted to scream but found herself incapable of making a single sound, a single movement. They could not take her away from Sandro because of that one moment of tired despondency, she thought desperately! They could not take her away from the man she loved!

As suddenly as it had begun, the bizarre mirage ended, as if all it had been waiting for was that one admission. Adrienne found herself staring at her reflection again. Her features remained the same. Only the eyes had changed. Now they held an awareness that had not been there just moments before. Within the space of seconds, her quest had become deeply and intensely personal. Within the space of seconds, she had realized that she loved Alessandro di Montefiore beyond all measure.

Adrienne dropped her face into her hands and began to cry.

Chapter Eight

Daria, her mouth slightly open with surprise, watched her mistress cry, her shoulders shaking with fierce, soundless sobs. She had seen Isabella cry before, but never without an obvious motive, never so silently and *never* without an appropriate audience to appreciate her performance.

She frowned. She had been Isabella's slave for five terrible years and she knew her better than she had ever wanted to know anyone. But she had never seen her as she had been this day. Rising from her kneeling position at the foot of the bed, she took a fine linen handkerchief from one of the *cassoni*, the painted chests containing the finery that had been part of Isabella's dowry, and knelt again next to her mistress, waiting.

She watched Isabella's sobs quiet. She heard her exhale on a long, shuddering breath and tensed, waiting for impatient, angry words or perhaps one of those backhanded slaps that Isabella was so fond of meting out. She passed her finger over the scar below her cheekbone, which had come from one of Isabella's rings, but the hatred that had been her main source of strength did not arise. Reaching inside herself, she strove to recapture it, but no matter how hard she tried, it remained out of her grasp.

Was it because today Isabella had called her by her real name for the first time? For five years she had called her Barbara, always with that taunting lilt in her voice. But today she had looked her in the eyes as if she were a real person and called her Daria.

Adrienne raised her head, starting at the slight movement at her elbow. Next to her stool, Daria knelt, proffering a handkerchief that lay on her crossed hands like a sacrifice. As she took it, she saw the young woman watching her through lowered lashes.

"Why do you look at me like that, Daria?" Adrienne felt a flash of apprehension. Could it be that Isabella's slave was the only one to recognize her as an impostor?

The young woman immediately lowered her head to her knees, her shoulders hunched against the expected blows. "Forgive me, *madonna*," she murmured.

Adrienne touched her shoulder. "Look at me, Daria." But the young slave seemed to curl her body still further.

"Forgive me," she repeated. "Madonna Isabella has warned me many times to keep my unworthy eyes lowered on pain of flogging."

"No one will flog you, Daria. I command you to look at me."

Hesitantly Daria straightened and raised her eyes to Adrienne's face. There was confusion in her eyes, and fear. Adrienne decided to take a risk. She needed a friend desperately and she cared not if this friend was a slave girl.

"You find me much changed, do you not?"

Daria gave a quick, choppy nod and lowered her gaze again. But Adrienne reached out and tipped her face upward. "Tell me," she said softly. "I command you."

Daria's wide mouth worked for a moment before she began to speak. "*Madonna* sent the other women away and allowed me to prepare her for the banquet. *Madonna* chose only two rings to wear."

She would have looked down again, but Adrienne kept her fingers under her chin, needing to see the emotions mirrored in those extraordinary turquoise eyes. "But there is more, is there not?"

Daria nodded but did not speak until Adrienne repeated her command.

"Madonna Isabella did not slap me while I was dressing her hair. And for the first time *madonna* did not call me Barbara but by my real name." Daria held her breath and waited for the blow that would surely come now.

"Do you know why I called you Barbara—" she paused to swallow "—before?"

"Because it means barbarian woman."

Adrienne wanted to close her eyes against the shame she felt. She wanted to beg Daria's forgiveness. "I will not call you Barbara again," she said, knowing that she could not say more.

She saw the unspoken question in the girl's eyes. A question she dared not answer.

Daria stared at her mistress. She had recounted the changes she saw in Isabella, but she had not made mention of the greatest change of all. The eyes that had looked out at the world with ruthlessness cold enough to freeze the blood in one's veins now seemed to hold warmth and kindness.

When had she changed? And why? Had the marriage bed changed her thus? Or had it been her strange disappearance for a day and a night, which everyone whispered about? Had the change been wrought by a pure spirit or by witchcraft? Her Russian soul was prepared to believe in either. Under the cover of her left hand, she pressed her thumb and the first two fingers of her right hand together and made a tiny sign of the cross beneath her breasts.

Adrienne let her hand fall back into her lap and turned away from the questioning eyes. "Unfasten the jewels in my hair first, Daria."

Sandro stood in the doorway of the bedchamber. In her white linen nightgown Isabella looked as pure and virginal as one of Mantegna's Madonnas. As the slave girl drew the ivory comb through Isabella's hair, he could feel the heat begin to curl through his loins. Just the thought of twisting his hand in those strands of golden silk made his body spring to life.

She had bewitched him, he thought. He had lain with her and now he craved her like a drug. If it had only been her body that he hungered for, he could have sated himself and been done with it. But it was more, he acknowledged. It had been more from the moment he had taken his dagger and shed his blood instead of hers.

He knew it would be wiser to stay away from her bed tonight. To prove that he was not reduced to utter submission by the warmth in her brown gold eyes, by her gentle touch. To prove that he cared not that her brother had kissed her hand like a lover. But as surely, as inexorably as a bee is drawn to drink of the nectar of a blossom, he was drawn to her to drink of her sweetness.

Despising himself for his weakness, full of the black thoughts he had cultivated all evening, Sandro watched Isabella. When the slave girl laid down the comb and began to plait her mistress's hair, he moved forward.

Adrienne had closed her eyes as Daria drew the comb through strand after strand and willed the strain of the past hours, which still tightened her muscles, to drain out of her. But instead, the tension grew, pulling her nerves even tauter until she felt brittle enough to snap.

"*Madonna.*"

The surge of joy, of relief she felt at the sound of Sandro's voice was almost painful. As she turned toward him, the movement pulled her half-plaited braid out of Daria's hands.

"Sandro!" But her welcoming smile died on her lips and her hands, which she had begun to raise toward him, fell back down into her lap as she saw his grim mien.

The joy in her eyes and her smile seemed so profound, so artless, that Sandro had to clench his fists in the folds of his robe to prevent himself from taking her into his arms. He watched the joyous light die and forced himself not to look away.

"Leave us, Daria," Adrienne said softly, without taking her eyes from Sandro. Then she laced her hands and waited.

For long, silent moments they watched each other like two wild animals, taking each other's measure, waiting for the other to make the first move.

"Well, are you going to say something?" he finally demanded, annoyed that she had again done the unexpected and made no attempt to cajole him out of his anger.

"Not until I know what I am defending myself against."

Sandro narrowed his eyes at her calmly spoken words. She possessed even more audacity than he had expected. Or more innocence. Brushing aside that unsettling thought, he spoke quickly.

"There were whispers that your relations with your brothers were, shall we say, more intimate than is generally accepted, *madonna*. What I saw tonight would seem to bear those rumors out."

So he had seen Piero's revolting advances, Adrienne thought. She wanted to cry out, to scream at him that those whispers were about the other Isabella. Not her. But what could she say? And if she repeated Piero's words to her, Sandro would kill him. Even though an inner voice reminded her that Piero had not given up hope to supplant the Montefiores as ruler of Siena, reminded her that he continued to conspire against Sandro and his father, she could not bring herself to condemn him to death.

"My brother gets carried away at times."

"Then I suggest that you advise him to bridle himself." He stepped closer. "Do you understand me or do I have to be more explicit?" He kept his voice soft in an attempt to hide from himself how murderous was the jealous rage he felt.

"I understand that I have done nothing wrong and that you are reproaching me for my brother's conduct." She paused and looked him directly in the eyes.

"But I have understood the line you have drawn and I will thus inform my brother."

Again Sandro felt an unwilling admiration for her courage.

"Since we are at the business of drawing lines," she went on, "I will tell you this." His expression was still so grim that Adrienne almost lost her nerve. But then she remembered how he had smiled at Luisa. She took a deep breath. "I will not stand by and watch as you take mistresses and sire bastards."

Sandro felt his breath catch as if he had taken a sharp blow to his middle. He had become accustomed to the word in his twenty-four years. Why did it pain him now, simply because it came from her lips? "What do you expect, *madonna,* from a man who is naught but a bastard himself?"

She smothered a gasp at the flash of pain that shot into his eyes. If she could have taken back that one word she would have. If she thought that he would accept it, she would have offered him her touch. Because she knew he wouldn't, she laced her hands still more tightly.

"Your father's wife could bear no children. I ask only that you give me the same chance he gave her before you turn to other women." Even as Adrienne said the words, she remembered. She remembered that Isabella had miscarried twice. And she remembered the circumstances. Because she was determined to break the old mold, she lifted her chin. "I will not be a complacent wife, Sandro."

Sandro looked at his wife. Her hands were still locked in her lap, but that was the only docile thing about her. There was fire in her eyes and the air around her seemed to crackle with energy like the air

before a summer storm. For a moment he was caught
between anger and amusement.

"Is that a threat, *madonna?*" Despite himself, the
corners of his mouth curved upward with the beginnings of a smile.

Adrienne raised her eyebrows. "Am I a barbarian,
Don Alessandro?" she asked, echoing the words he
had once said to her. "Only a friendly warning."

Needing to touch her, he stepped closer. Needing,
just as much, to keep some distance, he picked up her
braid and began to unplait it. When her hair was
loose, he combed through the golden strands with his
fingers.

He had not anticipated how arousing that simple
gesture would be. Needing more, he brought his
hands, still full of her spun-gold hair, forward to cup
her face, her neck. She made a small sound of pleasure and he looked into the mirror.

Her head was tipped back to allow him better ac-
cess to her throat. His hands looked dark and rough
against the delicate skin the color of pale honey, and
the contrast had him drawing her back toward him.

The contact with Sandro's aroused body brought
Adrienne's eyes open and a soft gasp to her lips. Their
eyes met in the mirror and Adrienne watched in fascination as his hands slipped downward to untie the
laces of her nightgown, nudged it off her shoulders
and slid further to cup her breasts, which were already swelling with the ache for his touch.

He bent then and, picking her up as easily as if she
were a child, carried her to the bed and laid her down.
Letting his robe fall on the floor, he sat on the edge of
the bed. Because he wanted to touch her so badly, he
did not touch her at all.

But his eyes touched her, and Adrienne felt his gaze as surely as if it were his hands that were roaming her skin. She could feel the heat that he aroused in her with his eyes alone. First a flush that dampened her skin. Then the sparks that began to dance in the pit of her stomach. And then the flame between her thighs that made her want to beg.

Was it different now that she knew she loved him? More intense? Even more arousing? Or had she loved him from the very beginning? Or perhaps even before that? Needing proof that he was here, that he was real, she reached for him and placed her fingers against his mouth.

As long as he was not touching her he could believe that he still had a choice. But now, even though her fingers were barely brushing his lips, he surrendered. He curled his hand around hers, anchoring it, and pressed his mouth against her palm.

"You are mine, Isabella. Only mine."

Adrienne smiled. "Show me."

He stretched out at her side and slipped his hand between her thighs, which she had parted in welcome. She was slick and hot, and if every fragment of his attention had not been trained on her, he might have missed the almost inaudible sound she made, the barely perceptible tensing of her body. If he had been indifferent to anything but his own pleasure, he might have ignored it.

"Why did you not tell me that I was hurting you?" His tone was brusque with anger at his own thoughtlessness. He had made love to her all through the past day. Had he thought to make love to her all night, as well?

"I can hardly warn you away from other women with one breath and then deny you my body with the next."

Because the simple way she had said the words moved him, he frowned. "I do not enjoy making love to women in pain."

"I could take exception of your use of the plural, Sandro, but I shall let it go this time." Adrienne smiled, although the flash of jealousy was still humming through her. "It must be difficult to go from having half the women in Italy to only one wife." She traced the chiseled line of his cheekbone with a finger.

Even though she was smiling, he could see the fire in her eyes. He remembered his vow earlier that evening to prove to himself that he could find other women as desirable. That might turn out to be more difficult than he had foreseen, he thought, in more ways than one. Needing distance again, he swung his legs over the side of the bed and reached for his robe. He stiffened when he felt Isabella's hand at the base of his spine.

"Will you sleep with me, Sandro?"

He looked at her over his shoulder, his eyebrows curving up mockingly. "Would you chain me to your bed like a pet monkey to make certain that I do not stray?"

"No. I trust you not to stray." She smiled a little sadly and wished that she could tell him what was in her heart. "But I would like to feel you next to me through the night."

He fought the warmth in her eyes, but it was useless. "But I have made no promises, Isabella."

"I know." Her fingers spread against the skin of his back. "I have not asked for any."

If she had weighed out her words like ounces of gold, she could not have chosen better ones.

Disarmed by both her words and touch, which did not issue demands but tendered invitations instead, Sandro let the robe slide from his fingers and lay down beside her.

Controlling the temptation to take her mouth, he turned her onto her side and pulled her into the curve of his body.

Wanting to look at him one more time before she slept, Adrienne shifted, sliding her body against his still-aroused flesh.

His hand on her hip stilled her movement. "You are not making it any easier for me."

"I am sorry." Her heart was so full that the words began to spill out of her before she could stop them. "Sandro, I l—" At the last moment she broke off, realizing that he would never believe her.

"What?"

She shook her head. "Good night."

Sandro hooked his arm around her, his hand splaying on one soft breast. He would never have admitted it, but there was no place in the world where he would rather be than here, now.

Chapter Nine

"*Madonna*'s brothers and Donna Luisa are here."

Adrienne looked up at Angela and smiled. Of all her ladies she had come to like Angela, with her flirtatious dark eyes and cheerful disposition, best. "Have wine and fruit brought to them in the library, Angela, and tell them that I will be with them in a few moments."

"Don Piero asks leave to keep *madonna* company in her chambers."

"No!" Adrienne's breath caught in her throat. Desperately she searched for an excuse, then decided that, as Isabella di Montefiore, she did not need one. "Ask him to wait with the others."

It did not look as though she would have a problem with Alfonso, she thought as she stared blindly into the mirror. Whatever had transpired between him and Isabella in the past, he was now much too intent on enjoying the favors of Luisa Barbiano to have more than a passing interest in his sister. But Piero was another matter. She still was not quite clear how she would deal with him.

Throughout the wedding festivities, which had lasted for weeks, he had stalked her. It had been fairly simple to avoid him or make certain that she was never alone with him. Yet she had been constantly aware of his eyes upon her. And so had Sandro.

The festivities had come to an end, and now Adrienne found the days at her disposal with no banquets, no hunts, no plays, no acrobats, no musicians, no parades to fill her time. Sandro had returned to his business of training and drilling Siena's troops, which, together with his own military services, earned the city-state a good portion of its revenues. And Adrienne was faced with the alternative of locking herself into her apartments or facing her dilemma head-on.

Flanked by two of her ladies, Adrienne walked into the library. Alfonso had backed Luisa into a corner, while Piero paced back and forth, a wine goblet in one hand. The minute he saw her, he set the goblet down so carelessly that the wine sloshed over the edge. Hurrying toward her, he took both her hands in his and brushed his lips over the knuckles.

"You look lovely, as always, *piccolina.*" As he kissed her on both cheeks, he whispered, "I want to speak to you alone today, Bella. No excuses."

Adrienne sent him a smile that did not reach her eyes. "My life is no longer as simple as it was when I was merely Isabella Gennaro."

His eyes narrowed. "What do you mean?"

"I am told that Isabella di Montefiore's position demands that she always be accompanied by at least one of her ladies." Her voice dropped to a whisper. "And I think it would be politic for my conduct to be beyond reproach." Piero's hands on hers tightened and she added, "For now."

Extricating her hands from Piero's, she gestured toward the two women who had stopped a few steps behind her. "I believe that you all know Angela and Lucrezia. They will be attending me today."

She heard Piero murmur something obscene under his breath, but she ignored him and turned to Alfonso.

Alfonso deposited a casual kiss on his sister's cheek. "It would seem that marriage agrees with you, Bella." He smiled suggestively. "Do you not think so, Piero?"

Piero grumbled something that could have been agreement and turned away.

When Luisa glided up to her and took her hands in greeting, Adrienne could barely mask her shiver of distaste.

"Of course marriage agrees with her. She has the most beautiful man in Siena in her bed."

Adrienne watched her send her lover a heavy-eyed look that belied her words, making Alfonso preen like a peacock. At the same time, she saw Luisa brush Piero discreetly with her gaze. A satisfied, malicious light came into her eyes when she had ascertained that his expression had grown still darker. The exercise had taken mere seconds, but Adrienne began to understand how intricate Luisa's little game was and how good she was at it.

Luisa then turned to look squarely at Adrienne, and for the space of a moment her sky blue eyes were bright with provocation. Then her gaze softened and took on that practiced, conscious warmth, but Adrienne understood that the silent warning she had given her days ago had not done its work. The gauntlet had been thrown down as surely as if it lay on the floor between them.

* * *

The six of them rode out to Vignano, where the new Gennaro summer villa was in the last stages of construction. It was a spacious, airy building, adorned and decorated by the very best artisans and artists that money, earned by generations of bankers and merchants, could buy.

A delicious meal of cold partridge, cheeses, sausage from Milan and thinly sliced ham from Parma was laid for them *al fresco* on the terrace, which was shaded by old oak trees. After they had eaten, Alfonso dragged Luisa off to the villa with ill-disguised haste, ostensibly to see to some detail of the work, while Adrienne made a production of eating another apple she did not want.

Piero rose and with an innocuous smile offered her his hand. "Shall we see if the gardens are to your liking, *sorellina?*"

"Do not ask me to leave my ladies behind, Piero," Adrienne murmured as she took his arm. She saw the flare of anger in his eyes, but before he could speak, she continued. "This is a new fact of my life that we must become accustomed to." She tapped his hand. "Please?"

He sent her a dark look and muttered his assent.

As they started down the path, the pattern the gardeners had raked into the gravel brought the image of the paths at the Château de Beaufort and of the people who had walked them into Adrienne's mind so suddenly that she was defenseless against the memory. Unexpected, unwanted tears shot into her eyes as she was caught for a moment in an ache for a life that no longer existed. During the past weeks her life as Adrienne de Beaufort had faded into some shadowy realm that lived on the outer fringes of her consciousness, but now the memories were almost too vivid to bear.

Even as she blinked back the tears, Piero stopped and, his eyes warm with real concern, tipped her face up to his. "What is wrong, Bella?" he asked as his fingers stroked her cheek.

She shook her head, unable to speak.

Suddenly the hatred was distorting his face. "If that bastard is being cruel to you, I will kill him like a mad dog without waiting for a promising opportunity."

Stunned, Adrienne stared at him as the vicious words penetrated her brain. Oh God, she thought, how would she ever be able to reconcile all these conflicting emotions! She had known that he sought Sandro's life. She had *known* it. Known it long before she had come to inhabit Isabella's body. But hearing him say the words aloud intensified the knowledge, making it even more pernicious. Making her an accomplice. Making her, Adrienne, responsible.

Her thoughts began to race. The moment she returned to the city she would go to Sandro and tell him everything. That Piero wanted to kill him. That he intended, one way or another, to be the ruler of Siena. That he lusted after her. Oh God, she thought, Piero would then suffer questioning and abuse, trial and death or at best imprisonment. And how could she do that to him when just a moment ago he had looked at her with affection and brotherly concern?

Twisting away from him, she half walked, half ran down the path, but she had not gone far when the constricting, heavy clothes had her leaning against a piece of statuary to catch her breath. No, she thought, this was wrong. All wrong. If she had come here to change Sandro's destiny, surely she could change Piero's, as well. If she saved Sandro's life, she would prevent Piero from having Sandro's blood on his hands.

By the time Piero reached her, the plan, born of desperation, had formed in her mind. She whipped around to face him, projecting a fury that was only marginally exaggerated.

"You are a fool, Piero," she lashed out. "Have you schemed and intrigued and greased palms all your life only to ruin all your plans with one stab of your dagger? Only to satisfy your male pride?"

"What are you talking about? I only want to protect you." He reached out to touch her, but she slapped his hands away.

"If you truly want to protect me, you will bide your time."

"What are you talking about?" His eyes narrowed. "We said that we would wait only as long as it took for you to find a discreet way to—" He stopped and his eyes shifted to the two women before returning to his sister.

"There are better ways." Adrienne dragged in a ragged breath and prayed that she wasn't making a terrible mistake. "Listen to me. If we act now, the suspicions, the whispers, could ruin us."

"Why did you not think of this before? Or are you stalling for time because you will lose the services—" Piero spat the word "—of your husband?"

"You are a greater fool than I took you for, Piero." She hid her horror behind contempt. "If we let nature take its course—" she saw Piero open his mouth to interrupt her and held up her hand to silence him

"—with a little discreet help from us *if* it should become necessary, it would be so much easier."

She lowered her voice. "If the Duke of Montefiore dies, my husband will succeed him. If he dies, then my firstborn son will succeed him. Who better to guide him through his minority than his uncle?"

"This is not what I am interested in and well you know it, little sister. I have no wish to wait for years, only to be regent for a spawn of the Montefiores." He narrowed his eyes. "Why have you changed your mind, Bella? Our plans—"

"Forget about our plans for a moment." She stamped her foot. "Do you not understand how much easier that would make everything?" She pressed her clenched fists to her forehead. "You would ease into the position legitimately. It would be a tidy little package."

"What do I care for legitimacy?" He made an obscene gesture. "Look around you, Bella. What does anyone care about legitimacy? All I care about, all *anyone* cares about, is power."

"You will have the power, I tell you. All I need is a little time and I will hand you your power on a silver platter." Her lips curved in a cold smile.

"What about the Montefiores?"

"You will leave them to me, Piero. I will choose the time and the place."

"No!" He spun away from her. "They are mine, both of them. But especially the bastard." His voice lowered until it was only a hoarse whisper. "Especially the bastard."

Adrienne stepped back and looked Piero up and down. The fear was lodged in her throat, but her eyes were full of cold contempt as she met his gaze. "So you prefer to have everything smeared with blood and gore. Is that what you need to prove that you are a man?''

His face was so distorted with rage that Adrienne thought she had gone too far. But within moments the rage disappeared, replaced by that covetous look that she already knew too well.

"No, Bella." His voice took on a musical, seductive lilt. "You know far better than anyone what I need." Again he reached out to touch her.

"No." She stepped back. "Remember that we are not alone." She flicked her eyes to where the two women stood, far enough away not to overhear them.

"When, Bella?" he demanded. "Tell me when."

"Will you do this my way?"

Piero saw the fierce determination in his sister's eyes. "All right," he conceded. He knew how contrary Isabella could be if she was thwarted. If her way took too long, his dagger would be ready, he swore silently. Or the purse to pay for someone else's weapon.

"Swear it."

"I swear it on the graves of our parents," he said easily, with no qualms about swearing falsely. Then he gripped her arm. "I have given you what you wanted. Now you will tell me when you will give me what I want. What you promised me."

Her gaze went from his hand, which was digging into her arm, to his eyes and remained there. Only when he had released her did she speak. "There have been rumors, Piero. And I will not have the paternity of my child questioned." She saw his mouth twist with anger again and raised her hand. "You swore to do it my way. Remember that."

Piero clenched his fists. "I will wait until Monte-fiore plants his spawn in your belly, little sister." The words were as bitter as gall on his tongue. "And then I will take what has always been mine."

Even as the disgust at his words rolled over her, Adrienne felt a wave of relief. She had won a little precious time. This would keep Piero at bay, away from Sandro. Away from Sandro's father. Away from herself. She had won at least a few months. And in that time, much could happen.

Francesco di Montefiore stood at the window of his study. When the group of riders rode into the *piazza*, his gaze brushed over them. Only when he recognized that his daughter-in-law led the group, her brother Piero at her side, did he focus his eyes on them. They were too far away for him to be able to read their expressions, but their stiff posture told him that neither one of them was pleased.

"Tell Donna Lucrezia to excuse herself discreetly from her mistress. I wish her report immediately." He spoke without turning around to the scribe who sat behind him.

As the man scurried out of the room, Francesco sighed. There had been so much he had not been able to give his only son. He would have wanted at least to give him a wife he could trust. A wife whose morals were not highly questionable.

Almost an hour later, long after the lady-in-waiting had come and gone, he had still not moved from his post by the window. He heard the door open behind him. He heard his chamberlain announce his daughter-in-law. Still he did not move.

He had watched her throughout the weeks of festivities as carefully as any beast of prey watches his quarry, but he had seen none of the impatient arrogance, none of the loose, tainted charm that she was famous for. The charm that had every man she looked at groveling at her feet. He remembered her wide, panicked eyes as she had stood in the middle of the rowdy crowd that had come to bed the newlyweds. He remembered the innocent sensuality in her gaze when her eyes had rested on Alessandro. It was as if there were two Isabellas, he thought. And then there was that mysterious disappearance of hers, which both she and Alessandro stubbornly refused to discuss.

The word *witch* crossed his mind but he rejected it, the thought too terrible to consider. Still, when he turned to face her, under the cover of one hand, he made the sign against the evil eye.

"Donna Isabella."

"*Altezza.*"

He watched her face carefully as she rose from her curtsy, but there was neither impatience nor annoyance in her eyes at his rudeness, no sign of contempt for the title he had bought for twenty thousand ducats and a gold collar worth twice that.

Adrienne looked at her father-in-law, trying to guess why he had requested her presence. She had realized the very first day that he neither liked nor trusted her. Well, she had seen the cool, slightly pained expression in his eyes when he looked at Sandro and she did not much like him, either.

For a long time he said nothing, merely observed her with his tired, pale eyes. There was a deep weariness echoed in the stoop of his shoulders, and all of a sudden she felt a surge of compassion for this man who already carried within him the illness she knew would bring him an early grave. This was something she would not be able to change, she thought sadly. She tried to mask the shiver that passed through her and wished for a moment that she did not know what the future would bring.

Francesco felt a flash of irritation that she stood there quietly, expectantly, with none of the Gennaro insolence he was all too familiar with. It would have been much easier to be unkind to her. Could it be that he had misjudged her? he asked himself. Had he been unfair to her, judging her by the behavior of her family, who had made nothing but trouble for him for years? He had tried to question Alessandro about her, but his son had looked him in the eye and coolly told him that his marriage was his own affair.

All of a sudden he felt like a fool to have summoned her here. What could he reproach her with? That she had spent the day with her brothers? That she had apparently had a lively argument with her brother Piero? No matter how he had questioned Donna Lucrezia, the lady-in-waiting had insisted that Isabella's conduct had been impeccable.

"I do not wish to forbid you the company of your brothers, *madonna*," he said in a more polite tone than was his wont, "but I would look upon it with favor if you curtailed the time you spent with them."

Adrienne could have shouted with elation at his words. Finally she was being given a reason, an excuse, to stay away from Piero and Alfonso. Instead, she raised her eyebrows and looked the duke in the eyes. "Is there a particular reason for this request?"

"You are an intelligent young woman, Donna Isabella. And you have eyes and ears." He crossed his arms. "I think you well know the reason."

"All this effort because of a little gossip?" She hated her cool, slightly mocking tone, but she knew that Isabella would not have capitulated to the duke's request easily.

"I want what is best for my son." Francesco found himself bristling under the chit's self-possessed gaze.

"Ah, yes." All of a sudden it was easy to feel derision for this man who spoke of what he wanted for his son and yet had been the one to deal him the greatest hurt.

"What does that mean?" He took a step toward her.

"As you said yourself, I am an intelligent woman and I have eyes and ears."

"And?"

"Your head may want what is best for your son—" her voice and her eyes softened as she forgot to play the role of Isabella "—but your heart cannot give it to him."

His mouth slightly open, he stared into her eyes, which had lost all mockery and were filled with warmth and sadness. Then he shook his head as if to clear it. "What would you, a Gennaro, know about the heart?" he jeered.

His words hurt, even though she knew they were not truly aimed at her but at the other Isabella. "Since I have become your daughter-in-law, there are days I think I know more about the heart than I ever wanted to," she said softly, half to herself. She turned away, not wanting him to see the pain she was sure was legible on her face.

She had come into this life the first time by some accident, the second time on a wave of impulse. She had known what she wanted—no, what she needed to do. But she had certainly not thought about the implications or about the cost to herself.

She had not expected to fall in love with Alessandro di Montefiore. And even if she had known it, the thought would not have frightened her. No, she would have welcomed it, for she had lived all her life with the dream that someday there would be someone for her who would fill her life with light.

What she had not known was how much love could hurt. She had not known how helpless it would make her feel to see desire in Sandro's eyes, and to know when that desire had been slaked, the shadows and the mistrust would return. Sometimes he would make love to her and then leave her bed, as if he could bear her nearness only when it was coupled with passion. The only thing that gave her hope was those moments of reluctant tenderness when he would lie with her after passion was spent and let his fingers drift dreamily over her skin or play with the ends of her hair. Or when he would murmur her name in sleep and reach for her to pull her into the curve of his body.

She heard the duke's steps behind her and breathed deeply, willing the pain out of her face, her eyes. It was her pain, as it was her love, and she was unwilling to share it with this man who had never given Sandro what he had needed from him. When she turned to face him again, pride had stiffened her spine and composed her features.

"If I did not know that you were Isabella Gennaro," he whispered, "I would swear that it could not be so."

Adrienne hid the panic that slammed into her under a shrug. She started to move away, but the duke's large hand curved around her shoulder to turn her back to face him.

She looked him in the eyes. "I am not Isabella Gennaro, *Altezza*." She saw his eyes widen and tilted up her chin. "I am Isabella di Montefiore." And in that moment, Adrienne knew that she truly was.

He looked at her for a long time in silence. Then, as the hand that still held her shoulder fell away, he gave a single nod of acknowledgment.

"You love him." It was more a statement of fact than a question.

She raised her head another notch. "Yes."

"And Alessandro?" Francesco saw the pain flash into her eyes, but her head remained high.

"I do not speak for Alessandro. You will have to ask him yourself."

The duke moved away from her, knowing full well that he did not have the right to ask his son a question of such intimacy. He felt a surge of jealousy as he understood that this young woman was closer to his son after sharing his bed for a few weeks than he had become in twenty-four years. There had been a chasm between them from the moment he had looked upon the newborn babe in the arms of the woman whom he had taken to his bed only because his wife could not bear him the son he needed. And the chasm had remained, he knew, through his own inability to breach it.

"Perhaps I have misjudged you, Donna Isabella," he said, turning back to face her. "For the sake of my son's happiness, I hope so."

He said no more and Adrienne understood the unspoken implications. She understood that she would still be watched. But she also understood that, in time, she might have an ally, albeit an unwilling one. As she rose from her curtsy, she looked the duke directly in the eyes one more time before she turned and left the room.

Chapter Ten

Sandro listened to Michele Vanucci's amusing account of his latest amorous adventures with only half an ear as they rode toward the city. He had driven his men hard during the past days and he knew that he could be well satisfied with both his troops and his equipment. Why then did he feel a discontent that was sharp and bitter on his tongue? Why did he feel an impatience that plagued him like a thorn in his flesh?

It was because of the enforced idleness of the past months, he told himself. With the prospect of more idleness to come in the months ahead. Although his contract to fight for the Papacy, if need arose, would run for a few months more, the chances that his men would see more than the environs of their camp seemed slim.

Italy was enjoying a rare stretch of peace, and the rumors that Louis, King of France, was planning a new Italian campaign seemed to be no more than just that. Sandro knew he would have little to do except drill his men in the daytime and at night provide them with enough wine and enough whores to keep them docile. Of course it was the excessive time on his hands that made him edgy, he repeated. But he was lying to himself and he knew it.

"And then I slung her over my shoulder, carried her down the main staircase, past her father and brothers, who applauded and waved me on, and into the street."

"You what?" Sandro turned toward his lieutenant and best friend with a frown.

Michele's full-bodied laugh rang out, sending a flock of starlings up from a nearby vineyard where the grapes were already beginning to take on their deep purple color. "Just making sure that you were listening to me, Alessandro."

"I was listening." His voice and his expression were sullen.

"But most of your thoughts were somewhere else, eh?" Grinning, Michele leaned over and gave Sandro a friendly cuff on the shoulder. "And I have a fairly good idea where they were, too."

Sandro sent his friend a dark look and grumbled something short and obscene under his breath. This had to stop, he railed at himself. Ever since he had first stood in the doorway of his bride's bedchamber those weeks ago, she filled his waking thoughts as she filled his dreams. Her scent was ever in his nostrils, even when he was surrounded by the smell of dust and sweat. Even as he gripped the hilt of his sword, he knew just what her skin felt like. Her image would rise up before his eyes to taunt him.

"Why are you fighting it so, Alessandro?" Michele asked, his hazel eyes warm with affection. "Be glad that they have given you a beautiful wife and enjoy her. Imagine if you had been given some fat, cross-eyed crone." He laughed again. "You would have to blindfold yourself and think of Mona Diana's women to beget your sons."

Sandro stared ahead, his face surly. He still distrusted Isabella, despite the aura of innocence and purity that seemed to surround her, just as he distrusted her brothers, and yet he could stay away from her no more than a bee could stay away from a luscious rose. How could he explain to Michele that in mere weeks Isabella had taken hold of him in a way that was far beyond desire? In a way he could no longer control? And the thought terrified him.

"Speaking of Mona Diana—" Michele swatted at Sandro with the back of his gloved hand and there was a devilish sparkle in his eyes "—what do you say we pay her a visit tonight? Maybe one of her beauties will take your mind off that wife of yours." His teeth flashed in a quick grin. "If that is what you *really* want."

Sandro nodded in agreement, but he felt no pleasure at the prospect, nor did his mood lighten. The women in Mona Diana's house of pleasure were pretty, well trained and healthy—and he had absolutely no desire to sample their charms. But by the time they had reached the Montefiore *palazzo,* he had convinced himself that maybe Michele was right. Maybe that was what he needed.

The entry hall was dark and cool. As their boots clattered over the marble tiles, they stripped off their gloves and short capes, tossing them to the lackeys who had run to meet them.

"And now a cup of wine to wash down the dust of the day and something to eat, Michele."

Sandro loosened the fastenings of his leather doublet. His foot already on the lowest step of the staircase, he snapped his fingers at one of the lackeys to approach so that he could give him his orders. It was then that he looked up the stairs and saw her.

Isabella stood halfway up the wide staircase. She had just untwined the rope of pearls that had bound her hair in its habitual simple plait and the jewels still hung from her fingers like a milky waterfall. She did not speak, but she smiled and took a few steps toward him.

Forgetting Michele, forgetting the orders he had been about to give, Sandro continued up the stairs and stopped on the step below her, their faces level.

"Madonna." His nod was curt. He was not accustomed to feeling guilt, but he felt a flash of it now and wondered if she—with her uncanny instincts—would be able to read it in his eyes.

"I am well pleased to see you, Don Alessandro." She tipped her head to one side and her mouth curved in a smile. "Especially since you are apparently in such a charming mood this evening," she teased gently.

Sandro looked away to get his mind off what it would feel like to wipe that smile off her mouth with his kiss.

"Will we have the pleasure of your company at supper?"

"No." His tone was sharp. "I am going out with Michele." He sent her a black look, irritated at himself that he had felt the need to qualify his no.

Without looking back, he snapped his fingers in wordless command and moved past her, knowing that had he remained, he would not have been able to resist touching her.

* * *

Adrienne lay in the soft, wide bed and stared up at the gods and nymphs who frolicked on the roof of the canopy. For Sandro she was still like one of the nymphs up there, she thought, a body to be used and discarded. Even though she understood the reasons why he still did not trust her, why he would not allow her within the barriers he protected himself with, the realization still hurt.

All that would perhaps have been bearable if she had had unlimited time at her disposal, but she did not. The burden of knowledge hung heavy on her. Knowledge she could share with no one. She knew that the King of France was already setting out for Italy, bringing discord. And in his wake was Cesare Borgia, burning with ambition to carve his own dukedom out of the city-states of central Italy. She dug the heels of her hands into her eyes, wondering how she would be able to use this terrible knowledge she had of the future without being burned for a witch.

But there was one dread point where her knowledge failed her. She did not know how much time she had left. Her gaze fell on Isabella's portrait across the room, a continuous reminder. She did not know if she would suddenly wake up in Adrienne de Beaufort's life and find that the universe had played a terrible trick on her. As they always did, her nerves began to jump at the thought.

She heard the door open and knew from the gliding step that it was Daria with a cup of mare's milk, sweetened with honey and spiced with orange oil and cinnamon. Sitting up in bed, she took the cup from the young slave and sipped the sweet beverage.

Daria knelt next to the bed and watched her mistress drink. Her hands were folded at her waist and she could feel the metal capsule that she had sewn into her tunic. How many nights had she brought Isabella her cup of milk, wanting to add the contents of the capsule to the brew? How many nights had she carried the empty cup away, hating herself for her cowardice in preferring a life full of terror and pain to a quick death? But now, since the sorceress, as she had come to think of her, had entered her mistress's body, she was glad for her cowardice. She could never go home again because she was soiled, but there were still sunsets to watch and flowers to smell.

Adrienne drained the cup, the taste as familiar to her as if she had drunk this spiced milk all her life. As she turned to hand the cup to Daria, she heard the sound of boots on the tiles.

The heavy door crashed open and Sandro stood framed in the doorway, the flickering candlelight throwing shadows across his face.

He stared across the room at his wife. She looked small and fragile in the large bed, although he knew that she was neither. He wanted to hate her and knew that he could not. He wanted to make love to her. He refused to put a name to the madness he felt for her, but whatever it was, it was stifling him.

He had just spent the most frustrating evening of his life drinking cup after cup of wine, surrounded by a bevy of Mona Diana's pretty women, who had used all their skills to arouse him. And he had not been able to bring himself to touch any of them.

Furious, Sandro strode forward until he stood at the bedside.

Adrienne looked up at him and saw the fury in his turbulent eyes. Even from where he stood, she caught the smell of wine and a heavily sweet, musky perfume. Within the space of a breath, her fury matched his.

"How dare you come to my bed with the smell of wine and other women on you?"

He reached for her, but she slapped his hand away. The wine he had consumed had not dulled his reflexes and he caught her wrists so quickly that she gasped.

"Let go of me." She tried to twist out of his grasp but he held her as tightly as if his fingers were iron manacles.

He pulled her up onto her knees and still there was no fear in her eyes, only fury, and it fueled his own.

"You are a witch." His nostrils fluttered with rage. "A few weeks, Isabella. In a few weeks you have pushed me to the wall. Every time I breathe I smell only your scent." In that moment he dragged in a ragged breath that brought him her fragrance. He almost closed his eyes with the pleasure of it. "Every time I look at another woman, I see only your face." Although he was not aware of it, his fingers loosened and his merciless grip became a caress.

Adrienne could have escaped him easily now, but she let her hands lie in the circle of his fingers.

"I spent the evening surrounded by beautiful women and I could not touch a single one of them, damn you."

Her anger was gone as quickly as it had risen, and she bit the inside of her lower lip to prevent a smile. His tone was the slightly petulant one of a small boy complaining about not being able to eat a sweetmeat because he had eaten more than his fill beforehand.

She turned her hands and placed them flat against his chest. "Am I supposed to sympathize with you now?"

Sandro looked down at her, her mouth serious, her eyes smiling up at him. Something snapped inside of him then. A door opened, releasing a surge of emotion that flowed through him like a warm river. If he had not drunk too much wine, he might have recognized it for the emotion it was. Though even if he had recognized it, he would have denied it.

But Adrienne knew what it was. If she had been a different woman, if she had been the other Isabella, she might have felt triumph. Instead she felt gratitude, hope and an immeasurable joy. She let her head fall forward so that her forehead rested against his chest. His heartbeat was fast and a little uneven and she felt it seep into her until both their hearts beat with the same rhythm.

"Isabella."

She lifted her head. The words of love were on her lips, but Adrienne knew that she would have to wait before she would be able to say them. Oh God, she thought as fear shot through her, please, please let me be here to say them.

Sandro saw the brief flicker of fear in his wife's eyes, and remembering how he had dragged her up from the bed, he felt a surge of guilt. "Do not be afraid, Isabella." His hands still circling her wrists, he sank down to kneel at the edge of the bed. "I will not hurt you."

One by one he kissed her fingers and then lowered his mouth into the palm of her hand.

Sitting back on her heels, Adrienne watched Sandro kiss her fingers. Somehow watching his mouth move over her hands aroused her even more than feeling his lips on her skin. He turned one hand and lowered his mouth to the palm, his hot breath singeing her. She felt him draw a circle on her palm with the tip of his tongue and that touch brought a soft moan to her lips.

Her hand still at his mouth, Sandro looked up at his wife. Her eyes were half-closed with incipient pleasure, her lips parted as if they were already eager to welcome his kiss. Could she truly have forgiven him for his roughness? he wondered.

Adrienne gazed down at Sandro. For the first time there was uncertainty in his eyes, a vulnerability put there by his new, unacknowledged feelings. Slowly she slid her hand away from his mouth, across his cheek, until her fingers tunneled into his hair. Her hand closed over the black silky strands and pulled him down until his face nestled against the softness of her belly.

As the heat shot through him, he realized that she had given him an answer to his unspoken question. Lifting his head, he drew her hands to the laces of his shirt.

With her eyes on his, Adrienne began to undress him.

Chapter Eleven

Her hopes had not been quite fulfilled after all, Adrienne mused sadly as her fingers plied the needle. Several weeks had passed since the night she had seen such deep emotion mirrored in Sandro's eyes, but she had never seen it again, and she had begun to ask herself if it had been there at all. Perhaps she had deceived herself because she had wanted to see it so badly.

He was avoiding her. Every day he and Michele rode out to the camp, although she had gathered from occasional remarks that the troops were in top form and his constant presence would not have been necessary. Often enough they did not even return to the city in the evenings, electing to stay in a summer villa in Costalpino, a village halfway between the city and the camp. Despite herself, Adrienne sometimes could not help wondering just whose company he kept on those evenings.

Left to her own devices, she felt the hot summer days drag endlessly. It was not long before she decided that she was having no more of it. She did not know exactly how Isabella had spent her time. From what she remembered from the diaries she had pored over, plus what she had pieced together, Isabella had spent the days in hedonistic pleasure. She had held court for an endless procession of lovesick men, expecting to be continually amused and diverted, and when she was not, she had not hesitated to strike out quickly and cruelly. Adrienne understood that there was a measure of risk in changing her behavior so radically, but she also knew that she could not bear to live Isabella's indolent, sybaritic, selfish life.

She had put away one tiny linen garment that she had finished hemming and picked up another, when there was a commotion at the door. The other women's fingers stilled in their sewing and Gianni the dwarf, who had been singing a *canzone* in his surprisingly pure tenor to the accompaniment of his lute, fell silent as Luisa swept in, clothed in a gown of brilliant blue that matched her eyes and trailing a cloud of cloyingly sweet scent.

"So it is true!" she cried. Gliding through the room like a caravel in full sail, she snatched the small linen shirt from Adrienne's fingers. "You are shut away in your apartments sewing for the poor. Good God, Isabella, you might as well have taken the veil." She crouched down, her velvet skirt billowing around her. "Are they forcing you to do this, *cara?*"

Silently Adrienne held her hand out for her sewing. When Luisa had handed it back to her, she began to stitch again.

"No one is forcing me to do anything, Luisa," Adrienne said quietly. "And there is nothing strange about this." She tried to keep her voice light. "My responsibilities have changed and I have changed with them." She lifted her eyes briefly to Luisa's.

"And this business that you cannot see your brothers? What is this?".

"I can hardly ignore a request made by my father-in-law." One who did not know better would have said that she was bristling with righteous indignation, Adrienne thought as she put her sewing down in her lap and looked Luisa full in the face. "I explained everything to Piero and Alfonso and told them to take the matter up with the duke if they so desired. Apparently they preferred to send you." She smiled to soften her words. "Or is that not so?"

As she rose, Luisa rose with her, stumbling over Gianni, who had been sitting at Adrienne's feet. "Get out of my way, you freak," she muttered. She aimed a kick at him, but he somersaulted aside with surprising agility. With a shrug Luisa turned toward Adrienne.

Adrienne swept her gaze coolly over her visitor. "Those who serve me are mine to reward or punish, Luisa." She paused. "Only mine." Her voice was low but carried a distinct tone of command. "I would thank you to remember that." Swiveling around, she strode toward the window.

"Bella." Following her, Luisa put her hand on Adrienne's arm. "I have never seen you like this before. Talk to me, I beg you. I am your oldest, your best friend."

Yes, Adrienne thought, *and you would not hesitate to become my husband's mistress to increase your power.* She stepped away from Luisa's touch. When she spoke again, she kept her face toward the window, knowing that she would not be able to keep her feelings out of her eyes. "What can I tell you, Luisa, but that my life has changed whether I like it or not, and I must make the best with what I have." And that was not far from the truth, she thought ruefully.

"And this business with the hospitals?" Luisa demanded. "God knows, you could be infected by some foul disease." She gestured dramatically. "Alfonso and Piero are worried to death about you."

"They need not worry." Adrienne shrugged. "I do not care for the sick. I only try to make certain that the hospitals have what they need." Her voice softened. "As for the children in the Foundlings' Hospital, the only disease they suffer from is loneliness."

"Is this truly you talking, Bella?"

Before Adrienne could avoid her hand, Luisa had reached out and turned her so that they stood face-to-face. Although the fear was cold in her belly, she fought to keep it out of her eyes.

"Ah, so that is it." Luisa's sky blue eyes lighted up with sudden awareness and malice.

"What?" Her stomach beginning to churn, Adrienne pressed a hand against her middle. "What are you talking about?"

"You are with child, little one. I can see it in your eyes." She laughed softly. "You have the same look as one of Botticelli's Madonnas." Luisa cupped her cheek with a gentleness that seemed real. "Small wonder that you are acting odd."

So that was it! Adrienne swayed slightly as the realization penetrated. She had paid scant attention to the fact that her monthly courses had failed to appear. And she had simply attributed the other small changes in her body to the heat.

Even as the joy that she carried Sandro's child surged through her, she remembered. Her words to Piero. Remembered the words in Isabella's diary. An icy shiver snaked along her spine. She was here to change history, she reminded herself. And change it she would. Her hand still lay against her belly as if to soothe the child who slept there. Silently, fervently, she promised her son that she would keep him safe.

"I truly do not know yet if that is so." She moved her shoulders in what she hoped was a casual shrug.

"*Poverina,* poor girl, of course it is so." Luisa's flutelike voice dripped honey. "Well, perhaps you shall be fortunate and your time will not be too cumbersome."

Adrienne could fairly see the wheels turning in Luisa's calculating head. She breathed deeply and clenched her fists against the desire to raise her hand and bodily strike the despicable thoughts from Luisa's mind.

"You will excuse me now, Luisa." Adrienne's voice was cool as she stepped back. "I promised the Mother Superior at the Foundlings' Hospital those shirts by the morrow. You are welcome to join us. We can always use another pair of hands."

Luisa's laugh tinkled through the room. "Oh, *cara,* you must truly not be yourself." She pressed her perfumed cheek to Adrienne's and swept out of the room.

Slowly Adrienne returned to her seat, and as she picked up her sewing again, she began to plan.

It was barely dawn when Adrienne arose. She had kept her servants and ladies up until midnight with preparations and now she could hardly wait to begin her journey to Costalpino. The journey would be brief, but she had no illusions about just how great a distance she would have to travel.

She had sent a message to the duke, wording it clearly enough so that he would know she was not asking for permission but merely being polite enough to inform him of her plans.

The litter that had been part of Isabella's dowry stood ready in the courtyard when Adrienne and those whom she had chosen to accompany her descended. It was an elaborate, ostentatious affair, its wooden undercarriage decorated with hammered gold, the frame painted in a brilliant azure, the curtains of gold brocade and wine red velvet doubled to keep out the dust of the road.

"Donna Isabella."

Adrienne turned to see her father-in-law framed by one of the arches of the arcade that went around three sides of the courtyard. His face was stern as she approached him.

"Alessandro will return to the city for the council meeting by the end of the week."

"I have news for him that will not keep."

"News?" The duke straightened, his eyebrows drawing together. "What news?"

Adrienne lowered her head slightly in a gesture of apology. "News that Alessandro should hear first, *Altezza.*"

Understanding dawned in the duke's eyes and he almost smiled. "Additional men-at-arms will ride with you." He raised his hand as if to preclude an expected protest. "To make certain your horses are well behaved."

Nodding lightly in acknowledgment, Adrienne turned to go.

* * *

The journey to Costalpino took barely two hours
and yet to Adrienne it seemed like an eternity. She re-
clined among the silk pillows while Gianni played his
lute and Daria moved a large fan fashioned of colorful Chinese silk back and forth in a vain effort to cool
the hot, still air inside the litter. By the time the horses
stopped in front of the high wrought-iron gate of the
villa, Adrienne felt half-stifled and her stomach was
rebelling against the constant swaying motion of the
litter.

She tore the curtains aside, ignoring the cloud of
dust that rose from them, and drew in the fresh air
greedily. Already Sandro's chamberlain was at the
gate, bowing low to greet her.

"When does your master return?" she asked as one
of the men-at-arms handed her down from the litter.

"Toward evening, Madonna Isabella."

"Good." Adrienne nodded. "Show me to Don
Alessandro's apartments and have my baggage
brought. And send me the cook, Peppino." Her use of
the man's pet name and the warm smile she sent him
made him her slave for life. "I want him to prepare
something especially delicious for supper tonight."

She had been pacing for more than an hour when
she heard the horses. Although she wanted to run toward the entry, she forced herself to remain standing
in the doorway of the chamber. When the footman
threw open the front door, she heard voices, followed
by a ripple of feminine laughter. The welcoming smile
on her face froze, and if her pride had allowed her to,
she would have fled.

Sandro strode in, followed by Michele, who had his arm slung casually around the shoulders of a girl in simple peasant dress.

"I bid you good-evening, Don Alessandro." Her voice, its cool, haughty tone masking her hurt, rang through the entry hall.

Swiveling around, his short cape and gloves still in his hands, Sandro stared across the hall. Isabella stood framed in a doorway, a vision of loveliness in a gown the color of emeralds. Before he could arm himself against them, joy and pleasure leapt within him, lighting his eyes. But within a moment he had himself under control again, reminding himself harshly that he had no wish to feel either. Tossing the garments he held into the hands of a waiting footman, he moved toward her, his brows knit in a frown.

Adrienne felt her heart start to pound when she saw pleasure flame in his eyes. But it was quickly gone. He moved toward her, his steps smooth and gliding like a jungle cat about to strike.

"And a good-evening to you, *madonna*." He took her hand, its slight unsteadiness, at such variance with her coolly distant expression, surprising him. As he lowered his head toward her hand, the fragrance of roses drifted toward him. He knew that he would find the same fragrance in the hollow of her throat, in the valley between her breasts, and his senses began to swim with desire so quickly that he could not check it. Determined to fight it, he brushed her fingers with a perfunctory kiss and dropped her hand.

"What are you doing here?" His voice lowered to a furious whisper. "I do not remember extending an invitation to you to visit me here."

"I am your wife." Adrienne struggled to hold on to the joyful anticipation she had felt. "I did not think that I would need an invitation."

"Indeed you are my wife, *madonna,* and it is my right to decide when I do not choose to be badgered by your presence," he snapped. "It is time you learned your place." He felt a flare of disgust at his words, his tone. Simply by being the woman she was, Isabella touched some weak spot in his spirit, he admitted to himself, and he was punishing her for it.

"Badgered? My place?" Temper began to simmer in Adrienne's eyes. "Your choice of words is, to put it mildly, unfortunate."

She glanced beyond him to where Michele stood, his arm still around the girl's shoulders, and her eyes narrowed. "I told you that I would not be a complacent wife, Sandro. I did not speak less than the truth."

"What will you do?" He gestured over his shoulder with his chin, his eyes goading her even more than his words. "Fight over me like a fishwife?"

"If I must."

Sandro felt a jolt of male pride at her words. Pride and something else. Something warmer, gentler.

Adrienne stepped closer, her gown brushing against his legs. "Are you callous enough, cruel enough, to provoke me into it?" She tilted her head up so that their mouths were separated by no more than a handbreadth. Something flickered in his eyes and she felt a little of the anticipation, the confidence, begin to return. She shook her head. "I do not think so."

Her sweet breath drifted over his mouth as she spoke and he needed all his control not to close the distance between them.

Michele watched the interplay between Sandro and his wife. Poor Alessandro, he thought. He had fallen into the trap. He just did not realize yet how deeply. There was no pity in his thought but rather a gentle amusement and a touch of envy. Beckoning to a footman, he bade him to bring the girl to his apartments. Then he released her, dismissing her with a casual pat on her derriere, and moved toward his friend.

Sandro had stepped back at the sound of footsteps behind him and Michele executed an elegant, low bow before his friend's wife.

"Forgive me, *madonna,* for disgracing your house with my companion for this night."

"*Your* companion?"

Michele smiled at the mixture of confusion and relief in Isabella's eyes. Well now, he thought to himself with something resembling satisfaction, my friend Alessandro is in good company in his trap then. "Yes," he said. "My companion."

Adrienne's gaze flitted between the two men—Michele smiling, Sandro scowling.

"In earlier days we might have shared her." Michele shrugged and sent her a charming, unselfconscious grin. "But you, *madonna*—" he bowed again "—have tamed Alessandro as thoroughly as Saint Francis of Assisi tamed the wolf of Gubbio." He gestured melodramatically to underline his reference to the legend that the saint had tamed a rapacious wolf who had been terrorizing the city of Gubbio.

His eyes full of gentle amusement, Michele curved his hand around his friend's shoulder. "You will forgive me, Alessandro, for revealing your secrets, eh?" He leaned closer and his voice lowered. "But knowing your fondness for the truth, I am sure you do not mind.''

Michele's words effectively took the wind out of Sandro's sails. His scowl dissipated and he laughed, as much at himself as at his friend's words. He was a fool, he thought. Why should he not enjoy what was his for as long as he wanted it?

He cuffed Michele on the shoulder. ''Get out of my sight before I am tempted to have your tongue cut out.''

As Michele strode away, Sandro turned toward his wife, the desire to possess already stirring his blood. Her eyes had softened, darkened, so that only a shimmer of the golden lights was visible. Her mouth was barely curved with the hint of a smile. Despite himself, he found the desire mellowing.

''Sandro.'' Her voice was low and husky. ''I do not want to tame you. I just do not want to share you with other women.'' Too proud to chance a rebuff, Adrienne laced her hands to stop herself from reaching out to him.

Lost in her eyes, he opened his mouth to tell her that there was not a woman in the world who could tempt him now that he had made love to her. But at the last moment he remembered that she was a Gennaro, and no matter how much he wanted her, he would never be able to allow himself to trust her completely.

Because it was easier than words, he lifted his hand to cup her chin, his eyes drifting closed at the sheer pleasure of feeling her velvet skin beneath his fingers. He allowed his hand to drift down her neck and felt her pulse begin to drum. As if that had been the signal to ride into battle, he lowered his head to her mouth with a kind of desperation.

As he came closer, Adrienne could smell the dust and sweat, the horseflesh and leather and, underlying that, the scent of his skin. Even before he touched her mouth, she could feel her knees weakening. His mouth took hers ruthlessly, his teeth scraping over her lips as his tongue filled her. But instead of frightening her, this sign of uncontrolled passion fueled her own and she matched his kiss.

When he dragged his mouth away from hers, his breath was shuddering in and out of his lungs. He stared down at her, her eyes half-closed, her lips wet and parted, inviting him to take her mouth again, and he knew that if he did not move away now, in another moment he would take her here, on the floor, in full view of the servants. He stepped away, but unable to separate himself from her completely, he slid his hand down the unbelievably soft skin that swelled above the square neckline of her gown and cupped her breast. For a moment he let his hand rest there before he spun away and strode toward the staircase.

Adrienne watched him go, still half-lost in the haze of incipient passion. In her girlhood fantasies she had dreamt of her ideal lover. She had dreamed of a man with tranquil eyes and gentle hands. A man who would walk with her hand in hand in the summer twilight. A man who would read her poetry underneath an apple tree.

Instead she found that her ideal lover was a warrior, with eyes like a stormy night and hands that could be rough. Hands that were relentless when they drove her to the peak of a passion she had not believed possible. But they were gentle, too, she reminded herself, remembering how they would drift over her skin when the passion had been sated, as if she were something infinitely lovely, infinitely precious.

Her lips curved in a smile as she moved toward the staircase.

Sandro slid down in the copper tub, flipping his long black hair over the edge to drip on the marble floor. The warm water had soothed him, even as it had washed away the sweat and dust of the day, but no matter how he tried to empty his mind, he could not banish Isabella from it. And he knew that it was not only because the mere thought of her aroused him. With her spirit tempered by gentleness, her kindness, her wit, she had touched something in him he had not known he possessed.

She had bewitched him, he told himself, still unwilling, still unable to admit the true depth of his feelings. And then there were the doubts, the suspicions. He could not deny what he saw in her eyes, yet how could he reconcile that with what he knew of her? How could he be sure that she was not involved in some plan hatched by her brothers? And then there was still the matter of her disappearance on the night of their wedding.

Oddly enough, that last, which might have driven another man to violence, troubled him the least. In some strange way he accepted it, as he had accepted it from the first, like an unsolvable puzzle one tolerates without seeming to need to explore its significance.

He closed his eyes and dozed.

He awoke with the fragrance of roses in his nostrils. Opening his eyes, he saw Isabella sitting on a stool next to the tub and pleasure eddied through him.

He raised his hand and touched his fingers to her cheek.

Adrienne took his hand and touched her lips to the center of his palm as he had touched her so many times. The warm, wet skin against her mouth set off an ache within her, and keeping her eyes on his, she traced a circle with her tongue. She felt the muscles in his hand tense, but he did not move.

Her gaze was still meshed with his, as her mouth slid down toward his wrist, where it came to rest against the small, thin scar that had remained from the wound his own dagger had made. Her eyes widened as she remembered how his scarlet blood had trickled onto the white sheet, and she wished that she could explain to him how much it had meant to her that he had not taken her that night.

As Sandro felt Isabella's lips against the scar on his wrist, he was struck by how much that secret, which neither one of them would ever share with anyone else, bound them together. He felt something flare inside him. Something warm. Something vital and at the same time almost unbearably sweet. And still he told himself that what he felt was only desire for her luscious body, which satisfied him as no other.

Suddenly he could not wait to make love to her. Yes, to spill his desire into her. But even more to absorb her desire, her passion, which he aroused so easily, into himself.

He rose, the water flowing down his body, which was already more than half-aroused. Adrienne felt the warmth pool between her thighs as she looked at his magnificent body—whipcord lean with the long, subtle muscles of the expert swordsman.

He stepped out of the tub and ignoring the bath sheet she held out to him, he reached for her, curling his hand around her neck to bring her closer.

"You are wearing too many clothes." He hooked a finger into the neckline of her gown.

Adrienne shook her head. She wanted to share her news with him now. Now, before they were steeped with passion. She stepped away, but he reached out and pulled her back toward him.

"Did your father confessor not instruct you that it is a wife's duty to accept her husband whenever he wants to couple with her?" The line of gentle kisses that he drew down the side of her neck belied his callous words.

"Indeed." She placed her hands lightly on his hips and had to check the desire to rub them over the wet, sleek skin. She stepped back again and smiled up at him. "In order to procreate."

"Precisely." He began to draw her closer again, but she resisted.

"But what if one has already?" Above eyes that were smiling, her eyebrows curved upward in question. "Is it still a duty then?"

Sandro's hands tightened on her shoulders. "What are you saying, Isabella?"

She reached up and, taking both his hands, brought them down to lie against her belly. "I am with child, Sandro," she whispered. "I will give you a son."

Her heart lurched as she remembered again. Remembered Piero's words. Remembered that Isabella had confided to her diary that she had miscarried her child after giving her brothers what she had denied them before her marriage. But she was here to change history, Adrienne told herself, as she had told herself again and again. And she would.

She squeezed his hands. "God willing, I will give you a son."

Sandro looked down at his wife. He had married her against his will. He had been ready to hate and despise her, and yet he had found himself wanting her as he had never wanted another woman. That he could accept. But now he found himself crowded by other feelings, other needs. He wanted to deny them and he did, but only up to a point. He could not deny that he had felt something move within him when he had returned to the villa today to find her there. Even less could he deny the tempest within him now. Yes, there was the pride that he had planted a child within her womb. But even stronger was the emotion that he felt for her and her alone.

Adrienne felt the tension in Sandro's hands. She saw the storm of emotions in his black eyes. That and her own feelings, welling up inside her like an effervescent spring, gave her the courage to speak.

"I love you, Sandro."

He went completely still at her words. Then, tearing his hands out of her grasp, he whirled away.

"No!" When he spun back to face her, his features were sharp with fury. "Do not say that! I do not want to hear your lies."

Adrienne felt the joy within her fade a little. But she had seen the emotions in his eyes and she held on to that.

"Why are you so furious, Sandro?" She forced herself to speak very softly, wanting him to have to strain to hear her, wanting nothing to detract from the strength of her words. "Because I told you that I love you? Or because you love me but are afraid to admit it?''

He opened his mouth to speak, to refute her accusations, but he found the words sticking in his throat as the truth flashed through him. Something within him softened, like wax against a flame. He felt himself surrendering to the seductive warmth that spread through him.

Adrienne's eyes filled with tears of joy as she watched the light come into his eyes. She opened her arms and he came into them.

Chapter Twelve

The days slipped by, as harmonious as the tranquil countryside that surrounded Costalpino. The fields of growing corn and yellowing wheat, the vineyards, the rolling hills, occasionally topped by fieldstone farmhouses with their roofs of faded brick red tile or the ubiquitous cypresses, breathed an ageless serenity.

Although large and airy, the villa seemed intimate after the huge dimensions of the *palazzo* in Siena. The architect had made the rooms appear cozy by covering the walls with Gobelin tapestries in muted colors and ivory-colored brocade with appliqué work in wine red velvet.

But it was the gardens that Adrienne loved best. There was the small formal garden with its maze of neat, graveled paths bordered by cypresses and trimmed box trees, in the center of which was a fountain presided over by Neptune and his nymphs. Beyond it, a gently sloping lawn was dotted with oak trees so ancient and gnarled that they were full of crevices and hollows big enough for a child to hide in.

There was only one part of the garden that she learned to avoid, even though it was an inviting place with a small pool populated by a family of swans and rimmed by a Roman colonnade and benches to enjoy either sun or shade. There she had found a sculpture of a winged cherub riding a dolphin. A sculpture that she had grown up with, for it had stood in the garden of the Château de Beaufort.

She had been walking through the garden on Sandro's arm the first time she had seen it. Her feet had faltered and she had blanched so visibly that, alarmed, Sandro had lifted her into his arms and carried her to the nearest bench. It had been simple to explain the moment away with a passing reference to her delicate condition, but she had taken care that they not walk that way again. She had enough reminders that she was perhaps merely an interloper, a visitor, whose time here might be horribly temporary.

Her fingers brushed the cool marble of the balustrade that bordered the formal garden as she watched the road for the cloud of dust that would signal Sandro's return. Yes, she thought, the days were harmonious. And the nights—she closed her eyes—the nights were full of passion and tenderness. More and more their lives seemed to interlace like the weft and warp of a single piece of fabric. And yet there was always a fine line of tension present in both of them, like a bank of thunderclouds on the farthest horizon of a perfect summer day.

Adrienne had not repeated her vow of love, nor had Sandro found his way to the words she herself needed so badly to hear. As if they would be a talisman against the lingering doubt and suspicion that she knew still lived within Sandro's mind. Sometimes she caught him looking at her with questions in his eyes, and the pain that he still did not trust her would roll through her.

July had slipped into August. Many of the fields had been harvested, leaving only a stubble of grain stalks and exposing the rich, reddish brown earth. The grapes were starting to turn fat and purple on their vines.

Adrienne knew that this quiet time was coming to an end. As she had known it would, the news had come that Louis, King of France, was on his way over the Alps to stake his claim on Milan. There had been a brief mention that Cesare Borgia, the pope's illegitimate son, was in the king's retinue, but it had been no more than that. Even when the news had arrived that the pope had excommunicated the papal vicars who ruled the cities of Forlì and Imola, Pesaro, Cesena and Rimini for ostensibly failing to pay the taxes due the Papacy, no one had drawn the connection. But she knew, Adrienne thought as dread and fear gathered in the pit of her stomach like lead weights.

She knew that soon Borgia, under the cover of reclaiming the cities for the Papacy, would start carving out his own dukedom in central Italy. She knew that he would hire the best *condottieri* in Italy to help him. And she knew that Sandro, with his superbly trained troops and modern artillery, would be one of the first. And no matter how many nights she lay awake, she saw no way of preventing it.

Unseeing, she stared out over the countryside, her gaze focused on the future. She knew the future, she thought, and yet she did not. She knew nothing of the details, the nuances, which might have helped her. She knew nothing of what she had perhaps already set into motion. And what she did know gave her no clue as to what she could do to change the terrible, terrible outcome.

Her hands tightened on the balustrade so that the slightly uneven edge dug into her palms. What had been the sense in exchanging her own life for Isabella's if she was not going to be able to change what was most vital? But she would not give up. Somehow, somehow, she swore, she would find a way.

When her eyes focused again, she saw the already settling line of dust on the sunbaked road leading to the villa. Sandro was back! Her heart gave a little skip. Her skirts belling, she turned.

"Sandro!" Her hands rose to her breast in an instinctive gesture of surprise.

"Your thoughts must have taken you far away." He stepped up to her and took her hands in his as he brushed her cheek with his lips. "I called out, but you did not hear me."

"I was just—thinking," she murmured, and although she would have lowered her forehead to rest against his chest, he tipped her face up toward his.

Sandro saw the shadows in her eyes and he had seen how the skin had stretched whitely over her knuckles as she had stood there lost in thought. Before he could do anything about it, the old doubts rose to cloud the clarity of his emotions like silt rises up to cloud a glass-clear stream.

"Is something wrong?"

"No—yes." Adrienne shrugged helplessly. "It is just that I do not want to go back."

"Is that all?" Sandro felt an unreasonable wave of relief even as a tiny, unnoticed fragment of doubt remained behind.

Smiling, he slid his arm around her shoulders and steered her down the path. "We cannot hide here forever. Besides, the second race of the *palio* will be run the day after tomorrow.'' His eyes sparkled with anticipation and pleasure. The two races, run in early July and the day after the Feast of the Assumption of the Virgin, had been the high point of his childhood and youth, as they were for every Sienese male. "And we have an important visitor to welcome."

"A visitor?" Adrienne felt the surface of her skin ice over despite the heat of the August day. "Who?" she managed, knowing, fearing, whose name she would hear.

"Cesare Borgia."

Adrienne's heart seemed to stop for a moment and then began to pound.

"Now it seems that all our speculation on what the pope's intentions are can end." Sandro's step was springy as he spoke. "Apparently he is planning a campaign to reclaim the cities for the Papacy."

"And he wants to give you a *condotta,*" she whispered.

"Indeed. He is offering forty-five thousand ducats a year." He sent her a cocky grin. "And I am sure that with a little skillful negotiation, I can get at least another five thousand out of him. After all, he knows that my artillery is even better than Vitelli's."

"No."

Sandro stopped and looked down at his wife, frowning.

"Do not do it." Adrienne turned to face him and gripped the front of Sandro's doublet. "Oh God, Sandro, promise me that you will not do it."

"Isabella, do you know what you are saying?" Her eyes were huge and terrified, and not understanding what was wrong, he laid his hand against her cheek.

"Yes—no, I do not care," she stammered, her thoughts scattering like hunted rabbits. "You will be in danger. You must not have anything to do with Cesare Borgia." Her fingers curled even more convulsively into his doublet. "Ever. Do you understand?"

"Isabella, my treasure." He cupped her face and stroked his thumbs over her cheekbones, trying to soothe her. "Making war is my profession."

Caught in the horror, Adrienne barely noticed that he had used an endearment for the first time outside the bedroom. "Make war if you must, but not for Borgia." With the last of her control, she choked back the full truth. "This man is dangerous. You would be in danger of losing your life if you threw in your lot with him."

Sandro laughed. "Come now, surely you do not believe all those rumors about the Borgias. That is just the talk of people jealous of their skill and their power." Like most of his contemporaries Sandro had a healthy respect for both. He was also a realist. "Besides, if you believe the rumors circulating about them, they are single-handedly responsible for half the deaths in Italy."

"Do not laugh, Sandro." Adrienne shook him so that the fabric of his doublet groaned under her fingers. "I mean it. They are evil." Her breath quickened. "Cesare Borgia is evil and he will do you harm."

"Listen to me, Isabella." Tenderness warred with impatience. "Cesare Borgia is no more and no less evil than most other men. Besides, what would you have me do?" He brought his hands down to her shoulders and gave her a little shake. "Say no to the son of the pope? Say no to money that will represent a good portion of Siena's income? Say no and be the laughingstock of Italy?''

''I do not care if you are the laughingstock of Italy, Sandro. I want you alive.'' She reached upward, bringing him still closer. ''Do you hear me? Alive!''

She pulled in a long, shuddering breath. ''Listen to me. We can sell my jewels. Not just the ones from the dowry but the ones that are my personal possessions. I can get money from my brothers. The Gennaro bank is rich and lends money to half of Europe.'' The words poured out of her in an urgent flood. ''We can think of something, find some way. I know we can. Please.''

Sandro looked down at her. She was serious, he realized. She meant exactly what she said. Her eyes were brimming with desperation, but they carried only a bare sheen of moisture. Her voice shook with the depth of her emotion, but she was far from incoherence or hysteria.

Surely her fears were irrational, he thought, a product of a too fertile imagination, stimulated by her condition. And yet there was something else, something... He stared into her eyes. For some reason the memory of her disappearance the night of their wedding brushed his consciousness.

Her breath quick and uneven as if she had been running, Adrienne waited for Sandro to say something. But he remained silent, his black eyes unfathomable.

Then he raised his hand and feathered the backs of his fingers down her cheek. ''Even if I wanted to do as you ask, I could not.''

All strength that her tension and fear had given her to try to change his mind flowed out of her, weakening her knees, and if she had not been still gripping his doublet, she might have slid to the ground. She let her head fall forward to his chest, unmindful of the leather laces that pressed into her forehead.

He did not believe her, she thought as the feeling of failure crept into her bones, making her feel cold despite the heat of the summer day. She had told him as much as she could and he did not believe her.

She resisted at first when he tipped her face up to his, but he persisted. He felt something move inside him as he looked down at her, her eyes clouded and dull with sadness. Still, somewhere in the back of his mind, there was a whisper of a voice asking him if he was truly certain that this was not some kind of convoluted plan concocted by the Gennaros to ruin him. But the need to comfort Isabella pushed the dark whisper away.

"It will be all right. You will see."

Adrienne managed to nod. "Will you let me stay here in Costalpino at least so that there are no additional...complications?"

He shook his head, not understanding or not wanting to understand her implication. "You are my wife, Isabella. The wife of the heir to the Dukedom of Siena. It is necessary that you appear at my side."

The adamant look in his eyes told her that she did not have a choice. Slowly she nodded, hoping fervently that in retreating she could regroup to be strong enough to fight again another day.

Sandro slid his thumbs along her jaw. "That is more like it." He leaned down to taste her lips. "You forget that I know just how much spirit you have. Firsthand."

But the tiny taste was not enough and he came back for more. The heat between them spiraled quickly,

fueled perhaps by the danger that lurked ahead.
Picking her up, Sandro strode toward the villa.

They returned to a city that was one huge pageant
from morning till late at night. The *palio* race repre-
sented the culmination of the rivalry between the sev-
enteen city wards. Each *contrada*, with its own flag
and its heraldic motif, was determined to outdo its rivals, so the parades were almost as competitive as the
race itself. Dressed in rich costumes, drummers
pounded out ever more complicated rhythms and flag
twirlers performed their *sbandierata*, which lay somewhere between complicated acrobatics and a courtly -
dance.

Despite her fears, Adrienne watched the preparations for the race with a wide-eyed fascination that she
was unable to hide, even though she knew that it must
seem strange for Isabella, who had grown up with the
tradition of the *palio*, to show such an avid interest. As
representatives of the duke, she and Sandro visited
each of the ten *contrade* who had been chosen by lot
to participate in the race. The race would lead through
the narrow streets of town and end with three laps
around the Campo, the main square, which did not
belong to any of the wards and was thus the only neu-
tral ground in the city.

Everywhere they went they were enthusiastically
cheered. Throughout the more than twenty-five years
of his rule, Francesco di Montefiore had always been
respected and well liked. He had grasped the reins of
power from a communal government weakened by
internal strife and the economic decline that had af-
flicted the city since the plague had wiped out seventy
percent of its population one hundred and fifty years

before. Now Siena was strong again and the people were grateful and loyal to Francesco, but the relationship between ruler and subjects remained a distant one.

It was Alessandro di Montefiore whom they loved—not just for his bravery and his physical beauty but because they considered him one of their very own. Every year at *palio* time, the story of how Sandro had, as a fifteen-year-old boy, disguised himself as one of the jockeys and won the race was told and retold.

The day of the *palio* dawned warm and clear, promising to send the heat and tempers soaring by the time the race was run in the early evening hours. Adrienne lay on her side, her hand tucked under her cheek, and watched Sandro awaken. He stirred and then his eyes opened, immediately awake and aware, a habit long ingrained from his earliest soldier's training.

Propping himself up on his elbow, he looked down at his wife, her eyes large and dark with smudges beneath that told of a sleepless night. The tenderness that flooded through him was mirrored in his eyes.

He tucked a strand of golden hair behind her ear and his fingers lingered to caress. "Why did you not wake me up, if you could not sleep?"

"So that both of us could spend a sleepless night?" Her tone was light and cool, although the thought alone was enough to send the first flashes of heat through her.

"It would not be the first time." The corners of Sandro's mouth curved upward. "We might have found something...satisfactory to pass the time." His hand traced down her neck and he felt a tug of desire as she turned onto her back, exposing her white throat to his touch.

Adrienne looked up at Sandro, love and fear welling inside her, but she knew better than to speak now. It would simply try his patience, doing more harm than good. It was better to save her strength and her words for another day. Instead she sent him a brilliant smile. "Yes, I expect we might have found a thing or two." Turning her face into his palm, she scraped her teeth over the fleshy mound under his thumb.

Sandro's breath stumbled in his throat and his hand slid into her hair, twining the silky strands around his fingers. "Temptress." He lowered his lips to hers. "Tonight." Even as he spoke, he wondered how he would keep the desire that was already heating his blood in check that long.

It took all of his strength to pull back. As always something inside him moved as he looked down at Isabella, the words that lived in some secret compartment of his heart rising to his lips. For a moment he measured the need to say them against his pride. Then he quickly sat up in bed, telling himself that he was only removing himself from the temptation of her body. The need receded and pride won. Barely.

"I have to go now. I sent Borgia a message that I would ride out to escort him into the city."

"I know." Adrienne pushed herself up against the pillows and managed to give him a creditable smile. "I shall be waiting for you when you return."

Sandro smiled back. The shadows were still in her eyes, but her head was held high. Because he could feel the words of love rising to his lips, words of love that he could not afford to speak, he turned away and swung his legs off the bed.

* * *

Adrienne stared into her Venetian mirror. For a crazy moment the idea of making herself look ugly crossed her mind. She might not be able to make herself into an old, diseased crone, but if she used enough paint and paste and powder, she could certainly make herself look unattractive, undesirable, couldn't she? Slowly she traced her features, her cheekbones, her jawline with her fingertips, acknowledging with a shake of her head what she had already known. No, she thought. This she would not be able to change. There was no way she could make her face look less than beautiful.

Her face! She realized that during the past ten weeks she had slipped so thoroughly into Isabella's life that she had begun to think of the body she lived in as her body. The face that she saw daily in the mirror had become her face. She closed her eyes and tried to remember what she, Adrienne de Beaufort, had looked like. She remembered black curls and pert, sharp features, but the face itself remained a blur, like a long-ago memory.

She watched carefully as Daria and her women prepared her. Her hair was coiled and caught up off her neck and shoulders in a jeweled net. She donned the gown of cloth of gold with its underskirt of scarlet velvet and the elaborate necklace of sapphires and diamonds as if they were armor. And when she studied her reflection in the mirror, she knew that she looked more beautiful, more desirable than ever before.

The shadows were beginning to lengthen when Adrienne descended from her apartments to the great hall.

She had known that this moment would come when she would stand face-to-face with the man she had to outwit, to defeat. Even as she had tried so desperately to dissuade Sandro two days ago, deep within her heart she had known that she would not be spared this. This was, after all, why she had been sent into this life, this body. No, she corrected herself. She had chosen.

Although something seemed to skitter over the surface of her skin, her step was sure as she approached the men, who had straightened from the table still covered with maps and drawings. Sandro strode toward her to meet her halfway across the hall. Although she would have wanted to go into his arms, she smiled and laid her fingers lightly on the arm he held out to her. In step they moved forward.

Her hand still on Sandro's arm, she curtsied before her father-in-law. *"Altezza."*

Then, slowly, she turned and saw him.

"May I present my wife?" Sandro's mouth was curved in a proud smile, his wife's warnings already half-forgotten. "Isabella, the Duke of Valentinois, Don Cesare Borgia."

She dropped into a curtsy again. *"Altezza,"* she repeated.

Borgia reached for her hand and raised her from her curtsy. "As I told your husband, I prefer to leave the titles to the others. Don Cesare is good enough." A certain harshness in the inflection of his voice hinted at the fact that his language of preference was Spanish, his father's native tongue.

Keeping her hand lightly between his fingers, he smiled easily as he allowed his gaze to travel over her face. "Donna Isabella, you are even more beautiful than the reputation that precedes you."

His smile was innocuous, but Adrienne thought to catch an intonation in his voice that insinuated ... what? Scandal? Easy virtue? How much did he know about her? she wondered. And who had been his informants? Piero and Alfonso perhaps?

"I had not realized that I have a reputation to precede me, Don Cesare." Discreetly but firmly she removed the tips of her fingers from his hand. "Especially not as far as the court of France," she said, referring to his stay in Paris, which had lasted almost a year.

Borgia threw back his head and laughed, then reached out and clapped Sandro's shoulder. "You are most fortunate, Montefiore. A wife who is not only beautiful but witty, as well." For a moment he thought of the wife he had left behind in France, who had been neither. Her only advantages had been her name and her connections. He shrugged inwardly. The fact that he had a wife would not prevent him from taking as many women as he pleased. Just as the cardinal's hat he had renounced exactly one year ago had never kept him from his pleasures.

"Your husband and I have come to a mutually advantageous agreement, *madonna*." His light brown eyes twinkled and his slender, mobile hands gestured freely. "He drives a hard bargain."

Adrienne smiled noncommittally. "So I hear."

Nodding, Borgia began to chat about the race that would soon begin, drawing out even the taciturn Duke of Montefiore. Outwardly he was still relaxed, although he could feel the sexual tension gather in his loins as he breathed in Isabella di Montefiore's scent.

He would have to be careful and discreet this time, he warned himself. Ordinarily he cared to be neither, but it would be a shame to lose Montefiore's services. There was too much at stake this time. For him personally. Gesturing to an equerry to roll up the maps and drawings, he sent Adrienne a smile of apology and returned to the conversation she had interrupted.

History had painted Cesare Borgia as a monster. And Adrienne knew from Isabella's diaries that he could extinguish a man's life as casually as he would squash a bug. What was she to make of this slender, polite young man who looked no different than many other men? His well-tended auburn hair stopped just short of his shoulders. He was dressed in elegant black, relieved by the white shirt collar at his neck and the buttons of his doublet—gold-rimmed rubies the size of a thumbnail.

Were his easy, charming manners only a pretense, or had Sandro been right? she wondered. Was he perhaps no more evil than other men? There was an aura of command around him, but was it more than the mastery that any man of power projected? The tension began to seep out of Adrienne. It was then, in the middle of something he was saying to her father-in-law, that their eyes met. For the fraction of an instant she glimpsed what lay beneath the congenial surface—the cruelty, the lust for power and pleasure, the utter ruthlessness in obtaining both. Then he smiled, the amiable mask returning.

Adrienne lowered her gaze, wondering if she had betrayed her knowledge. Her heart was pounding as if she had run a mile. The battle had begun.

Chapter Thirteen

The knowledge that Sandro's life was at stake made it possible for Adrienne to reach inside herself for the control she needed. She knew that if she showed fear or weakness now, Borgia would pursue his purposes even more quickly, more ruthlessly. She resolved to play the part of radiant, confident, self-assured consort of the heir to the Dukedom of Siena. As they made their way to the places from which they would view the race, the strength she had been hoping for came pouring back into her. And she found that she no longer needed to play a role.

The windows of every building on the Campo had been decorated with festive banners, their colors bright and rich against the reddish brown stone. A dais, sheltered by a canopy in the blue and white Montefiore colors, had been readied for them. All around the square tiers of benches for visitors and especially honored members of the community had been set up. The simple folk were relegated behind a guardrail around the center of the Campo and the tension that rose from the tightly packed mass was so thick it was as palpable as the heat of the August day.

The silk-covered armchairs on the dais were embroidered with the Montefiore crest—crossed swords over a blue-and-white checkered shield—and Adrienne felt a wave of pride swell within her as they took their places. Suddenly it was important not only to save Sandro's life but to assure that the child she carried would someday succeed him.

Suddenly a voice rose above the muted roar of the crowd. "*Evviva* Montefiore. *Evviva il Duca.*" Other voices took up the cry until the whole huge square echoed with the tribute, the high brick buildings throwing back the sound and amplifying it.

Duke Francesco stood and raised his hand in thanks. Then he gestured to his son to rise and accept the salute with him. Within moments the mass of people were shouting as one, "Alessandro, Alessandro."

Alessandro raised both arms and waved to the crowd in boyish pleasure. His plan had worked even better than he had imagined. And all it had taken was Michele, dressed in simple tradesman's clothing, and that one first shout.

For long moments the deafening shouts went on until Alessandro gestured for silence. When the uproar had abated, he cupped his hands to his mouth. "Now to the festivities!" he called out. Cries of *evviva* erupted again, but he had already given the master of ceremonies a sign to send in the first drummers.

Cesare Borgia looked at the elder Montefiore and nodded in appreciation of the spectacle whose goal he well understood. "Very impressive." Then, turning to Sandro, he said, "And you, my friend, seem especially well loved."

Sandro laughed. "When I was fifteen, I disguised myself as a jockey and won the *palio* for the *contrada* I was born in. Ever since..." He moved his shoulders in a self-deprecating shrug.

Borgia forced an ounce more amiability into his smile. Yes, he thought. He would be especially careful. Alessandro di Montefiore was apparently even cleverer than he had thought.

The parade was endless, with every *contrada* in the race presenting its very best drummers and flag twirlers. Finally the large wagon pulled by four white oxen that carried the Council of Elders lumbered onto the sanded path. The cheers that went up among the crowd signaled their joy that the long-awaited race was about to begin even more than their very real respect for the elders.

Within moments after the oxen had been coaxed off the track, the pens that had been holding back the horses were opened and the spirited, nervous animals burst onto the sand-strewn cobblestones. Even as they moved toward the mark in front of the dais that was both the starting and finishing line, the jockeys, each dressed in the colors of the *contrada* he rode for, were jostling one another for the best position.

In those last edgy moments before the signal to start was given, under the cover of the whinnying of the high-strung horses, last-minute threats were exchanged, bribes offered, refused and offered again. It was a tumultuous, rough-and-tumble race that had but a single fixed rule—the jockeys were forbidden to manipulate one another's reins. Otherwise it was a relentless free-for-all, allowing the riders to flog an opponent or an opponent's horse, to try to unseat a rival with hands, feet or any other means. It was not an uncommon spectacle for a jockey to lose his seat and have to scramble for safety from the pounding hooves. Just as it had happened more than once that a horse had passed the finishing line without a rider—and won—for in this race it was solely the performance of the horse that counted in the end.

As she watched the handsome animals pawing the ground with barely controlled violence and smelled the dust and the sweat of thousands of people swirling around her, Adrienne felt a surge of the duality that she always fought. Her Gallic pragmatism warred suddenly with the almost sexual excitement that surged through her blood in anticipation of the wild, anarchic race.

Sandro turned to his wife. The oddly unfocused, bewildered look in her eyes reminded him that there were still many things about her he did not know, did not understand. The suspicion that had dwindled to a faint recollection in the recesses of his mind suddenly stirred more strongly. But then, as if prompted by the suspicion, that nameless emotion flooded his heart.

He curved his hand around her shoulder. "Is something wrong, Isabella? Are you feeling all right?"

Adrienne looked into his black eyes and smiled, pushing away the disconnected, disoriented feeling that had left her pale and shaky. "No, Sandro. There is nothing wrong."

She felt the heated excitement surge through her again, and as if in answer, the signal for the race to begin sounded. "Everything is right." As she turned toward the sound of the pounding hooves, she took a deep breath and prayed that she spoke the truth.

*   *   *

With a rustle of her tunic Daria rose from where she lay on the pallet at the foot of the bed as Adrienne stepped into the bedchamber on Sandro's arm.

The excitement of the race and the exhilaration of having given Cesare Borgia a vivid demonstration of the relationship between the Montefiores and their subjects were still rushing through Sandro's blood like a heady wine. As he closed the door behind them, Isabella's fragrance rose to tease his nostrils, and in the space of a heartbeat the excitement and exhilaration was compressed into a surge of desire for her. He stopped and turned his wife to face him. She was tired, he thought as he looked down at her, her eyes shadowed, and the concern he felt mellowed the sharp desire to a softer longing.

"I will sit with you until you sleep." He drew the backs of his fingers down her cheek.

Adrienne shook her head. "Go on and rest. It has been a long day for you, too."

"But a good one." Sandro grinned. He gave her a gentle push toward the slave girl who awaited her and then settled down in a chair.

Adrienne did not look toward him as Daria undressed her and took down her hair. But she felt him watching her, his gaze as arousing as if his hands had been upon her skin. She felt the fatigue of the day seep away to be replaced by the desire that began to course through her.

Only when she had slipped into the high bed did her eyes wander to where Sandro sat.

"Shall I bring *madonna* the spiced milk?" Daria asked softly as she tucked the light silk coverlet around her.

Adrienne shook her head. "Make your bed in the anteroom tonight." She patted the girl's arm as she spoke, but her gaze did not stray from Sandro's.

Neither one of them noticed as the slave girl picked up her pallet and scurried out of the room.

"Will you bring me a cup of wine, Sandro?"

Sandro filled a goblet with the ruby wine of the Sienese hills. Moving toward the bed, he saw that although Isabella's eyes were still shaded with the exhaustion of the day, the soft glow of invitation lay in them. He sat on the edge of the bed but made no move to give her the cup.

"I am thirsty."

Although his pulse had begun to speed, his movements were slow as he lifted the cup to his lips. He filled his mouth with the wine, and keeping his eyes on hers, lowered his head.

Adrienne's breath caught in her throat as she watched his face come closer. The nostrils of his straight nose flared lightly in that sign of beginning passion she had come to know so well, and she forgot that her mouth was dry with thirst. Her eyes closed as his mouth touched hers, and the gentle pressure parted her lips.

When the first drops of wine trickled into her mouth, her eyes flew open. While surprise held her still, he slowly filled her mouth with his tongue and more wine.

Adrienne swallowed the wine, which tasted of sunlight and Sandro, and she felt an insidious heat snake through her, dampening her skin, quickening her already rapid heartbeat.

"More wine, *tesoro?*"

Unable to speak, she lowered her eyelids briefly in assent.

Again she watched him fill his mouth with wine, and even though this time she was expecting it, her pulses began to hammer as he sent a slow stream of wine into her mouth.

Her breath had begun to hitch by the time she had swallowed the wine. "Sandro." Her fingers reached up to twist in his hair. "Make love to me."

"I am," he whispered. Then he stood and, without taking his eyes from hers, shrugged out of his clothes.

When the last of his garments had dropped to the floor, Adrienne drew away the coverlet and knelt on the bed. She unlaced the nightgown and drew it over her head.

Because his needs were pumping fiercely through his blood, he moved slowly. Again he sat down at the edge of the bed and cupped her face. Then he let his hand drift downward until it splayed on her stomach. Her belly was still flat, yet just knowing that she carried the child they had made together aroused him. He felt the power surge through him, power so potent, so boundless that he almost drew back, afraid that he would hurt her.

Adrienne felt the power pour through him and felt an answering power stream through her. She reached out and drew him closer. "Now, Sandro, now.

He moved forward and let the madness take him.

A faint noise woke Adrienne from her afternoon nap. Her eyes still closed, she fought her way out of the confusion she always felt in that fuzzy state between wakefulness and sleep. It was a moment when the two identities of Adrienne and Isabella seemed to interlace, making her unsure which identity she would open her eyes to. She reached out across the pillow, hoping to find the warm reality of Sandro's body, but the linen was smooth and cool.

She opened her eyes as she turned onto her back, her gaze meeting the cavorting gods and nymphs on the bed canopy. The nervous little skip in her belly signaled the return to full awareness and relief that she was who and where she was.

Sitting up as the noise that had woken her increased, she wondered if it was Gianni, scuffling again with one of the Montefiore servants who had mocked his size. She slipped out of bed and, picking up the robe of azure-colored silk, moved toward the anteroom.

The closer she came to the door that separated the two rooms, the louder the sounds of a struggle became. When she heard a woman's high-pitched scream, which was quickly muffled, she ran the last few steps and pulled open the door.

The spectacle that greeted her interrupted her momentum but only for the space of a breath, and she rushed forward.

"What are you doing?" she cried.

As he raised his head at the sound of his sister's voice, the openmouthed surprise on Piero's face might have been comical. He lay partly over Daria, whom he had bent over a table, his hands in her undone hair. The bodice of her tunic was torn, the skirt hiked up to her thighs.

Adrienne pushed at Piero with both hands and he staggered back, pulling Daria up. Only then did Adrienne realize that he had twisted her servant's hair around his hands like ropes, and she gripped his doublet at the shoulder. "Let her go, damn you!" She shook him. "You are mad!"

Piero's hands slackened, releasing the heavy strands of the slave girl's flaxen hair, and he stared at Adrienne as if it were she who had gone mad.

Catching Daria before she slid down to the floor, Adrienne put an arm around her shoulders and propped her up against her own body. "It is all right," she said softly. "I am here now. He will not hurt you."

She had barely said the words when the girl began to tremble like a leaf being buffeted by a strong wind. Half supporting, half dragging her, Adrienne pulled her to one of the clothing chests. The moment she had lowered her onto it, Daria pulled her legs up to her chest and curled herself into a tight ball.

Adrienne crouched down. "You will be all right," she repeated, and laid a hand against the girl's cheek, but Daria jerked back as if she had been struck.

The click of boot soles on marble tile had her up and whirling in one movement. Piero was advancing toward her, his eyes glittering.

"Dame Fortune smiles upon me today, *sorellina.*"

Adrienne forced herself to stand still, although all her instincts screamed at her to run.

Piero stopped in front of her and looked down into her face for a long time without speaking. Then, his eyes still on hers, he raised his hand and ran the tips of his fingers down the azure silk of her robe from the shoulder to the wrist. He slid his palm under hers and raised her hand to his lips.

He had barely lowered his moist mouth to her hand when Adrienne snatched it back. "Piero, I will not tolerate..."

"Shh, my little one." He raised a finger to her lips to silence her. "You know that I always took *la barbara* only because I could not have you." His soft mouth curved in a lover's smile. "But now that you are here..." He began to run his hand over her face.

Adrienne choked back the nausea that rose to clog her throat. Closing her fingers around Piero's wrist, she removed his hand from her face. "Piero, no."

"No?" His eyes narrowed. "Do you not you remember our agreement that day in Vignano?" His gaze slid down to her belly and then back up to her face. "Do not deny that Montefiore has planted his spawn in your belly. Even if Luisa had not told me, I would have known."

Adrienne spun away, knowing that she needed to hide the disgust that threatened to overcome her. Suddenly the panic rose, robbing her of breath, as she remembered yet again Isabella's careless words.

Two days ago my body spewed forth the Montefiore heir that had begun to grow in my belly. It is just as well if the brat was too weak to withstand the coupling that Piero and I had been waiting for so long.

Oh God, she thought, she had begun to feel safe from that particular danger, and yet here it was, threatening her. The fear sent her blood pounding through her as she wondered if he would try to take her against her will.

She pressed her hands against her middle as if to shield the child who slept there. It was that touch that calmed her. That touch and the knowledge that she had to play her hand with utmost care.

She heard his footsteps behind her again and turned to face him. Forcing her lips to curve in a smile, she put her palm against his chest. "Not like this, Piero.

My ladies will return at any moment to help me dress."
She shrugged. "And I never know when my husband
will return."

"Do not try to put me off, Bella. You promised and
I am here to take what you promised." He filled his
hands with the silk of her robe. "Do you think that I
will be satisfied to couple with your slave yet again?"

Oh Lord, she thought as the full understanding
penetrated her brain. Now she understood the hatred
she had seen in Daria's eyes that first day. Now she
understood that she had stopped Piero from raping
the girl as he had done many times before. Now she
understood why Daria had jerked back from her
touch. Adrienne lowered her eyes to hide the horror
that she was sure would be mirrored in them.

Masking the horror with rage she did not have to
pretend to, Adrienne looked up at Piero. "If he had
even the vaguest suspicion of this, Alessandro would
kill you!" She struck his shoulder with the heel of her
hand. "Do you not understand? I do not want to lose
you like this!"

Her breath caught as she realized that in some
strange way she had spoken the truth. Despite the revulsion, the loathing, she felt an odd sense of kinship
to him that she seemed to have no control over.

"Listen to me, Bella. It will be all right."

"Yes," she hissed, "but only if you stop being a
fool before you ruin everything."

"Listen, Bella. I have a plan."

She opened her mouth to rail at him, but as his
words sank in, she snapped it shut.

"We are going to get rid of him for you." His words
lowered to a murmur. "Just a little while longer and
you will be rid of him."

Adrienne felt as if someone had put a fist into her stomach. "How?" she managed.

He shrugged. "Montefiore has enemies, rivals." Piero's soft mouth curved in a malicious smile. "Now that he has thrown in his lot with Borgia, the possibilities are endless."

"But what are you going to do?" She fought to keep her voice calm and steady. "What is your plan?"

"The less you know about it, the better it will be." Piero patted her cheek with two fingers.

"No!" She grabbed his arm with both hands. "I told you once before that I want to be informed of what goes on." She shook him. "I meant it, Piero."

"Piccolina..."

"All right, all right," he soothed. "I will tell you as soon as we've arranged something."

She looked into his eyes, so like her own, and knew that he was lying. Even as she nodded her agreement, her mind was working furiously, looking for a way to cross his purpose.

Chapter Fourteen

"**I** will make certain that you receive the food and herbs you need as soon as possible, Sister." Adrienne tucked the list into a leather pouch and handed it to Angela. Before she could move to prevent it, the nun had lowered her head to kiss her sleeve.

"May the Lord bless *madonna* and the house of Montefiore."

Adrienne nodded her thanks and wondered what the good sister would say if she knew what business she would be conducting in a few moments in the house of the Lord. As she turned to step out of the hospital, Angela moved to follow her, but Adrienne stopped her with a choppy movement of her hand.

"Wait here for me. I would spend a few moments in prayer," she said, gesturing with her chin toward the cathedral across the *piazza*.

"I will accompany *madonna*."

"I need to be alone, Angela. You will wait for me here." Nerves made her voice sharp and she felt a surge of guilt at Angela's crestfallen look. She gave Angela's hand a quick squeeze and hurried outside.

The cold wind whipped her cloak around her. Pulling the hood over her face to protect herself from the rain, she hurried across the slippery cobblestones that slanted up toward the steps of the cathedral.

Inside the huge church, the handful of candles that burned did little to mitigate the gloom of the gray September day. Barely remembering to genuflect and cross herself, Adrienne hurried down the left side of the nave, her gaze darting around nervously. Empty, thank God, she thought, grateful that the weather was keeping the good folk of Siena indoors.

Pausing as she reached the intricately worked bronze grating that separated the small chapel of Saint John the Baptist from the rest of the church, she threw back her hood and covered her head with a thickly meshed veil that obscured her face. The gesture, which implied subterfuge and deception, brought home to her what she was risking. But she had no choice, she told herself. She had to act. She could not allow the control to slip from her hands to Piero's.

Suddenly her heart began to beat so wildly that her breath shuddered in and out of her lungs. She pressed her hand against her chest and leaned against one of the columns of black-and-white marble. For a moment she let her eyelids close. But immediately they flew open again in horror at the image that rose before her mind's eye. The image of Sandro and herself in a dark street with blood everywhere.

Ever since that last time she had spoken to Piero, images had begun to haunt her every time she closed her eyes. Images of blood flowing. So much blood. She had tried to comfort herself that she was only imagining the scene she remembered from Isabella's diaries.

Pretending weakness, I bade Alessandro to send his bodyguard for the litter while we took shelter under

*the wooden scaffolding of a half-built house. I saw the
shadow approaching and moaned to distract my husband. The shadow was almost upon us when I realized that I was not ready to forgo the pleasure his
services in the bedchamber brought to me. Not even
for my brothers. Not yet. I shifted to the side, pulling
Alessandro with me, and the knife, which would have
buried itself in the center of his back, plunged into his
shoulder.*

But no matter how she tried to convince herself,
Adrienne knew that the images she saw were somehow different.

She took a deep breath and then another. She had
already changed so much, she told herself. She stroked
a hand over her stomach. She had kept her child safe.
And she would keep Sandro safe, as well. She held on
to that thought, and her step was sure as she walked
into the chapel.

At first she thought the chapel, which was lighted
only by a flickering votive light that hung above the
silver relic shrine, was empty. When what had looked
like a shadow detached itself from the side wall, her
hands flew to her mouth to muffle a cry.

As if she had been riveted to the floor, she remained standing there in the center of the chapel as the
figure, wrapped in a hooded cloak that shaded his
face, moved toward her. When the man was an arm's
length from her, he let his cloak fall away and held out
his hand, palm upward. In his rough hand lay the
pearl-and-gold rosary she had given to Gianni when
she had entrusted him with the task of scouring the
dregs of the city to find a man willing to do anything
for a price. She had not waited to hear from Piero,
afraid that he would do his plotting in secret. Unable

to do what was necessary herself, she had turned to
Gianni, for he, at least, could leave the *palazzo* at will.

His overlarge head bobbing slightly, Gianni had
watched her as she had explained what she wanted him
to do, her words alternately faltering or spilling from
her tongue like a waterfall. When she had finished, he
had looked at her with that disconcertingly piercing
look that mirrored the insight that had made more
than one person fear his sharp jester's tongue and
said, "I would not do this for Isabella Gennaro, *madonna,* but I will do this for Isabella di Montefiore."

Adrienne had nodded, realizing that of all the people in her life, the only ones who had in some way understood that she was an impostor were Gianni and
Daria.

Now she stood in the cold chapel, paralyzed before
the ghoulish creature who held the rosary.

"The dwarf said that *madonna* would recognize the
rosary."

At the sound of the man's rasping voice, her eyes
darted from the rosary to his face. His features looked
as if they had been hewn from granite with a rough
hand. One cheek was seamed with a livid scar and his
dark hair hung lank and straight, almost to his shoulders. Apparently not insulted at her wide-eyed silence, he smiled, the strong white teeth making his skin
look even swarthier.

"You have a piece of work to do, *madonna?*" He
jiggled the rosary in his hand.

The matter-of-fact words snapped Adrienne out of
her inertness. "Yes, a piece of work." She laced her
fingers beneath the folds of her cloak. "You will go to
a man whom I will name to you." As she began to
speak, the strength began to flow back into her. "You

will show him the rosary and tell him that the woman who gave it to you sends you to perform the piece of work that was spoken of.''

"And this piece of work. What is it?"

Adrienne opened her mouth to speak but found the terrible words sticking in her throat.

"I am a *bravo, madonna,* and there is little I will not do for the right price." Again he spoke as directly as if he were an honest merchant offering his wares.

"He will hire you to kill a man."

"Ten ducats for a baseborn man and twenty ducats for a highborn gentleman, *madonna.*"

Adrienne had no way of knowing that he had gauged her fur-lined cloak and her speech and quadrupled his ordinary price for a life. "But you will not kill him." She raised a hand in warning. "Not even wound him. Do you understand?" She took half a step toward him. "Your knife will carry no trace of his blood."

"Then the price is forty ducats, *madonna.*" The man frowned. "A clumsy piece of work is bad for the reputation that is my sole fortune."

"All right," Adrienne agreed. "If you perform to my satisfaction, there will be another forty ducats for you afterward."

The man's eyes lighted up with the spark of greed. "How? When?"

"Here in the chapel, the day after." Reaching into a leather pouch, she counted out the coins, filling his hands with gold. Then she repeated her instructions until she was sure he had understood her.

He bowed and, swinging his wide cloak over a shoulder, turned to go.

"One moment."

The man stopped but did not turn around.

"Say a prayer that you discharge my instructions precisely. Otherwise you will not live to enjoy even this first payment. *Capisci?*" Her voice sounded so harsh and menacing even to her own ears that she almost believed her words.

"*Ho ben capito, madonna.*" His hoarse whisper floated over his shoulder and then he was gone.

"What did she look like, this woman who you say sent you here?" Piero Gennaro forced himself to stand still, although he badly wanted to pace away the vicious rage he had felt when he'd seen the rosary he himself had given Isabella in the hands of this *bravo*.

"I do not know, *messere,* for she wore a veil. She said that you would know who sent me when you saw the rosary. All I know is that her cloak was rich and lined with fine fur." The man drew a corner of his mouth upward in the caricature of a smile. "And she did not quibble when I told her my price."

"And what is the price you asked?"

"Twenty ducats, *messere.*"

The man's marginal hesitation before he named the price told Piero that he was lying. He exchanged a glance with Alfonso and saw that his brother, too, had drawn the same conclusion. "Tell me again what she said," he ordered. Perhaps the cutthroat would let a word slip in the retelling.

"She said that you needed to be disburdened of a certain person."

"And you are sure she did not say who that person was?"

"She said no name, *messere.*"

"Go now," Piero snapped. "But first the rosary." He held out his hand.

The man hesitated, obviously loath to give it up.

"Do not make me come after it."

The cutthroat scurried forward and dropped the rosary into Piero's palm. His fingers closed around it, and giving in to the impulse, Piero grabbed a fistful of the man's cloak before he could turn away. "You will not leave this house until the time has come to do what you have been paid for." He released the man, pushing him at the same time so that he staggered backward.

Warily the man retreated, starting when he almost backed into a large man who had entered the room behind him.

"You will lodge the gentleman downstairs, Bernardo." He gave the servant a sharp look and was satisfied to see his almost imperceptible nod, indicating that he had understood that the man would be brought to the dungeon. "He will be our guest for a time."

The door closed behind the two men and Piero twisted the rosary around his fingers as the footsteps receded down the corridor. Then he turned to his younger brother. "Well? What do you say?"

"Since it was obvious that he lied about his price, Bella probably gave him at least double that." Alfonso laughed. "It seems that our little sister is even more impatient than you are."

Piero shook his head. "Something is not right here, Alfonso." He struck his fist into the palm of his other hand. "I can feel it."

"The only thing you can feel right now is what is between your legs." Alfonso laughed again and thought of Luisa, who would be waiting for him to-night.

"And you?" Piero flared. "Do not try to make me believe that you have stopped wanting Bella."

"I have a talented mistress." Alfonso shrugged. "I am in no hurry. Besides," he added softly, "she is young yet. Let Montefiore break her in."

Piero whirled around, rage in his eyes, and spat, "Damn you!"

Alfonso grinned and, splashing some wine into a cup, lifted it in a mocking toast before he drank.

"Why is she going to such lengths?" Piero began to pace again. "That day in Vignano she insisted that we wait and let nature take its course. That we wait until her child is born and Montefiore succeeds his father before we act." He gripped the back of a chair, the skin stretching tightly over his knuckles. "And now she sends me a hired assassin. It does not make sense."

"Calm down, Piero. Just because you have an ul-terior motive for everything you do does not mean that everyone else does." He drank again deeply. "Our pleasure-loving little sister has probably grown tired of being shut up in that gloomy *palazzo* with her good works and her ladies and has decided to take the mat-ter into her own hands."

"I do not trust her, Alfonso. I have seen how she and Montefiore look at each other."

"Come now, Piero. You know as well as I do that the little bitch is a Messalina and could play any role she puts her mind to. Anyway, she would hardly be sending you an assassin if she were not looking for-ward to widowhood." Alfonso slung an arm around his brother's shoulders. "Besides, if you do not trust her, all you have to do is use your own assassin." Piero looked up sharply. "I happen to know for a fact that you have already hired one."

"And what do you suggest we do with Isabella's man?"

"Have his throat cut." Alfonso gestured carelessly. "I hardly think that anyone will miss him."

"A good idea, little brother." Piero smiled. "For all your easy ways, your soul is just as black as mine."

"Yes, but I enjoy it far more." Alfonso laughed and clapped his brother on the shoulder. "You take things far too seriously."

"Tell Bernardo that I have work for him to do." Piero poured himself a cup of wine but did not drink as he meticulously began to plan.

"Isabella?" Sandro's voice was tinged with impatience as he strode into the bedchamber. "Isabella, where are you?"

Adrienne's head snapped upward from the railing of the *prie-dieu* that stood in a far corner of the room in front of a small statue of the Madonna. She had knelt to pray for help, for guidance that she was doing the right thing, but she had received no answer.

Almost a month had passed since Piero had sent her the rosary to tell her that her message and her messenger had arrived. Still he had made her wait until her nerves were chafed raw. Even after they had met secretly in the same chapel where she had spoken to the assassin, he had made her wait, and she had not dared to prod him too energetically for fear of betraying herself. Now she had known for three days when she and Sandro would meet his would-be killer, and every one of those days had seemed a lifetime in hell.

Every hour of every day since then she had told herself that it had been the right thing, the only thing to do. The danger was there. She *knew* that if she had not hired the assassin, Piero would have done it. Surely it was better to meet the danger prepared. But now that the moment had come, all her confidence seemed to have evaporated as if it had never been, and she was consumed by nameless fears and premonitions.

"Forgive me. I did not mean to interrupt your prayers." Sandro looked down at his wife, her golden brown eyes wide with fear, unshed tears trembling on her lashes like tiny diamonds.

He crouched down so that they were at eye level. "Is something wrong, *tesoro?*" The concern and tenderness that rushed through him were tainted with that ever present streak of suspicion, but he had learned to ignore it as one learns to ignore a chronic ache.

She moved her head from side to side in denial, unable to speak.

He reached out and curved his hands around her shoulders. "You are shaking." He rose, lifting her with him, and closed his arms around her.

As he held her, Adrienne felt some of his strength seep into her, and little by little the faith that she was doing the right thing began to return.

"I am sorry. I was being foolish." She lifted her head and pulled her mouth into the semblance of a smile. "But they tell me that is normal for women with child."

Her body was still pressed against his. He could feel the quick, uneven beat of her heart against his own, and for a moment it seemed an even greater intimacy than when their bodies were joined. What would it have been like, he wondered, if they had been simply one man and one woman? If their families had not feuded with one another with cold-blooded ruthlessness for generations? If there had been trust between them to build on? Would he have then been able to put the emotions that pulsed through him into words? Or would he still have resisted that moment of surrender to another human being for fear that it would make him weak and vulnerable?

He saw the emotions in her eyes. Emotions that echoed his own. Emotions that threatened him. Calling on the control he had so mercilessly taught himself, he pushed them away, blocking them out like a shutter darkens and cools a room against warm sunlight.

"Sandro, I l—"

Afraid of his own feelings, which were still too close to the surface, he cut off her words with a kiss, plundering her mouth until the spiraling arousal pushed all thought from their minds.

"Do you think my mother would forgive us if we did not come to visit after all?" he whispered as he let his mouth drift down her throat.

"Sandro." Adrienne brought her hands forward and pushed at his shoulders. "We promised and you know how she waits for your visits."

"Then we will just be a little late," he murmured against her ear, his hands already busy with the fastenings of her gown.

She was already growing pliant, giving in to his persuasive hands and mouth, when she remembered what was going to happen tonight. And what, pray God, would not happen. The awareness swept over her like an ice-cold wave, dousing the passion, and she slipped from Sandro's embrace.

"We will be on time, my dear husband." She sent him a brittle smile over her shoulder. "It is past time you learned that you can not have every wish fulfilled immediately."

"Witch." He started toward her again, but she held up her hand, the arrogant slant of her eyebrows reducing him to a small boy demanding an additional sweetmeat.

Stopping, he held out his arm to her. When she had placed her hand there, he sent her a wicked smile. "You win, Isabella." He bent closer to her so that his breath feathered over her mouth. "For now."

It was late when they left the modest house where Sandro had spent the first years of his life. Adrienne was exhausted from the strain of maintaining a cheerful mien and keeping up a stream of casual conversation.

The evening was warm with a touch of that October freshness that heralded fall. As they stepped out into the small courtyard where the litter and Sandro's mount waited, Adrienne looked up at Sandro.

"Shall we send them all on ahead and pretend that instead of being the heir to the Dukedom of Siena and his consort we are simply husband and wife enjoying the evening before the autumn rains come?" She held her breath.

"You wish to walk home?"

"It is only a few steps." Adrienne pursed her lips in a small pout. "And soon I will be too fat to walk farther than from my bed to the privy."

"But that will be a while yet. Thank God." Sandro drew a finger down his wife's neck and shoulder and smiled at the light shiver that passed over her skin. "I have heard it said that when a woman is with child she needs to be humored." He spoke easily and beckoned to one of the guards to give him instructions.

The men moved out into the narrow street, and as Sandro stepped out onto the cobblestones behind them, Adrienne fingered the hilt of the dagger she had surreptitiously strapped to her hammered gold belt.

Chapter Fifteen

Adrienne felt her stomach begin to knot as they started down the dim street. With each step the knot tightened and tightened yet again.

She could not go through with it! The realization streaked through her mind like a thunderbolt. She could not allow this terrible charade to go on any longer! How could she have ever made the cavalier assumption that the man she had bought would follow the instructions she had given him? What had possessed her to trust the word of a paid assassin? What if he had changed his mind? What if Piero had given him more gold than she had promised him? What if his hand faltered?

The questions, the doubts battered her, waking all the fears, all the nightmares that had haunted her for the past weeks. She had to confess everything to Sandro, to warn him. The thought struck her that he would perhaps not believe her, or if he did, he would hate her for what she had done. At the very least he would never trust her again.

The terrible fear seemed to rise up from her stomach through her chest to close off her throat, to cut off her air, and her ears began to ring. Vaguely she noticed that the litter had just turned a corner ahead of them. Focused on the words she would say to Sandro, she never heard the telltale creak of a door behind them.

But Sandro heard it. Even as he spun around, he was dragging her back, pushing her behind him, while with the other hand he whipped out his dagger. The rough movement shook Adrienne out of her terrified daze and her gaze focused on the assailant. In that split second as both men paused, their daggers poised in midair, Adrienne saw that the attacker was not the man she had hired.

The realization translated itself directly into movement. With an inarticulate cry, Adrienne launched herself forward as the assassin plunged his dagger downward.

She felt nothing as the knife passed through the side of her breast into her ribs. Nothing but an overwhelming rage and the need to protect.

"Isabella!" Even as he screamed her name, Sandro bore the man backward to the wall of the house from which he had emerged with such force that the man's head crashed against the stone.

Alerted by the sound of the struggle, the guards and the litter carriers raced back to their master. As they approached from both sides, their lances pointed at the assassin, Sandro whirled toward his wife, just in time to catch her before her legs gave way.

"Isabella, are you—" The words stuck in his throat as he saw the spreading scarlet stain on her ivory-colored gown.

"No!" The single word tore out of his throat like a primal scream.

As he picked her up in his arms, he heard sounds of a scuffle behind him.

He swung around and shouted, "Alive! I want him alive!" But even as his words bounced off the dark walls of the houses, he saw the lances slide into the man's body.

As the lances held the man pinned to the wall, Sandro moved forward. "Who hired you?" he screamed. "Damn you, tell me who hired you!"

But the man's eyes were already emptying of all expression as his life drained away. When his head and shoulders slumped forward, Sandro knew that it was too late.

Turning, his wife's limp body in his arms, he began to run.

Adrienne came awake in a haze of pain that seemed to have taken possession of her whole body. Some self-protective instinct fought the returning awareness, but one by one the sounds around her intruded. The thump of a pestle grinding something in a mortar. The monotonous murmur of a woman's voice as she prayed softly. The crackle of a fire.

"Please, Don Alessandro, I beg you. Leave us. There is nothing you can do. Nothing."

"Do your duty, *dottore*. I will not leave until it is over and I know that she will be all right."

"But that could be hours, Don Alessandro," the doctor remonstrated, discomfited by the presence of a husband in a birthing room. "Even days."

Sandro looked up at the doctor, his black eyes opaque with grief and self-condemnation. "This—" He swallowed, unable to use more explicit words. "This is happening because she took a knife thrust meant for me." His voice was harsh with exhaustion and heartache. "I will wait."

Adrienne heard the voices, but unable to understand the words, she wanted to call out to Sandro. She filled her lungs with air. As she opened her mouth, a pain sliced through her abdomen like a razor and the words she had wanted to speak came out as a moan.

Within seconds she felt Sandro's fingers on her face and turned toward him, seeking comfort.

"It will be all right, *tesoro.*"

Again she opened her mouth to speak. Again the razor sliced through her so that her hips arched off the mattress. As the pain receded she fell back. There was a warm, sticky wetness on her thighs and underneath her. She sucked in air and with it came the metallic smell of blood.

Suddenly her mind was utterly and horribly clear and she did not need to understand the urgent whispers to know exactly what was happening. This she had not been able to change, she thought as despair descended upon her like a black curtain. She had failed and she would never see the child Sandro had given her. The child that the blood was flushing out of her body. Just like Isabella's child, her child would not live to take its first breath. All she had been able to do was change the circumstances of her child's destruction.

If she had failed in this, would she be able to save Sandro? The question followed with a terrible logic. Or would all her striving be for naught? Would she perhaps only change the details of his end without changing the fact?

"Fight, Isabella. Fight."

Her eyelids fluttered open at the sound of Sandro's voice, but his beloved face was blurred behind the curtain of constant pain. No, she thought, she would not fight. It would be better to slip away now than to be forced to look upon Sandro's death. Besides, with her death, the catalyst for his destruction would disappear. Perhaps this was what she had come here for, she thought. To die so that Sandro could live. Of course, that was it. The conclusion was so clear, so logical, that she almost smiled. She closed her eyes again and began the long, slow slide down toward the darkness.

"Isabella, I love you. Do you hear me?"

The urgent sound of the words pulled her out of the shadowy realm toward the light.

Sandro saw Isabella's eyelids twitch. When they began to rise, hope flared within him. But her eyes were dull with pain and had the faraway look of one about to take the final journey.

"I love you." He repeated the words again and again, like a magic incantation, a prayer. When he saw her eyes clear a little, he almost shouted with joy, but then they were clouding again as her body tensed under another onslaught of pain.

The guilt tore through him. Guilt because he had brought her out of her unconsciousness into pain. Guilt because the knife had been meant for him. Guilt that Isabella had had to be near death for him to voice the love that had lived within him for so long.

Something had brought her back, Adrienne thought as the wave of pain ebbed away, allowing her to breathe again. Sandro's voice. Sandro had called to her and brought her back. No. She moved her head from side to side. It could not have been Sandro's voice. She had heard...

"I love you."

Slowly her eyes opened, focused. "Sandro?"

"Yes, love."

"What—" She moistened her dry, cracked lips with her tongue. "What did you say?"

"I love you." Sandro found the words flowing easily from his lips.

Adrienne closed her eyes against the welling tears. What incredible irony, she thought. Now, hours or perhaps just minutes before she died, she was hearing the words she had wanted so badly. The cushioned darkness where there was no pain, no smell of blood, was beckoning again.

"Do not leave me, Isabella. I need you."

Almost against her will, Sandro's words dragged her back. Again and again, every time she began to drift toward the shadows, he brought her back.

"It is over and Donna Isabella has stopped bleeding."

Sandro raised his eyes, bleary and bloodshot, to the doctor in his dark robes. "Will she live?"

"She is young and strong, Don Alessandro. If there is no fever, then, God willing, she will live." The doctor allowed himself a faint smile. "And she will bear you other sons."

Sandro lowered his head to the pillow to lie next to Isabella's, and for the first time since he had been a very small boy, he wept.

Sandro stood at his wife's bedside and watched her sleep. Now, two weeks after she had been wounded and endured the nightmare of the miscarriage that had almost cost her her life, the color was beginning to seep back into her cheeks. But the fathomless sadness in her eyes had remained and he had found himself helpless to do anything to ease it.

He should have left days ago for Cesena, where he and his troops were to rendezvous with the other *condottieri* Cesare Borgia had hired. Instead, he had sent the troops ahead under Michele's command, needing to stay at his wife's side. But today he had received his friend's message that Borgia himself, together with the troops he had on loan from the King of France, would soon be arriving in Cesena, and he knew that he could no longer put off his departure.

So much was still unspoken between them, he reflected as he sat down on the edge of her bed. Although he had spent hours at her bedside, they had both shied away from speaking of the attack and of the son lost to them. And in the face of his guilt that he had been powerless to prevent what had happened, he had been incapable of repeating the words of love with which, time and time again, he had pulled her from the edge of death.

Nor had he shared the information that painstaking inquiry and a sizable amount of gold had bought him. He still had no proof, but he had enough bits and pieces to warrant a strong suspicion that the *bravo* who had attacked them had been bought by his brothers-in-law.

Over and over again he had told himself that Isabella could not possibly have known about the attack. Over and over again he had reminded himself that she had, after all, rushed forward to take the dagger meant for him. And just as often he had remembered that she had been the one to suggest that they send away the guards and walk the dark, narrow streets back to their *palazzo.*

No matter how many times Alessandro told himself that it had been a terrible coincidence, no matter what his own eyes had seen, no matter how strongly the emotions flowed through him, the voice inside his head would whisper a malicious reminder of his suspicions often enough so that he did not forget them.

But now she looked so fragile, so innocent, with her flawless face nestled in the white pillow. Needing to touch her, he reached out and tucked a strand of hair behind her ear. She stirred and shifted onto her back.

One of the women approached with a steaming cup that smelled of herbs and a tray of confections and set them down on the small table next to the bed. Sandro gestured to her to leave them, and she in turn gestured to the others. Silently the women slipped from the room, leaving them alone.

As always, Adrienne had that moment of alarmed disorientation as she came awake. But when she opened her eyes to see Sandro smiling down at her, the relief streamed through her like sunlight through a thundercloud. She struggled to sit up and Sandro lifted her with a firm, careful hand and settled her against the pillows.

"You see?" Because he wanted to hold her in a tight embrace, he allowed himself only to touch his fingers lightly to her cheek. "I have become as skillful as any of your attendants."

Adrienne's eyes clouded. "I am sorry I have been such an invalid..."

"Shh." Sandro covered her mouth with his hand. "It is I who should be sorry, Isabella. I was the one who failed. I was the one who did not protect you."

He turned away from her and Adrienne saw the muscle twitching furiously in his cheek. The guilt, doubly strong now, swept over her. Unable to speak, she reached out and curled her fingers around his arm.

But he shook her hand off and jumped up to pace beside the bed. "Stop being kind, Isabella. Rage at me, by God. Tell me that I was incapable of protecting you and our child." His hands curled into fists. "You are entitled." Vaguely he was aware of the inconsistency between what he was saying and the terrible suspicions that still gnawed at him, but what is logical thought when every possible emotion is warring within a man's soul?

"Where are your accusations?" he demanded. "I deserve every single one of them." Whirling away, he paced to the window and, propping his arms on either side, lowered his forehead to the cool glass.

"No! You do not understand," she cried, leaning forward. "It was not like that at all!" The words bubbled up inside of her like a volcano threatening to erupt. She drew breath to absolve him of the guilt. To accuse her brothers. And herself. Most of all herself.

But as her lips formed the first word, the realization hit her like a tidal wave. If she told him the truth, she would have gained nothing but to have selfishly unburdened her conscience. She would saddle him with a terrible knowledge. She would plant more mistrust of herself in his mind than he had ever felt for the other Isabella. And that would make it that much more difficult, perhaps impossible, to do what she had come here for.

She let herself fall back against the pillows. For her, there would be none of the relief that came with confession. She would live with secrets forever, she acknowledged. No matter how long she stayed in this body, in this life, she was condemned to living with secrets she could not share with anyone. Ever.

And as she looked across the room at the tense lines of Sandro's body, she knew that it was a price that she would pay. And pay gladly.

"Sandro, come here," she called softly. "I will come after you in a moment if you do not."

Her words had the desired effect, and he pushed away from the window and returned to her bedside but did not sit down.

"It is I who should beg your forgiveness." She stretched her hand out to him.

For a moment the desire, strong and sharp and urgent, to confess everything surfaced again. She could almost feel the relief of sharing the burden of knowledge with him, and if she had not seen the flicker of mistrust in Sandro's eyes, she might have given in to the temptation. But she knew that more than anything she needed his trust to protect him. And she knew that a confession would serve only to fan the flames of suspicion. Her hand, which he had still not taken, trembled slightly.

"If I had not had the whim to send away the guards, the man might never have attacked. If I had not moved when I did, you would have killed him before he had a chance to strike." She inhaled deeply, telling herself that if her words were not quite the truth, then neither were they a lie. "I will always have to live with the knowledge." Her eyes filled with tears. "And the guilt."

Sandro took her hand in both of his and, turning it upward, pressed his lips into the palm. Lowering himself to the bed, he framed her face with his hands. He gazed into her eyes, the evil voice in his head for once silent.

Up to now his life had been simple and straightforward, he thought. He had acquitted himself well of the studies that had been expected of the heir to the Dukedom of Siena. He had made war with skill and a minimum of cruelty. He had taken the women who caught his eye, carelessly perhaps, but never roughly. He had never indulged in introspection or emotions before, he told himself, forgetting the boy who had held his mother's hand as she had wept for a man who had not loved her. Forgetting the boy who had wanted the man who was his father to look at him once, just once, with warmth and approval.

Now everything had changed and he found his life centering around this one woman. He had told himself that it would stop once he had sated the hunger of his body for hers, but instead of ending, it had only become worse. And now as he looked into her sad eyes, which were swimming with tears, he felt the need to comfort her so acutely that it was almost physical.

"We will both live with it, Isabella. Together." He lowered his head and brushed his lips over her forehead.

The touch of his mouth on her skin was gentle and held no overtones of desire, and as Adrienne's eyes closed with the sweetness of it, the tears spilled down her cheeks.

Sandro tipped her face upward and wiped her tears away with his thumbs and his mouth. He felt his heart fill and overflow with tenderness, and yet no words found their way to his lips.

Her alabaster-cool skin warmed beneath the touch of his fingers and his lips and he found his pulse quickening with the first stirrings of desire. Knowing that this was not the time for it, he stroked her skin one last time and dropped his hands.

"When I return, we will deal with it together."

"When you return?" she echoed, noticing for the first time that he was not wearing colorful silk or velvet but a laced leather doublet over the simple, drab garb he wore when training his soldiers.

"I ride to Cesena today. Michele is already there with the troops."

Adrienne reached for his hands and gripped them, wanting to hold him back, even though she knew that it was only much later that the real danger would come. Fighting back the desolation, she smiled bravely.

"Godspeed then, my love," she whispered, and reaching into the neckline of her nightgown, she drew a gold chain that held a small cross over her head. Slipping the chain around Sandro's neck, she hooked her fingers into the collar of his shirt and worked the cross and chain inside.

Sandro felt the cross, still warm from her skin, come to rest against his chest. He lifted his hand and pressed it against the cross as if he could absorb even more of her warmth.

She saw his gesture, saw the emotions in his coal black eyes. She chided herself for wanting too much, yet she could not help wanting to hear the words now that she was well and her mind was clear. Inside her was a memory of Sandro telling her that he loved her, but it was vague and marred by pain and fear.

Cupping her face in his hands, his fingers tunneling into her hair, he lowered his mouth to hers. He felt her lips part beneath his, felt her unconditional welcome and let himself sink into the kiss. Desire was swirling through his blood when he dragged himself away from her mouth, appalled at his lack of self-control.

"Isabella, I am..."

Adrienne silenced him with a light touch, the stricken look in his eyes telling her what he was feeling. "When you return, Sandro," she whispered, her voice rich with promise. "When you return."

Sandro rose, knowing that it was past time for him to leave. He would have to drive himself and his mounts to be in Cesena by nightfall. At the doorway he stopped and turned back toward her. Briefly he touched his chest where the cross lay against his skin. Then, while he still could, he spun around and quickly strode downstairs.

Chapter Sixteen

Sensing his master's need, Sandro's mount stood perfectly still, barely twitching his ears against the mid-December wind that whistled over the hilltop.

From his vantage point on one of the low hills to the south of the city, Sandro watched the sack of Forlì. Or rather he imagined it, as the smoke and the screams from inside the city's walls were carried toward him on the wind.

Around him was the all but abandoned camp that held the ten thousand men Cesare Borgia had gathered for his campaign. Now it was occupied by a few sick and wounded being tended in the hospital tents and by his own fifteen hundred men, who sat around the campfires throwing dice and drinking the extra allotment of wine he had distributed among them. He was proud that the men he had trained had declined to take part in the rape and plunder of the fallen city, even though he knew well that the reason for their discipline lay in the additional pay that awaited them at the end of the campaign rather than in a distaste for what was taking place within Forlì's walls.

He had seen Cesare Borgia's devilishly clever strategy firsthand. When Forlì's sister city, Imola, had surrendered two weeks ago, he had controlled his troops with an iron hand, forbidding any looting or rape. So when Forlì's time came, its citizens had cheered as Borgia and his lieutenants entered the city, little knowing that he was about to loose his motley army of Spaniards, Frenchmen, Gascons, Germans and Italians upon them.

It had not been revenge that motivated Borgia, but the wish to set a grim example—and to execute a ghastly tableau meant to weaken the resolve of Caterina Sforza, barricaded in her fortress at the edge of the city. Now, Sandro thought, every city that Borgia besieged would tremble and sue for peace, remembering how easily Borgia could reward or punish.

From childhood Sandro had been trained to be a warrior and never questioned it. At fifteen he had first seen battle, and at eighteen, he had been given his own command. He had survived the campaign against the French and the carnage at Fornovo. But now, five years later, as he watched smoke rise over the conquered city, his stomach turned at the thought of what was happening within the walls and at the knowledge that his military prowess had led to this end.

He slipped his hand under his heavy cloak and rubbed his chest with his fingers. Through doublet and shirt he could make out the outline of the cross Isabella had given him, and for a moment the ugliness around him seemed to fade. Even though he chided himself for a fool, something in him softened as he remembered her eyes when she had put the cross around his neck. But even as the sweetness moved through him, the doubts and questions were not far behind.

His hands dropped to the reins of his mount. Suddenly he found himself needing motion, speed, something—anything—to drive out †he feelings that tugged at his nerves. He dug in his heels and gave the stallion his head.

A packet of Sandro's letters in her hands, Adrienne sat in the embrasure of a window looking down onto the Campo, which was covered with a rare dusting of snow. She had read and reread each one of his letters, hoping to find a soft word. But there were none. Even as she comforted herself that Sandro had other cares than to write *billets-doux,* she admitted that she would have given a great deal to read more than the formal, stilted wish that she was enjoying renewed health.

His letters were terse and to the point, more military bulletins than love letters. The siege and surrender of Imola. The surrender and the sack of Forlì. The bombardment of the Rocca di Ravaldino and Caterina Sforza's continued resistance. The breaching of the fortress's wall and Caterina's capture.

Her fingers rubbed the uppermost letter absently, the one Sandro had scrawled in haste on the march from Forlì to Pesaro, Cesare Borgia's next victim. She knew that there would be no battle for Pesaro. The campaign would soon be over and Sandro would be coming home. But instead of joy, Adrienne felt icy dread creeping through her bones. Soon Sandro would be coming home and he would not come alone.

Adrienne tried to summon up gratitude that she was not helpless. That she *knew* what lay before her. That her knowledge would enable her to fight what was to come more effectively. Yet the only thing she felt was dread.

Yes, she thought as she closed her eyes, leaning her temple against the cold glass, she knew. But had it helped her to know two months ago? She had saved Sandro from a knife wound, but she had paid with her child's life and almost with her own.

And now she grieved far beyond the grief of a woman who has lost her child. For she had not been able to change history after all. Now all trace of the confidence with which she had come into this life had faded and she trembled when she thought of Sandro's homecoming.

"Donna Isabella?"

Adrienne straightened immediately and opened her eyes. "What is it, Angela?" It crossed her mind that if someone had called out "Adrienne," she probably would not have reacted any more.

"Madonna's brothers are here."

Adrienne sighed. Throughout the festivities that had marked the Christmas holidays and the advent of the new year and the new century, she had skillfully avoided any situation that would have made it possible for either of them to hold a confidential conversation with her. She knew she could have refused to see them privately on any number of pretexts, but she also knew she had to face them sometime. So she had sent for them in order to face them when and where she chose. She straightened. And, by God, face them she would.

Rising from the window seat, she gestured to her ladies to remain where they sat with their sewing. She stopped next at one of the massive, inlaid chests, where Gianni sat cross-legged, his oversize head cocked to one side as he tuned his lute.

"Will you sing something merry for me, Gianni?" She smiled and tugged gently at one of his brown curls. "So that I hear at least one thing pleasant in the next half hour?"

The dwarf stared up at her, his mouth half-open. After years of cuffs and kicks and sharp, cruel words, he still had not become accustomed to this new, gentle mistress. Finally he managed to close his mouth and nod.

While Angela disappeared into the anteroom to show Piero and Alfonso in, Adrienne walked to the table, where fruit, wine and confections stood. Curling her fingers around the back of a chair, she waited, schooling her face to an expression of contempt she had no trouble feeling.

"*Sorellina!*"

"Bella."

They strode toward her, arms outstretched, smiling, confident.

Forcing herself to loosen her fingers until they only curved lightly around the comfortingly solid wood, she made no move toward them.

"Well, well, so you dare to show your faces in my presence." Though her nerves were singing, her voice was bold and scornful. "I did not think you had it in you."

"What are you talking about, Bella?" Alfonso slid an arm around her shoulders. "It is you who have not bothered to give us the time of day." As he lowered his head to kiss her, she gave him a sharp jab in the chest with the heel of her hand, sending him a step back.

Ignoring his squawk of annoyed surprise, she trained her narrowed gaze on Piero. "And I wonder just what *you* have to say for yourself." Before he could come closer, she gestured him toward a chair.

"Pour us some wine, Angela," she said as she sat down. "Then you may go back to your sewing." Adrienne smiled to soften her imperious tone.

Piero opened his mouth to speak, but Adrienne silenced him with a glance. Only when Angela had returned to the far end of the room where the others sat did she raise her hands from the arms of her chair to make a languid gesture. "You were saying, brother?"

"Why have you kept us away from you like this, Isabella?" Piero demanded, his low voice hot and angry.

She shot forward. "You ask, Piero? You dare to ask?" Her knuckles whitened as she gripped the edge of the table. "If I had known what a fool you were, I would never have confided in you. Never." The rage in her voice was very real. "If I had known that your stupidity—" she spat the last word "—would cost my son's life and almost kill me, I would have sent the cutthroat to your door instead!"

"Isabella, you—"

"Be quiet!" She pushed herself from the table and sat back in her chair. "If you had left things to me, most of our problems would have been solved by now."

"But you had said that you wanted to wait—" Piero lowered his voice "—until Alessandro succeeded his father." He leaned forward, placing his hands flat on the table. "So when you sent the man to me, I thought that—I thought you—" Both his gaze and his words faltered, and when he curled his hands into fists, damp spots remained on the dark, polished wood.

"You thought, you thought," she taunted. "With what, pray tell? With that brain of yours that would feel right at home in a sparrow's head?"

"Now listen to me, Isabella." A dull flush crept up his face. "It was only logical—"

"You speak of logic to me, Piero?" She interrupted him with a laugh. "You, who could never even win a game of chess against me?"

Adrienne felt herself stiffen as the words left her mouth; it was as if her blood had, in the space of a breath, turned to ice. How had she known that? she asked herself desperately. This had not happened to her since those first unsettling days when she had found herself recognizing faces, knowing names.

"What is wrong, Bella?" Alfonso reached for her hands, which had suddenly grown ice-cold.

"Here, *piccolina.*" Piero held a goblet of wine to her lips. "Oh God, Bella, can you ever forgive me?"

Adrienne saw the fear, the remorse in Piero's eyes and something within her softened, bringing yet another wave of panic. It was as if she were truly looking at him with the eyes of a sister who had known the boy before he had become a cruel, unscrupulous man. She pushed his hand that held the wine away and closed her eyes in an attempt to gather her thoughts, which had scattered like a flock of frightened birds.

She had to think this through, she thought, forcing herself to breathe deeply and evenly. But now she still had to bring this conversation to a good end. Opening her eyes, she fixed her gaze on Piero.

"You promised me, you swore once before that you would do nothing without my consent, but you lied and I almost died as a consequence of your meddling."

"Tell me that you forgive me, Bella." Piero reached for her hand, but she moved it out of his reach.

"I will not ask for your promise again, because I would not believe you if you swore on the True Cross." Adrienne felt a wave of anger, hate even, and that strengthened and reassured her. She had not turned into that other Isabella after all. "But if you cross me again, Piero, then be warned." She balled her hand into a fist and shook it.

Her blood seemed to thaw, seemed to start flowing again. She felt the stiffness leave her limbs and she reached for the cup of wine.

"Do we understand each other, Piero?" Her eyes did not move from his face as she observed him over the rim of the goblet.

He flushed again, like a boy being dressed down by a schoolmaster. "And what of your promises, Bella?" he asked belligerently. "When do you plan to keep those?"

"When everything has been done *my* way, to *my* satisfaction, we will speak about them again." She smiled. "Until then, consider it your penance to wait."

She stood. "Now you must excuse me. I find that I tire easily these days." She held her fingers out to each one in turn for a kiss, her posture precluding a more familiar touch.

When they were gone, she sank back down into the chair, struggling against the anxiety that had returned to threaten her. Her gaze roamed to the window seat where the packet of Sandro's letters still lay. Suddenly the sureness, the confidence, surged back into her as his image filled her vision. She would do it, she swore to herself. Somehow she would find a way to accomplish what she had come here to do.

When Adrienne rose to return to where her women sat, she was smiling.

Piero and Alfonso Gennaro walked back to their *palazzo* in silence. The wide, arched doors of the gray-stoned building closed behind them and Alfonso trotted up the staircase behind his brother, as he had done for most of his life. At the doors of his apartments, Piero shoved aside an assiduous servant who had stepped forward to take his cloak and stalked inside, leaving Alfonso to close the door.

Stripping off his gloves, he hurled them across the luxuriously appointed room, sending his plumed velvet hat and cloak after them. With jerky movements he splashed wine into a cup, but instead of drinking, he flung the goblet at the nearest wall with a hoarse cry of rage. As the red stain spread over the ivory damask, Piero spun around to face his brother.

"This situation is driving me mad." He ground his clenched fists against each other. "*She* is driving me mad."

Alfonso chuckled, drawing a glare from his brother. "She was in fine mettle today." He poured himself a cup of wine and savored it before he continued. "You know, Piero," he said thoughtfully, staring into his wine "there have been times during the past months when I thought that some evil spirit had put a virgin's soul into our Bella's body." He looked up with a shrug and laughed again, taking another drink of the wine. "But today it was just like old times."

His eyes widened at Alfonso's words, and with one hand under the cover of the other, Piero made the sign against the evil eye. There had been times during the last six months when, he, too, had surprised a look in her eyes, a smile on her lips that he had never seen before. He had blamed it on Montefiore and then on her condition, but now that he heard his brother's carelessly spoken words, something snapped in him and he began to tremble.

"Is something wrong?" Alfonso set his goblet down on the table. "You look as if you have seen a ghost."

Paling still further, Piero turned away, unwilling to let his brother share in the sudden suspicion that flared into a conviction as quickly as a spark becomes a flame. Within seconds a myriad of minute gestures and glances and words merged with all the irrational notions of his superstitious nature to become the portrait of sorcery.

It all fit, he realized as his thoughts tumbled head over heels like drunkards who had lost their foothold. Could it be that the evil spirits had played a terrible joke on him and had brought another woman to live in his Isabella's beautiful body? Was that why she did not want to keep the promises she had made so fervently? Why she did not want him to touch her anymore? Why she sometimes looked at him with scorn, even hatred?

No, he denied, balling his hands into fists. That could not be possible. The fates could not be so cruel that they would take his Isabella away from him that way. Not now, when he was so close to getting everything he had ever wanted.

He stared outside at the lengthening shadows, his eyes glazing with horror at the possibilities that had opened before him.

Despite her velvet cloak lined with the finest Russian sable, Adrienne shivered, but she knew it was not from the chill air. She could already hear the cacophony of sounds beyond the gate in the Campo—the horses' hooves, the clatter of weapons and armor, an occasional shout or a hoot of laughter. She felt her father-in-law's eyes on her. They had reached a measure of cautious understanding and respect during the last two months. Adrienne believed that with a little effort they could be friends. She looked up at him, ready to smile.

"Are you cold, Donna Isabella? Or afraid?" His pale eyes, so unlike Sandro's, were cool and observant.

"Neither, *Altezza,*" she answered, stiffening her spine.

In the six months since she had married his son, his daughter-in-law had done nothing to make him even suspect that her behavior was anything short of exemplary, and yet Francesco di Montefiore's unyielding character drove him to probe and probe again. He saw the defensive stiffening of her spine, but he also saw the angry, proud light that came into her eyes. Saw and approved.

"I was less than enthusiastic when his holiness decided to play the peacemaker between the Montefiores and the Gennaros," he said in that slow, measured way of speaking he had. "But Alessandro could have done worse. Much worse."

Adrienne saw the ghost of a smile touch his mouth before he turned back to face the entry, and she felt tears prick her eyes. He was a hard, harsh man, but life had not dealt easily with him. Being the woman she was, she felt a need to acknowledge this first sign of approval from him.

Turning toward him, she touched a gloved hand to his elbow. His head swiveled toward her, eyebrows knitted, eyes questioning, but instead of removing her hand, she gave his arm a light squeeze.

"I, too, could have done worse, *Altezza*." She paused and sent him the smile she had suppressed a moment ago. "In more ways than one."

Francesco di Montefiore looked down into his daughter-in-law's warm golden brown eyes and envied his son.

The clatter of hooves came closer and they both turned from the intimate moment toward the entry to the courtyard, where the footmen were already rushing forward to take the bridles of the dismounting men.

As true as a well-aimed arrow, Adrienne's gaze flew to Sandro and she felt her heart begin a fast, strong drumbeat. He was safe. He was here. He was hers. For a moment the others faded into blurred shadows and she saw only him.

Sandro felt Isabella's gaze on him as surely as if she had reached out across the courtyard and touched him. The reins still in his hands, he turned. The emotion that shot through him was so strong, so unexpected, that he did not even think to camouflage it beneath a casual exterior. He stared across the courtyard, the fire in his heart reflected in his eyes.

Adrienne felt the answering flame within her. It would be all right, she told herself. Something so beautiful, so strong, could not fall victim to evil.

Oblivious to the observers around them, they stood for a magic moment in their very own world circumscribed by love and yearning.

Chapter Seventeen

Sandro broke the spell, striding quickly across the courtyard, his gaze never swerving from his wife. Only his training and his ingrained sense of duty brought him to greet his father first. Touching the duke's outstretched hand lightly with his still-gloved fingers, he bent his knee to kiss the seal ring his father wore on his index finger.

"Welcome home, my son." Even as he wondered what it would be like to reach out and embrace his son, the duke knew it was too late. "We are pleased that you have acquitted yourself well."

He had expected no more and no less, Sandro thought, but he felt the disappointment like pressure on an old wound that produces a nagging ache. He acknowledged the coolly spoken praise with a bow but remained silent, still acutely aware of the foul taste the campaign had left in his mouth. Then he turned toward Isabella and everything was forgotten.

Lost in Sandro's gaze, Adrienne remained perfectly still. Then his mouth curved in that appealing, boyish smile he gave so rarely and he moved to stand in front of her.

Her eyes never leaving his, she pulled off her right glove and held her hand out to him. "*Benvenuto,* Sandro."

Her whisper was as soft and insubstantial as her breath, which clouded in the cold air, but it made him quiver as if she had caressed him. Stripping off his own right glove with a single sharp tug, Sandro took her fingers in his and lowered his head.

He felt her hand tense as his lips touched her cool skin. Tense and then slacken, as if his touch had melted not only the tension but the bones. He straightened, his lips lightly touching the backs of her fingers, and met her eyes. He saw the welcome there, saw the promises, and for the first time in his life he had the feeling that he had truly come home.

For the second time in minutes, they stood oblivious to their surroundings, not hearing the greetings exchanged between Duke Francesco and the guests Sandro had brought with him.

"Ah, Montefiore, still in the first flush of love. We will have to make certain that the festivities do not last too long tonight, eh?"

Cesare Borgia's slightly mocking voice broke into their private world. Sandro released his wife's hand, reluctant to let her go and at the same time unwilling to share the intimacy of the moment with anyone.

Fighting to control her distaste, Adrienne held her hand out to Borgia. "Welcome back to Siena, Don Cesare. It seems that your name is a harbinger of your military success."

"Thank you for your kind words, *madonna.*" He took her hand with a flourish and bent to kiss it. "I am looking forward to spending a few days in civilized surroundings—" he paused, raising his eyes to hers "—in the company of a virtuous woman."

As he straightened, Adrienne saw the challenge, the threat, the taunt in his eyes and fought to keep her expression aloof. But she felt the familiar skip of fear in her blood, followed by anger, and even as she suppressed them, she knew he had seen both.

Borgia smiled. He was glad that she was not going to be an easy mark. Women like his sister-in-law, Sancia, who fell into his bed before he had even issued an invitation, held little appeal for him. He far preferred women who fought him, the more the better. That way it was so much more satisfying when he broke their resistance. And he always did.

Looking over his shoulder to where Caterina Sforza was emerging from a litter at the far end of the courtyard, he felt the pleasurable tingle the combination of sex and power always gave him. She had fought him like a man from her fortress and fought him like a tigress when the fortress had fallen. Her gown was awry, her hair disheveled, dark circles under her eyes bearing witness to the use he had made of her every night since the fortress of Forlì had fallen. But still she fought him.

The disapproving frown on the face of the commander of the French troops as he intercepted the look Cesare sent Caterina did not escape his notice. The Frenchman had been the first to arrest Caterina and had tried his best to place her under the protection of King Louis, proclaiming that the French did not take women prisoners of war. But Cesare had insisted and won. After all, being the illegitimate son of the pope did have its advantages.

Now, with a disarming smile and an elegant gesture that hinted at conciliation, he invited the man to come closer. "May I present the captain of the French troops King Louis has so graciously lent me?" Borgia took a step back to let the slight man pass. "Donna Isabella di Montefiore . . . Yves, the Count de Beaufort."

No matter that she had tried to prepare herself for this moment, Adrienne still felt her breath freeze in her lungs as she stared at her ancestor. At first glance she found nothing familiar about his chin-length light brown hair and blue eyes. But when she looked closer, she noticed the slight frame, the delicate bone structure and the almost feminine features that he had passed on to generations of Beauforts.

She would not panic, she told herself. She could not afford to show weakness. Besides, it was not he who was the enemy. He was only the final tool Sandro's enemies would use. But even as she told herself all that, the fact that she was facing the man whom Isabella had married after Sandro had been slaughtered, whose child she had borne, made her body and her mind grow numb. Suddenly all control was sliding through her fingers like a greased rope and she felt the seconds slipping by.

Then the anger returned, a spurt that became a wave, and like someone falling down a cliff who finds a final handhold, Adrienne grasped the last threads of her control. As she held out her hand to the count, it occurred to her that her language would give her away. What would the count say when she began speaking a French of almost three hundred years hence. But even as that one last, panicked thought whipped through her mind, she found that the words emerging from her mouth had the cadence of François Villon and Rabelais, and the Count de Beaufort was smiling, telling her that he was charmed that she spoke his tongue so well.

For the remainder of the day and evening there was barely time to exchange word or a glance with Sandro. The hours passed in a whirl of dutiful conversation and dancing with their guests. Even though Adrienne was relieved to find that she had her emotions well under control, the tension within her kept growing until it felt as if it were interwoven with her muscles, her bones. Tension from weighing every word she spoke on a scale fine enough to weigh a pinch of gold dust. Tension from measuring each smile to be charming without giving encouragement. Tension from the sight of the sullen, desperate Caterina Sforza being relentlessly bent to Borgia's will. Tension from hiding the effort she was making from Sandro.

When they were finally able to leave the hall, the only sound that accompanied them down the corridors were the echoes of footsteps, theirs and those of the torchbearers.

The door of their chambers had barely closed behind them when Sandro moved away from her so quickly that her hand, which had lain on his arm, fell to her side. Without saying a word, he poured himself a cup of wine and walked to the window to stare out into the night.

He had been very quiet all evening, rarely joining in either the dancing or the conversation, and Adrienne had been too intent on not making any tactical errors to think about the reasons. Now, as she watched him stand in front of the window, she found that, instead of easing, her tension was building, digging relent-

lessly into her back along the shoulder blades and at
the base of her neck.

With a glance and a curt gesture she dismissed all
her women. Slowly she walked to stand behind Sandro. Was he angry with her for some reason? she
wondered. Had someone filled his ears with lies? But
she remembered what she had read in his eyes that afternoon, and that gave her the strength to place her
palm against his back.

She felt the marginal tightening of muscles beneath
the velvet and knew that although he had not moved
away from her touch, he would have liked to. She
knew that it would perhaps be wiser to coax or seduce
what she wanted from him, but she also realized that
she did not have the strength, the nerves, or the patience for it now. She took a step back.

"Would you like to tell me what is wrong, Sandro?"

"Nothing," he muttered. "You seem to have spent
a highly diverting evening."

"If you have anything, anything at all to say to
me—" the innuendo in his voice had her temper rising even as her voice softened "—then the least you
could do is look me in the eye when you say it."

Carefully Sandro set his wine cup down on the window seat and turned around—slowly, because he knew
that the fuse on his temper was already burning
brightly. He almost swayed under the impact as the
same feelings that had rushed through him only hours
ago rushed through him again. Within the space of a
breath everything was forgotten, everything save the
wild emotions that had pulled him into a relentless
vortex.

With half a step he closed the distance between them. Cupping her face with an ungentle, desperate grip, he took her mouth.

Even as she wanted to give in to the passion she tasted on his lips, Adrienne knew that it was not the answer to whatever was troubling him. There were too many other uncertainties in her life and that she could not afford to let anything between them go unresolved. Bringing her hands up, she pushed at his shoulders, although her knees were already weakening from the power of his kiss.

Her resistance had him remembering why he had spent the evening in sullen silence. Remembering how she had danced with Borgia and with that fop of a Frenchman with his mincing gait and effeminate features. How her laughter had cascaded like a cool waterfall. How beneath the easy conversation he had scented two males of the species readying for the hunt.

Sandro raised his head but kept his hands curved around her face. There was temper in her eyes now, but the welcome, the promises he had seen there this afternoon were still there, as well, and he felt a little of his tension begin to unravel.

"They were sniffing around you all evening and you—"

Understanding now, Adrienne smiled and put a finger on his lips to silence him. "And I was a perfect hostess." She felt the ache between her shoulders ease a little. "What would you have had me do, Sandro? You would not have thanked me had I sat there like a sulky child."

"You might have shown a little less enthusiasm," he muttered, beginning to feel foolish and hating it.

"Is that right?" Adrienne raised her eyebrows. "Jealous?"

"Yes, damn you." His hands, still framing her face, tightened again. "Yes."

Twin rivers of relief and love flowed through her. "But you have no need to be jealous, my love." This time it was she who closed the distance between them. "Shall I show you?"

Before he could answer, she rose on tiptoe and pressed her lips to his. He slanted her head so that he could deepen the kiss, but she was already retreating. Raising her hands to his, she loosened them and guided them downward, sliding them over her neck, her breasts, to lie at her waist.

She heard the cadence of his breathing change and smiled. Her eyes on his, she moistened a fingertip with her tongue and outlined his mouth with it. Then she came closer and closer still and retraced the path her finger had taken with the tip of her tongue.

Her palms, which lay against his chest, picked up the quickened beat of his heart. Her lips felt the renewed catch of his breath. She wanted to seduce and yet she found that it was she who was seduced.

The heaviness of beginning desire stole into her muscles, her bones, tempting her to melt into his arms. Yet at the same time an energy surged through her, driving her to arouse, to excite.

Mimicking what Sandro had often done to her, she let her mouth slide along the angle of his jaw, up and back to his lips for another taste. Then, as her fingers began to loosen the sapphire-and-gold buttons of his doublet, she took the path downward.

Sandro let his eyes fall closed as her mouth began to travel down his neck. He felt her warm, moist breath flow over his skin. He felt the occasional flick of her tongue. Even as he felt the urge to stop this game that she was playing and take control, he found himself seduced and remained passive.

Wanting to reveal more of his skin, Adrienne began to unlace his shirt, but the laces were stubborn and she was forced to tip her head back to examine what her fingers were doing. As the laces came undone to reveal his sharp collarbone, she traced her fingertips over the taut skin and then, unable to resist, lowered her mouth to the hollow at the base of his throat.

The butterfly touch of her fingers as she fought with the laces of his shirt was almost more than Sandro could bear, but he remained still, even though every muscle in his body had tightened. Then he felt her lips, her tongue, in the hollow of his throat and groaned, unable to bear what she was doing to him.

They both stilled at the sound. Then Adrienne raised her head to look at him, suddenly unsure.

"Enough." His voice was hoarse and raspy. "Do not touch me anymore. I forbid you."

He lifted his hands and curved them around hers, pulling them down, bending her arms backward until he had captured them behind her back. The movement brought her lower body forward so that it pushed against his loins, and despite her voluminous skirts, she could feel the pressure of his aroused body.

"Now it is your turn, Isabella."

He began to tease her, his mouth far more expert than hers, knowing exactly where to kiss, where to nip, where to soothe. Within moments her breath was shuddering, her skin moist from his tongue and her own desire. When he released her hands, her knees buckled, and had he not caught her, she would have fallen.

Picking her up as easily as if she were a child, he shouldered open the door to the bedchamber.

Quickly, easily, Sandro began to undress her, as if the fastenings of a woman's clothing held no secrets for him. For a moment Adrienne felt a twinge of disappointment as his hands unclothed her as lightly, as impersonally as if he were one of her servants. But when she opened her eyes to look at him, she saw his skin shining with dampness, his nostrils quivering, the muscles in his neck corded with tension, and she realized with a flutter of nervous excitement how thin the thread of his control was.

She was still wearing her linen undershirt when he stepped away from her.

"Go." He jerked his chin toward the bed.

Although she thought to understand the needs driving him, she could not prevent the disappointment that settled like a weight within her. She started to protest, but he had already turned away and begun to shed his own clothes.

"Sandro, I—"

Even before she touched him, he was whirling around, gripping her shoulders. "Did you not understand what I said, Isabella?" Without giving her a chance to respond to his question, he continued, "I am but a breath away from taking you now, here, where we stand."

Adrienne felt the needs, not just those of the body but of the heart, as well, shimmer through him, and although she was sure it was impossible, her love expanded and grew.

Her eyes shone with warmth, with—love. Sandro had seen it there before—many times—but now, for the first time, he allowed himself to name it. And believe it. For one precious moment he believed totally, unconditionally. His grip on her shoulders eased and became a caress. Closing his eyes, he lowered his head so that his forehead rested against hers.

"Please, Isabella, I beg you, give me a moment." He raised his head. "I want to make love to you, not take you like a beast."

His hands fell away from her shoulders and Adrienne moved back to kneel on the bed. Never taking her eyes from him, she began to loosen the pearls that bound her hair.

Although Sandro tried to slow his movements, to even his breath, he found himself peeling his clothes away with quick, rough movements that did nothing to quiet the urgency within him. His gaze on Isabella, he approached the bed. She looked pale and virginal in her white shirt, her eyes serious. He sat down on the edge of the bed and reached out to bring her closer, but she shifted back.

Slowly Adrienne worked the white linen of her shirt up over her knees, her thighs, her hips. Then, cross ing her arms, she pulled it over her head with one quick tug. Suddenly her breath hitched at her own boldness and she curled her fingers into the cloth and pressed it against her middle.

Her shy movement coaxed a smile to Sandro's lips. "It is a little late for modesty." He reached out, plucked the shift from her fingers and tossed it aside.

His gaze drifted over her body. It seemed to have retained the lushness it had acquired during the brief months of her pregnancy and he ached to mold her curves with his hands. It was then that he saw the scar from the assassin's knife.

The rage, the guilt that went through him made his blood run hot, then cold. He had never seen the wound itself, he realized. All he had seen had been the blood soaking through her gown. Now he saw the terrible path the knife had taken, passing through the side of her breast to plunge into her again between her ribs.

As Adrienne saw the horrified look on Sandro's face, her stomach began to knot. Would her marred body repulse him? Would it forever remind him of the child they had lost?

"Do you still have pain?" His voice was slow, halting.

She shook her head, swallowing before she found the voice to answer. "An occasional twinge. No more."

Sandro placed his palm against the side of her breast. The scar had healed cleanly, but he could feel the slightly puckered flesh against his skin. Pain and guilt surged through him again. For the rest of their lives, the scar would remind him that he had not been able to protect what was his. "Tell me you forgive me."

The words were a demand, but she saw the plea in his eyes. Covering his hand with both of hers, she smiled and shook her head in gentle reproach. "Have I not told you before?"

"Yes." He was utterly still. "I need to hear it again."

"Let me show you." Still holding his hand in both of hers, she lifted it away from her breast and up to her lips. "Come closer," she whispered, her breath flowing over his fingers.

With a graceful twist of his body, Sandro shifted so that he, too, knelt on the bed. Suddenly he was afraid to touch her, afraid that his passion would make him too quick, too rough. He lifted his free hand and brushed the backs of his fingers across her cheek, her mouth. Tentatively he let his hand drift lower, between her breasts, across her belly, until it lay against the curls that guarded her femininity.

His hand trembled as he remembered how her body had arched in pain. How her blood had flowed until he had thought it was impossible for someone to lose so much blood and still live. His gaze traveled down and then back up to her face. "Are you healed here, too?"

"Yes," she breathed. "Touch me and see for yourself."

Slowly his hand slid between her legs. They gasped in unison as his fingers encountered flesh that was slick and swollen with desire. And still he kept his touch feather-light, not daring to touch her more ardently.

Adrienne felt the muscles in her thighs tense with the incredible sensations the gliding touch of his fingers was producing. But she wanted more.

"I will not break, Sandro," she whispered. Her hand skimmed over his face in invitation.

The heat that his fingers made grew unbearable and she knew that the only relief was the still greater heat that was to come. Her hand slipped into his hair and twisted in the silky strands. Using that as leverage, she slid the last few inches across the silk coverlet until her body was flush against his.

The last of his control snapped at the sensation of her heated skin against his. With a sound that was half triumph, half surrender, he took her mouth even as he bore her back. His hands explored. His mouth tasted. His breath caressed.

Stunned by the onslaught of his passion, Adrienne lay still. But only for a moment. Then she began to make her own demands.

They tangled, rolling across the bed. When he surged above her, his aroused flesh flexing against her, demanding entry, she welcomed him, twining her legs around his. And still he hesitated, afraid to hurt her with the force of his passion.

Adrienne reached between their bodies, already damp with sweat, and guided him to her. "Come into me now, Sandro," she whispered. "Come into me and give me a child."

He tensed, remembering her pain again, and yet the softly spoken request had his arousal spiraling still further. Sandro felt her hands on him, gently urging him closer and closer still. Unable to resist, he slid into her. He had barely begun to thrust into her when the climax took him and he stilled. His body was still pulsing with his release when he began to move again.

This time they climbed the mountain together, balancing on the top, where pleasure was so intense that it was almost pain. Then, in a burst of shooting stars, lost in each other, they tumbled off.

Still sheathed in her, Sandro rolled to his side. His mouth brushed over her closed eyelids.

"Isabella?"

"Mmm."

"Look at me."

Lazy with pleasure, Adrienne finally managed to open her eyes.

Sandro let his fingers drift over her cheek and down the impossibly soft skin of her neck. "I love you," he murmured. Then he closed his eyes and slept.

Chapter Eighteen

"I wish you could see my château. It is very lovely." Yves de Beaufort sent Isabella di Montefiore an enamored look. "Oh, you would like it. It is but a twenty-minute walk from the sea and—"

Even though she continued to step and turn and sway in the rhythm of the pavane, Adrienne suddenly lost all awareness of her surroundings. She no longer saw the brightly lighted hall or the other dancers in their lavish, brilliantly colored costumes. She no longer heard the stately melody played by the violas and lutes. She no longer smelled the rich aroma of food that still drifted through the hall to blend with the smell of the crowd. Instead she found herself transported into the world of her childhood with such clarity that she could identify every sound, every scent.

"You can smell the water even in the middle of the rose garden." The words slipped out so spontaneously, so naturally, that if Beaufort's hand on hers had not tightened, Adrienne might not have noticed that she had said them.

"But—" Beaufort sent her a look that was more baffled than surprised "—how did you know?"

Adrienne covered the alarm that streaked through her with an edgy laugh. "Know what, my dear count?"

"Why, that there is a rose garden at the Château de Beaufort and that you can smell the sea even if you bury your nose in a rosebush."

She moved her shoulders in a shrug. "I am quite sure that every self-respecting château in France has a rose garden. And if it is only a twenty-minute walk from the sea, it stands to reason that the smell of the water is everywhere." Adrienne laughed again, a sharp, brittle sound. "Does it not?"

Yves de Beaufort smiled and nodded because it was not his way to contradict a woman. The explanation Isabella di Montefiore had given him had sounded very simple, very logical, but he had seen the strange, faraway look in her eyes when she had spoken. It had been as if she were seeing the garden he was describing, and for some reason the image had saddened her. She had secrets. He had seen them in her eyes that very first afternoon in the courtyard. And he wanted to be the one to discover them all.

For the rest of the dance, Adrienne avoided looking at Beaufort and concentrated on keeping her hands steady. No matter how skillfully she had glossed over the words that had spilled out of her mouth, she had seen the thoughtful look in his blue eyes. He had noticed something odd. She was sure of it. But what was it that he had seen or thought to see? And what could she do about it?

When the dance ended, Yves de Beaufort proffered his arm to his hostess, his precise Gallic mind already planning his next avenue of attack. Suddenly he found his way blocked by Alessandro di Montefiore. The *condottiere* bowed with perfect politeness, his mouth curving in a smile. But his black eyes were glacial.

"My apologies for intruding. I fear that I must deprive you of my wife's company for a little while, Beaufort."

Yves de Beaufort ignored the rich sarcasm in Montefiore's voice. "But of course." He smiled mildly. "I shall be devastated, but I will console myself with your excellent wine, my dear Montefiore."

His eyes followed them as they moved away. He was a man who not only enjoyed the pleasure a woman could bring but liked women for their own sake, as many men did not. But he felt something for Isabella di Montefiore beyond what he had ever felt for a woman before—an attachment, a kinship even. It would be difficult to pry her away from the husband she was so obviously in love with, he thought, but one never knew. No, he smiled, in these uncertain times one never knew.

They walked down the length of the hall in strained silence, the quick pace that Sandro set and the grim line of his mouth precluding anyone from stopping them for some desultory conversation.

"Is something wrong?" Adrienne finally demanded.

"Wrong?" Sandro's eyebrows curved in question like raven's wings. "Why should there be? You are being the perfect hostess. Again."

Despite the turmoil inside her, Adrienne was tempted to smile. "And you are being jealous. Again."

Sandro stopped and pulled his wife to face him. As their guests had lingered, putting off the continuation of their journey to Rome time and time again, he had found it more and more difficult to keep things in perspective.

There had been no way to exclude the Gennaro brothers from the festivities and their presence grated on his nerves. He could not fault Borgia's conduct toward Isabella, but he had seen how often he looked her way with those inscrutable eyes of his. And the Frenchman was forever sniffing at her heels and sometimes she would look at him with an odd expression in her eyes that he could not quite classify. And then there were his own emotions, which were strangling him. He felt like a fool and he hated it.

He had made love to her every night since he had returned, but they had never regained the perfect, unmarred union of that first night. It was not only the distractions and duties of their days that were making things difficult. But the old doubts and suspicions had returned to plague him again. Yes, he saw the love in Isabella's eyes, the love he wanted so badly to believe in. But he also saw the disquiet, the anxiety that flickered there in unguarded moments, and he found himself questioning the honesty of her feelings.

"And I do not need to be jealous." He brushed his fingers over her cheek and let his hand drift down her neck to lie at the base of her throat. "Is that what you were going to say?"

"Yes." Even as Adrienne spoke, the memory welled up of that strange moment when the words to complete the sentence the Count de Beaufort had begun had tumbled from her mouth.

Before she could push the memory aside, her surroundings seemed to blur again and the smell of the sea filled her nostrils. The moment passed so quickly that she could almost make herself believe she had imagined it. But she knew she had not. She was surrounded with uncertainties, with enigmas, and no matter how she tried to reassure herself, she was afraid.

Sandro felt the quick leap of her pulse, felt her convulsive swallow, saw the odd, remote look come into her eyes. He felt a spurt of panic that was followed so quickly by anger that it was easy to deny that he had felt the former.

"You have not forgotten what I said to you, Isabella?" His voice was even, but his eyes were turbulent.

She did not need a more precise explanation to know exactly what he meant. She remembered their first night together and felt the chill of the jeweled dagger sheath against her breast so clearly that she would not have been surprised to look down and find it pressing against her skin.

Because the scent of the sea was still in her nostrils, because in this moment she remembered so clearly that she had had a life of her own before she had chosen, for his sake, to take another one, there was defiance in her eyes when she focused on him again.

"No, Sandro, I have not forgotten." Her chin tilted upward. "There are a great many other things that I have not forgotten, either." It was pain rather than anger that thinned her mouth. "Now I would thank you to take your hands off me."

"You dismiss me?" His eyes widened at her insolence.

"I will not be mauled by you." The anger surged up, eclipsing the pain. "Not in private and especially not in public." She jerked her hand upward and struck away the hand that still lay at her throat.

He reached for her again, but the fury that she radiated stopped him. It was too strong, he thought with a wave of relief. Too strong to be anything but honest. He lifted his hand again, this time in a gesture of conciliation, but she stepped away from him.

"I would not advise you to touch me again, Sandro. Not unless you want a scene on your hands that will keep tongues buzzing from here to kingdom come."

Her skirts belled as she turned swiftly and stalked away. His unwilling admiration disappeared as Sandro watched her smile at Beaufort. He felt the tension begin to gather at the base of his spine, and although he was not aware of it, the evil voice in his head was whispering again.

Piero smiled as he watched Isabella stalk away from her husband. So there was trouble in paradise, he thought as he tapped his finger against his cheek. Perhaps it would be easier than he had anticipated to put his plans into action.

Yes, he still wanted her. And often enough the desire was so strong that he found himself willing to forget those suspicions that Alfonso's words had planted in his mind. There were even times when he could push them away and pretend that everything was as it always had been. But underneath, the irrational conviction remained that some power had put another woman into the body of his sister. And he knew that he was willing to sacrifice this other Isabella on the altar of his ambition. And his ambition was to rule Siena.

Piero saw that Cesare Borgia's eyes had also followed the little scene between Montefiore and Isabella. He sidled up to him with the vague idea that it would do no harm to lay a little ground.

"I see that my sister's beauty does not leave your grace indifferent," he murmured.

Borgia, his arms crossed over his black velvet doublet, turned toward him, and for a moment Piero quailed before the power of the opaque dark eyes that were Cesare Borgia's strongest weapon. Eyes that remained utterly without expression whether he was in a merry mood or seething with anger, whether he was about to set a prisoner free or send him to the torture chamber.

"I assume that you do not make this observation for its own sake."

Taken aback by Borgia's directness, Piero opened his mouth and then shut it, unsure suddenly of how to continue.

"Well, what is it, Gennaro?" Borgia prodded. "Do you have something important to say or are you just pimping for your sister?"

The bluntly vulgar words stirred his anger. No, Piero thought, the time was not yet ripe. "I was just making conversation, *Altezza*. And I allow myself the comment that someone of such rare beauty as Donna Isabella needs no one to pimp for her." He bowed and backed away.

Borgia turned back toward the hall. His inscrutable gaze flickered over Isabella, then wandered to Montefiore. He was not accustomed to waiting for his pleasure, but this time he would make an exception, he mused. After all, Montefiore's troops and his skill were still needed, and he had recognized the burning ambition in Piero Gennaro's eyes. Who knows? Perhaps there was business to be done here before he indulged himself with Isabella's body.

In the meantime he would go to Rome. For the time being it suited him to keep up the charade that the cities he had conquered were destined to enrich the coffers of the Papacy, so it was time that he paid obeisance to his father.

Borgia's slender fingers played with the enormous ruby he wore on his index finger. Yes, he would go to Rome to plan his next campaign and wait. After all, he had learned patience well in the years he had been merely the second son destined for a career in the church. He had been patient until fate had offered an opportunity and then he had struck. And now his brother Juan's body had been providing a feast for the worms for nigh on three years and he was the pope's eldest son. He smiled and beckoned to Caterina Sforza to come closer.

She was dreaming. Adrienne was sure she was dreaming. And yet everything was so real that she grew unsure, unable to distinguish between dream and reality. The well-raked gravel on the path crunched beneath her feet. She could see the familiar shimmer of weathered rose-gray stone through the trees. The cool breeze that ruffled her hair brought with it the smell of the sea.

Suddenly Yves de Beaufort appeared in front of her. He held out his hand and his smile was gentle.

"You belong to me now, Isabella. Alessandro di Montefiore is dead and you belong to me."

"No! It is not true!" she cried and covered her eyes with her hands, palm outward. "It cannot be true!"

He took her hands and pulled them gently away from her eyes. "You will be happy at the Château de Beaufort. I will make you forget him and you will be happy." He kissed her fingers. "You will see."

His lips on her fingers were cold and repellent, but she had no strength to wrest her hands from his grasp.

Abruptly, everything around her seemed to dim, disappearing behind a thick veil, and she saw Sandro, kneeling, the executioner's sword raised above his head. In a flash of silver the sword fell and the world turned crimson, crimson with Sandro's blood. She went rigid, the horror cutting off her breathing as blood poured over her. Then she managed to drag in a lungful of air and began to scream.

"Shh. It is all right."

The voice and someone holding her brought her out of the worst of the nightmare. Her screams subsided to whimpers as she lay there, her breath heaving, her nightgown soaked with sweat. But the horror of what she had dreamt hung over her like a miasma.

Sandro stroked back her damp, matted hair. "You were only dreaming again."

The voice penetrated the hideousness and Adrienne's eyelids fluttered open onto a dark, hazy world. But through the dimness she saw Sandro's face. It was Sandro's face, was it not? She lifted a trembling hand to reassure herself.

"Sandro?"

"Yes, I am here."

She allowed herself to sink back, relief filling her eyes with tears that flowed down her cheeks in rivulets.

"Don't cry." He wiped away the tears with his fingers. "It is all right now. It is over."

But even as he said the words, he knew he was lying. How could it be all right when he lay next to her every night, sleepless, waiting for her dreams to come? He already knew the rhythm. She would grow restless, begin to murmur words only half-understood, cry out. Then those terrible screams would begin. The screams that chilled his blood and sharpened his guilt that he had not woken her earlier.

Every time she began to dream he told himself that he would wake her. This time he would wake her. But every night he let her sleep on, dream on, because every night he listened for a murmur, a word that would confirm the suspicions that lived and festered within him.

Her tears dried, her breathing evened, and finally Adrienne lay against him, relaxed except for a thin band of tension that ran from her neck to the base of her spine. She shifted to ease it, sighing when it persisted.

He trailed his hand down her back with enough pressure so that the last bit of tension began to drain out of her. Curling toward him, she grew pliant and drowsy.

"Do you want to tell me about it?" he asked softly, telling himself that what he was doing was not a treacherous ploy.

"It was the same awful dream. I dreamt—" Suddenly remembering that the dream was another thing she could not—dared not—share with him, she shook her head. "I don't want to think about it. I just want to forget," she whispered, and burrowed her face more deeply into his chest. "Help me to forget."

He felt her shoulders tense again, and in contradiction to the doubts pelting him, he experienced a wave of love as deep and clear as the sea. Tipping her face up to his, he lowered his mouth.

Chapter Nineteen

Restlessness and impatience drove Sandro out of the brightly lighted hall onto the small, narrow balcony. Below him the Campo spread out, peaceful and empty. Above him the night sky was veiled with a white moonlit haze. It was one of those mild nights that come at the end of winter. A night that hinted at the warmth that would soon be spreading over the land. He filled his lungs with the fresh air and closed his eyes.

With the power of concentration that he had possessed even as a small boy, he blocked out the music and laughter and the din of voices that spilled out from the hall behind him. Their guests would finally be leaving early in the morning and he and Isabella would have at least a few days to themselves before he, too, would have to travel to Rome. Cesare Borgia had requested that all his *condottieri* be present for the triumphal entry he planned to make into the Eternal City, and in the past months Sandro had seen more than one example of what happened to people who treated Borgia's requests as less than an order.

Would Isabella's nightmares stop once they were alone? he wondered. Did he want them to stop? Or did some perverse, cruel part of him want her to suffer until a murmured word, a name, would prove or disprove his own doubts?

The double doors behind him creaked open and he swore under his breath that his solitude was about to be disturbed. But no one stepped outside to join him and he again leaned back against the cool brick.

"I do not think you know quite how much you have given me during these past days, Donna Isabella."

At the sound of the mild voice Sandro stiffened. The soft, familiar laugh that answered the words had him curling his hands around the wrought-iron railing that bordered the balcony.

"Come now, my dear count. Surely you exaggerate."

"But I do not, fair lady. When I leave Siena, my heart will remain in your keeping."

The glass rattled lightly as the doors closed. He heard the laugh again, faint now, but even more flirtatious and seductive.

Even after the voices had faded, Sandro remained on the balcony, his hands gripping the railing, not noticing that the cold from the wrought iron was seeping into his body. So she had betrayed him after all. Was this what she dreamed every night? Was it guilt that drove her to wake up screaming?

She has betrayed me. The words ran on and on in his head like an endless litany.

For long moments he felt nothing—no anger, no pain—only emptiness that stretched out in front of him like a boundless desert. Even his pulse, his heartbeat, seemed to have stopped, as if his blood had ceased flowing and turned to ice.

When the pain came, it was in a wave that pushed him under and took his breath away. He tried to deny it, tried to deny that his heart was breaking. If he could have, he would have torn it from his body. Then his sense of survival took over and he began to fight the pain.

He fought it desperately, fought it with the weapon that had stood him in good stead all his life. Deliberately he drew on the anger until all his nerves were vibrating with it. And still there was more.

Finally the rage filled him, filled him to the exclusion of all else. He burned with it, but it was not the kind of fire that warmed, only destroyed. Knowing that if he returned to the festivities now he would be capable of killing her and Beaufort, Sandro harnessed his fury. He let himself into the hall and, shutting eyes and ears against the revelry, cut across a corner and slipped out into the corridor.

Not bothering to wake any of the stable hands, he saddled his mount himself. His tension communicated itself to the animal, and by the time he was ready to mount, the stallion was prancing in the hay-strewn stall. Even as he leapt into the saddle, the horse bounded forward. Hooves pounding on the damp cobblestones, the stallion galloped into the night.

With that sixth sense she seemed to have where Sandro was concerned, Adrienne knew that something was wrong. She had not seen him for what seemed like hours and she looked for him now as carefully, as discreetly as she could, but he was nowhere to be seen.

"I fear I have been neglecting my other guests." She managed to smile creditably at Yves de Beaufort, although her stomach was suddenly roiling with fear and premonition. "Will you excuse me now?"

She lifted her fingers from his arm and began to move away from him, but he captured her hand in his.

"You would leave me like this? Without a word of encouragement, a word of promise?"

Adrienne's gaze flew up in surprise to meet his. Suddenly Beaufort's voice had lost its habitual mildness and grown urgent. His good-natured look had turned intrusive. Even his delicate features seemed to have sharpened, taking on the aspect of a hungry ferret.

He had lulled her into a feeling of safety, she realized. With his easy manner and his chivalrous, undemanding compliments he had made her forget who he was. During the past two weeks she had found it increasingly comfortable, dangerously comfortable, to spend time with him. Besides, she had thought herself so clever that the attention he was paying her helped her to stay out of Cesare Borgia's way. After all, it was Borgia who was the real danger.

Now she wondered if, in her eagerness to avoid ancient patterns, she had made another fatal error. Had she miscalculated yet again? Had she prevented one catastrophe only to cause another? She could feel the cold shiver of fear slither along her spine, but she ruthlessly controlled it.

"Indeed, my dear count, I have given all my promises already and have no more to give." Her lips curved in a smile that did not reach her eyes. "As far as encouragement is concerned, I would encourage you to look for a wife of your own."

A new flash of fear skimmed over her nerve endings at her own words. This was just what he was doing, after all. She managed to keep her eyes steady on his as she extricated her hand from his grasp.

"I bid you a good-night," she said softly, and turned, forcing herself to walk away slowly, even though she wanted to run and hide.

Yves de Beaufort watched her walk away with a philosophical shrug. He was a pragmatic man not given to beating his head against the wall. He would be leaving Siena tomorrow, and although he had never been one to believe in premonitions, something told him he would be seeing Isabella di Montefiore again. Who knows, he thought, perhaps next time she would be less proud and haughty.

Adrienne tossed and turned in her canopied bed beneath the gods and nymphs, who seemed to mock her. The festivities had long since ended, but Sandro had not appeared. Neither Michele, nor her father-in-law nor any of the servants whom she had questioned had known Sandro's whereabouts and she had spent the remainder of the evening keeping a nervous eye on the brightly dressed throng.

She had finally managed to fall into an uneasy sleep when an urgent, breathless whisper woke her. She opened her eyes to find Gianni tugging at the sleeve of her nightgown.

"Donna Isabella, wake up." He dragged in a breath on a sob. "Please!"

Realizing somehow that it was imperative that she do so, Adrienne beat back the disorientation that always came upon awakening.

"Gianni?" She propped herself up on an elbow. "What is it?"

"It is Don Alessandro." Needing more air, he jerked at his collar so that the top button of his doublet popped and fell to the floor with a metallic tinkle.

"What has happened?" Adrienne threw back the covers and swung her feet over the side of the bed. "Has something happened to him?" She dug her fingers into Gianni's doublet and shook him. "Answer me!"

"No. No, *madonna.*" He shook his oversize head so vigorously that it looked as if his thin neck would snap. "He is here."

"Here? Thank God!" Adrienne released the dwarf's doublet so quickly that he staggered backward.

As she turned toward the door, he grabbed her nightgown, wanting to hold her back. The unexpected jerk made her stumble and her head whipped back in annoyance.

"Wait, *madonna,* please. Don Alessandro looks—"

The door to the bedchamber opened with a crash.

"Ready to kill," Gianni finished in a hoarse whisper, and made the sign of the cross.

For long moments they stood there, as still as if they had been turned to stone. The first to move was Sandro.

"Out." He jerked a hand in the dwarf's direction without bothering even to glance at him.

With a beseeching look at his mistress that begged forgiveness, Gianni scurried out of the room. If only he could go to someone, he thought desperately as he ran through the silent rooms. Someone who would protect this new, gentle Donna Isabella. But there was no one. Then he remembered his dagger, the dagger

Donna Isabella had given him when she had thrown away his hated jester's costume and presented him with clothes of fine velvet. Fingering the cool hilt of the knife, he crept back to the door of the bedchamber and curled up on the floor, his ear to the door.

"You were going somewhere, *madonna?*" Sandro advanced into the room with slow, supple movements, like a large cat getting ready to strike.

Adrienne ran toward him. "Where were you? I looked for you all evening. What happened? Where did you go?"

She reached out to touch him, but he stretched out his arm to stop her, the heel of his hand striking her breastbone.

"I asked you where you were going."

Bewildered, Adrienne shook her head. "To find you." She spoke haltingly, still dazed from sleep and worry. "Gianni came to wake me. To tell me you were back."

Sandro curled his fingers into her nightgown. "So that you could get rid of your lover?" The low timbre of his voice made the underlying tone of menace even more palpable.

She stared at him, sure that she had misunderstood his words.

"Well?" He tightened his grip, his knuckles pressing painfully into her flesh.

Adrienne began to struggle. "Are you mad?" She tried to loosen his grip, but she might as well have been fighting against an iron vise. "What are you talking about?"

Sandro looked down at her, her eyes wide with alarm, confusion and the beginnings of anger. But he could see no guilt. Was she so callous, so depraved, that she felt no guilt? Somehow that was even more of an insult.

Even as a renewed spurt of rage prodded him, he hesitated. Could he possibly be mistaken? No, he told himself. He had heard them. Heard Beaufort's suggestive tone, Isabella's seductive laughter. And then there were the dreams. And the fact that tainted Gennaro blood flowed in her veins. She had made him believe that she was different, but she was like the rest of them—born and bred for baseness and deceit.

"I heard you and Beaufort, so you need not bother to deny it, *madonna*. You have betrayed me and I will have my revenge."

But even as he spoke, as he looked into her face, he could already feel himself softening. He heard his treacherous heart clamoring for him to believe her lies because he wanted them so badly to be true. It would be so easy to forget that she had betrayed him, he thought. So easy. All he had to do was to close off his mind and he would lose himself in her fragrance, her warmth.

Adrienne could feel the fury emanating from him like a wall of flames, ready to scorch anything in its wake. When she felt it ease, hope surged within her.

Reaching out, she touched her fingers to his face. "I have never betrayed you, Sandro. Never. Not in reality, nor in my heart."

The sound of her voice brought the rage back. "Be silent," he snarled, and he struck her hands away, too afraid of their seductive touch.

"Sandro, believe me, I—" Her words faltered as she remembered the words Beaufort had spoken just hours ago and her own fears. Her vision blurred, and a wave of dizziness made her head spin. Oh God, she thought.

Was Sandro right? Had she allowed herself to be pulled into a new net, betraying him without even knowing that she did so?

Sandro saw the flicker in her eyes. Guilt. There it was, he thought, wondering why he felt no triumph, no justification. He wanted to kill her for what she had done to him, but he knew he could not. No matter what she had done, he could not.

The fury, the love, the sorrow, the loss merged into a single tempest of emotion within him. Yes, she had betrayed him. But she was still his and he would prove it to both of them.

With a single movement he dragged her against him. Coiling her braid around one hand, he pulled her head back, exposing her white throat to him. He raised his other hand to curve roughly around her neck, as if he were daring her to fight him.

Adrienne saw the sudden flare of desire in his eyes that was reflected in the tautness of his features. She saw his nostrils begin their telltale fluttering. She knew that if she touched his skin it would vibrate with barely suppressed passion.

Then he was forcing her head back, filling her mouth with his tongue. She felt the power of his hands and knew that struggling would be useless. In minutes, perhaps in seconds, he would take her. The realization flashed through her, bringing fear that tasted cold and bitter on her tongue. But this was Sandro, she reminded herself. Sandro whom she loved above all else. Sandro for whom she had forfeited her own life.

The love flowed through her then, warming her, erasing the fear. But suddenly it was vital that she stop him. Vital that he not take her now, quickly, roughly, with nothing but this desire, edged in violence, simmering between them. Suddenly it was important that even this moment have a measure of tenderness.

He wanted her to fight him, to provoke him, but instead she lay against his body, pliant in surrender as she accepted his brutal kiss. Releasing her braid, he pushed her away.

"Take off your nightgown."

Her eyes on his, she tugged the laces open and then worked the gown off her shoulders until it fell to pool at her feet.

He watched her as she obeyed him. Her skin was flushed, but she stood straight, her eyes clear and fearless. A hot wave of shame welled up in him, but he tamped it down and turned away to shed his own clothes.

When he turned back to face her, she still stood perfectly motionless in the pool of white linen. With a gesture so simple and yet so real, so true, she held out her hand to him.

In that one moment he understood that what she was offering was not unconditional surrender but unconditional love. He took her hand and together they walked to the bed.

Chapter Twenty

The days turned into weeks. Spring came, warm and rainy this year, bringing the scent of damp earth and fresh green leaves into the narrow streets of the city. As she looked out of the open window onto the Campo, Adrienne could smell both, even though all she saw was brick and stone.

She leaned a little further out of the window, wondering if today was the day that Sandro would finally come. There had been no word from him for six long weeks and her only news of him had come from a Venetian dignitary who had passed through Siena on his way from Rome. Cesare Borgia's entrance into the Eternal City had been triumphant and ostentatious beyond compare, he had reported. And the entertainments that followed were lavish and lascivious to say the least. He had smiled discreetly when he mentioned that Sandro frequented them all with a grim, resentful mien.

Without warning, the weariness from the wakeful nights overcame her. Needing to rest, if only for a moment, she lowered herself to the floor and half knelt, half sat, pillowing her head on the cradle of her arms. But the moment she closed her eyes, Sandro's image rose to torment her. Oh God, she thought as her eyes flew open. Would she ever be able to rest again?

She had thought, hoped, that all would be well when she had taken him by the hand to give him freely what he had started to take so violently. He had made love to her with a passion tempered by so much gentleness that for the space of a few hours her joy had known no bounds. He believed her! He trusted her!

But when the new day had come, she saw that again she had become victim to an illusion. Sandro had risen from her bed before dawn with barely a word and left to make his preparations to depart from Siena with Borgia and his retinue.

She had gone through the necessary motions that morning, mercifully numb. Beaufort had whispered his last insinuating compliments to her, but they had hardly registered. Borgia's words to her had been innocuous, but they had barely penetrated her pain-dulled mind as he lifted her hand to his mouth and let a single finger slide along her palm in silent message. And Sandro. Sandro had not met her eyes once. Not even at the very last moment of farewell. But it wasn't until much later that the pain had come. And the fear.

The rustle of bedclothes and a stifled moan behind her brought her back to the present and she swiftly closed the window and returned to her father-in-law's side. She would have wanted to reach out to the nearly spent man who lay, pale and gaunt, in the middle of the huge bed. She would have wanted to give him the comfort of a touch at least, since he would not allow her to ease his pain with the sweet Turkish poppy syrup she had obtained. But she knew that he did not suffer gladly any touch that he deemed unnecessary. He was as harsh to himself as he was to others.

*Today Francesco di Montefiore died, alone and un-
mourned. I made certain that the messenger bearing
the news did not leave for Rome until the old man had
taken his last breath. I am told that he suffered greatly,
calling for Alessandro at the end and begging his forgiveness. It is only just. Now I have paid him back, at
least a little, for the mean, spiteful way he has always
treated me.*

Adrienne remembered Isabella's words and wondered if this was fated to happen again. Would Francesco di Montefiore die calling for his son? She had
sent Sandro message after urgent message, but still he
did not come. And time was running out.

"Is there anything I can do?" she asked softly,
bending down toward him.

The worst of the pain had passed and Duke Francesco di Montefiore raised his eyelids and looked at his
daughter-in-law. He had misjudged Isabella, he
thought ruefully. She looked pale and fragile from the
days and nights she had spent at his bedside and he
knew that he should send her to rest. But her serene
presence seemed to comfort him and ease his pain, and
he found himself unable to forgo it. He tried to gesture to her to sit down, but his hand was too weak to
do more than twitch helplessly.

"Shall I sit with you for a while?" she said, seeing
the futile attempt he had made.

"Yes." He breathed the word rather than said it.

Tucking one foot under her, Adrienne sat down on
the edge of the bed. She had spent almost all her time
in the duke's sickroom since he had taken to his bed
three weeks ago. She had not needed to hear the di-
agnosis of the doctor to know that the time left him
would be short and painful.

She thought back to that day many months ago when he had summoned her to lecture her about her brothers. She well remembered the sadness in her heart as she had looked at him, knowing that he already carried the source of his death within him. Knowing that whatever she would be able to change, to change this would be beyond her power.

The old man saw the grief in her eyes. Yes, he thought again, he had misjudged her badly. And that had been only the last mistake of the many he had made in the course of his life. He sighed. So many mistakes. He wondered briefly, longingly, if God would give him the chance to make amends in this life, or if it would be his lot to suffer in the hell Dante had described so well.

"You had the same look in your eyes that day when I summoned you to forbid you to see your brothers." The words were spaced and slow, as if he had to painfully drag every word out of his throat.

Adrienne smiled sadly. "Perhaps because I was remembering that day just now."

"You—" He gasped as a spasm savaged him. "You knew already then, did you not?"

Neither one of them needed further elaboration on what he meant.

"Yes." Adrienne tensed and laced her hands a little tighter, not sure where the question was leading.

"How?"

She shook her head helplessly. How could she explain to him that three hundred years from now she had read a diary and thus had known months ago that he already carried his fatal illness within him? How could she explain who she truly was? How could she explain it when she did not even know it herself? Was she still Adrienne? Or had she become Isabella in every way? And if she had, which Isabella was she?

"I just knew." She spread her hands palm upward in a helpless gesture. "I just knew."

The duke's eyes closed, and when he said nothing, she thought that he had fallen asleep and her tension began to ease. When he spoke again, she started.

"From the moment I saw you in the midst of that ribald crowd in your bedchamber you seemed different from the Isabella Gennaro I had seen. From the other Isabella." The words came haltingly. "First I thought it was an illusion." His lids lifted. "Then I thought you were a witch."

She met his gaze steadily, though her heart had begun to race at his words. "But I am not."

"I know."

As his eyes closed, a ghost of a smile touched his almost colorless lips as if he were privy to her secret.

She sat with him until she was sure that he had slipped back into sleep. Then she stood and went back to the window, needing a breath of fresh spring air to dispel the smell of the sickroom. Where was Sandro? she asked herself again as she tugged the window sash wide open. She stared outside absently kneading her middle, where a knot of queasiness seemed to have taken up permanent residence from the nervous tension of the past weeks.

"Madonna?"

The unexpected sound of Daria's voice had her whirling around. The sudden movement turned the queasy feeling into a flash of full-blown nausea that brought a sheen of cold sweat to her skin.

Taking her mistress's elbow, the young slave woman maneuvered her into a nearby chair.

Adrienne leaned back and, trying to breathe evenly and deeply, waited for the nausea to pass. What was wrong with her? She felt a flash of impatience, of anger even, that her body was betraying her with weakness when she had need of all the strength she could muster.

When she opened her eyes, Daria was kneeling at her feet, an odd look in her incredible turquoise eyes. "What is it, Daria?"

"*Madonna* should be taking better care of herself now."

Adrienne stared at the young woman as the realization took hold of her. Instinctively, her hands moved to lie flat against her belly. She closed her eyes against the tears that sprang into them, not knowing whether to cry with joy that Sandro had given her another child or to cry with sorrow because history was repeating itself again. Oh God, she thought, her hands balling into fists. Would it be granted to her to hold this child in her arms, or would this child, too, be lost?

She shook her head. There was no sense in asking herself questions she could not answer. She would go mad if she did. Mad! All she could do was go on and live this life as best she could. No, she corrected herself, forcing herself to unclench the hands that lay on her belly, it was *her* life. By God, she had made it her life.

The thought had a surge of strength flowing through her, reviving her. She took a long, deep breath and found the nausea gone. It was then that she saw the thin line between Daria's pale eyebrows and sat forward.

"Is something wrong, Daria?"

"One of the messengers *madonna* sent to Don Alessandro has returned."

"Oh, thank God. Perhaps he has a message from—" She was half out of her seat when the look on Daria's face stopped her.

"The man never got to Rome, *madonna*. He is half-dead."

Daria at her heels, Adrienne ran downstairs, where the messenger, his blue-and-white livery filthy with blood and grime, had been bedded in the entry on a makeshift pallet. Instructing that the doctor come immediately to tend him, she knelt at his side, ordering everyone but Daria away so that she could speak to him in privacy.

"Can you hear me?" She laid her hand against the man's ravaged face.

He opened his eyes and, recognizing her, tried to struggle up. Gently but firmly she held him down.

"Rest now. The doctor will be here to tend to your wounds in a moment." The man subsided and lay still. "Bring water," she ordered over her shoulder, but Daria was already handing her a cup.

After the man had painfully downed a few swallows, she returned the cup to Daria's waiting hands and tried to curb her impatience. "Can you tell me what happened?"

"Barely an hour out of the city—" he winced as he drew breath "—horse tripped. Rope stretched—across road." His words came in spurts. "Tried to get up—but they were upon me—like hyenas."

"Who?"

"I do not know, *madonna*." He looked at her apologetically. "Masked."

"Did they rob you?"

The man rolled his head from side to side in denial. "They beat me, but took nothing. Did not even search my saddlebags. His breath shuddered and he coughed. "Trussed me up. Brought me to small farmhouse. Threw me down stairs into cellar." His eyes closed in pain and exhaustion.

Adrienne wanted to shake him, to shout at him to go on quickly. Instead she laced her fingers tightly in her lap and asked softly, "What happened then?"

"The other two were there, too."

"Other two?"

"Messengers. Messengers *madonna* sent—Rome—Don Alessandro."

"What?" Adrienne felt as if someone had put a fist into her stomach. "Both messengers?"

The man nodded. "Once we heard the men talking that they would sell us into Turkish slavery." A tremor went through him. "I managed to free myself and stole one of the horses."

Adrienne heard the footsteps of the doctor. "You will be taken care of now." She put a hand on his shoulder. "I thank you for your loyalty. It will not go unrewarded."

Her head reeling from what she had heard, she stood. Her steps stiff, as if she were sleepwalking, she made her way toward the staircase. What was happening? Who had done this? Was she surrounded by traitors? The thoughts chased one another, each more frightening than the next.

She started to climb the stairs, but all of a sudden everything around her seemed to dim. To turn into wisps of smoke and shadow. For a moment it seemed that the only real thing in her universe was the marble of the balustrade, cool and solid under her hand. She wanted to run and hide, she thought desperately. She wanted Sandro to come home and put everything right. But she knew that the responsibility rested squarely on her shoulders.

"Is *madonna* all right?"

Adrienne heard Daria's voice behind her and she shook her head. "No, I am not all right. I have to think," she whispered, her voice harsh and urgent. "I have to get to the bottom of this. Find out who did this."

Unmindful of the picture she presented, she sat down on the step and lowered her head to her knees. She had been walking a razor's edge ever since she had come into this life, she thought, menaced by dangers, by suspicions, by hatred or lust from all around her. But at least they had threatened her directly, so that she had been able to react in some way. Now she and her father-in-law and Sandro were faced with an intrigue, a conspiracy of such magnitude that she had no idea what she could do about it.

When the realization hit her, her head snapped up abruptly. How could she have been so incredibly stupid? She slapped both hands against her forehead. Because she was so tired, because it was a little different than she had expected it, she had not seen that the machinery for Sandro's downfall had already been set into motion.

Even as the first surge of panic rushed through her, she was fighting it. She had not begun this to be beaten now, she swore to herself. Somehow, somehow she would manage.

But how? a cynical inner voice demanded. She was completely alone with no friends, no servants she could truly trust except a Russian slave girl and a dwarf. She could have trusted her father-in-law, but she could not burden a dying man.

Why not? she asked herself, remembering the strange yearning she had seen in his eyes. Perhaps sharing this burden with her for the good of the son he had never been able to love enough would ease him.

She sprang up, ignoring the dizziness that blurred her vision. Grabbing Daria's arm, she pulled her up to stand next to her.

"Find Gianni," she whispered, her mouth close to the young woman's ear. "Bring him to the duke's chamber."

Daria stared at her mistress. The unnerved, dispirited woman of a moment ago was gone and in her place was an avenging angel with fire in her eyes.

Adrienne grabbed her shoulders and gave her a little push. "Go, quickly now."

Galvanized by the energy that suddenly radiated from her mistress, the slave girl turned and, picking up the hem of her tunic, flew up the stairs.

Within minutes, Adrienne had turned everyone out of the duke's chamber and locked the door behind Daria and Gianni. If she felt a moment of doubt, if misgivings came to trouble her, she gave no indication as she approached the bed.

"*Altezza.*"

Francesco heard the urgency that vibrated through the soft voice and he opened his eyes, alert and aware that something was very wrong.

Adrienne released a breath in relief that his eyes were clear and, for the moment at least, free of pain.

"What is it?"

"Forgive me for disturbing your grace, but something terrible and dangerous is happening and I need your counsel. The only other ones I can trust not to betray me are Daria and Gianni here." She gestured toward the two servants, who had taken their customary position at her feet, Daria on her knees and Gianni sitting cross-legged.

"What is it?" the duke repeated more strongly, the authority of years audible in his voice.

"I have sent three messengers to Alessandro, asking him to come home. Just minutes ago I learned why he has not." Adrienne drew in a deep breath. Then she quickly, succinctly repeated what the messenger had told her.

"Every single one of my messengers has been set upon. That means there is someone in the *palazzo* who is conspiring against the house of Montefiore—" she paused "—or reporting to whoever has contrived this plot." She swallowed before continuing.

"If your grace were to die while Alessandro is still in Rome, it would be simple for someone to seize the reins of the state." She leaned forward in her urgency. "If my reasoning is just, the most logical candidates are my brothers."

"You accuse your own flesh and blood?"

"They are my brothers, but I have no illusions about what they are capable of." As Adrienne said the words, she felt a heaviness, a sadness in her heart.

Then she gave a quick shake of her head. "Besides, I told your grace once before. I am not Isabella Gennaro." Pride had her tilting her chin upward, pride that had nothing to do with arrogance and everything to do with love. "I am Isabella di Montefiore."

The duke nodded once in silent approval. "And if this is as you say? How do you think to stop them?"

"There is no one I can send to Rome, so I will ride myself."

"Are you mad?" The duke struggled up against his pillows.

Adrienne reached out to calm him. "It is the only way. I can send neither Daria nor Gianni and there is no one else I can trust." She paused. "Besides, perhaps then Alessandro will believe me. Believe *in* me."

She gripped his hands. "No one must know that I am gone. Is there someone who can come and care for your grace? Someone with enough authority to keep all but the most necessary away and make everyone believe that I am somewhere in your chambers?" Her voice rose as panic began to pull at her. "No one must know that I am gone! No one!"

"No, this is impossible." The duke pushed her restraining hands away. "Do you have any idea just how dangerous the roads are? Do you know what will happen to you if some brigand realizes you are a woman? We will find someone to whom we can entrust this mission."

But even as he spoke the words, the duke felt a pang of doubt. Whom could he trust implicitly? His counselors? His secretaries? His officials? Some nameless servant? No, he acknowledged. It was a sorry admission to have to make after being a stern but just ruler for more than thirty years, but now, when everything was stripped down to the bare truth, he knew that there was not a single man in his entourage whose loyalty, whose heart, he could unreservedly trust.

If the Gennaros were indeed plotting to seize power, they could have bribed his whole court and every single one of his subjects by now. He had seen enough in this life to know that everyone had a price. It was not always a price that could be paid in coin, but a price nevertheless.

"Please, your grace." Adrienne took a deep breath. "I am with child. I do not want it to grow up without a home and perhaps without a father."

"Are you mad?" The duke's thin fingers twisted in the bedclothes. "How can you even think to ride to Rome if you are breeding?"

"Do you have someone you can entrust with this?" she demanded softly. "Someone you are absolutely sure of?" For a moment it crossed her mind that he might not be absolutely sure of her, either.

"It is our only chance." Adrienne met her father-in-law's eyes and played her last card. "What do you think will happen to a Montefiore child, especially if it is a son, if the Gennaros rule Siena?"

The duke fell back, both his physical pain and his mental anguish mirrored in his emaciated features.

"No, I cannot allow it. No matter what the outcome is, I cannot allow it."

Adrienne took his hands again. "But—" She fell silent when his fingers stiffened as a wave of pain overtook him.

"No," he whispered when the worst of the pain had passed. "I must keep you safe, Isabella. You and your child." A deep breath shuddered in and out of his lungs. "I have never been able to give Alessandro what he needed from me, but I can give him this."

When he opened his eyes, they were keen and alert. "Send to the order of the Dominicans for Friar Bernardo. We were like brothers before he took orders and he will not deny me this last service."

Within an hour Friar Bernardo, his hands tucked into the wide sleeves of his rough black habit, stood in the duke's austerely luxurious bedchamber and listened silently to his old friend's request. His face was gaunt and creased from thirty years of ascetic living and he had the blazing eyes of a man prepared to suffer anything for his faith.

"You are the only one I can trust." Exhausted, the duke lay back against his pillows. "Will you do this for me?"

Friar Bernardo nodded. "I need to ask the abbot for permission, but since I have never asked for anything, there is no reason for him to refuse me."

Feeling their need to exchange a few words in private, Adrienne left the two men alone. Although part of her was relieved that she and her unborn child would be spared the dangers of the journey, she chafed against her enforced inactivity and against the lost opportunity to prove herself to Sandro. Besides, although her father-in-law seemed to trust the monk implicitly, she had her doubts.

When Friar Bernardo emerged from the bedchamber she approached him.

"Will your abbot wish to know why you want leave?"

"He will consider it his duty to ask."

"Will you tell him the truth?" she demanded.

The friar tucked his hands into his sleeves. "Would *madonna* have me lie to a man of the church?"

She twisted her hands. "The church, these days, means allegiance to a Borgia pope." The monk's face remained impassive, but there was a tiny flicker of dislike in his eyes. Going with her impulse, Adrienne decided to trust him. "My brothers will strike a bargain with Borgia if they have not already."

"*Madonna* can rest easy. No one will know my destination."

When Adrienne held out a pouch containing a small fortune in gold coins, he lifted his hands in refusal, but she pressed it on him. "You will need to purchase a good mount—our stables are probably being watched," she said quickly. "And I beg you, Father, to change horses as often as you can get a fresh one, no matter what the cost."

The friar slid the pouch into one of the deep pockets of his habit and turned to go. He was almost at the door when Adrienne ran after him and gripped his sleeve.

"Tell my husband—" she stopped the words of love that rose to her lips "—that I pray for his quick and safe return."

Friar Bernardo's severe features softened and he nodded. Then he slipped through the door, his sandals making barely a sound on the brick tiles.

Chapter Twenty-one

Cesare Borgia's eyes did not waver as he watched Piero Gennaro over his steepled fingers. He had listened for some minutes to Gennaro's ambiguous rambling about the unfortunate conditions in Siena, which he well understood was aimed at provoking some kind of statement or proposition from him. But it was his special skill to get precise and, more often than not, self-incriminating information from others while giving nothing away himself. "Just what is it that you want from me?" Borgia's even tone sounded mildly interested at best.

Piero Gennaro felt the rivulet of sweat run down his spine and he barely restrained himself from squirming in the massive, carved chair that Borgia had offered him. "Francesco di Montefiore is dying."

"So you said."

The terse reminder that he was repeating himself made him feel like a fool.

"His death could make it possible to reverse the unfavorable effects Montefiore rule has had on my beloved city."

Borgia made a noncommittal sound and gestured to Gennaro to continue.

Piero swallowed reflexively although his mouth was dry. "It is the opinion of many that there are others better suited to rule Siena than Montefiore's heir."

"This is very interesting, Don Piero, and I am honored that you have come all the way to Rome to share your cares with me, but—" he gestured briefly with his elegant hands and then steepled them again "—is there something particular you wanted to inform me of?"

Surreptitiously, Piero slid his damp palms along his thighs, wishing that he dared to look away from Borgia's opaque, expressionless eyes, which were paralyzing his ability to think. Damnation, why did Borgia not say something? he thought. Realizing that he had no choice but to spread all his cards on the table, he leaned forward.

"As Don Cesare surely knows, there was a time when the Gennaros were the ruling force in Siena. The Montefiores are naught but usurpers." He made a sound of disgust, underscoring it with a choppy gesture of his hands. "Upstarts who have either killed for or bought their titles."

His breath caught in his throat, making the last words sound strangled. This, he realized, was not quite the right thing to say to someone whose family had gone from nothing to the highest power within a single generation by just those means.

"There are many in Siena who would welcome a return of the Gennaros to power." Hoping to cover his blunder, he blurted out the lie. "And my brother and I are well prepared to wield that power justly and for the good of all." He continued without flinching.

"That is very commendable, but I repeat the question I put to you once before. Just what do you want from me?"

Was that a touch of impatience that he heard in Borgia's mellow voice? Piero paled. No, he admitted, there was no other choice but to use plain words.

"If my family fights Alessandro di Montefiore's succession, there will be civil war. I have no desire to rule a ruined city-state and—" he paused "—it is not in Don Cesare's interest, or in the interest of his holiness and the papal states, that Siena be beggared." Piero lowered his voice. "Nor is it perhaps in Don Cesare's personal interest that Alessandro di Montefiore become master of Siena."

"How so? Alessandro is an excellent *condottiere* who has served me well and who, no doubt, will serve me well again, whether he is the ruler of Siena's son or himself the ruler."

Piero's nerves began to hum. Perhaps it had not been a good idea to come to Borgia with this matter after all. Perhaps he would have been better off hiring a simple cutthroat who asked no questions or purchasing a reliable poison from an alchemist. But then he reminded himself that he needed to be rid of Alessandro tidily. He wanted no blood on his hands. When he became ruler of Siena, he wanted no whispers following him that his brother-in-law's death had been his doing.

"When—if—he becomes master of Siena, his power will be incomparably greater than it is now." Piero relaxed slightly, knowing that he was about to deliver his most convincing argument. "It would not be the first time that a powerful *condottiere* turned against his master."

A fractional narrowing of Borgia's eyes was the only indication that he had hit a sensitive spot, but it was enough, and Piero allowed himself a sigh of relief and a small smile.

"Even in the unlikely case that your theory is correct, Don Piero, would it not be to my disadvantage to deprive myself of my most skilled *condottiere* at a time when I am planning my next campaign?" He lowered his hands and picked up a penknife with a jewel-encrusted handle and began to toy with it. "Or do you perchance possess proof for your theory?"

"My proof is my knowledge of Alessandro di Montefiore," Piero said with as much assurance as deceit. "I have known him all my life and he is, after all, married to my sister."

"Your sister. Ah, yes." Borgia's mouth curved. "Isabella *la bella*. Since you are planning Alessandro's demise with such care, do I presume correctly that you already have plans for her remarriage—" he paused, raising his eyes from the penknife he still fingered to Piero's face "—or whatever?" Briefly it occurred to him that it was time that he thought about his own brother-in-law's demise and his sister Lucrezia's remarriage.

Piero shook his head. "Not yet. I rather thought to wait and see if I had any—suitable offers."

"It is indeed a pity that I already have a wife in France, Don Piero," Borgia said, probing. "Otherwise I might even have been tempted."

"Both of us are men of the world, Don Cesare." He had taken the bait! By God, Borgia had taken the bait! Piero needed all his control not to break out in relieved laughter. "And we know that marriage—even for a well-born lady—is not always the most advantageous path."

"So I was right after all. You do pimp for your sister." Tossing the penknife down, Borgia strode to a table and poured himself a cup of wine.

"I beg to differ, Don Cesare." Piero carefully controlled the rage that rose within him, reminding himself that the woman whom Borgia was talking about was a witch who had somehow supplanted his beloved Bella. With ease, he ignored the fact that he would not have hesitated to sell his Bella to the highest bidder, either.

"Whoever succeeds Alessandro di Montefiore in my sister's bed will not have an easy time of it. She is completely besotted with him."

Borgia drank again. Then he set down the cup and sauntered back to his desk. He leaned forward, slapping his palms on the polished wood with such suddenness that Gennaro shot backward in his chair as if he had been struck. "What do you want from me?" His voice was insidiously low.

"It—it would b-be easy for D-Don Cesare to eliminate Montefiore," he stammered.

"Do you take me for a *bravo* perhaps?"

"N-no, of course not." Piero's eyes began to bulge. "Don Cesare h-has possibilities I can only dream of."

Borgia pushed himself back. What a piddling, miserable excuse for a man, he thought contemptuously. He strode to the window and stared down into the courtyard, where the pope's guard was changing, their yellow-and-black uniforms bright against the pale marble of the building.

As his mind worked like a piece of well-oiled machinery, spinning one thought after another, he unconsciously slid his hand under his shoulder-length dark auburn hair and ran his finger around the edge of an almost healed sore on his neck. He had learned to live with the French disease that was a souvenir of his stay in Naples three years ago.

He would let Alessandro be crowned Duke of Siena, he mused. That would make the worm now sweating behind him sweat a little more. Then he would use Montefiore's skills and his men to besiege his next victim. And when that was done, he would confiscate Montefiore's lances and his artillery before he rid himself the man. And then—he smiled. Then he would play a little game of cat and mouse with Isabella, and when he was done with her, her haughtiness would be a thing of the past.

At his leisure, he would turn his attention to Siena. He had no doubts that it would fall into his lap like a ripe plum from the soft, weak hands of the Gennaros. It was a fat prize and he would make it the jewel of his possessions. He felt a flash of arousal at the thought. Power was the best aphrodisiac. Better than any woman. Better even than the lovely, haughty Isabella.

He turned and rapped out his instructions to Piero Gennaro.

Sandro brooded in the luxurious rooms Cesare Borgia had placed at his disposal. The entrance into the city, with its parade of soldiers and prisoners, was six weeks past. The plans for Borgia's next campaign had been discussed at length and were clear-cut.

He had dispatched all of his duties and knew full well that he could have gone back to Siena weeks ago. Instead, he was still in Rome, attending the amusements and entertainments that vied with one another in extravagance, excess and wantonness, although he found them revolting.

If he were to admit the truth, he was still in the city simply because he was too ashamed of what he had done to return home. Too ashamed to look Isabella in the face.

He rubbed his eyes with the heels of his hands. The bile rose in his throat when he remembered how violently he had touched her, marking her delicate skin. He had been one step away from raping her. He tunneled his fingers into his long hair and tightened them viciously, as if that small pain could somehow begin to expiate the vileness of his actions.

And what had she done? She had reached her hand out to him and given him everything. His stomach contracted as he remembered. And he had taken. Taken everything she had offered because his desire, his need, had been so great that he could not have refused it any more than he could have refused to breathe.

Yet when the light of the new day had come, the enormity of what he had done struck him and he had fled like the basest coward, unable even to contemplate looking her in the face. And now, for the first time in his life, the fear of something paralyzed him to the point of utter inertia. And every day the shame and the fear grew greater and greater still.

When the footman came to tell him that a Dominican friar was urgently asking for an audience, Sandro did not bother to raise his head.

"Later," he snarled. Then his head snapped up as he felt the familiar tingle at the base of his neck. The tingle that had saved his life more than once in battle.

"Wait!"

The footman stopped, his hand already on the ornate door handle.

"Bring him in."

Moments later, Friar Bernardo stumbled into the room, his creased face gray with fatigue, his black habit dusty and travel-stained.

"I bear an urgent message from the duke, your excellency's father."

Frowning, Sandro bade the friar to sit and poured him a cup of wine.

In a low, halting voice that bespoke how close to the brink of exhaustion he was, the elder monk recounted what he himself had been told.

Perching on the corner of a table, Sandro listened. His father was dying. Something moved within him— sadness, regret for opportunities lost, but no true grief. He had schooled himself too well not to care about his father's indifference to feel grief.

"You say that the Gennaros waylaid the other messengers?"

"That is what Donna Isabella believes."

Was this perhaps some kind of elaborate trick? The reflexive moment of doubt, of suspicion, rose to torment him, but he shoved it away. "How do I know that my father really sent you?" he demanded.

"Forgive me." The friar shook his head. "Age and fatigue have softened my brain." He reached inside the shirt he wore under his habit and pulled a leather cord over his head. Then he stretched out his hand, the Duke of Siena's great seal ring on his leathery palm.

In one fluid motion Sandro was up and shouting for his servants.

"Prepare to return to Siena and ready my horse. Tell Don Michele that we ride in one hour." He turned toward the friar. "You will rest, *padre,* and return to Siena at your leisure."

Friar Bernardo shook his head. "If it is the same to your excellency, I will leave, also. I would rather not rest my head in a Vatican ruled by a Borgia."

Already on his way out of his apartment, Sandro nodded.

"Your excellency?"

"Yes?" He turned, impatience vibrating in his voice.

"Donna Isabella also gave me a message."

"Yes?" Suddenly every muscle, every nerve in Sandro's body tensed with anticipation.

"She asked me to wish your excellency a speedy and safe return home."

Sandro felt his throat tighten with disappointment. He knew he did not deserve it, but what he would have given to hear a word of forgiveness, of love.

Friar Bernardo saw the pain in Alessandro's eyes as he had seen the unspoken love in the pale, drawn face of his wife. He could have said something, but he knew that that was something the two young people needed to straighten out alone.

"I shall return momentarily, *padre.*"

"Will Borgia let your excellency leave?"

Sandro tossed his head so that his hair swung behind his shoulders. "I am not planning to ask him for permission."

Chapter Twenty-two

Sandro's feet touched the ground even before his mount, lathered with sweat and foaming at the mouth, had come to a stop. He had left Michele and the two men-at-arms who had accompanied him behind hours ago and galloped ahead. Waving the servants who rushed toward him aside, he took the stairs two at a time, shedding his gloves, his mud-caked cloak and plumed beret as he went.

The ride from Rome had been hellish, the roads turned to a morass by the sudden rains blown in from the sea. His body was so close to exhaustion that he could not have defined what his emotions were. The physical fatigue had numbed him, distilling every thought, every feeling, down to a blind sense of urgency that kept him moving.

When he burst into his father's apartments, there was a flurry of movement among the courtiers who stood about in small groups despite the early hour. Some only stared. Some spoke. Some moved toward him. But he ignored them as he tore through the rooms. As he flung open the door to the anteroom, the guards shifted to attention, their lances crossing in front of the door to the bedchamber.

Seeing who they had before them, the men stepped aside immediately to let him pass. Sandro heard one of the guards begin to speak as he pressed down the heavy brass handle of the door and found it locked.

"What in damnation—" Sandro whirled around to face the guards again.

"Madonna Isabella keeps the door locked from the inside, your excellency."

The mention of his wife's name, followed within seconds by the grate of a key in the lock, had Sandro stiffening. Suddenly a fear the likes of which he had never felt before—not in battle, not in hand-to-hand combat—iced his skin. Gathering all his courage, he slowly turned around.

The sound of galloping hooves across the Campo had startled Adrienne from a fitful sleep. Within seconds she was out of her chair and at the window, but there was no one to be seen. Only the empty square in the rain-washed dawn.

Restless, she did not return to her chair but began to wander around the bedchamber. She was beyond weariness. Her muscles throbbed. Even her bones seemed to ache. But the pain was faraway, fuzzy, almost as if it belonged to someone else.

She stopped at the duke's bedside. Unable to watch him suffer constant pain, she had begged him to permit her to give him the drug she had obtained and he had finally acceded. Now he lay still, drifting in and out of consciousness as he had for the past days. He was waiting, she knew. Holding on tenaciously to that last thread of life until his son would come.

Suddenly sounds in the anteroom penetrated her consciousness. She heard a door bounce off a wall.

Heard the clang of the guards' lances. Oh God, she thought, had her brother come already? Had they somehow learned about Friar Bernardo's mission and decided to speed the duke's death?

Then she heard the voices. They were muffled beyond recognition by the massive oak door and she had not understood the words that had been spoken, but she knew, she suddenly knew beyond all doubt, that finally, finally Sandro had come home.

Her heart pounding, Adrienne ran across the room and without hesitation turned the key and pulled open the door.

For long moments the world around them ceased to exist as both stood perfectly still, their eyes a mirror of their souls, where emotions flowed like a fast-running river.

She had waited so long for this moment, Adrienne thought. She wanted to run into his arms, but she found herself hesitating, unsure of what his reaction—and hers—would be.

She was so pale and so fragile, Sandro thought, her eyes so bruised and heavy with sorrow. How much of the blame lay at his door? he wondered. Staggered by the depth, the purity of the emotions that surged through him, he lifted a hand toward her face. He half expected her to shrink away from his touch, but she did not. On a wave of gratitude and hope, he brushed his fingertips over her cheek.

"Are you all right, Isabella?"

"Yes." She laid her hand against his chest. "And you?" Now that he stood here before her, whole and, for the moment at least, safe, relief flooded through her. She could feel the strong, quick beat of his heart

against her palm and the rhythm seeped into her like
a magic elixir, lending her strength.

Behind him, the anteroom began to fill with courtiers expecting to witness the ceremony of the transfer
of power and the dying of their prince.

Looking past Sandro's shoulder, she gave a quick
shake of her head. "Do not let them in yet. He needs
to see you alone."

Sandro nodded and Adrienne stepped back to let
him pass, locking the door behind him. She moved by
him to lead the way toward the bed, but he stopped her
with a light, undemanding touch on her arm.

"Wait, Isabella. Please."

She looked over her shoulder at Sandro and then
back toward the bed. "It will keep."

Sandro shook his head and gently turned her
around to face him. "Let me say it now, Isabella,
while I still have the courage to do it."

Adrienne opened her mouth to deny the necessity
for words, for apologies. She wanted to tell him that
she understood, that her heart was so full of love for
him that there was no room left for rancor, for bitterness. But then she remembered how close Sandro had
come to taking something precious, something irre-
placeable, from them both, and she remained silent.
He needed to say the words, she realized. And she
needed to hear them.

"There is no excuse for what I did, Isabella." He
met her eyes and held them. "There are reasons—my
own stupidity, my blindness, my compulsion to believe the worst—but no excuses." Sandro paused. He
needed badly to touch her, but that would make it too
easy, he knew, so he kept his hands at his sides.

"Despite what I saw every time you looked at me, despite what I felt every time you touched me, I could not bring myself to believe that there were no lies in you. That what you were offering me was real."

Adrienne had been so sure that she had already long forgiven him, but now, suddenly, unexpectedly, anger surged up within her. "And do you believe now?" she demanded. "Or will I see the doubts and suspicions in your eyes the next time a man looks at me?" She took a deep breath. "And what of my brothers? Will you judge me by the same measuring stick that you judge them?"

"No—"

She held up her hand to silence him. "When Friar Bernardo came to you, Sandro, tell me that your first thought was not that I had plotted with my brothers to betray you." She saw the truth in his eyes and was tempted to close her eyes against it, but she did not.

"I cannot make you a promise I may not be able to keep, Isabella. In time—" he laced his fingers in an uncharacteristic gesture of nervousness "—if you give me that time, perhaps I will be able to give you all the promises you ask for."

Time! Panic sliced through her. How could she give him time, when she did not know if she had it to give? How could she give him time when she lived in constant awareness, constant fear, that the next breath would find her in another world, another body?

"Why did you not come home sooner?" Driven by her fears, she lashed out at him. "Do you know what would have happened if—" Her hand flew up to her mouth as the long-suppressed tears rose to clog her throat. She had not cried for six long, terrible weeks, but now that he was here, she was suddenly losing the control she had held on to so desperately.

"I was ashamed. And afraid." He exhaled with relief as he spoke the words, as if he had lanced a festering wound within himself. He raised his hands to cup her face.

"Can you understand that, Isabella? I had almost raped you to avenge myself for an imagined betrayal, and in answer you had given me yourself and your love, holding nothing back." The memory took the bottom out of his stomach. For a moment Sandro closed his eyes and remembered how she had stood there in the pool of her white nightgown and held her hand out to him.

"That is why I could not look into your eyes the next morning. And because I was afraid that I would find disgust there. Or worse yet, fear."

He filled his lungs with a long, trembling breath. "I spent six weeks only half-alive at best. I was paralyzed with shame and terrified that when I found the courage to come back you would not want me anymore." His thumbs feathered over her cheekbones in a silent plea. "Can you forgive me, Isabella?"

When she said nothing, he felt a flash of pure terror. "If you can forgive me, then tell me, I beg you. I need to hear you say the words."

Her heart had been cleansed by his words and Adrienne felt it fill with love for this beautiful, tormented man. A love so great, so pure, that it left no room for anger or bitterness or resentment. She raised her hands to touch his face.

"Yes, Sandro." She smiled. "I forgive you with all my heart." Suddenly she felt light, so light, so unfettered, that she had the physical sensation of floating.

She had freed him, she thought, but she had also freed herself.

Rising on her toes, she brushed her lips over his mouth to seal her pledge. "Come now, my love," she whispered. "He is waiting."

Hand in hand they approached the bed where Duke Francesco di Montefiore lay dying.

Sandro knelt at his father's bedside and looked at the emaciated old man who had become a ghost of his former self. Now, when he was filled to overflowing with the love he felt for Isabella, he would have wanted to feel at least a shadow of love for this man who had given him life. But all he felt was a deep regret for chances missed.

Reaching inside his shirt, he took out the golden seal ring that Friar Bernardo had brought him. Taking his father's frail hand in his, he slipped the ring back onto the old man's index finger.

"Alessandro?"

"Yes, Father."

"Thank God." The duke's lids lifted and he rolled his head to the side. "I do not have much time left, my son." He grimaced as pain cut through him.

Adrienne moved to get the stoppered bottle with the poppy syrup.

"No." The duke raised his hand a fraction of an inch off the coverlet. "I do not want to blur these last few moments.

"Alessandro, there was so much I could never give you, but—" he rested for a moment before he continued "—I have always been proud of you."

Sandro felt a wave of sadness. What would he have given to have heard those words years ago? When he had been a boy trying desperately to earn the love of

a grim and distant but nevertheless beloved father.
When he had been a youth trying to secure at least his
father's respect.

"Forgive me for not giving you these words—and
others—long ago," he said, as if reading Sandro's
thoughts. "But I could not. I loved my wife beyond all
measure, but our love was not blessed by children. I
never forgave your mother for bearing me my only
child."

The pain winded him, but he spoke quickly, afraid
that time would be too short. "And you—you, Alessandro, were the constant reminder that I had betrayed my wife to beget myself an heir. Perhaps
now—" his eyes shifted to Isabella and back to his son
"—you will understand just what that means." Exhausted, he let his eyes fall closed. "Perhaps now you
will not judge me as harshly."

"Father, I—"

The duke cut Sandro off with a shake of his head.
"Your wife—" He glanced toward his daughter-in-
law, his eyes sending her a silent thank-you. "You are
fortunate, Alessandro. May she bear you sons."

His breath whistled past his lips as another wave of
pain took him. "Call them in now," he said, the effort distorting his voice to a strained whisper. "This
duty to you I will fulfill."

Silently Sandro walked to the door and unlocked it.
As he pulled it open, the hum of conversation in the
anteroom ceased as all eyes turned to him. At his gesture, the courtiers crowded into the bedchamber.

"All of you—" the old man's stern gaze swept
around the room with his accustomed authority
"—shall witness that I bequeath my title and my
power to my son and heir, Alessandro di Monte-

fiore." His voice was thin and reedy but audible in every corner of the large chamber. "I have prepared him well for the tasks that lie before him and he will rule you fairly and to your greater good."

With the last remnants of his strength, the duke slipped the seal ring from his finger and onto Sandro's. "I bless you." As he raised his hand to make the sign of the cross, his thin body arched up in pain. When he fell back, his eyes stayed open, staring into eternity.

As Sandro reached to close his father's eyes, a priest on the other side of the bed was already chanting a prayer for the dead. He raised his wife to stand beside him and faced his courtiers.

"The duke is dead. Long live the duke." The courtiers' cries echoed through the chamber.

Seeing that Isabella was close to collapsing, Sandro slid an arm around her and pulled her against him to lend her the support of his body. And so they stood, flank against flank, as the courtiers filed by to affirm their allegiance to their duke by kissing Sandro's ring and the hem of the new duchess's gown.

By the time the ceremony was finished, Adrienne was holding herself on her feet by sheer willpower. When the courtiers had filed out of the bedchamber, she and Sandro turned to face the bed one more time. Then slowly, they, too, left the chamber.

They had just departed the ducal apartments when Sandro felt Isabella's arm tremble on his and her step falter. Ignoring the guards, ignoring the courtiers who still loitered in the corridor, he picked her up in his arms and strode toward their apartments.

Chapter Twenty-three

Sandro shouldered his way into Isabella's rooms and glared at his wife's ladies, who knelt in deep curtsies before them.

"Up, all of you!" he ordered, his voice rough with worry and his own exhaustion. "Help *madonna*."

Gently he lowered her onto a bench strewn with pillows and knelt at her side. She had gone as white as a linen sheet, her skin drawn tightly over her cheekbones, and only the uneven pulse that fluttered at the base of her throat indicated that she was still breathing.

Feeling utterly helpless, he watched as the women placed cool, wet cloths on her forehead and at the nape of her neck. When Daria dipped a thin cambric handkerchief in a cup that held a dark liquid smelling strongly of brandy and something medicinal, he stayed her hand.

"What is that?"

"Arnica flowers steeped in brandy, your grace. It is a restorative and will not harm *madonna*."

He nodded and released her. He knew of the strange bond between his wife and the slave girl, but still he watched her like a hawk as she squeezed a few drops onto Isabella's lips and rubbed her temples and the pulses behind her ears with the liquid-soaked handkerchief.

"*Madonna* will be all right," she whispered. "All she needs is rest." She sent her master an oblique look. "She has not slept in a bed since your grace's father fell ill."

All the while he had been sulking in Rome, drowning in his fears and his self-pity, Isabella had been depleting herself at his father's deathbed. This knowledge sapped his own strength and Sandro lowered his head, leaning it against her hip.

When he felt her shift, his head snapped up.

Her head spinning, Adrienne found her vision blurred and suddenly was terrified that she had returned to her own body, her own time. "Sandro?"

"Yes, *tesoro*." He cupped her face with one hand. "How are you feeling?"

Relief flowed through her at the sound of his voice, returning a little color to her face. Adrienne blinked and slowly the world around her came back into focus. "What happened?"

"You fainted." He fought to keep his touch light when what he really wanted to do was crush her against him. "Daria tells me that you have not slept in a bed for weeks."

She shrugged off his words.

"Will you be all right now? I need to get out of these clothes." He did not want to leave her, but he could smell the sweat and the scent of horseflesh on himself and he knew that he looked as if he had taken a mud bath in his clothes.

"Of course." She pushed herself up so that she was half sitting on the bench.

Daria melted away, leaving them alone. Sandro opened his mouth to tell Isabella that he would be back as soon as possible, but without warning, the memory of the last time they had been together, here, in this room, returned to torment him. Suddenly he was terribly unsure. Would she welcome him? Could she? If the memory of his violence turned his own stomach, what would she feel when she had been its victim?

"What is wrong?" Adrienne touched Sandro's unshaven cheek.

"I am not sure that you want me to come back." He looked away from her face. "I would not blame you if you did not."

"Sandro, look at me." When he had met her eyes, she continued. "We put it to rest—with your words and mine." She reached for his hands and laced his fingers with hers. "Yes, we will remember it, as one remembers pain. But the memory will fade. Believe me." She smiled and gave his hands a little squeeze to emphasize her words. "If memories of pain did not fade, no woman would have more than one child."

Sandro's stomach lurched at this new reminder of pain Isabella had suffered because of him.

Adrienne saw the shadow that crossed Sandro's face and she would have wanted to tell him that she was not afraid of the pain of bearing the child who was already growing in her belly. She was afraid, yes, but not of that.

She unlinked their hands and touched her fingers to his cheek. "Go now." Her mouth curved. "I shall be waiting for you."

While Sandro bathed, Adrienne lay in the warm, rose-scented water her women had prepared for her and felt the tension, the fatigue, the sorrow of the past weeks drain out of her. She let herself empty of all thought, all anxiety, knowing instinctively that she desperately needed a few hours of respite.

Afterward, Daria brought her one of the simple white nightgowns she preferred and she slipped into it, covering it with the jeweled brocade robe she had woken up in so many months ago. Her women had washed her hair and brushed it in front of the fire until it dried. Now it hung in a golden curtain down her back, its only adornment a thin circlet of pearls.

When all the women had gone, Adrienne wandered through the chamber, which was redolent with the fragrance of sweet-smelling herbs and flower petals that simmered in a pot on top of a glowing coal brazier. She stopped at the table, which was full of dishes with tasty tidbits to tempt the palate—flaky crescent pastries, thin slices of tender peacock meat, artichoke hearts spiced with nutmeg and ginger, dark red cherries cooked in wine and honey. But her momentary weariness was too great even to reach out for a taste.

The couch, covered with a throw of lynx fur, beckoned. Adrienne lay down to wait for Sandro. Within moments she was asleep.

When Sandro stepped inside the bedchamber, his gaze went immediately to where Isabella lay, her robe shimmering like the plumage of a rare bird against the pale fur. He shut the door behind him with an audible click, but still she did not move. Controlling the desire to race across the room and wake her, he stayed where he was and watched her instead. She lay against the colorful silk pillows, her hand tucked, childlike, under her cheek. Although she was still pale, a trace of color had returned to her skin.

He had not been able to come to terms with her apparently boundless capacity for love and forgiveness, her generosity of spirit. Would he ever become accustomed to it? he asked himself. It made him feel so inadequate, so paltry.

His gaze wandered around the room and stopped at the almost life-size portrait of her that had been painted before their wedding. He looked from the painting to the living, breathing woman and then back again. What could Pinturicchio have been thinking of? he asked himself. The woman in the portrait was arrogant and cold, her eyes covetous and calculating. Only the features and body were the same. It was as if Pinturicchio had painted Isabella's evil twin.

But then he remembered that this was indeed the Isabella he had first seen at their wedding. The Isabella who had scrutinized him like a housewife inspecting a side of beef. He shook his head. It was an enigma beyond his understanding. An enigma like her disappearance, which, strangely enough, he had not questioned very deeply. Why had he accepted that so easily while he had painstakingly kept all his other suspicions, his doubts, alive? He had no answer to that. It had simply been a point of faith that had slipped into his brain and his heart without a ripple and taken hold.

Slowly he crossed the room toward her. She did not even stir when he picked her up and carried her toward the bed. He worked the robe off easily and laid her onto the soft mattress, then shed his own robe together with the loose shirt and hose he wore under it. When he slipped into the bed beside her, she did not wake, but with a soft sigh she turned into his body as if seeking his warmth.

Sandro slid his arms around her. His face nestled against her hair and he inhaled her fragrance of roses and woman. He had come home, he thought as his fingers sifted through her hair, gleaming like spun gold in the candlelight. He had finally come home.

As Adrienne came awake, her habitual disorientation dissipated immediately, even before she had opened her eyes. For once, she knew exactly where she was, for every single one of her sensory perceptions was of Sandro. Her palm lay against the hard planes of his chest and she felt his strong, even heartbeat beneath it. She heard his regular breathing, his breath lightly ruffling the fine hair at the crown of her head. Her face was nestled against his shoulder, and every time she inhaled, she drew in the familiar scent of his skin.

She had fallen asleep on the couch, she realized, and he had carried her to bed without waking her. The thought brought a smile to her mouth. Now, as she lay here within the curve of Sandro's arm, the past weeks seemed almost unreal—a nightmare viewed from the vantage point of a sunny morning. The sickness, the pain, the death that she had lived with had receded, and suddenly she felt so incredibly alive that her skin tingled.

Careful not to wake him, she shifted to lean on her elbow. The candles were still burning brightly so she knew that she had not slept long. Still, she felt refreshed as if she had slept for hours and hours. She stretched luxuriously, the movement bringing her whole body flush against Sandro.

Adrienne felt the rhythm of his heartbeat change a fraction of a moment before he opened his eyes. He awoke as he always did, alert, eyes clear.

"Did I wake you?" The fingers of the hand that lay on his chest spread in an unconscious caress. "I am sorry."

"It has been a long time since I have been woken quite so pleasantly." He saw her eyes narrow and flash and almost laughed aloud with pure joy.

With a deft tug, he pulled her to lie partway across his body. "I am glad to see that some things do not change. You—" The rest of the teasing words died on his lips as he fell into her eyes. He framed her face with his hands.

"God, I have missed you, Isabella." His thumbs stroked the soft skin under her chin and then slid upward to trace the line of her lower lip. "Do you know just how much I have missed you?"

Adrienne gave a barely perceptible shake of her head. "Show me."

"Are you sure, Isabella?" His hands stilled. "Are you sure you want my hands on you?"

Her eyes lit up with a mischievous light. "Try it and see."

His hands tightened as her breath brushed his mouth. "Do not tease me." His blood was beginning to swim with desire from her words alone.

"I do not think—" she stretched upward, punctuating her words with a row of tiny kisses along the line of his jaw "—I said anything about teasing."

Sandro groaned softly as her leg shifted over his aroused body. Turning slightly, he rolled her off him and moved to put at least a handbreadth of distance between their bodies, knowing that unless he did, it would be over before it had truly begun. Then, as he bent to take her mouth, his fingers began to undo the laces of her nightgown.

Unsure of his own control, he did not take off her gown. Although he wanted to touch her so badly, to feel the texture of her skin against his fingertips, he only smoothed back the thin linen to expose her breasts.

Adrienne kept her eyes on Sandro's face as he peeled back her nightgown. Already half-aroused, she felt desire surge through her blood as she watched his face. Watched his eyes widen with arousal, watched his nostrils begin to quiver and a muscle jump uncontrollably in his cheek. She knew him well enough to know how close he was to the edge, but still he did not touch her.

Instead he lowered his head and let his mouth roam over her face. He brushed a kiss over her temple. He tasted the tender skin beneath her ear. He outlined the curve of her jaw with the tip of his tongue.

He wanted to linger over her. To show her all the gentleness that he was capable of—so much gentleness that it would drive the memory of his transgressions from her mind.

Shifting, Adrienne offered him her mouth, but he only feathered his lips briefly over hers, ignoring her invitation. Again and again he teased her with light touches of his lips. Even when she started to move beneath him, her hips restless and seeking, he did not take more.

"Sandro." His name came out on a sob. "Please." She hooked a foot behind his calf to bring him closer and still he resisted. She had needed the tenderness, but now she needed the blaze of passion that would burn away her burdens, her fears. Desperate, she reached up and, twining both hands in his hair, pulled him toward her until they were mouth against mouth. Anchoring him there, she slid her tongue past his lips.

He had been holding on to his control by a thread. But when he felt the wet heat of her tongue in his mouth, the thread was severed with one stroke.

Suddenly they were both frantic. Their mouths fused, they raced their hands over skin already damp, driving each other upward.

Sandro broke away from her mouth, wanting to slow the relentless momentum of their passion, but she dragged him back. She didn't want gentleness now. She wanted a passionate affirmation of life in the midst of death and danger. Yielding to her demands, he gave it to her.

The nightgown tore as he stripped it off. As she kicked it away, she was already entwining her legs with his, opening for him.

Suddenly afraid of his own strength, Sandro rolled over onto his back, pulling her with him. He saw bewilderment in her eyes as she found herself lying on top of him, but then he was taking her mouth again.

It was an unaccustomed, erotic feeling to lie on top of Sandro's body, his aroused flesh pressing into her belly. Then she felt him hook his hands behind her thighs and bring her knees forward so that she straddled him. Slowly he swept his hands up over her hips, her ribs, pushing her up.

"What are you doing?" Even though she was dizzy with the passion he had already awoken in her, she flushed with embarrassment at her brazen posture.

"Have you not read Ovid?" He smiled wickedly. "The ancient Romans did this all the time."

Not giving her a chance to reply, he slid his fingers between their bodies to stroke her. He watched her melt against his touch and was sure that he had never seen anything so arousing.

Her body overwhelmed by sensation, Adrienne was unable to move. His fingertips and the flexing of his aroused body against her sensitive flesh, brought her so close to the peak that she could almost taste the release. Her head tipped back and her eyes closed in anticipation of the ultimate pleasure.

Then he was lifting her, fitting her to him. Poised at the gate of her body, he slid his hands up her rib cage until he cupped her breasts.

"Look at me, Isabella." He brushed his thumbs over the crests.

Her eyes, heavy with passion, opened and met his. Slowly he slid her down, down until their bodies melded completely.

She had never felt so open to him before, Adrienne thought as he filled her. As she settled fully onto him, he brought his hands back down to her hips. Gripping her, he began to lift her, a little at first, then more and more.

The pressure and pleasure began to build and her hands curved around his arms, seeking purchase in the midst of the tempest. When he arched his own hips upward as he brought her down, she crested with a cry.

But he did not let her come down from the peak. Instead his hips kept moving. Freeing his arms from her grip, he braced her palms flat against his shoulders and began to touch her.

She stilled at his first touch, but he shook his head. "No, keep moving," he urged. "Ride me." His fingers slid to the point where their bodies were joined. "Ride me."

And she rode him as the pleasure rose and rose farther. Then when it finally began to peak, she went utterly still again, paralyzed by the beginnings of release. Now Sandro took over. Took over her movement and his. He moved, coaxing a wave of pleasure from her and then another until she was sure that she would go mad. When the final blinding climax came, they both held still and shattered.

She lay on top of him, their bodies still joined, the sweat pooling between them. His hand stroked lazily up and down her back and they both drifted in that half-conscious world where the pleasure had catapulted them.

"I love you," she murmured into his neck, already more than half-asleep.

"And I love you." Sandro shifted and brushed his mouth over her temple. Keeping their bodies fused, he rolled to the side.

Adrienne's lids lifted and she gave him a sleepy smile. "Are you going to make love to me again?"

"Later." He kissed her on the tip of her nose. "When you are not half-asleep."

"Mmm." She burrowed her face into his shoulder. "You have given me a child, you know."

He smiled into her hair. "Is not ten minutes afterward a little soon to tell, love?"

"No," she murmured. "Not ten minutes." The words were beginning to slur as she slipped into sleep. "Six weeks."

Sandro's head shot up from the pillow. "What are you talking about?" He tipped her face up to his, but she was fast asleep.

He closed his eyes and lowered his forehead to touch Isabella's. If it had not been for her, their child would have been conceived in anger and violence. He gathered her close and wondered if he would ever be able to forgive himself. It was a long time before he slept.

Chapter Twenty-four

Adrienne recognized the scarlet Borgia seal with its charging bull even before the messenger handed it to Sandro. She tried to keep still as she watched him slit it open but she failed and began to pace, lacing and unlacing her hands.

She heard the rustle of paper as Sandro tossed the message onto his desk, but she did not turn around. Pressing her linked hands against her midriff, she waited for him to tell her what she already knew. Even when he had begun to speak, she hoped that the words she would hear would be other than those she expected.

"Borgia writes that he has decided to begin the siege of Pesaro as soon as possible." Sandro laughed grimly. "Poor Giovanni Sforza will now pay through the nose for having been Lucrezia Borgia's first husband."

"And?" Her throat was so tight that she could hardly speak. "What else does he write?"

"He asks me to send my troops ahead to Pesaro under the command of my lieutenant and—"

Adrienne stiffened as if in expectation of a physical blow.

"—to come to Forlì before I join them."

The world darkened around her and she swayed.

"He wants to take counsel with his *condottieri* before the campaign begins."

She heard his words indistinctly, as if they came from somewhere far away.

"What in God's name does he want to take counsel with us for?" Sandro grumbled. "Everything was discussed in Rome down to the last detail." Exasperated, he tunneled both hands through his hair, wishing for a moment that his father were still alive. No matter what their differences, their difficulties, had been, he had had a healthy respect for his father's opinion.

As she reached for the back of a chair to support herself, Adrienne concentrated on filling her lungs with sufficient air, but her throat was locked.

"Isabella!"

Her legs crumpled and the last thing she heard before the black curtain descended was Sandro calling her name.

When she regained consciousness, she was still lying on the floor, her head cradled in Sandro's lap. Immediately she struggled to get up, but he held her firmly yet gently.

"Shh, lie still, *tesoro.* The doctor will be here in a moment.

"No!" Her eyes wide and terrified, she twisted out of his grasp. From the corners of her eyes she saw that there were servants standing about. "Get them out of here!" She gripped the front of his doublet with both hands. "Get them all out of here." She gave him a little shake. "Please."

"Isabella, you fainted," he soothed in a slow and patient tone, as if she were a fractious child. "You must let the doctor examine you."

"No, I tell you!" The fear left a metallic taste on her tongue, not unlike the taste of blood. "Get everyone out of here." She lowered her voice to a desperate whisper. "I have to speak to you alone."

Seeing her agitation, Sandro decided that giving in to her would do her less harm for the moment than insisting on having the doctor look at her.

He beckoned to the nearest footman and gave him his orders. Within moments the door had closed behind the last servant.

Adrienne was half sitting, half kneeling on the floor, her hands still clutching Sandro's doublet. Gently he loosened her fingers. "We are alone now, love." He curled his hands around hers and kissed first one palm then the other. "What is it?"

That first surge of panic had receded, and now Sandro's calm, forbearing tone made Adrienne feel foolish. But she had no reason to feel foolish, she reminded herself. She knew. *She knew.*

For months she had tried to prepare herself for this moment. She had reflected long and hard about the words, the reasoning she would choose. She had told herself that she would speak calmly. But now, in the face of the actual event, the words spilled out rashly, disregarding all tact, all diplomacy, all logic.

"You must not go, Sandro. You cannot. You have to stay clear of Cesare Borgia." Her heartbeat was so loud in her ears that she could barely hear her own words. "Borgia means you harm, as do my brothers. Do you not understand?" She tried to free her hands, but he held her fast, so she pounded his chest with their linked hands in impotent fury. "Do you not understand that he will kill you?"

Sandro was watching her with a patient, indulgent smile and she knew exactly what he was thinking. He would humor her a little and then he would coax and cosset her out of what he was sure was the irrational mood of a woman with child.

"I grant you that your brothers would do me harm, but I have faith in their ineptness." He sent her a cocky smile. "As far as Borgia is concerned, I have no quarrel with him. He is paying me and my troops a very handsome sum, but we are easily worth that and more. It would be to his own detriment to harm me now, when the campaign is about to begin."

Adrienne shook her head at his foolish confidence. "Have you not seen that Borgia does not always need reasons for his cruelty?" she demanded. "Have you not seen that he enjoys cruelty for its own sake?" She bit her lip to stop herself from saying more.

"Of course I have seen that." Sandro dismissed the observation with a shrug. "But I have also seen that he does not let his penchant for cruelty or violence get in the way of his own personal advantage."

"That is exactly it!" Adrienne cried. "His own personal advantage." She shifted onto her knees to lend strength to her words.

Sandro was looking at her as if she had gone a little mad and she wanted to shake him until he understood, really understood, what she was saying.

"He wants Siena." She paused. "And he wants me."

His eyes narrowed and cooled and she suddenly wondered if she had made a terrible mistake.

"What are you talking about?"

She paused for a moment, yet she had no choice but to continue. She had said too much already. "Oh, Sandro, do you not remember how he looked at me?"

"A man would have to be dead not to look at you, Isabella. But as I remember it—" his black eyebrows drew together in a frown "—it was not Borgia who courted you with extraordinary persistence."

He was withdrawing from her. Even though he still held her hands, she could feel his touch grow remote.

"But that is the least of it. He would use me and discard me with no compunctions." She pressed his hands, willing him to believe her. "It is Siena that he is greedy for."

Saying nothing, Sandro looked into her eyes for a long time. Then he disengaged their hands and stood in one lithe motion. He paced the length of the study to stare out of a window, his head warring with his heart.

Borgia was a cruel, power-hungry man, but he was no fool, Sandro reflected. Attacking cities that were papal vicarates, cities he had been authorized to make war against by his father, Pope Alexander, was one thing. Usurping the power in the independent city-state of Siena, where the Montefiores had wielded power since his grandfather had been chosen over a Gennaro, would be an entirely different matter.

And if it were true, how could Isabella possibly know what Borgia was planning? Unless— He shook his head as his mind obstinately took the old road again. But in his heart he knew better, he assured himself. With a sigh he turned and strode back to where she still knelt on the floor.

She saw the doubts in his eyes. She had failed, she thought, and the awful, hollow feeling inside her grew.

She had known from the beginning that what she needed most was his trust. She had known that the moment would come when he would have to trust her, to believe her implicitly in order to survive. Now the moment was here and she had failed. Oh, God, she thought. If only the old duke were still alive. Perhaps she would have had an ally.

Then he held out both hands to her and Adrienne felt hope leap up in her heart. She put her hands in his and he lifted her up, the only sound in the room the rustle of velvet and the light *chink* of the teardrops of onyx that decorated her gown.

"You are really sure?"

Adrienne nodded, afraid to trust her voice.

"How do you know this?" The moment the words were out Sandro was already half regretting his question. But the words were said, and although he found his mouth suddenly gone dry in anticipation of her answer, he pushed on. "Are your brothers involved in this? Have they taken you into their confidence?"

"If they had, do you truly think that I would have been silent until now?" Almost afraid to breathe, she waited for his answer.

"No." He repeated the denial, more strongly this time. "No."

Relief flowed through Adrienne, weakening her muscles, and she leaned her forehead against his chest.

"But why are you so sure?" His logical mind still demanded answers. "How do you know?"

She looked up at him and shook her head. This was one of the burdens she would always live with, she thought. This knowledge was hers and hers alone and she would never be able to share it with anyone.

"Call it intuition. Or second sight. Or whatever you will." She squeezed Sandro's hands. "But I know."

Again he gazed into her eyes for a long, long time. For so long that she began to tense again.

"I cannot avoid Borgia completely. A contract has been signed. Money has changed hands. And I have an obligation to fulfill." He spoke quickly, thrusting out his chin in an instinctive gesture of pride. "A Montefiore does not go back on his word." He grazed her cheek lightly with the back of his hand. "Do you understand that?"

Realizing just how much he was giving her, Adrienne nodded, feeling a wave of relief. "Yes. But stay away from Forlì. Please." She lifted her hands to his face. "Promise me that you will stay away from Forlì, no matter what. No matter what," she repeated.

"I told you once before that I do not want to make promises I cannot keep."

She drew breath to interrupt him, but he placed a finger on her lips to silence her.

"No, hear me out, Isabella. I will do my best to stay away from Forlì. If, for some reason, I cannot avoid going there, I will exercise extreme caution." He smiled confidently, sure that he had satisfied her. "Is that good enough?" He took the finger he had used to silence her on a leisurely journey of her lips.

"Sandro, have you not understood a single word?" The relief disappeared and Adrienne felt the knot in her stomach form again. "All the caution in the world will do you no good if you go to Forlì." Her voice rose, reflecting her agitation. "You are one man. How well do you think you can protect yourself, alone, against Borgia and his henchmen once he gets you inside the fortress?"

"Isabella—" Sandro shook his head, his patience fraying. "I have promised you what I can. Would you have me lie?"

"No, I do not want you to lie," she cried. "I want you to promise and mean it." Her fingers curled again into his doublet. "Sandro, I love you." Her voice grew shrill. "I love you." Panic was rising within her like thick swirls of smoke. "I cannot lose you. I cannot lo—"

Suddenly she stopped and stilled completely. So completely that even her breathing became unnoticeable. Her eyes, huge and terrified, were trained on Sandro's face, but she did not see him. Instead she found herself witnessing the last grisly scene of the life of Alessandro di Montefiore. But she was not merely observing what Isabella had described in her diary. She was *there*.

Her hands were curled around the cold marble of the balustrade of the spectator's gallery that looked onto the huge hall, which was draped in scarlet. She could smell the fresh sawdust that had been strewn beneath the executioner's block. She heard the drumroll reverberate from the gray stone walls. She saw Sandro, head high, eyes blazing, being led into the hall from a side door.

Sandro stared at his wife. She had fallen silent, her frenetic outburst cut off in the middle of a word. Her hands remained twisted in the fabric of his doublet, and she had stilled so totally that she looked as if she had turned to stone. She stared, her eyes glassy and unfocused, their expression as terrified as if she were gazing upon all the horrors of hell.

The unearthly silence, the utter rigidity of her body, the hideous fear in her eyes sent shivers of dread down his spine. Every second, every heartbeat seemed to last an eternity. And still she did not move.

"Isabella?" His voice was a hoarse whisper. "Isabella?" When she gave no answer, he raised his hand toward her shoulder.

Caught in the terrible tableau, Adrienne watched the procession move toward the dais, where the executioner's block stood. Watched Sandro mount the stairs and contemptuously push away the servant who offered him a blindfold. He knelt and lowered his head to the block, running his hands through his long hair to bring it forward and remove it from his neck. The hooded executioner stepped forward. When he raised his sword, she began to scream.

Just as his fingers brushed her shoulder, the room began to echo with her screams.

For a split second he remained motionless. Then he gripped her arms. "Isabella! What is it? What is wrong?" He cupped her chin with one hand and shook her desperately, trying to stop her screams, trying to efface that glassy, unfocused look in her eyes.

"Isabella," he shouted. "Look at me!"

Adrienne heard shouting and the tableau trembled as if shaken by an earthquake. Then abruptly it shattered like a picture made of glass and disappeared.

The first thing she was aware of was Sandro's face an inch from hers. He was shaking her. Shouting at her. Then pressing her face against his chest.

She felt an incredible surge of relief, followed immediately by a new wave of panic. She had seen Sandro's end. The recognition sliced through her like a red-hot knife. That could only mean one thing. She would not be able to keep him safe. Just like the other

Isabella, she would watch him die under the sword of Borgia's executioner.

Sandro held her pressed against him, his face buried in her hair. The rigidity had drained from her body and she was resting quietly in his arms—too quietly. He closed his eyes. At least the terrible screams had stopped. And she had looked at him and really seen him. Unsure of what had happened, for the moment he was content just to hold her. Later, he thought, later there would be time enough to figure out what had happened.

Even though Adrienne lay against him, boneless, sapped of her strength by the terrible vision, her mind raced. Like an animal being hunted by a predator, thought after thought darted, leapt, retraced a path, found itself backed up against a wall.

Then the seed of an idea took root. Took root and within seconds sprouted and grew. That had to be the answer. She felt her heart begin to race as hope sprang up again. If she could not keep him safe in this life, then the only possible solution could be to leave it. Her decision made, she raised her head and straightened, going from passiveness to lightning-fast movement within the space of a breath.

With a twist of her shoulders, she freed herself from Sandro's embrace. Before he could even react, she had gripped his hand and was pulling him toward the door.

"Isabella, what are you doing?" he managed, but she was already unlocking the door.

With Sandro in tow, she plowed through the gaping crowd gathered in the anteroom.

Unsure of how to deal with Isabella's overwrought state, Sandro followed her, allowing himself to be pulled up the staircase, along the corridor toward their apartments. She stumbled once over the hem of her gown, falling on one knee, but before Sandro could bend to help her, she was up and running again.

Wide-eyed, her ladies stared at them as Adrienne dragged Sandro through her apartments. Gasping, she tore the door to her bedchamber open and tumbled inside. Her eyes darted around the room. Empty! Thank God! A sob of relief ripped out of her throat. She twisted the key and for a moment collapsed against the locked door, her chest heaving.

"Isabella, talk to me." Sandro ran his hands up her arms. "What are you doing? What do you want?" He fought to keep his voice low and even, afraid to push her over the edge into hysteria.

Adrienne looked up him, her breath burning in her throat. There was no way she could explain to him what she was going to do. Even if she could find words to explain it, he would not believe her. He would think she had gone mad.

Would he hate her for what she was about to do? For depriving him of his life? She pushed the questions away. That was the chance she would have to take. But she had to do it now, quickly, before the courage deserted her.

She shook her head, and seizing Sandro's hand again, she bolted across the room. Her knees were threatening to give way, but through sheer willpower she kept herself upright. One step and then another. As she reached the far wall, her legs finally collapsed and she fell to her knees underneath the portrait.

Sandro raised her and started to speak, but she shook her head again, placing her hand over his mouth.

"Please, Sandro, do not say anything. Do not ask any questions." Her hands trembled as they slid along his face and into his hair, and yet their grip was strong as she cradled his head. "Trust me. Just for a few moments. Please." Her words were quick and breathless. "Will you do that?" She gave him an impatient shake. "Will you?"

"All right," Sandro agreed, afraid of aggravating her agitation.

Lacing her fingers with his, Adrienne began to run her free hand over the portrait—up and then down again. Nothing. Again. Still nothing. Her breath started coming in spurts. She heard Sandro speak her name, but she only shook her head, concentrating on the task before her.

Sweat beaded on her brow. She felt the rivulets trickling down her body. Yet, at the same time, an icy chill crawled along her spine.

She tried to force herself to move her hand slowly over the smooth canvas, but her hand seemed to take on a momentum she could not control. It moved faster and faster until it began to fly wildly over the portrait.

Hysteria started bubbling up inside her. She heard a high voice and then the crying of a woman without realizing that the sounds came from her mouth. Suddenly she felt the jolt.

But instead of being sucked fully into the darkness, she found herself balancing on its perimeter. She felt the force of the black void at her back pulling at her, but at the same time there was a counterforce resisting it. She was a pin that was being buffeted between two powerful magnets. A boat adrift upon the open sea between two storms.

Her fingers, which had been gripping Sandro's hand, began to grow tired and lax. Oh God, no, she thought. She had to make certain that Sandro made the journey with her! Although the muscles in the back of her hand were cramping with the effort, her fingers were disobeying her, loosening, separating from his.

Desperate, she removed her other hand from the canvas and reached for him. In that moment a second jolt propelled her forward.

She crashed into Sandro, knocking him off balance. Together they fell and Adrienne felt the darkness enclose her.

They had done it. That was her first thought as she regained awareness. They had done it. She turned onto her back, an arm flung wide in a gesture of relief.

Her eyes still closed, she took a deep breath. And then another. Where was the scent of the sea? The dampness? Stiffening, she took another breath. The scent of rose oil and jasmine filled her nostrils.

She opened her eyes. Across the room she saw the canopied bed with the curtains of aquamarine velvet. Her gaze darted around the chamber, taking in the heavy, ornate furniture. She squeezed her eyes shut and then opened them again, but nothing had changed. Something had gone terribly wrong and she was still lying on the floor of Isabella di Montefiore's bedchamber.

One last, mad hope flashed through her. Perhaps Sandro had made the journey without her. Perhaps he was safe, at least.

Then she felt a light touch and tipped her head to the side. Sandro lay on the floor two arm's lengths away and he had stretched out his hand to touch his fingertips to hers.

The last bit of strength that she possessed flowed out of her and she began to weep.

Chapter Twenty-five

Although she did not stir, Sandro knew the moment that Isabella awoke—not so much because he heard the change in her breathing but simply because he was so attuned to her. Still he did not understand her. Still there were secrets, barriers.

What had she been trying to do that day with her portrait? Had she acted so bizarrely simply because she had been terrified and hysterical? Had she wanted to conjure a spell? And then there had been an unearthly moment when she had seemed to turn transparent, when his hands seemed to be gripping not flesh but air.

Afterwards, when she had wept so bitterly, he had not had the courage to press her for answers. But he still felt an icy chill in the pit of his stomach when he remembered. And wondered.

As Adrienne surfaced from sleep, she knew immediately where she was. Ever since her abortive attempt to escape back to her life as Adrienne de Beaufort, she had stopped experiencing those disoriented, paralyzing moments upon awakening. Now she woke up knowing exactly where she was. Who she was. Her mouth curved in a wistful smile. It was as if that mad, unsuccessful flight had proved to her that she belonged here irrevocably.

Yes, she belonged here. She understood that now. For some reason, fate had set her down in this life and it would be up to her, Adrienne de Beaufort, to complete the destiny of Isabella di Montefiore.

The realization of that inevitability had brought her a measure of peace. Yet she could not help asking herself just what that destiny would be. There had been things she had been able to change. Others had been beyond her grasp. There was little sense in playing the doubtful intellectual game of trying to foresee that destiny, which was something she had finally understood.

Nevertheless, she could not prevent her thoughts from drifting in that direction this morning. After all, today was not a day like any other. Today Sandro was leaving to join his troops in Pesaro. And then he would be in Cesare Borgia's terrible orbit of power and she knew—knew much too well—what fate awaited him there unless she somehow managed to keep him safe.

Even though she found it strange, perhaps even unnatural, she was grateful for the calmness she felt. She did not want her last hours with Sandro to be marred by tears and panic. Somewhere in the distance, the thought brushed her mind that it was perhaps one last gift that the Fates were giving them.

She turned onto her side, her body flowing along the curve of Sandro's back. The instant her skin connected with his, she felt the tiny jolt that went through him and realized he was already awake.

Deciding to ignore that fact for a few moments, she propped herself up on one elbow and planted a leisurely row of kisses along his shoulder. An hour, she thought. For an hour she would pretend this was a morning like any other. As her fingers drifted down his side to curve over his hip, she began to trace a pattern on his skin with the tip of her tongue.

Sandro had not been able to prevent a small jolt of awareness when he felt Isabella nestle herself against his back. Now, trying to prolong the teasing, he struggled to hold himself still as she trailed her mouth and her fingers over his skin.

For long minutes he allowed the sweet, easy pleasure to wash over him. But when her knee slipped between his thighs and her fingers drifted down from his hip, over his belly, to touch his awakening flesh, he groaned and turned onto his back, pulling her to lie on top of him.

"Temptress."

As she gazed into Sandro's beautiful face, the enormity of her love for him struck Adrienne so strongly that she felt it like a physical shock. Her love was a flame and her whole being, body and soul, seemed to glow with it.

She raised her hands and traced the planes and angles of his face as if she wanted to memorize them with her fingers. Then she twisted her fingers in his long, silky black hair, the texture of which never failed to arouse her.

"Make love to me, Sandro." She lowered her mouth to his for a brief taste. "Make love to me—" She stopped abruptly, horrified at what she had almost said.

Sandro heard her breath catch. "Make love to me," she had said. The cold feeling in the pit of his stomach returned. She had not said them aloud, but the rest of her words hung in the room as surely as if she had spoken them. "As if it were the last time."

They saw the knowledge in each other's eyes. They saw it, accepted it and put it aside.

Sandro smiled and trailed his hands up his wife's body. "No, love. I will make love to you as if it were the first time." His fingers began to trace a sensuous pattern on her back. "Do you remember?"

Something softened inside Adrienne and she brushed his mouth with hers. "Yes, I remember. But perhaps you would like to refresh my memory."

He laughed and brought her head down to his.

"Sit down."

Cesare Borgia's perfectly even, melodious voice had the same impact as the crack of a whip, and Piero Gennaro skidded to a stop on the brick red tiles and scurried back to one of the massive, high-backed chairs that stood in front of the desk.

"I find it very peculiar indeed that Montefiore has refused to come to Forlì. Have you shared our plans with someone?" His eyes narrowed. "Your sister, perhaps?"

"No, Don Cesare," Piero quickly assured him. "No one but Alfonso and myself know." He rubbed his damp palms against his hose. "Believe me, I beg you."

"I have no reason to doubt your word, Don Piero." Borgia smiled with his mouth only. "However, I suggest that you make it your business to see that I can greet your brother-in-law here as my guest shortly. My campaign will soon begin and my time is limited."

"But, Don Cesare, how—"

Borgia silenced him with a look whose blandness gave no hint of the irritation he felt. It was time that he got rid of the Gennaro brothers, he mused. They were bumbling idiots who could not see beyond their own ambition to rule Siena. Once he had what he wanted, he would hand them over to Michelotto and be done with them. No one would care about what happened to them, and for them there would be no need of the elaborate preparations he was making for Alessandro di Montefiore's demise.

"Don Piero." Borgia propped his chin on his laced hands. "When you came to me, you baited your hook quite nicely with your sister's luscious flesh." He smiled again. "I imagine if you do the same now, Montefiore will find this bait irresistible."

He leaned back in his chair. "Yes, I believe I would enjoy having both husband and wife here in Forlì."

Realizing that he was dismissed, Piero rose. He wished he had the nerve to ask Borgia just how he was supposed to get Isabella here. After all, she had not been exactly forthcoming to him since she had fallen under Montefiore's spell. He could not imagine how he would do it short of putting her in chains and abducting her.

"Do not use force, Don Piero."

Piero started, wondering if Borgia could read his mind with those eerie, expressionless eyes of his.

"I do not care for damaged goods." His fingertips tapped lightly on the highly polished surface of the desk. "Do we understand each other?"

"Yes, Don Cesare." Piero began to back away. "Of course."

When Piero turned around, he could feel Borgia's eyes boring into his back and he had to forcibly control the desire to break into a run to escape them.

"Don Piero."

Piero stiffened as if he had felt the prick of a knife between his shoulder blades and turned around.

Borgia gestured at the chair Piero had just vacated with one finger. In the time it had taken Piero to cross to the door, he had decided to take the matter in hand himself.

"Your sister will get a note. A cry for help from her imprisoned husband." He rapped out his instructions.

"But she will not believe—"

"At the same time, she will receive a letter in my own hand, telling her that her husband is my guest and requesting her presence." Borgia smiled. "Once she is here in Forlì, Montefiore will be informed. I have no doubt that we will have him here within a day."

"What—what if the signals somehow get crossed?" Piero stammered. "What if she receives an actual message from Montefiore at the same time?"

"I would suggest—" Borgia leaned forward and lowered his voice "—strongly suggest that you make certain that does not happen."

Adrienne smiled with satisfaction as she signed the last of the documents and letters for the day. She had protested when Sandro had told her that he was placing full authority for the Dukedom of Siena into her hands for the duration of his absence, suspecting that he was doing so only to take her mind off her fears. But she had taken to the work like the proverbial duck to water.

Granted, there had been no heavy political decisions to make. Most of her duties up to now had pertained to the administration of the vast Montefiore land holdings or petitions from citizens. But she found it enormously gratifying that she was doing something useful. And the work kept the loneliness at bay. In her life as Adrienne she had dealt with being alone as a matter of course, never defining it as loneliness. But now she was lonely for Sandro's nearness and she missed the companionship of the old duke.

When the last of the counselors and scribes had left the room, she threw open a window. The Campo was lively in the late afternoon sunlight. In one corner a traveling company had set up a makeshift stage and was performing a play in the *commedia dell'arte* style with Harlequin and Columbine cavorting in their multicolored dress. At the other end of the *piazza* a small crowd had gathered around a juggler and two acrobats who vied with each other for the crowd's praise and coins. Near the fountain a lone piper played a haunting melody. Above the Campo the swallows screeched as they swooped and dove for their supper.

She was so caught up in the wonderfully alive tableau below her that she did not hear the chamberlain until he addressed her.

"Yes, Don Federico, what is it?" She spoke without turning around.

"There are messages, your grace."

"Messages?" She whirled around. "From Don Alessandro?"

"It would seem so, your grace. This man—" he took a step to the side "—says he bears a message from the duke but will deliver it only into your grace's hands."

Adrienne's eyes widened at the sight of the man. His skin was mottled from illness or drink and a tic affected one eye; his clothes and smell suggested that he made his home in the gutter. She stretched out her hand and the man came a step closer but made no move to hand her the grimy scrap of paper he clutched in his bony fingers.

"I was promised payment, *madonna*."

"Give him a coin, Don Federico."

The man snatched the gold piece from the chamberlain, thrust the note at Adrienne and whirled around to flee the room, but Don Federico reached out with a surprisingly agile movement and grabbed him by the edge of his short cloak.

Adrienne stared down at the folded scrap of paper, which was stained a rusty color. Her fingers stiff and icy with dread, she unfolded it. The barely legible scrawl danced in front of her eyes before she could finally decipher it. "Held in Forlì. Help. A."

Thoughts, feelings came in waves. Denial. Anger. Panic. So the worst of her nightmares had come true, she acknowledged as her heart constricted within her chest. Or had it? Hope flared as she fixed her gaze on the writing again. Why was the note signed "A," when she had never called him anything but Sandro? Was this some kind of a trap contrived by her brothers?

She stepped closer to the man, almost gagging from his stench. "Who gave you this?" she demanded, brandishing the scrap of paper in front of his face. "What did the man look like?"

"One of the jailers at the Forlì dungeon, *madonna*." He shrugged. "God knows, they all look like butchers."

Adrienne blanched. "You did not see the man who wrote this?"

He shook his head and screwed up his eyes trying to remember what the masked man who had given him the piece of paper had said. ''The turnkey said the fellow who wrote this is not as pretty as he used to be.'' He cackled, pleased that he had remembered. ''And he had to write the words in his own blood.'' He smiled, showing the blackened stumps of his teeth. ''No ink.''

Adrienne turned away, her stomach roiling. But how could she be sure that this scum was telling the truth? And if he were, why had Sandro not used some word, or phrase to assure her that the note came from him?

Then the entire meaning of the man's words dawned on her and she pressed her knuckles to her mouth to keep from crying out. If he had been tortured, he would not have the strength to write more. Her gaze returned to the scrap of paper. Had the scrawled words been written by hands broken and mutilated?

''Your grace?''

Turning, she saw the letter in Don Federico's hand, Borgia's seal spreading on it like a bloodstain. Even before she reached for it and broke the seal, she knew what she would find there.

She scanned the brief lines and all hope died. Adrienne understood that despite all her knowledge, all her warnings, she had been able to do nothing. Sandro really was Borgia's prisoner in the dungeon of Forlì.

Chapter Twenty-six

Adrienne's knees almost buckled as she slid down from the back of her mount. One of the men who had accompanied her on the ride from Siena steadied her and she nodded her thanks as she moved away.

Despite the early hour, the May morning was already hot and she did not bother to wipe away the rivulets of sweat that trickled down the sides of her face and her neck. Leaning against one of the trees in the small copse where they had stopped, she wrapped her arms around herself, as much for her own solace as to soothe the child who slept within her. They had come to the end of their journey.

What an irony of fate, she mused. Isabella had ridden to Forlì, a willing decoy to lure her husband into Borgia's captivity. And now she had made the same journey, brought here by Sandro, who had apparently been too careless, too foolhardy.

As they had ridden, fear had been lodged in the back of her throat, its taste constantly on her tongue. Now as she looked at the buff-colored walls of the city of Forlì just ahead, she felt an almost eerie calmness.

In the southernmost corner of the city, the Rocca di Ravaldino thrust out into the countryside like the prow of a ship. Adrienne watched the drawbridge of the fortress being lowered to allow a lone rider to pass and wished for an army that would gallop in his wake and free Sandro.

The men who had accompanied her belonged to Sandro's personal guard, a detachment of which had remained in Siena at her disposal. She knew that they would go to their deaths without question, but she was realist enough to recognize that they had absolutely no chance of freeing Sandro by force. It had taken Cesare Borgia, armed with ten thousand men and the best artillery in Europe, two weeks to force the citadel of Forlì to surrender.

Adrienne knew that her only hope was to bribe her way inside. The men who had been with Sandro during the siege of the city had tried to warn her how difficult that would be, but she had refused to listen. It gave her hope to think that if Sandro had been able to get a note out of the dungeon of the fortress, she would be able to get herself in and both of them out again.

She felt a movement at her side and looked down at Gianni. He had begged to be allowed to accompany her, and realizing that his experience at things clandestine was far greater than hers, she had agreed.

"It will be all right, Donna Isabella." He held out a small bundle toward her.

Adrienne nodded, not trusting her voice to speak. Taking the bundle, she disappeared behind some bushes to slip into her costume. Quickly she stripped off the dusty, drab men's clothes she had worn for the ride and put on the simple dress, grateful that her pregnancy was not yet showing. She smoothed out the rough linen and then knelt to pick up a handful of earth. As she rubbed dirt into her face and hands, Adrienne prayed that her disguise would allow her to pass for a young peasant woman going to market.

Tucking the small bundle of cured animal skins under her arm, she set out on that last dusty stretch of road. The narrow thoroughfare was crowded on this market day. Men, women and children jostled one another as they carried baskets and burlap sacks or pulled handcarts. Envious looks followed the occasional more prosperous peasant who could afford to carry his wares to market on a donkey. The dust-filled air rang with shouts and curses and laughter.

Adrienne walked purposefully, ignoring her exhaustion, ignoring the people around her, and fully concentrated on the task before her. There had been no time to work out a real plan. The men, wearing their own disguises as tradesmen or peasants, would enter the city later. God give that they would meet at the right time, the right place.

A crowd milled at the city gate as voices rose, arguing with the guards about the price of entry to be paid in coin or goods. As she moved closer, Adrienne saw that behind the table where the guards haggled with the crowd, a man-at-arms wearing the scarlet-and-yellow Borgia colors sat on horseback, impassively overseeing the proceedings. Grateful for the crush of bodies around her, she rounded her shoulders and ducked her head to make herself as unobtrusive as possible.

The guards waved a group past the gate into the city and an impatient surge of the throng behind her sent Adrienne forward so quickly that she stumbled, falling to her knees.

"This one will not win any prizes for grace."
Mocking laughter rose from the guards.

"She may be clumsy, but the wench is comely
enough for my bed," one of the guards called out.

Ignoring the taunts and the laughter, Adrienne
picked up her bundle of animal skins and rose, keeping her eyes stubbornly on the ground.

"What is the matter, girl?" A rough hand reached
across the table and jerked her chin up. "Have you not
been taught to look a man who is addressing you in the
face?"

Adrienne's hands tightened on her bundle as she
looked into the face of the guard. His crude features
appeared to have been hewn from a piece of wood.
She had hoped to slip into the city unobtrusively under cover of the crowd, and now a single misstep could
be the ruin of her plan.

"You are here to collect the tolls, not find yourself
a body to keep you warm tonight," the man on
horseback ordered.

Adrienne allowed herself the briefest of glances at
him, half expecting to recognize one of Borgia's
henchmen. But the man looked completely unfamiliar. She dropped her eyes again as the relief that
flooded through her brought a flush to her cheeks.

The guard straightened at the sound of the soft,
even voice behind him. "All right," he snarled at
Adrienne, "give me two of those sorry skins of
yours."

She worked two skins out from underneath the rope
that bound them, then snatched up her bundle and
darted away.

Her heart beating quickly, she followed the other
vendors toward the marketplace. Several times she

stopped to fiddle with her shoes, glancing around her surreptitiously to make certain that none of the men she had seen at the gate were following her. Finally deciding that she had taken as much care as she could afford, she turned off the main thoroughfare and plunged into the warren of dark, cramped streets that led toward the Rocca.

One moment she was in the narrow, sunless street and the next Adrienne found herself blinded by the sunlight on a wall of sand-colored brick. The buttressed wall that rose from a foundation of craggy rock was so high that she had to tip her head back to see its crenellated top. As her gaze traveled upward, she saw that the only windows were narrow slits protected by iron bars.

The sheer size and solidity of the fortress struck her like a fist and she felt her confidence began to dwindle. For long minutes she stood there as if rooted to the ground, desperately trying to decide where she would start her search. Finally forcing herself to move, she began to walk around the perimeter of the citadel to investigate the points of entry from the city.

She had barely gone more than a few steps when a man appeared from an alleyway and barred her path.

"Don Cesare welcomes you to Forlì, *madonna*."

The shock of the man's words was so great that for a moment the meaning of his words barely registered and Adrienne stared at him. Then suddenly her heart leapt into her throat and began to race.

"What?" The single word came out in a croak. Instinctively she pressed her bundle against her middle as if that could protect her. "You must be mistaking me for someone else." She rounded her shoulders in a subservient gesture.

"No, *madonna.*" The man's grin was a slash of white in his swarthy face. "I do not mistake you." With a mocking bow, he offered her his arm. "You will accompany me now."

No, Adrienne's mind screamed, it could not be! It could not be! She would not allow it! She took a step back. And then another. Hearing a sound behind her, she whirled, only to find herself face-to-face with two men-at-arms who stood straddle-legged and impassive, blocking her way.

It was over, she realized. It was over before it had begun. An incredible weariness seemed to come over her and her arms dropped to her sides, letting the bundle of skins tumble to the cobblestones. Dispassionately she watched it roll and come to rest against the boots of one of the men. She felt the exhaustion flow through her until her muscles, her very bones, seemed to turn to water.

Even as her knees began to buckle, she was reaching inside herself, dipping into that one last reservoir of strength. She would not give up, she told herself. If this was the way it had to be, she would confront Borgia. Confront him and bargain with him for Sandro's life. Her stomach contracted with the knowledge that the only thing she could bargain with was herself. Even so, she consciously drew on the strength until energy began to surge through her again, giving her back her sense of self.

A heavy hand descended onto her shoulder. Adrienne stiffened and turned around, fixing her gaze on Borgia's henchman.

Shedding her role as peasant girl, she straightened. "Take your hands off me."

Although his eyes narrowed with hostility, the man jerked his hand back as if he had been burned.

"I will accompany *madonna* to Don Cesare now. But please remember that the men behind us are quick." He grinned again as his composure returned. "And they take orders only from me."

Insolently he offered her his arm again. Ignoring it, Adrienne began to walk.

They entered the fortress through a well-guarded door so low that they had to bend to get through it. A lone torch burned in the arched passageway that led through the wall of the citadel. When they had emerged again into the sunlight of the courtyard, Adrienne realized how naive she had been to believe that she would be able to bribe her way inside.

The huge courtyard was bustling with activity, making it look, at first glance, like the *piazza* of a harmless village. Women were at the well bringing up buckets of water. A servant trudged by, carrying a huge basket of laundry. A trio of dogs chased one another playfully. Only the well-armed guards in the scarlet-and-yellow livery were a vivid reminder that this was no mere village. And who the master was.

As she followed her captor, Adrienne tried to memorize every door, every staircase, every turn of the corridor. Soon—too soon—they stopped in front of a massive oaken door. The man knocked once and it opened immediately. Stepping across the threshold, Adrienne found herself in a well-guarded anteroom. As she crossed the room, her heart pounding, her hands damp, she felt the men's eyes following her.

A guard pushed open the door on the other side of the room as she approached, and she found herself staring into the handsome, cold face of Cesare Borgia.

"Welcome to Forlì, Donna Isabella." Borgia stood but remained behind his desk.

As their eyes met, Adrienne felt the panic fall away from her. It was as if she had stepped on a stage. And she knew that Sandro's life—and hers in the end—would depend on the performance she would give.

"Thank you, Michelotto." Borgia nodded at the man behind her. "You have done your work well. As usual."

Adrienne felt a jolt as she realized that the man who had brought her here was the infamous Michelotto Corella, Borgia's favored assassin, whose expertise with the garotte and the dagger had disposed of many an adversary.

Then the door behind her snapped shut and she and Borgia were alone. She remained standing where she was and watched him slowly move around his desk and approach her.

"To what do I owe the honor of your visit, *madonna?*" Keeping his eyes on hers, Borgia picked up her hand and lifted it to his mouth.

Adrienne did not retreat, but she could not prevent a ripple of revulsion as his lips brushed over her skin. "I believe you know better than anyone why I am here, Don Cesare."

"Indeed." His lips curved in a smile, and keeping her hand in his, he steered her toward his desk. He reached for a letter and, with a casually insolent movement of his wrist, handed it to her.

*Your wife is my guest at Forlì. Should you wish to
see her, I would be pleased to welcome you, also.*

In disbelief, Adrienne's eyes flew over the lines
again and again. Then with mounting horror she understood that despite all her knowledge, all her pre-
cautions, she had done unwittingly what Isabella had
done deliberately. She had betrayed her husband. She
had led him into the trap that would cost him his life.

How could she have been so stupid? How could she
not have seen the note the beggar had brought her for
the trap it was? For a brief moment she felt defeat
weaken her before she pushed it away. The war was
not yet over, she thought. She may have lost this battle but, by God, she would not stop fighting. When she
raised her gaze to Borgia's face, her eyes were defi-
ant.

Borgia saw the anger, the combative expression in
her eyes. So she would not disappoint him by giving
in meekly after all. He would enjoy both the battle and
the spoils. He felt his body stir in anticipation.

The anger surged through Adrienne with such violence that her ears rang with it. Tossing the letter back
down on the desk, she opened her mouth to tell Borgia that he was a despicable, perfidious knave who
deserved to burn in hell.

"The fire in your eyes is very provocative, *madonna*." Borgia raised his hand and brushed the backs
of his fingers across her mouth. "But do not say anything you might regret."

Fighting for control, Adrienne whirled away, her
fingers laced so tightly that the knuckles cracked.
What could she say to him that would make him
change his mind? How could she buy his promise not
to send the letter to Sandro? She rubbed her hands

over her face as her thoughts raced desperately. And
even if he made such a promise, how could she be sure
that he would keep it?

She turned around to face him again. "What do you
want from my husband?" she demanded. "Has he not
served you loyally and well?"

"Indeed he has," Borgia agreed with equanimity.

"What do you want from him, then?" she repeated.

"It is the mark of a good leader not only to judge
the past—" he lifted his hands in an elegant gesture
"—but also the future."

"What are you talking about? Alessandro di Montefiore would not betray where he has given his word."

"Perhaps not." One dark eyebrow curved upward.
"Perhaps it is not the question of his loyalty that gives
me pause."

She clasped her hands together again to prevent
herself from attacking him bodily. "What then?" It
was an utterly bizarre situation, she thought. Here she
was asking questions, the answers to which she knew
only too well. And yet . . . and yet the historical reality
had shifted enough so that she realized that she really
knew nothing at all.

Borgia smiled and shook his head. "You shall be my
guest for a time, Donna Isabella. It would be a shame
to exhaust our topics of conversation so quickly." He
stepped closer. "Would it not?"

"It was my brothers." She wanted answers, and she
would provoke him for them if need be. "Because they
were too weak, too inept to destroy my husband, they
came to you to do their dirty work for them."

Borgia's eyebrows rose slightly at her tone. "You
err, *madonna*. I do no one's dirty work but my own."

"Do you deny then what I said?"

"I have spoken with your brothers. Yes." He crossed his arms across his chest. "We have some mutual . . . interests."

Adrienne's eyes narrowed. "And one of those interests is to murder my husband."

"Murder is a crude word, *madonna*. There are situations in which a prince has no choice but to send men to their death." He shrugged. "Both on the battlefield and off."

Adrienne stared at him—the cold eyes heated only by a spark of lust, the cruel, well-formed mouth. So it was going to happen, she thought. He was going to send Sandro to the block and she would be there to see him die. A wave of pain surged through her, so acute that she almost cried out.

"Will you not be merciful?" she asked softly. "Just this once?"

"Ah, Donna Isabella." His mellow voice sounded almost regretful. "Mercy is a virtue a prince can ill afford."

"But you *can* afford it." She lunged forward and dug her fingers into the black velvet of his doublet. "You are the Duke of Valentinois, the Duke of the Romagna, the most powerful man in Italy save the pope. What is one life to you?" Even as she begged for Sandro's life, she knew that her words were like leaves in a storm that would be swept away and forgotten. And still she begged.

"He has done nothing to harm you." Unshed tears trembled on her lashes. "Will you not spare him?" Desperation tightened her fingers, and even though Borgia raised his hands to circle her wrists, she refused to release him. "If not for the sake of your immortal soul, then at least for your own gain."

"My own gain?" His tone was offhand, but it contained a shadow of true interest. "How so?"

"I am wealthy in my own right. I will give you anything that is within my power to give." Her words rushed out on one breath.

"Anything?"

"Anything."

His hands on her wrists loosened now and his thumbs began to stroke.

Adrienne stilled, realizing what she had said, what she had promised. She let go of his doublet, but when she tried to lower her hands, Borgia's fingers tightened painfully until they were like iron manacles. For long moments they stared at each other. Then he laughed harshly and released her so suddenly that her hands fell as if they had been weighted.

"I could take you now, this minute, without offering anything in return. Do you think anyone would move a muscle to help you?" he asked. "At best, the guards in the anteroom would lay bets on how quickly your screams would turn to moans of pleasure."

She stared at him, horrified as much by his casual tone as by what he was saying. Instinctively, her hands went to her middle, as if that gesture could protect her child from the words he spoke so calmly. She backed away from him. One step and then another.

Borgia laughed again. "Do not fear, Donna Isabella. I will wait. At least until you have bathed off the dust of the road." He closed the gap between them again and lifted his fingers to her cheek. "And who knows? Perhaps I *will* give you something in return."

He traced the line of her jaw. "You will have to wait and see."

Adrienne's stomach roiled at his words, his touch, and she twisted her head aside.

Suddenly his hand was cupping her chin, his fingers biting cruelly into her cheeks. "Do not turn away from me," he said softly. "Do not ever turn away from me." His fingers tightened still further before he released her and swiveled away.

Swaying, she steadied herself against the back of a chair. The dagger! Her eyes widened as she remembered the dagger she had strapped to her leg. Her eyes flickered to where Borgia stood, his back to her, then to the desk where the letter lay. She could almost feel the cold metal in her hand. Her breathing grew quick and uneven.

She could do it. She was sure of it. She could do it without a qualm. Then she would destroy the letter and Sandro would be safe. And then ... Adrienne closed her eyes. Then Borgia's men would come and put her to death. Oh God, she thought, she did not want to die. She wanted to live. She wanted to give birth to the child within her. Somehow—somehow—she would find a way, she promised herself. She could not have been sent into this life only to fail. She had to believe that.

"*Madonna.*"

She jerked at the sound of Borgia's voice.

"Since you are obviously not wearing any jewelry your husband will recognize, may I ask you to add a few words to my letter?" He smiled. "Just in case your husband does not take me as easily at my word as you did."

"No!" Adrienne curled both hands around the back of the chair. "I will not."

"You may suit yourself, Donna Isabella." He shrugged. "If you refuse, then I will have to send something else." He paused before he continued in a conversational tone. "An ear perhaps. Or one of your fingers."

Adrienne felt another wave of nausea. He would do it, she thought as she looked into his inscrutable eyes. He would do it and enjoy it. Bowing her head in defeat, she moved forward.

Her hands were almost steady as she took the quill and began to write.

It is as he says. I am in Forlì.

Borgia laughed softly. "Very good, Donna Isabella."

Without looking up, Adrienne dipped the quill in the ink pot.

I was brought here by a ruse.

She heard Borgia make a sound of displeasure, but she continued to write.

I beg you, do not come here.

The quill scratched across the parchment as Borgia pulled it out from under her hand. He looked down at what she had written and began to laugh.

"I thank you, Donna Isabella. No man could possibly resist such an invitation to prove his valor."

Realizing that he was right, Adrienne reached for the letter, but Borgia stepped back beyond her grasp.

Desperate now, she jumped up. She had one more trump card, she thought, but she had no way of knowing if it would save Sandro or be the final ruin of them both. Yet she had no choice but to use it.

"If you spare him, I can offer you something that no one else can."

"And I have already told you that I can take you anytime I please."

Adrienne shook her head. "That is not what I mean." She took a deep breath. "I can see your future, Don Cesare. I know what will happen and when. As long as Alessandro di Montefiore is safe, I will tell you what lies ahead and then your power will be infinite."

Borgia's gaze sharpened. "You can foresee the future?" He laughed contemptuously. "You expect me to believe that? If you can foresee the future, why are you here?"

"My knowledge does not work for me. Only for others."

"Prove it."

She swallowed. "You have plans for your sister, Lucrezia, and her husband, Alfonso di Bisceglie, stands in your way." She saw the flicker of surprise in Borgia's eyes and plunged on.

"Alfonso will die by your command before the end of this year and your sister will marry the heir of the House of Este."

Borgia turned and strode to stand at a narrow window. How could she know something that existed only in his own head? He had confided in no one that Alfonso di Bisceglie's days were numbered, nor that he had chosen Alfonso d'Este to be Lucrezia's new husband. How did she know this unless she truly had the sight? He stilled as a long, cold shiver crawled the length of his spine. Or unless she was a witch. He pushed that unwelcome thought away, telling himself that it was far more important to know if she would be able to foresee his enemies' plans than how she came by the knowledge. The vista that opened before him was tempting beyond measure.

"Your...gift is of interest to me." As he turned to face her again, he tried to recapture the desire he had felt just minutes ago, but it eluded him.

A sigh of relief shuddered past her lips. "Then you will destroy the letter and leave my husband in peace?"

"No, *madonna*." His mouth curved in a hideous smile. "When your husband is my guest, we will speak again of your talent."

"You..." Adrienne started toward him.

"Silence." He raised his hand to stop her. "I have shown great patience with you, Donna Isabella. Do not try it further. Remember Caterina Sforza, whose apartments you will be occupying. She tried my patience a little too much and now she has much leisure to reflect on her actions." He paused. "In the dungeon of the Castel Sant'Angelo in Rome."

Without waiting for a reply, he strode past her and opened the door to the anteroom to call for Michelotto.

Chapter Twenty-seven

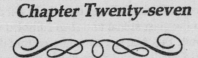

Adrienne stood at the window looking down into the huge courtyard, her fingers drumming against the glass. Two full days had passed since her interview with Borgia. At first she had been grateful that he had allowed her to remain in Caterina Sforza's apartments alone and undisturbed except for the occasional visit of servants who brought her food or came to help her dress in Caterina's clothes. But the more time passed, the more restless and uneasy she became, feeling like a becalmed ship in an uncharted, threatening ocean.

Her back was against the wall, she admitted. Unless Borgia chose to be placated by the offer of her body and her knowledge of the future, she would have no choice but to watch Sandro die. The pain welled up inside her, clogging her throat.

No, she told herself. She had one more choice. If it came to that, she would at the last moment use her dagger on Borgia. Perhaps Sandro would be able to escape in the chaos that would surely ensue. And for her? She looked down at the large ring on her middle finger, the only jewelry she had kept hidden deep in her pockets. For her there would be the deadly contents of the ring and then eternal sleep. A lone tear slipped unheeded down her cheek.

The sound of laughter rose from the courtyard and a flash of movement caught her attention. Leaning forward, she saw the stunted figure of a dwarf turning cartwheels. Gianni? Could it really be Gianni? Her fingers on the glass stilled and then fumbled with the window bolt. But then she remembered that it was secured with a small padlock and she had to be satisfied with pressing her face against the glass.

She tried to get a glimpse of his face, but even when he stopped to acknowledge the applause of the small crowd that had gathered to watch him, she could not be certain that it was Gianni.

Then she saw the dwarf run toward one of the servant women who were watching him and snatch several eggs from the basket she was holding. Ignoring the woman's shriek of protest, he began to juggle them so quickly that the eye could hardly keep up with them. After several minutes, he caught them one after another with casual dexterity and held them up so that the spectators could see that they were undamaged. With a courtly bow, he returned them to the woman's basket.

Her face still pressed against the glass, Adrienne closed her eyes as a half-hysterical mixture of laughter and sobs shook her. It really was Gianni. She was sure of it now. Somehow he had found a way into the fortress. Hope began to bloom again. Just the thought that there was at least one soul on her side in this hellish place seemed to be a sign that her prayers had been heard.

She paid no attention to the sound of the door in the adjoining room being opened, or to the sound of approaching footsteps, expecting it to be one of the silent servants who periodically brought her food and drink. When she felt a hand curve around her half-bare shoulder, she started, choking back a cry of alarm.

It was the scent that told her it was Borgia—that smell of sulfur overlaid by the spicy scent of cloves and coriander that always seemed to surround him. Stubbornly she kept her eyes on the goings-on in the courtyard. She felt his gaze travel over her, and even though her skin crawled, she fought to give no sign of her agitation.

Cesare Borgia felt his blood begin to heat as his eyes followed the graceful line of Isabella's neck. He was glad now that he had waited. The past two days had whetted his appetite still further. And now that Alessandro di Montefiore was his prisoner, it would be that much more arousing and satisfying to bed his wife. And if she was a witch? Angrily, he pushed away the question that had been whispering through his brain for the past two days. Witch or not, he would have her.

"I bring news, *madonna*."

Adrienne's heart began to pound.

"Montefiore has not disappointed me." Releasing her shoulder, he unlocked the padlock on the window, unfastened the bolt and pushed both casements open.

"Take your hands off me, Corella."

Adrienne pressed a hand against her mouth at the sound of Sandro's voice.

"Where is my wife, damn you?"

Corella's malevolent chuckle made her blood run cold.

"You will see her soon enough."

Self-reproaches filled Adrienne now, and her mind raced with a thousand thoughts. She realized that up until this moment she had, in her deepest heart, not quite given up hope that somehow Sandro would be able to evade captivity. A terrible pressure settled in her chest—the weight of guilt.

There was movement below and a group of men came into view, Sandro walking ahead of them, his head high, his hands bound with a length of rope.

"Stop!" At Corella's command, one of the men poked his lance at Sandro's back. "Look up to your left, Montefiore."

Sandro jerked his head up and saw Isabella. Her tormented eyes were huge in her pale face. The back of one hand was pressed against her mouth as if to muffle a scream. Oh God, he thought, what had Borgia done to her? Instinctively his hands worked against his fetters until the skin was raw and bleeding from the rope. His stomach churned against his own helplessness.

Then the figure behind her moved and he saw that it was Borgia himself, a triumphant smile on his face. As their eyes met and held, Borgia slid his hand possessively down Isabella's neck and curved it around her shoulder.

"Beast!" Sandro felt a wave of rage so black that he could have killed Borgia with his bare hands. He took a step forward, but again the point of a lance at his back stopped him.

He looked back at his wife, who still stood motionless. He saw the heartache, the grief in her eyes. And he was sure that she had never been more beautiful and he had never loved her more. The corners of his mouth lifted in a shadow of a smile and he nodded, wanting to let her know that he believed what she was silently trying to tell him—that he had not come to be here through her betrayal.

Would he see her again? Sandro was enough of a realist to know how slim his chances were. The small troop of men he had brought with him would be scaling the walls of the Rocca under the cover of darkness this night, but both he and the men who had volunteered for the undertaking knew that the odds they faced were not encouraging.

"Get moving." Sandro ignored Corella's harsh voice as one more time his eyes locked with Isabella's.

Emotions spun through him like a whirlwind, their intensity taking his breath away. There were still so many things he wanted to tell her. So many moments he wanted to share with her. He had wasted so much time on mistrust. Even though he knew that it was useless to regret the past, it gnawed at him.

He felt Corella's fist strike him on the back of his shoulder, but his gaze did not waver. Then, slowly, his eyes still on hers, he began to move.

Utterly still, Adrienne stood and watched as Sandro was led away. The pain was so great that she was numb with it. It was as if her heart were bleeding, her lifeblood seeping away. Her pain blinded her so she did not see Gianni tripping after the group, already engaging the men at the rear in jesting conversation.

Sandro and his guards had long disappeared from her field of vision when she again became aware that Borgia was touching her. He turned her around to face him.

"A very touching little pantomime, *madonna.*"

Adrienne said nothing, but the anger and hatred shot into her eyes. How dare he mock and belittle those precious moments?

"Tell me again, Donna Isabella—" he ran the tips of his fingers down from her shoulders and hooked them into the low neckline of her gown of wine red velvet "—how you will compensate me for sparing your husband's life."

She barely controlled the shiver of repulsion that went through her. "I told you." Adrienne swallowed. "I will foretell your future."

"And?" Borgia prompted.

"And I will—" She paused, fighting against the nausea that threatened to overwhelm her. "I will give you my body."

"I like the sound of that." He pushed his hands further down into her neckline so that the backs of his fingers brushed her nipples. "Say it again."

Adrienne began to tremble.

"Say it again." The pressure of his fingers grew.

"I will give you my body." Her voice was barely audible as she forced the words out.

"Yes, I like the sound of that," he repeated and smiled. "I believe that I will take the first portion of my payment now."

He was still smiling when, without warning, he tightened his hands on the neckline of her gown and pulled downward.

For a moment Adrienne was perfectly still, her brain not quite comprehending what was happening, even though the sound of fabric being torn was like a crack of thunder in the quiet room. Only the coolness of the air on her skin made her realize that she was naked to the waist. Then, in a flash, the memory of Fabien ripping the bodice of her gown rose before her and instinctively she reached for the dagger at Borgia's belt.

No sooner had she pulled the dagger out of its jeweled scabbard than his hand was on her wrist. With a cruel twist he wrenched her hand so that the dagger clattered down to the floor.

"You should not have done that, *madonna.*" His voice was soft, almost conversational, giving no indication of the murderous rage that had risen within him.

He bent down and picked up the dagger. Holding it loosely as if he were weighing it, he looked at her, then at the dagger, then back at her. Without warning, moving as quickly as a striking cobra, he slashed her gown and underskirt open from the waist down. As if he had all the time in the world, he slid the knife back into its scabbard. Then he gripped her by the shoulders and bore her back against the wall next to the open window.

Everything happened so quickly that Adrienne found herself incapable of moving a muscle in her own defense. She could feel his hot breath on her face. Then his mouth was on hers, wet and voracious, his tongue raping her mouth. He tore her slit skirts aside and she felt the roughness of his hose against her thighs. The nausea began to rise in her throat.

Finally, she was going to be his, Borgia thought. And when he was still wet from her body, he would visit Montefiore and vaunt his conquest. That would afford him more pleasure than putting him on the rack.

As his hands nestled at the closure of his hose, he realized with a flash of alarm that, although the tug of desire in his loins was still strong, his arousal had withered. The alarm turned into an icy rage and he gripped Isabella by the neck and took her mouth in another punishing kiss. And still his flesh did not re-awaken.

"You witch," he snarled. "Tomorrow you will be at my side to watch your beloved Alessandro die." He flung her aside so violently that she lost her footing and fell to the floor.

The thump her body made brought him back to his senses and he straightened and controlled his breathing until it was even again. His face once again impassive, he marked a small bow.

"Good night, *madonna,* and pleasant dreams." As he turned away, he heard her begin to retch, and again his jaw tightened with fury.

After her bout of nausea, Adrienne sat on the floor for a long time stroking her belly to quiet her child. She whispered to it, crooned to it, told it comforting lies that everything would be all right. Even when her gaze fell on her ring filled with the deadly poison, she did not stop reassuring the child that slept within her.

When she was sure that she was strong enough to stand, she rose and stripped off the sorry remains of the gown. Then she wrapped herself in a robe and, her dagger in easy reach, curled up against the pillows of the bed to wait for what the night would bring.

She was up long before dawn. From Caterina Sforza's dressing room she chose a snowy white chemise trimmed with Venetian lace and a gown of black velvet trimmed with teardrops of silver. Carefully she bound her dagger to her left arm so that it was well covered by the gown's wide sleeves. Ready for what-

ever destiny had in store for her that day, Adrienne
settled down to wait.

The sun had passed its zenith by the time one of
Borgia's men, accompanied by four men-at-arms,
came to summon her. Her head was high and her
hands steady as she moved through the cool corridors
of the fortress.

Wide doors guarded by men in scarlet and yellow
opened at her approach. As she stepped over the
threshold, she saw that she was on the gallery above
the great hall of the citadel. Her heart thumped against
her ribs as she realized that she had reached her destination.

"Good afternoon, Donna Isabella."

Borgia stepped in front of her, blocking her view
into the hall.

"I trust that you have rested well." He picked up her
hand and lifted it to his mouth, surprised and less than
pleased to find it dry and steady.

Adrienne said nothing, but she found that even the
sight of Borgia did not undermine the calmness she
felt. In the course of the long night, she had surrendered herself to whatever the fate that had brought her
here had in store for her, and that had given her the
strength she would need.

"Come, *madonna*." He increased the pressure on
her hand. "There is something I would like to show
you."

"I do not need to see it to know what it is, Don
Cesare."

Borgia's eyebrows rose in question.

"You have built a tribunal and covered it with red
fabric. Only the block is covered with white." She felt

a stab of satisfaction—and hope—when she saw the flicker of surprise in his eyes.

But he said nothing more as he led her down the steps toward the balustrade of the gallery. Two massive, high-backed chairs stood there on a small dais, and when Adrienne had taken her place she saw the scene she had just described.

Her strength faltered at the sight of the low platform, its bloodred fabric a startling contrast to the block draped in pristine white. Unprepared for the stark reality of what until now she had known only from the pages of a diary, Adrienne felt her strength falter. Before she had time to get herself under control again, the drums began to beat a slow, steady rhythm. The great doors of the hall opened and the procession began.

"Do you see the men in the gallery across from us?"

Adrienne lifted her gaze from the scene below and nodded.

Borgia gave a low chuckle. "They are good burghers of the city of Forlì, here to witness the lawful execution of a man found guilty of the lack of fidelity."

"Found guilty by whom?" The gaze that she turned on him was contemptuous. "And lawful in whose eyes?"

Borgia did not reply but laughed again and shrugged.

First in the procession were men from Borgia's personal guard. Armed with both lances and swords and dressed in unrelieved black, they took their positions around the platform. Adrienne felt the first wave of panic surge through her. With so many armed men guarding him, Sandro would need a miracle to escape.

Following them was the executioner, clad entirely in red. His head was completely covered by the pointed red hood, the holes cut out for eyes, nose and mouth making it even more diabolic. Before him he carried an enormous sword, holding it hilt upward so that it made a parody of a cross.

Adrienne sat without moving as she waited for Sandro to appear. Her hands curled around the arms of the chair so tightly that the carving cut into her palms. A shuddering sigh of relief escaped her as she caught sight of him. At least he walked freely, she thought. At least his body had not been broken on the rack.

His steps were slow and measured, but still they brought him toward the platform much too quickly. The closer he came to the scarlet-draped steps, the quicker her breathing became. Drops of sweat formed on her face and ran down the sides of her neck in trickles, mingling with the tears that had begun to flow.

Sandro knew that Isabella was in the hall watching. He knew it as certainly as if he had seen her. He felt her presence. He felt her grief. Slowly he mounted the steps of the platform and moved toward the block, where the executioner stood ready.

One glance, he thought. One last glance, so that he would go to his death with her image branded on his eyes. But he knew that if he looked into her beloved face, he would never find the courage to face his death with dignity.

He knelt and put his head down on the block. Then, lifting his hands, he drew his fingers through his long hair to bring it forward and off his neck.

Beside him, he felt the executioner shift as he bent down toward him. What mockery, he thought, and waited for the words with which the man who was about to behead him would ask his forgiveness. He stiffened in surprise when he heard Michele Vanucci's familiar voice.

"I do not know what shape you will be in when you get out of here, but if I have anything to say about it, your head will still be attached to your neck."

Chapter Twenty-eight

Panic had closed off her throat. Adrienne watched Sandro kneel. Watched him lower his head, his hair jet black against the white cloth that covered the block. Watched the executioner bend down to him. She knew she had to do something. But what? her mind screamed. What?

The rhythm of the drums quickened, filling the hall with an urgent rush of sound that begged for a climax. The executioner raised his huge sword aloft. A ray of sunlight struck it, sending a bolt of light streaking through the hall.

Suddenly the scent of fresh sawdust drifted up to her, reminding her sharply of that horrifyingly real vision that had driven her to try to save Sandro by pulling him into the portrait and taking him back through time.

The sights, the sounds, the smells were the same, but there was something subtly different about the scene she was seeing now, she realized. It was nothing tangible, nothing she could name, but it was no less real for that.

The air around her began to vibrate. Adrienne felt a jolt as she recognized the difference. Her vision had been engulfed in black despair. But here, now, the image was transparent and filled with light.

A desperate hope pulsed through her. As she pushed herself back from the banister, she whirled her head to the side so quickly that the ligaments in her neck snapped. Borgia sat in his chair, his body seemingly relaxed, but a muscle in his cheek was jumping furiously.

"I know the exact day that your father will die," she whispered, desperation making her voice as hoarse as an old crone's.

"And I know precisely what will happen to you after that. You will be as weak as a babe and all your power and riches will flow through your fingers like sand and you will not be able to hold them." Her breathing was quick and shallow as if she had been running. "And you will die a desperate, destitute man—" She paused. "The laughingstock of all who knew you."

He turned toward her, all pretense of casualness gone, his face a feral mask. His hand snaked out and circled her arm in a brutal grip.

"Tell me, damn you!" His eyes glowed like hot coals with fury. "Now!"

"No!" The pain in her arm was excruciating, but still she fought him. And the more she fought him, the more savage his grip became. With the resourcefulness of the desperate, she let her muscles go limp. The moment his grip eased in response, Adrienne wrenched her arm out of his grasp.

He reached for her, but she pushed herself out of the chair with such violence that it tipped backward with a crash. For a fraction of a second she faltered and then half fell, half jumped off the low dais out of his reach. Even as she backed away, Borgia advanced toward her.

"Stop!" She stretched out one hand defensively while she lifted the other toward her mouth.

"My ring is filled with poison so deadly that it will kill me in seconds. If you come closer, I will drink it." She paused, her breathing ragged. "And you will have nothing."

Borgia took one step toward her. She placed the cold metal of the ring closer to her lips. "Do not think I will not do it. I have nothing left to lose."

He raised both hands palm outward and took a small step back. "All right." His voice was tight with the fury that he was so ruthlessly controlling. "All right."

"Get back. I do not want you or anyone else close to me."

Borgia took another step back. He would make her pay, he thought as his gut contracted with hatred. He would make them both pay.

"What do you want?" His mellow voice had coarsened.

"You know what I want," she fired back. "I want you to let him go. Once I have seen him ride safely through the gates of Forlì, we will speak again."

Borgia stepped up to the balustrade. At his signal the drums stopped, filling the hall with a deafening silence. "Back to the dungeon with him," he called out. "For now," he added, needing to save face in front of his men and the stolid burghers on the opposite gallery who were gaping at the scene they had witnessed.

Keeping watch on Borgia out of the corner of her eye, Adrienne glanced down in time to see Sandro rise and look up to meet her gaze. There were questions in his eyes and something else, an élan that made her want to believe in miracles.

As she watched him being led out of the hall, her eyes filled with tears—tears of joy. She did not know what the future would bring. She did not know how the story of Isabella and Alessandro di Montefiore would end. But she knew that Sandro was leaving the great hall of the Rocca di Ravaldino alive. Alive! She had changed history. And she still had hope.

"I will accompany you back to your apartments."

Adrienne tilted her chin up and gave Borgia a sharp look through her tears. "But only from a safe distance."

She paced through the luxurious apartments like a caged lioness. Hours had passed since she had returned. Outside the light was softening with the approaching dusk. She had no way of knowing what was happening to Sandro and the waiting was driving her mad.

There were so many ways that Borgia could still take his revenge. So many ways. She stared down into the courtyard, where the only activity was limited to two cats strolling by, tails high. It was then that she felt the pain knife through her.

Even as her brain screamed denial, she eased herself down on the bed. Another pain, not quite as keen as the first, had her stretching into a bow. She forced herself to lie quietly and put both hands on her abdomen. No, she assured herself. It could not be happening. Her body was not rejecting this child, too. But she remembered too well that months ago she had changed history just as she had changed history today and she still had lost the child she had carried.

She breathed evenly, concentrating on the child within her. Occasionally she rubbed her thighs together and was relieved to find no trace of that sticky wetness she remembered all too well.

Gradually the even breathing and concentration eased her. The discomfort disappeared and she slept.

She came awake in the middle of a complicated, confused dream. All she remembered from it was a jumble of smells. The scent of the sea off the coast of Normandy. The slightly musty smell of the secret chamber behind Isabella's portrait. The fragrance of roses and lemon when she buried her face in her mother's soft shoulder.

Staring up at the bed's canopy, which portrayed a half-playful, half-erotic scene not unlike the one that had greeted her when she had awakened for the first time in the Palazzo Montefiore, Adrienne let the memory of the dream float through her. Why had she dreamt of her life as Adrienne de Beaufort? What had she dreamt so intensely that the smells had stayed with her? Did it mean that— Suddenly afraid, she sat bolt upright and rubbed her hands over her face.

"You are well rested now, I trust."

Adrienne's head snapped up. A few feet away Cesare Borgia lounged in a chair, his eyes shaded by a black beret pulled low on his forehead. A goblet of wine stood at his elbow. The flickering candles in a three-pronged candelabrum cast a ghostly light through the room.

The shock of seeing him there numbed her. She felt an icy shiver crawl down her spine. Carefully, discreetly, she shifted her left arm. The dagger was gone! Her gaze darted over the bed but it was nowhere to be seen.

"Is this what you were looking for?" Borgia lifted the knife briefly before he tossed it back onto the table. "You were sleeping so soundly that it was pitifully easy to relieve you of it." He smiled. "And of your ring."

With a cry of alarm Adrienne looked down at her hands and found them bare. Then, seeing that the ring lay in the middle of his outstretched palm, she lunged forward. But her feet had not touched the floor when he fisted his hand and pulled it back.

"Now tell me, *madonna*—" his voice was light, mocking "—what are you going to bargain with now?"

She stared at him, her mind fuzzy from sleep and the panic beginning to swirl through her.

"I have the knowledge you want in my head," she managed. "Where you cannot steal it."

He laughed softly, musically. "Do you know how easy it is to obtain knowledge? A touch of the boot, the screws, the rack. A little fire. A few clever instruments." Pausing for a moment, he let his gaze sweep over her. "It would be a pity to mark that lovely body of yours, Donna Isabella."

She told herself that she was not afraid, that she would withstand the torture, but her nerves were screaming.

"What are you going to do?" She hated the choked sound of her voice.

"I will have my information, one way or another. But first I am going to have you."

Instinctively she moved back on the bed.

Borgia picked up the goblet and watched her over its rim as he sipped. "I have decided to be generous and spare Don Alessandro's life."

The joy sprang up within her, only to be battled down by suspicion.

"Montefiore will live, but his days will be circumscribed by the boundaries of a cell," he continued. "If I am feeling especially generous, I may even allow you to visit him from time to time to sweeten his imprisonment." He toasted her with the wine and drank deeply. "But perhaps he will not want you in his bed after you have shared mine for fear that I have given you the French disease." He pulled off his beret and she saw the seeping sore on his forehead it had concealed.

Adrienne looked at him with loathing. "Do not fear," she said. "French disease or not, he will never touch me again, knowing that I have lain with Cesare Borgia."

Borgia's eyes narrowed. "And he *will* know. He will have seen it with his own eyes."

"What?" Her lips formed the word, but no sound emerged.

"My men should be bringing him any minute." Lightly he rubbed his hands together "It is a time-honored tradition, after all, to have the consummation witnessed."

Horror tightened her throat, numbed her limbs, making it impossible for her to speak or move. No, she thought. This could not be happening. Nothing this vile could possibly happen.

Even when she heard the door open, she could not move. The shadowy figures came through the anteroom. When she saw Sandro framed by the doorway, she blinked, sure that she was seeing an apparition. Even when he moved forward, she was not completely sure that he was real.

"Welcome, Montefiore." Borgia set down the goblet and rose. He kept his eyes trained on his rival's face, not wanting to miss a single expression.

"Lash him to the chair," he said without looking at the guards.

Sandro's mouth curved. "I think not."

Before Borgia could say a word, Sandro had whipped out a dagger from beneath his short cloak. With one hand he held its needle-sharp point to Borgia's throat while with the other he relieved Borgia of his own weapon.

Speechless, Adrienne watched the scene unfolding in front of her, still not certain that she was not seeing a mirage.

"Watch him." He waited until his men had their weapons trained on Borgia. Then he turned toward the bed.

He had purposely not looked at Isabella before this moment, afraid that seeing her would distract him. Now, as he looked at her for the first time, his heart sank. He saw no welcome on her face. Her eyes were glazed and full of desolation. Confusion. Disbelief. But no joy. He felt the pain shoot through him and it took all of his strength not to turn away.

Sandro took a step and then another. Still her expression did not change. Slowly he walked toward her until he stood at the edge of the bed. All he had to do was lift his hand and he could touch her. But he did not.

Adrienne watched Sandro come closer. And closer still. And still she did not move, sure now that she had conjured up an illusion. She wanted to close her eyes against the pain that the vision was causing her, but she did not, for it was such a sweet pain.

Then he was standing at the edge of the bed. She was tempted—oh, so tempted—to reach out, but she was too afraid that this apparition would dissipate if she moved or spoke. Then she felt the wave of heat that radiated from his body. Slowly, ever so slowly she began to believe.

She rose up onto her knees. Her hands reached out but stopped short of touching him.

"Sandro? Is it really you?" Her whisper was barely audible.

"Yes." The pain that was still reverberating through him made him cautious.

Her eyes focused, then softened before they began to fill. Even though it trembled, her mouth curved upward and she opened her arms.

It was not until she was running her hands over his back, not until she was enveloped in his embrace, her face pressed against his chest, that she truly began to believe that this was not a dream.

For long minutes they said nothing, content merely to touch, to feel. Then Adrienne lifted her head, needing to look into Sandro's face again.

He brushed his fingers over her cheeks and neck where Borgia's hands had left marks. He did not want to ask. He did not want to know. But he had to. Swallowing, he said haltingly, "Did he...hurt you?"

Knowing what he meant, she shook her head. "He was going to..." A shiver went through her and she found herself unable to say the words. "He wanted to make you watch...."

"I know." Sandro's mouth was grim. "My men and I were trying to find a way to get to you when the summons came."

"Your men?"

"They scaled the wall last night." The pride was evident in his quick grin. "I did not know it at the time, but half the guards at my execution were my own men."

Adrienne pressed her face against his chest again, content to hold and be held. "What are you going to do?"

"I'm going to kill him."

"You cannot!" Her eyes flew up to his.

"I have killed before, Isabella." His mouth was a thin line and his nostrils fluttered with fury. "I will see him punished for what he did to us, to you."

Adrienne pulled back and gripped his hands. "And how long do you think the pope will let you live after you have killed his son?" She drew his hands down and pressed them against her belly. "I do not want my child to grow up without a father."

"And how long do you think *he* will let us live if I let him go?" he demanded. "How soon will there be an assassin's knife in our backs or the Borgia poison in our food?"

"If we can stay alive for a few years, it will be all right," she whispered.

"What?"

Adrienne repeated her words.

"Isabella—"

"Sandro—" She reached up and framed his face with her hands "Do you trust me?"

He met her gaze, his black eyes shining with a calm, steady light. "Yes," he said simply.

Her breath skipped a little as she exhaled and she realized that she had been holding it. "Will you trust me with this?"

He touched his fingertips to her cheek and nodded once.

They had ridden slowly toward Siena—Adrienne and Gianni in a litter, Sandro and his men in careful formation around Cesare Borgia. Now, with the border of Siena's territories in sight, they stopped one last time to wait for the troops Sandro had recalled from the siege of Pesaro. As soon as they had arrived, they would go their way and allow Borgia to go his.

"I sincerely hope that we do not meet again." Sandro's eyes were cold as he regarded Borgia. "But if we do, only one of us will live to tell about it."

Borgia laughed contemptuously. "Do not vaunt your nonexistent courage, Montefiore. If you had any, we both know I would not be alive this moment."

Even though his hands itched to put his sword to Borgia's throat, Sandro left them at his belt. "You owe your life to my wife," he taunted. "She prefers a husband whose hands are not befouled with your tainted blood."

Flushing, Borgia took a step forward.

"You are outnumbered," Sandro warned softly.

Borgia's gaze darted around and saw that the others had closed in, hands at the hilt of their swords. He shrugged philosophically. "Today perhaps. But the day will come when the circumstances are reversed." He paused. "My arm is long."

"I do not doubt that, Don Cesare. But how long will your arm be if you are dead?"

"What are you talking about?"

"Who would revenge your death?"

"His holiness—" he began.

Sandro smiled. "Indeed. His holiness could buy someone. There are some of us who need not buy loyalty." He gave his adversary a long, hard look. "Even after our death." Then, satisfied that Borgia had understood, he turned away.

Adrienne had watched the exchange. She had seen the flash of hatred in Borgia's eyes, and wondered if she had made a mistake by staying Sandro's hand. In that moment she knew that she would not stay his hand when it came to her brothers. When Sandro slid his arm around her shoulders, she leaned her head against him.

"Doubts, *tesoro?*"

She shook her head. "Only for a moment."

Together they walked toward the edge of camp, breathing in the clear air of the hills that guarded the northern approach to their domain.

"What did you tell him that made him stop my execution?"

Adrienne had been expecting the question long before this, but still she tensed.

"I told him that I knew his future."

Sandro hooked a finger under her chin and turned her face up to his. "And you do?"

Her eyes cautious, she nodded, although she would have wanted to deny it. "But not by black magic or evil means."

He had told her that he trusted her, Adrienne thought, but as she looked into his eyes, she wondered if the day would come when he would demand to know things she could not tell him. Could never tell him.

"Sandro," she whispered, "I love you." Her fingers curled into his doublet and she repeated the words as if they were an incantation that would allow her to stay here even though her mission was complete.

Her words of love flowed over him as he looked down at her. There were secrets in her eyes. Mysteries that he would never fathom. He had known that from the beginning. Something moved in him. A knot uncoiled. Now, this very moment, he took all the questions, looked at them one more time and put them away forever, surrendering the need to know. He believed and that was enough.

He cupped her head, his fingers sliding into her golden hair. "I love you, Isabella." He bent and brushed a kiss over her mouth to seal his pledge.

Epilogue

Siena, August 25, 1504

"Isabella!"

Adrienne let her son Francesco's pudgy little hands go and straightened with difficulty as Sandro burst into the room.

His black eyes were lively with elation, and even as the joy and relief rushed through her, the knot of dread in the pit of her stomach tightened. For days—no, weeks, months—she had been preparing herself for the time when he would bring the news he bore today. She stood and took a step toward him.

"It is over!" He gripped her shoulders and bent to brush his lips with hers. "Read this."

With fingers suddenly awkward and clammy, she took the letter he thrust at her. Turning toward the window, she began to read.

Altezza, with pleasure I humbly inform you that on the twentieth of August, Don Cesare Borgia was brought aboard a ship, a prisoner of the

Spanish masters of the Kingdom of Naples. The ship has set sail for Valencia.

Her eyes skimmed over the words again and again. It was over, she thought.... It was truly over. She knew that for the two and a half years that Borgia had left to live, he would be too busy trying to save his own hide to be able to try to repay old debts. Just as she had foretold him, he had become a penniless, powerless man. It was truly over. An icy shiver shook her as the words echoed again within her. Was her time over, too?

Sandro came up behind her and slid his arms around her waist, which was swollen with yet another fruit of their love. "We are free of him at last, my love." He lowered his mouth to the spot where her neck met her shoulder. "We are free," he whispered against her skin.

Even as she let herself flow into his embrace, Adrienne felt fear snake up her spine. She did not want to look, but her gaze was drawn to the portrait of Isabella di Montefiore. The eyes were watching her. They beckoned, telling her that now that Sandro was truly safe, the time had come for her to leave.

I want my life back.

Adrienne stiffened as the words spoken in the voice she had long come to accept as her own echoed inside her head. *No,* she protested, her eyes on the portrait. *You are dead. You killed yourself, insane with guilt and love for your betrayed husband.*

The eyes grew colder, more imperious, more demanding. *Give me back my life.*

Adrienne shook her head, sure that she was going mad. *With my own eyes I read the last words in your diary, written on midsummer eve,* she argued. *That day is two months past. That day when you slit your own throat. You cannot come back and take what is mine. You cannot!*

But the woman in the portrait did not let go and Adrienne felt the pull physically. As the letter she held dropped to the floor, she curled her fingers around Sandro's wrists. No, she thought, she would not let her do this. She would not.

She met the eyes of the woman in the portrait. Met and held them, defying the menace. Suddenly she knew what she had to do. It was a risk and she accepted it as she had accepted other risks.

"Have a fire built," she said to Daria, who had knelt to play with Francesco. "A large one."

"Are you all right?" Sandro tightened his arms around her. He ran his hands over her belly and felt the child within move restlessly. "Let me get the doctor."

He turned to go, but she held on to his hands as if they were a lifeline.

"Stay. I need you."

Alarm tugged at his nerve endings as all the old questions rose toward his lips. But they slipped away as he concentrated on Isabella, her warmth, her fragrance and the ripe fullness of her body giving him all the answers he needed.

Together they stood as the servants came and built a fire, feeding it until it was a roaring blaze.

"Take the portrait out of the frame and roll it up."

Too well trained to question their mistress, the servants removed the painting from the ornate, carved frame and proceeded to roll it.

Conscious of the danger but knowing that this she had to do herself, Adrienne released Sandro's hand and took the heavy canvas from the footman. The moment her fingers closed around it, the palm of her hand began to tingle.

As she moved toward the fireplace, she could feel the black void on the other side. It was pulling at her, pulling like quicksand, and even as she fought against it, she felt herself growing weaker.

She heard her son babbling quietly behind her. She felt Sandro's gaze on her. And she closed her eyes against the desire to turn around and look at them one more time.

She was losing. She could feel herself begin to slip away. Knowing that it was the ultimate risk, she let go. She stopped fighting the pull. Instead she filled herself with the love she felt for Sandro, for Francesco, for the child within her. Emotion, pure and powerful, flooded through her whole being like a radiant golden light.

The pull grew weaker and weaker still. When it had died, she thrust the canvas into the fire. Stepping back from the shower of sparks, she watched the canvas burn, knowing that, finally, she was free. When only ashes were left, she turned to Sandro and held out her arms.

Sandro stepped into her embrace. He knew that something vital had just taken place. He did not understand it, but he did not need to. All he needed to know was that suddenly that edge of tension that had lived within her all these years was gone.

He smiled. "I love you, *tesoro.*"

She reached up to frame his face. "Say my name, Sandro," she demanded. "Say my name."

"I love you, Isabella."

"Yes." She smiled and drew him down toward her. As their lips met, she said farewell to Adrienne de Beaufort. She had journeyed across time, and now, for better, for worse, forever, she *was* Isabella di Montefiore. There was no other.

* * * * *

Author's Note

With one exception, all of the characters in this story are fictitious. That exception is Cesare Borgia, who was the illegitimate son of Pope Alexander VI. It is impossible to open a book about the Renaissance without running across the infamous exploits of the Borgia family, and Cesare Borgia as a villain was simply too good to miss.

I have followed historical accounts of the period very carefully except for one or two minor chronological details to accommodate my story.

The only major liberty I took was dictated by my choice of Siena as a setting. I could not resist giving my readers a taste of this city, which is a true jewel. Its harmonious atmosphere and ambience are unequaled even in a country of superlatives like Italy. This made it necessary for me to invent the Montefiore family as rulers of Siena. During the period of my story, Siena was a city-state ruled by a rather colorless small-time tyrant, Pandolfo Petrucci, whose greatest claim to fame was that he took part in a conspiracy against Cesare Borgia and lived to tell about it. But he would hardly have made an appealing hero.

Alessandro di Montefiore, however, embodies all the attributes of a hero—and a little more. Enjoy.

Harlequin® Historical

FIRST IMPRESSIONS THAT ARE SURE TO ENDURE!

It's March Madness time again! Each year, Harlequin Historicals picks the best and brightest new stars in historical romance and brings them to you in one exciting month!

The Heart's Desire by Gayle Wilson—When the hunt for a spy pairs a cynical duke with a determined young woman, caution is thrown to the wind in one night of passion.

Rain Shadow by Cheryl St.John—A widower in need of a wife falls in love with the wrong woman, an Indian-raised sharp-shooter more suited to a Wild West show than to a farm.

My Lord Beaumont by Madris Dupree—Adventure abounds in this tale about a rakish nobleman who learns a lesson in love when he rescues a young stowaway.

Capture by Emily French—The story of a courageous woman who is captured by Algonquin Indians, and the warrior whose dreams foretell her part in an ancient prophecy.

Four exciting historicals by four promising new authors who are certain to become your favorites. Look for them wherever Harlequin Historicals are sold. Don't be left behind!

Take 4 bestselling love stories FREE

Plus get a FREE surprise gift!

Special Limited-time Offer

Mail to Harlequin Reader Service®

3010 Walden Avenue
P.O. Box 1867
Buffalo, N.Y. 14269-1867

YES! Please send me 4 free Harlequin Historical™ novels and my free surprise gift. Then send me 4 brand-new novels every month, which I will receive before they appear in bookstores. Bill me at the low price of $3.19 each plus 25¢ delivery and applicable sales tax, if any.* That's the complete price and—compared to the cover prices of $3.99 each—quite a bargain! I understand that accepting the books and gift places me under no obligation ever to buy any books. I can always return a shipment and cancel at any time. Even if I never buy another book from Harlequin, the 4 free books and the surprise gift are mine to keep forever.

247 BPA ANRM

Name	(PLEASE PRINT)
Address	Apt. No.
City	State	Zip

This offer is limited to one order per household and not valid to present Harlequin Historical™ subscribers. *Terms and prices are subject to change without notice. Sales tax applicable in N.Y.

UHIS-94R   ©1990 Harlequin Enterprises Limited

Harlequin® Historical

A SON OF BRITAIN, A DAUGHTER OF ROME.
ENEMIES BY BIRTH, LOVERS BY DESTINY.

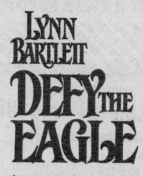

LYNN BARTLETT

DEFY THE EAGLE

From bestselling author Lynn Bartlett comes this tale of epic passion and ancient rebellion. Jilana, the daughter of a Roman merchant, and Caddaric, rebel warrior of Britain, are caught in the clash of two cultures amid one of the greatest eras in history.

Coming in February 1994
from Harlequin Historicals

Don't miss it! Available wherever Harlequin Books are sold.

My Valentine 1994

Celebrate the most romantic day of the year with
MY VALENTINE 1994
a collection of original stories, written by
four of Harlequin's most popular authors...

**MARGOT DALTON
MURIEL JENSEN
MARISA CARROLL
KAREN YOUNG**

*Available in February, wherever
Harlequin Books are sold.*

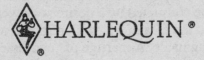

HARLEQUIN®

VAL94

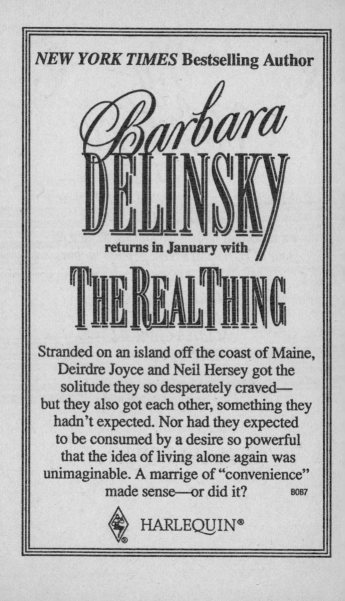

NEW YORK TIMES Bestselling Author

Barbara DELINSKY

returns in January with

THE REAL THING

Stranded on an island off the coast of Maine,
Deirdre Joyce and Neil Hersey got the
solitude they so desperately craved—
but they also got each other, something they
hadn't expected. Nor had they expected
to be consumed by a desire so powerful
that the idea of living alone again was
unimaginable. A marrige of "convenience"
made sense—or did it?

B087

HARLEQUIN®

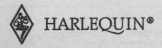

HARLEQUIN®

Don't miss these Harlequin favorites by some of our most distinguished authors!
And now, you can receive a discount by ordering two or more titles!

HT#25409	THE NIGHT IN SHINING ARMOR by JoAnn Ross	$2.99	☐
HT#25471	LOVESTORM by JoAnn Ross	$2.99	☐
HP#11463	THE WEDDING by Emma Darcy	$2.89	☐
HP#11592	THE LAST GRAND PASSION by Emma Darcy	$2.99	☐
HR#03188	DOUBLY DELICIOUS by Emma Goldrick	$2.89	☐
HR#03248	SAFE IN MY HEART by Leigh Michaels	$2.89	☐
HS#70464	CHILDREN OF THE HEART by Sally Garrett	$3.25	☐
HS#70524	STRING OF MIRACLES by Sally Garrett	$3.39	☐
HS#70500	THE SILENCE OF MIDNIGHT by Karen Young	$3.39	☐
HI#22178	SCHOOL FOR SPIES by Vickie York	$2.79	☐
HI#22212	DANGEROUS VINTAGE by Laura Pender	$2.89	☐
HI#22219	TORCH JOB by Patricia Rosemoor	$2.89	☐
HAR#16459	MACKENZIE'S BABY by Anne McAllister	$3.39	☐
HAR#16466	A COWBOY FOR CHRISTMAS by Anne McAllister	$3.39	☐
HAR#16462	THE PIRATE AND HIS LADY by Margaret St. George	$3.39	☐
HAR#16477	THE LAST REAL MAN by Rebecca Flanders	$3.39	☐
HH#28704	A CORNER OF HEAVEN by Theresa Michaels	$3.99	☐
HH#28707	LIGHT ON THE MOUNTAIN by Maura Seger	$3.99	☐

Harlequin Promotional Titles

#83247	YESTERDAY COMES TOMORROW by Rebecca Flanders	$4.99	☐
#83257	MY VALENTINE 1993	$4.99	☐
	(short-story collection featuring Anne Stuart, Judith Arnold, Anne McAllister, Linda Randall Wisdom)		

(limited quantities available on certain titles)

	AMOUNT	$
DEDUCT:	10% DISCOUNT FOR 2+ BOOKS	$
ADD:	POSTAGE & HANDLING	$
	($1.00 for one book, 50¢ for each additional)	
	APPLICABLE TAXES*	$ _____
	TOTAL PAYABLE	$ _____
	(check or money order—please do not send cash)	

To order, complete this form and send it, along with a check or money order for the total above, payable to Harlequin Books, to: **In the U.S.:** 3010 Walden Avenue, P.O. Box 9047, Buffalo, NY 14269-9047; **In Canada:** P.O. Box 613, Fort Erie, Ontario, L2A 5X3.

Name: _____

Address: _____ City: _____

State/Prov.: _____ Zip/Postal Code: _____

*New York residents remit applicable sales taxes.
 Canadian residents remit applicable GST and provincial taxes.

HBACK-JM